A MAGGOT

Books by John Fowles

JOHN FOWLES

A Maggot

Collins   Toronto

First published 1985
by Collins Publishers

This edition published 1986
by TOTEM BOOKS
a division of Collins Publishers
100 Lesmill Road, Don Mills, Ontario

© 1985 by J.R. Fowles Ltd.

Canadian Cataloguing in Publication Data
Fowles, John, 1926-
   A maggot
ISBN 0-00-223112-3

I. Title.

PR6056.085M33 1986 823'.914 C86-094223-6

Printed and bound in Canada

PROLOGUE

A MAGGOT is the larval stage of a winged creature; as is the written text, at least in the writer's hope. But an older though now obsolete sense of the word is that of whim or quirk. By extension it was sometimes used in the late seventeenth and early eighteenth century of dance-tunes and airs that otherwise had no special title . . . Mr. Beveridge's Maggot, My Lord Byron's Maggot, The Carpenters' Maggot, and so on. This fictional maggot was written very much for the same reason as those old musical ones of the period in which it is set; out of obsession with a theme. For some years before its writing a small group of travellers, faceless, without apparent motive, went in my mind towards an event. Evidently in some past, since they rode horses, and in a deserted landscape; but beyond this very primitive image, nothing. I do not know where it came from, or why it kept obstinately rising from my unconscious. The riders never progressed to any destination, but simply rode along a sky-line, like a sequence of looped film in a movie projector; or like a single line of verse, the last remnant of a lost myth.

What follows may seem like a historical novel; but it is not. It is maggot.

—*John Fowles, 1985*

A MAGGOT

IN THE LATE AND LAST AFTERNOON of an April long ago, a forlorn little group of travellers cross a remote upland in the far south-west of England. All are on horseback, proceeding at a walk along the moorland track. There lies about them, in the bleak landscape, too high to have yet felt the obvious effects of spring, in the uniform grey of the overcast sky, an aura of dismal monotony, an accepted tedium of both journey and season. The peaty track they follow traverses a waste of dead heather and ling; below, in a steep-sided valley, stand unbroken dark woodlands, still more in bud than in leaf. All the farthest distances fade into a mist, and the travellers' clothes are by chance similarly without accent. The day is quite windless, held in a dull suspension. Only in the extreme west does a thin wash of yellow light offer some hope of better weather to come.

A man in his late twenties, in a dark bistre greatcoat, boots and a tricorn hat, its upturned edges trimmed discreetly in silver braid, leads the silent caravan. The underparts of his bay, and of his clothes, like those of his companions, are mud-splashed, as if earlier in the day they have travelled in mirier places. He rides with a slack rein and a slight stoop, staring at the track ahead as if he does not see it. Some paces behind comes an older man on a smaller, plumper horse. His greatcoat is in dark grey, his hat black and plainer, and he too looks neither to left nor right, but reads a small volume held in his free hand, letting his placid pad tread its own way. Behind him, on a stouter beast, sit two people: a bareheaded man in a long-sleeved blouse, heavy drugget jerkin and leather breeches, his long hair tied in a knot, with in front of him, sitting sideways and resting against his breast — he supports her back with his right arm — a young woman. She is enveloped in a brown hooded cloak, and muffled so that only her eyes and nose are visible. Behind these two a leading-line runs back to a packhorse. The animal carries a seam, or wooden frame, with a large leather portmanteau tied to one side, and a smaller wooden box, brassbound at its corners, on the other. Various other bundles and bags lie bulkily distributed under a rope net. The overburdened beast plods with hanged head, and sets the pace for the rest.

They may travel in silence, but they do not go unobserved. The air across the valley opposite, above where its steepness breaks into rocks and small cliffs, is noisy with deep and ominous voices, complaining of this intrusion into their domain. These threatening voices come from a disturbed ravenry. The bird was then still far from its present rare and solitary state, but common and colonial, surviving even in many towns, and abundantly in isolated countryside. Though the mounted and circling black specks stay at a mile's distance, there is something foreboding in their alarm, their watchful hostility. All who ride that day, despite their difference in many other things, know their reputation; and secretly fear that snoring cry.

One might have supposed the two leading riders and the humble apparent journeyman and wife chance-met, merely keeping together for safety in this lonely place. That such a consideration — and not because of ravens — was then requisite is plain in the leading rider. The tip of a sword-sheath protrudes beneath his greatcoat, while on the other side a bulge in the way the coat falls suggests, quite correctly, that a pistol is hung behind the saddle. The journeyman also has a brass-ended holstered pistol, even readier to hand behind his saddle, while strung on top of the netted impedimenta on the dejected packhorse's back is a long-barrelled musket. Only the older, second rider seems not armed. It is he who is the exception for his time. Yet if they had been chance-met, the two gentlemen would surely have been exchanging some sort of conversation and riding abreast, which the track permitted. These two pass not a word; nor does the man with the woman behind him. All ride as if lost in their own separate worlds.

The track at last begins to slope diagonally down the upland towards the first of the woods in the valley below. A mile or so on, these woods give way to fields; and as far away again, where the valley runs into another, can just be made out, in a thin veil of wood-smoke, an obscure cluster of buildings and an imposing church-tower. In the west the sky begins to show amber glints from invisible breaks of cloud. That again, in other travellers, might have provoked some remark, some lighter heart; but in these, no reaction.

Then, dramatically, another figure on horseback appears from where the way enters the trees, mounting towards the travellers. He does provide colour, since he wears a faded scarlet riding-coat and what seems like a dragoon's hat; a squareset man of indeterminate age with a large moustache. The long cutlass behind his saddle and the massive wooden butt of a stout-cased blunderbuss suggest a familiar hazard; and so does the way in which, as soon as he sees the approaching file ahead, he kicks his horse and trots more briskly up the hill as if to halt and challenge them. But they show neither alarm nor excitement. Only the elder man who reads as he rides quietly closes his volume and slips it into his greatcoat pocket. The newcomer reins in some ten yards short of the leading younger gentleman, then touches his hat and turns his horse to walk beside him. He says something, and the gentleman nods, without looking at him. The newcomer touches his hat again, then pulls aside and waits until the last pair come abreast of him. They stop, and the newcomer leans across and unfastens the leading-line of the packhorse from its ring behind the saddle. No friendly word seems spoken, even here. The newcomer then takes his place, now leading the packhorse, at the rear of the procession; and very soon it is as if he has always been there, one more mute limb of the indifferent rest.

They enter the leafless trees. The track falls steeper and harsher, since it serves as a temporary stream-bed during the winter rains. More and more often comes the ring of iron shoes striking stone. They arrive at what is almost a ravine, sloping faces of half-buried rock, an awkward scramble even on foot. The leading rider seems not to notice it, though his horse hesitates nervously, picking its way. One of its hind feet slips, for a moment it seems it must fall, and trap its rider. But somehow it, and the lurching man, keep balance. They go a little slower, negotiate one more slip and scramble with a clatter of frantic hooves, then come to more level ground. The horse gives a little snorting whinny. The man rides on, without even a glance back to see how the others fare.

The older gentleman has stopped. He glances round at the pair behind him. The man there makes a little anti-clockwise circle with a finger and points to the ground: dismount and lead. The man in the scarlet coat at the rear, wise from his own recent upward passage, has already got down, and is tying the packhorse to an exposed root by the trackside. The older gentleman dismounts. Then his counsellor behind jumps off, with a singular dexterity, kicking free of his right stirrup and swinging his leg over the horse's back and slipping to the ground all in one lithe movement. He holds his arms out for the woman, who leans and half sinks towards him, to be caught, then swung free and set down.

The elderly man goes gingerly down the ravine, leading his cob, then the bareheaded man in the jerkin, and his horse. The woman walks behind, her skirts held slightly off the ground so that she can see her feet and where they are placed; then the last man, he in the faded scarlet coat. Once down, he extends the rein of his riding-horse to the man in the jerkin to hold, then turns and climbs heavily back for the packhorse. The older gentleman laboriously mounts again, and rides on. The woman raises her hands and pushes back the hood of her cloak, then loosens the white linen band she has swathed round the lower part of her face. She is young, hardly more than a girl, pale-faced, with dark hair bound severely back beneath a flat-crowned chip, or willow-shaving, hat. Its side-brims are tied down against her cheeks, almost into a bonnet, by the blue kissing-ribbons beneath her chin. Such a chip or wheat-straw hat is worn by every humbler English country-woman. A little fringe of white also appears beneath the bottom of her cloak: an apron. She is evidently a servant, a maid.

Unfastening the top of her cloak, and likewise undoing the kissing-ribbons, she goes beside the track a little ahead and stoops where some sweet-violets are still in flower on a bank. Her companion stares at her crouched back, the small movements of her hands, the left one picking, ruffling the heart-shaped green leaves to reveal the hidden flowers, the right one holding the small sprig of deep mauve heads she has found. He stares as if he does not comprehend why she should do this.

He has a strangely inscrutable face, which does not reveal whether its expressionlessness is that of an illiterate stupidity, an ignorant acceptance of destiny not far removed from that of the two horses he is holding; or whether it hides something deeper, some resentment of grace, some twisted sectarian suspicion of personable young women who waste time picking flowers. Yet it is also a strikingly regular, well-proportioned face, which, together with his evident agility, an innate athleticism and strength, adds an incongruous touch of the classical, of an Apollo, to one of plainly low-born origins and certainly not Greek ones, for his strangest features are his eyes, that are of a vacant blue, almost as if he were blind, though it is clear he is not. They add greatly to the impression of inscrutability, for they betray no sign of emotion, seem always to stare, to suggest their owner is somewhere else. So might twin camera lenses see, not normal human eyes.

Now the girl straightens and comes back towards him, smelling her minuscule posy; then gravely holds the purple flowers, with their little flecks of orange and silver, out and up for him to smell as well. Their eyes meet for a moment. Hers are of a more usual colour, a tawny brown, faintly challenging and mischievous, though she does not smile. She pushes the posy an inch or two nearer still. He briefly sniffs, nods; then as if they waste time, turns and mounts with the same agile grace and sense of balance that he showed before, still holding the other horse's rein. The girl watches him a moment more while he sits above, tightening the loosened linen muffler, pulling it to cover her mouth once more. She tucks her violets carefully inside the rim of white cloth, just below her nostrils.

The man in the military coat comes with the packhorse — he has stopped above to piss beside it — and takes his own horse from the man in the jerkin, and reties the leading-line. The girl stands waiting beside the pillion horse's withers; and now, in a seemingly familiar ritual, the military man comes round, faces her, then bends and enlaces his fingers to make a mounting stirrup. She sets her left foot in his hands, springs and is lightly lifted to her blanketed seat before the impassive man in the jerkin. She looks down, the bunch of violets like an absurd moustache beneath her nose. The man in the scarlet coat dryly tips his forefinger to his hat and winks. She looks away. Her companion, who has observed this, abruptly kicks the pillion horse's sides. It breaks into an immediate clumsy trot. He reins the beast sharply back, and she has to catch against him. Fists on hips, the man in the military coat watches them go for a moment or two, soon to settle to a walk, then mounts and follows.

A faint sound comes to his ears, as they wind down through the woodland. The young woman is singing, or rather humming a tune to herself. It is that of the melancholy old folk-air, "Daphne," already ancient in this time; yet it seems, this intrusion of a human voice in the previous silence, less melancholy than vaguely impudent. The man at the rear rides closer, to hear the voice better. The sound of hooves, an occasional creak of leather, a tiny jingle of harness metal; tumbling water below, and the sound of a missel-thrush also singing, from far across the valley, barely audible, as fragmented as the muffled girl's voice. Through the bare branches ahead, there is a gleam of luminous gold, where the sinking western sun has found a first direct interstice in the clouds.

Now the sound of rushing water dominates. They ride for a little way close above a fast and furious moorland stream and greener vegetation: more violets, wood-sorrel, first ferns, nests of primroses, emerald young rushes and grass. They come to a small clearing where the track descends to stream-level, then bends into the water, smoother here, at a ford. On the other side, facing them, wait the two gentlemen on their horses; and it is evident now, as masters wait for laggard servants. The elder, behind, takes snuff. The girl stops her singing. The three horses splash across, beside a line of stepping-stones, blundering their way among the small rocks beneath the swift-running water. The younger gentleman stares at the girl, at her floral moustache, as if she is in some way to blame for this delay. She does not look at him, but nestles close against her companion, whose arms surround her to keep her balanced. Only when all three horses and their burdens are safely across does the younger gentleman turn his horse and proceed, in the same order as before, and the same silence.

Some few minutes later this sombre cavalcade of five came out of the trees and once more upon an open prospect, for here the valley-bottom broadened considerably. The track ran slightly down-hill across a long open meadow. In those days a single animal dominated the agricultural economy of the West of England: the sheep — and the needs of its pasturing. The huge hundred-acre sheep-run was a much more frequent feature of cultivated landscapes than today's densely hedged and enclosed patchwork of small fields. In the distance could be seen the small town whose church-tower they had made out from the moorland above. Three or four flocks studded the long meadow before them; and as many shepherds, monolithic figures in cloaks of brown frieze, like primitive bishops with their crooks. One had two children beside him. Their sheep, Exmoor Horns, were smaller and scraggier than modern sheep, and tight-coated. To the travellers' left, where the hillside came down to the valley-bottom, was a massive stone pen, and yet another farther along.

The younger gentleman reined in slightly and let the older come beside him; and from then on they rode abreast, though still without talking. The two shepherd children ran across the close-cropped turf to the side of the open track, ahead of the party, and waited once they were there, with strangely intent eyes, watching beings from fable, not reality, approach; and as if they imagined themselves not seen in return. They made no greeting, this small upstaring boy and his sister, both barefoot; and received none. The younger gentleman ignored them completely, the elder gave no more than a casual glance. The manservant on the doubly laden horse similarly ignored them, while the man in the scarlet coat seemed to find himself, even before such a minute audience as this, put upon dignity. He rode a little more erect, staring ahead, like a would-be cavalry trooper. Only the young woman smiled, with her eyes, down at the small girl.

For three hundred yards the two children alternately walked and trotted beside the travellers; but then the boy ran ahead, for a first banked hedge and a gate now barred the road. He heaved it off its latch, then pushed it wide back and open; and stood there, staring at the ground, with a hand outstretched. The older gentleman felt in his greatcoat pocket, and tossed a farthing down. The boy and his sister both scrambled for it as it rolled on the ground, but the boy had it first. Now once more they both stood, with outstretched small arms, the palms upwards, heads bowed, as the rear of the cavalcade passed. The young woman raised her left hand and took a pinch of her spray of violets, then threw them at the small girl. They fell across the child's arm, over her bent crown of no doubt lice-ridden hair, then to the ground: where the child stared at them, the arm dropped, nonplussed by this useless, incomprehensible gift.

A quarter of an hour later the five came to the outskirts of the small town of C———. It was town more by virtue of being a few hundred inhabitants larger than any surrounding village in this thinly populated area than in any modern sense of the term; town also by virtue of an ancient charter, granted in palmier or more hopeful days four hundred years before; and which still absurdly permitted its somnolent mayor and tiny corporation to elect two members to parliament. It boasted also a few tradesmen and craftsmen, a weekly market, an inn besides its two or three ale- and ciderhouses, and even an ancient grammar-school, if one can call school one aged master, also parish clerk, and seven boys; but in all else it was a village.

Nothing, indeed, could have misled more than the majestic high-pinnacled and battlemented tower of its medieval church; it now dominated and surveyed a much less prosperous and confident place than the one that had built it nearly three centuries earlier, and stood far more relic than representative. No gentry lived permanently there, though a manor-house existed. The place was too remote, and like all remote Britain then, without turnpike or decent carriage-road. Above all it was without attraction to an age whose notion of natural beauty — in those few capable of forming such notions — was strictly confined to the French or Italianate formal garden at home and the denuded but ordered (through art) classical landscapes of Southern Europe abroad.

To the educated English traveller then there was nothing romantic or picturesque at all in domestic wild landscapes, and less than nothing in the cramped vernacular buildings of such townlets as C———. All this was so much desert, beneath the consideration of anyone who pretended to taste. The period had no sympathy with unregulated or primordial nature. It was aggressive wilderness, an ugly and all-invasive reminder of the Fall, of man's eternal exile from the Garden of Eden; and particularly aggressive, to a nation of profit-haunted puritans, on the threshold of an age of commerce, in its flagrant uselessness. The time had equally no sense (except among a few bookworms and scholars) of the antique outside the context of Greece and Rome; even its natural sciences, such as botany, though by now long founded, remained essentially hostile to wild nature, seeing it only as something to be tamed, classified, utilised, exploited. The narrow streets and alleys, the Tudor houses and crammed cottage closes of such towns conveyed nothing but an antediluvian barbarism, such as we can experience today only in some primitive foreign land . . . in an African village, perhaps, or an Arab *souk*.

A twentieth-century mind, could it have journeyed back and taken on the sensibilities and eyes of those two better-class travellers riding that day into the town, would have felt itself landed, or becalmed, in some strange doldrum of time, place and spirit; in one of those periods when Clio seems to stop and scratch her tousled head, and wonder where the devil to go next from here. This particular last day of April falls in a year very nearly equidistant from 1689, the culmination of the English Revolution, and 1789, the

start of the French; in a sort of dozing solstitial standstill, a stasis of
the kind predicted by those today who see all evolution as a punc-
tuated equilibrium, between those two zenith dates and all they
stand for; at a time of reaction from the intemperate extremisms of
the previous century, yet already hatching the seeds (perhaps even
in that farthing and careless strew of fallen violets) of the world-
changing upheaval to come. Certainly England as a whole was indulging in its favourite and sempiternal national hobby: retreating
deep within itself, and united only in a constipated hatred of
change of any kind.

Yet like so many seemingly inert troughs in history, it was not altogether a bad time for the six million or so there then were of the
English; and however humble they might be. The two begging
children by the road wore ragged and patched clothes; but at least
they were visibly neither starved nor starving. There were higher
real wages than for centuries past — and for very nearly two centuries to come. Indeed it was only just becoming anything but a
distinctly prosperous time for this county of Devon. Its ports, its
ships, its towns and villages lived, and largely thrived, as they had
for the last half-millennium, on one great staple: wool. In the
abrupt course of the next seventy years this trade was to be first
slowly throttled, then finally annihilated by a national change of
taste, towards lighter fabrics, and the more enterprising North of
England; but still at this time half of Europe, even colonial
America and imperial Russia, bought and made clothes from the
Devonshire dozen, its famous length of serge and perpetuana.

There was evidence of the cloth trade in nearly every thatched
doorway and open cottage shutter of C———; women spinning,
men spinning, children spinning, their hands so accustomed that
eyes and tongues were entirely free; or if not doing that, then engaged in cleaning, carding and combing the raw fleece-wool. Here
and there in a dark interior might be glimpsed or heard looms, but
the spinning predominated. The mechanical jenny was still several
decades in the future and the bottleneck in the ancient hand process always lay with the production of the yarn, for which the great
weaving, finishing and market centres like Tiverton and Exeter
and their rich clothiers had an insatiable greed. In all this, too, the

endless treadling, blurred wheels, distaffs, the very scent of raw wool, our travellers found nothing picturesque or of interest. Throughout the country, industry still lay inside the cottage, in outwork, in the domestic system.

This contempt, or blindness, was returned, in an inverse way. The riders were forced to go at an even slower pace by a lumbering ox-cart, which left no room to pass; and the doorway spinners, the townspeople about in the street, or attracted to their windows and thresholds by the horses' hooves, betrayed a similar sense of alienation by staring, as the shepherd's children had, at these strangers as if they were indeed foreigners, and not to be trusted. There was also the beginning of a political and a class feeling about this. It had been proved fifty years earlier, in the neighbouring counties of Somerset and Dorset, when nearly half of those who had flocked to join the Monmouth Rebellion had come from the cloth trade; most of the rest had come from the agricultural community, and virtually none at all from the local gentry. It would be wrong to speak yet of a trade-union-mindedness, or even of the mob spirit by then recognised and feared in larger cities; but of an inherent resentment of those who lived in a world not ruled by cloth, here was evidence.

The two gentlemen studiously avoided the watching eyes; and a sternness and gravity in their demeanour forebade greeting or enquiry, if not chowring comment. The young woman passenger did from time to time glance shyly sideways; but something bizarre in her muffled appearance puzzled the spectators. Only the man in the faded scarlet coat at the rear seemed like a normal traveller. He gave stare for stare; and even tipped his hat to two girls in a doorway.

Then a young man in a smock darted forward from the niche of a cob buttress supporting a leaning cottage wall and brandished an osier ring of dead birds up at the military-looking man. He had the sly grin of a yokel, half joker, half village idiot.

"Buy 'un, maister? Penny a 'oop, penny a 'oop!"

He was waved aside, but walked backwards, still thrusting the little ring of dead birds, each pierced through the neck, crimson and brown breasts and coal-black heads, up towards the rider.

Hoops, or bullfinches, then had a price on their head, paid against their bodies by parish vestries.

"Where be's 'ee to then, maister?"

The man in the scarlet coat rode on a pace or two in silence, and threw an answer back over his shoulder.

"The fleas in thy poxy inn."

"What business?"

Again the rider waited to answer, and this time did not turn his head.

"None o' thine."

The ox-cart now turned into a smith's yard, and the cavalcade could go more quickly. In a hundred yards or so they came to a more open square, paved with small dark setts sunk on edge. Though the sun had set, the sky had now cleared extensively in the west. Rose streaks of vapour floated in a honey-coloured light, suffusing the canopy still above with pink and amethyst tints. Somewhat finer and taller buildings surrounded this square and its central building, an open-sided shed, or market, made of massive oak timbers and with a steep-pitched and stone-tiled roof. There was a clothier's shop, a saddler's, a grocer's, an apothecary and barber-surgeon's, the latter being the nearest the place had to a doctor; a cord-wainer's. At the far end of the square beyond the market-house stood a knot of people, around a long wooden pole lying on its side, the central totem for the next day's celebrations, in process of being dressed with streamers.

Closer, beside the roof-supporting outer columns of the market-house, groups of children noisily played lamp-loo and tutball, those primitive forms of tag and baseball. Modern lovers of the second game would have been shocked to see that here it was preponderantly played by the girls (and perhaps also to know that its traditional prize, for the most skilled, was not the million-dollar contract, but a mere tansy pudding). An older group of lads, some men among them, stood all with short knob-ended sticks of heavy holly and hawthorn in their hands, and took turns to throw at a bizarre and ragged shape of stuffed red cloth, vaguely birdlike, set at the foot of the market-house wall. To the travellers this last was a familiar sight, no more than practice for the noble, ancient and universal English sport to be played on the morrow: that of cocks-quailing, or slaughtering cocks by throwing the weighted squailers, or sticks, at them. Its traditional main season was Shrovetide; but in Devon it was so popular, as cockfighting was among the gentry, that it was celebrated at other festivals. A very few hours would see a series of terrified living birds tied in place of the stuffed red puppet, and blood on the setts. Eighteenth-century man was truly Christian in his cruelty to animals. Was it not a blasphemous cock that crowed thrice, rejoicing each time the apostle Peter denied? What could be more virtuous than bludgeoning its descendants to death?

The two gentlemen reined in, as if somewhat taken aback by this unexpected open stage and animated crowd. The cock-throwers had already turned away from their rehearsal; the children as quickly dropped their games. The younger gentleman looked back to the man in the scarlet coat, who pointed across to the northern side of the square, at a ramshackle stone building with a crudely painted black stag on a wall-board above its porch and an archway to a stableyard beside it.

The clattering and clopping procession now headed up across the slightly sloping square. The maypole was also forsaken for this more interesting entertainment, which had already gathered a small train on its way to the square. Some seventy or eighty faces were waiting, when they approached the inn; but just before they came to dismount, the younger gentleman politely gestured the elder forward, as if he must take precedence. A florid-faced man with a paunch came out under the porch, a serving-girl and a pot-boy behind him; then a man with a bustling limp from the yard, the ostler. He took the older gentleman's horse as he slid stiffly to the ground; the potboy, the younger gentleman's behind him. The landlord bowed.

"Welcome, sirs. Puddicombe, at your service. Us trust you be come an easy journey."

The elder gentleman answered.

"All is ready?"

"As your man bespoke, sir. To the letter."

"Then show to our chambers. We are much fatigued."

The landlord backed, and offered entrance. But the younger gentleman waited a moment or two, watching the other three horses and their riders into the yard, to which they had headed direct. His senior eyed him, then the ring of onlookers, and spoke with a firm, even faintly testy, authority.

"Come, nephew. Enough of being the cynosure of nowhere."

With that he passed into the inn, leaving his nephew to follow.

In the best upstairs chamber, the uncle and nephew have just finished their supper. Candles have been lit on a wall-sconce by the door, three more in a pewter branch on the table. An ash-log fire burns in a wide open hearth not far away, and the faintly acrid smell of its smoke pervades the trembling shadows in the large old room. A four-poster bed, its curtains drawn, stands with its head against a side-wall opposite the fire, with a ewer and bowl on a stand beside it. There is another table and chair by the window. Two ancient and worm-eaten wooden-armed chairs with leather-padded seats face each other on either side of the hearth; a long seventeenth-century bench-stool guards the foot of the bed. There is no other furniture. The windows are hidden by folding shutters, now latched across; there are no hangings, drawings or pictures, except for a framed engraving, on the wall above the fire, of the last but one monarch, Queen Anne, and a small tarnished mirror by the wall-sconce.

Ranged by the door lie the leather trunk, lid flung open on clothes, and the brassbound wooden chest. The fire and its shifting lights and shadows somewhat hide the room's bareness, and at least the old half-panelling and uncarpeted yet polished broad-planks are warm.

The nephew fills his glass from a blue-and-white china decanter of Madeira, then rises and goes to the fire. He stares down at it for a few moments in silence. He has unbuckled his neck-stock and put on a damask night-gown (at that period a loose informal coat, not what it means today) over his long waistcoat and breeches. He has also taken his wig off, revealing that he is shaven-headed to the apparent point, in the poor light, of baldness; and indeed looks like nothing so much as a modern skinhead, did not his clothes deny it. His riding-coat and long suit-coat, and the fashionably brief campaign wig, hang from hooks by the door, the top-boots and sword stand below. His uncle has remained more formally dressed, and still wears his hat and much fuller wig, whose knot-ends lie against his coat. The two men bear little physical resemblance. The nephew is slightly built, and his face shows, as he stares at the fire, a blend of fastidiousness and intransigence. It is, with its aquiline nose and fine mouth, not an unhandsome face; but something broods in it. It certainly does not suggest any lack of breeding or urbanity, indeed he looks like a man confident, even certain, of his position in life, and of his general philosophy, despite his comparative youth. But unmistakably it suggests will, and an indifference to all that is not that will.

Its present meditative expression is in marked contrast to that of the corpulent uncle, at first sight a man of more imposing mien: jowly, doctorial, heavy-browed, incipiently choleric. Yet for all that he seems distinctly less at ease than his companion, whose stance in front of the fire, the downbent face, he now contemplates. His look reveals a certain wryness, not untinged with impatience. But he ends by looking down at his plate. His quick glance up, when suddenly the younger man speaks, although it is seemingly to the fire, suggests that the meal, like the journey, has lacked conversation.

"I thank you for bearing with me, Lacy. And my *vacua*."

"I had fair warning, sir. And fair fee."

"Even so. For one to whom speech must be the bread of life . . . I fear I have been poor company."

They do not speak like nephew and uncle. The older man produces a snuff-box; and slides a sly look under his eyebrows at his interlocutor.

"Speech has brought me rotten cabbages before now. And far worse rewards than yours." He takes snuff. "No more than the cabbages themselves, on occasion."

The man by the fire looks back then, with a faint smile.

"I'll wager never such a part as this."

"I can't deny you there, sir. Most assuredly no such part as this."

"I am grateful. You have played it well."

The older man bows, though with a perceptibly mock exaggeration.

"I might have played it better still had I — " but he breaks off, and opens his hands.

"Had you had more confidence in the author?"

"In his final design, Mr Bartholomew. With respect."

The younger man stares back at the fire.

"We might all say that, might we not? *In comœdia vitæ.*"

"True, sir." He takes a lace handkerchief out and dabs at his nose. "But our craft conforms us. We like to have our morrows fixed. Therein doth lie our art. Without we are disarmed of half our powers, sir."

"I have not remarked it."

The actor smiles down, and closes his snuff-box. The younger man walks slowly to the window and idly unlatches the shutters, and folds a creaking half-panel back. He looks out, almost as if he expects to see someone waiting below in the market-place. But it is empty now and dark. In one or two of the surrounding houses windows shine faintly with candlelight. There is still a very barely perceptible luminescence, a last breath of the gone day, in the western sky; and stars, some nearly overhead, announce that the sky continues to clear eastwards. He recloses the shutter and turns to face the man at the table.

"We may ride the same road for an hour tomorrow. Then we must part."

The older man looks down with a slight rise of his eyebrows and a tilted nod of reluctant acquiescence, like a chess-player forced to acknowledge he has met his master.

"I trust I may at least hope to meet you in more auspicious circumstances."

"If fortune wishes it."

The actor gives him a prolonged look.

"Come, sir. At this happy juncture — did you yourself not mock at superstition but a day or two ago? You speak as if fortune is your foe."

"Hazard is no superstition, Lacy."

"One throw of the dice, perhaps. But you may throw again."

"May one cross the Rubicon twice?"

"But the young lady —"

"This time . . . or never more."

Lacy is silent a moment.

"My dear sir, with all respect, you take too tragical a view of matters. You are no Romeo in a history, bound upon destiny's wheel. Such notions are but a poet's contrivance, to achieve his effect." He pauses, but gets no answer. "Very well, you may fail this time in your venture, as you tell me you failed before. But may you not try again — as true lovers must? The old adage warns us so."

The young man goes back to his chair and sits, and once more stares at the fire a long moment.

"Say it were a history that has neither Romeo nor Juliet. But another end, as dark as the darkest night." He looks up. There is a sudden force, a directness in his look. "What then, Lacy?"

"The comparison is better made between ourselves. When you speak thus, it is I who am thrown into darkest night."

Again the younger man is slow to reply.

"Allow me to put a strange fancy to you. You spake just now of fixed morrows. Suppose one came to you, to you alone, and said that he had pierced the secrets of the world to come — I mean not those of Heaven, but of this world we live in. Who could persuade you he was no fair-booth charlatan, but had truly discovered what he pretended by some secret study, mathematic science, astrology, what you will. Then told you of the world to come, what shall happen tomorrow, shall happen this day month, next year, a hundred, a thousand years from now. All, as in a history. Now — would you run crying it in the streets or keep silent?"

"I should first doubt my own mind."

"But if that doubt were removed by some irrefutable proof?"

"Then I should warn my fellow-men. So that they might consider to avoid what might harm them."

"Very well. But now further suppose that this prophet reveals that the predestinate future of this world is full of fire and plague, of civil commotion, of endless calamity. What then? Is the case the same?"

"I cannot conceive your case, sir. How it should be proven."

"Bear with me. It is but conjecture. Let us grant he shall find proof to convince you."

"You are too deep for me, Mr Bartholomew. If it be in the stars that my house shall be struck by a thunderbolt tomorrow, I grant you I may not avert that. Yet if it be also in the stars that I may be told as much, I can surely remove from my house in the expectation."

"But suppose the bolt will strike you, wheresoe'er you flee or shelter? You are none the better off. You should as well have stayed at home. Besides, he might not know how you in person should die, when such and such an evil shall fall on any one of mankind, no more than that one day it must fall on most. I would ask this, Lacy. Would you not, if such a man, before coming to you, advised you of his purpose in coming, so that you had time to reflect and conquer natural curiosity — would you not most wisely refuse to hear a single word from him?"

"Perhaps. I can allow that."

"And would not he, if he were Christian and kind — and mark you, even if his prophetic science foretold the very opposite, that this corrupt and cruel world should one day live in eternal peace and plenty — would not he still most wisely keep his secret to himself? If all were one day assured of Paradise, who would any longer trouble to stir himself to virtue or merit?"

"I take your general argument, sir. But not why you should speak so in present circumstance."

"This, Lacy. Suppose you were he that can read this most awful decree upon what shall come. Is it not best that you should accept to be its only victim? Might not a most condign divine anger at such blasphemous breaking of the seals of time be assuaged at the price of your silence — nay, your own life?"

"I cannot answer that. You touch upon matters . . . it is not for us to trespass upon the privilege of our Creator alone."

The younger man, his eyes still lost in the fire, bows his head a little in acquiescence.

"I but put a case. I mean no blasphemy."

Then he falls silent, as if he regrets having opened the subject at all. It is clear that this does not satisfy the actor, for now he rises, and in his turn slowly goes to the window, his hands behind his back. He stands there a moment before the shutters, then suddenly clasps his hands more firmly, and turns and addresses the back of the bald head that sits silhouetted between him and the fire.

"I must speak frankly, Mr Bartholomew, since we part tomorrow. One learns in my profession to read men by their physiognomies. By their looks, their gait, their cast of countenance. I have ventured to form an opinion of you. It is highly favourable, sir. Behind the subterfuges we are presently reduced to, I believe you an honest and honourable gentleman. I trust you know me well enough by now to permit me to say that I should never have entered upon this enterprise were I not persuaded that you had justice upon your side."

The younger man does not turn, and there is a tinge of dryness in his voice.

"But?"

"I can forgive you, sir, for hiding some circumstances in this our present business. I apprehend there is necessity and good sense in that. To use such necessity to deceive me as to the very business itself, that I could not forgive. I won't conceal it, sir. You may speak of fancies, but what am I to make —"

Suddenly the younger man stands, it seems almost in a rage, so abrupt is the movement. Yet he merely turns towards the actor with another of his direct looks.

"I give you my word, Lacy. You know I am a disobedient son, you know I have not told you all. If such be sins, I confess to 'em. You have my word that what I do breaks no law of this land." He comes forward and reaches out a hand. "I would have you believe that."

The actor hesitates, then takes the hand. The younger man fixes him with his eyes.

"Upon my honour, Lacy. You have not misjudged me there. And I pray you to remember this, whatever lies ahead." He drops the hand and turns away to the fire again, but looks back at the actor standing by the chair. "I have deceived you in much. I beg you to believe that it is to spare you much, also. No one shall ever find in you any but an innocent instrument. Should it come to that."

The older man's eyes are stern.

"None the less, something other than what you have led me to believe is afoot?"

The younger man looks back down to the fire.

"I seek a meeting with someone. That much is true."

"But not of the kind you have given me to suppose?" Mr Bartholomew is silent. "An affair of honour?"

Mr Bartholomew smiles faintly. "I should not be here without a friend, were that the case. Nor ride so many miles to do what may be done far closer London."

The actor opens his mouth to speak, in vain. There is the sound of a footstep outside the door, then a knock. The younger man calls. The landlord Puddicombe appears, and addresses the supposed uncle.

"Mr Brown, there be a gentleman below. His compliments, sir. With your pardon."

The actor throws a sharp look at the man by the fire. He shows no sign of expectation fulfilled, yet it is he who speaks impatiently to the landlord.

"Who?"

"Mr Beckford, sir."

"And who may Mr Beckford be?"

"Our parson, sir."

The man by the fire looks down, it seems almost with relief, then up again at the actor.

"Forgive me, uncle. I am tired. Let me not prevent you."

The actor smoothly, if belatedly, takes his cue. "Tell the reverend gentleman I shall be pleased to wait on him downstairs. My nephew craves his indulgence."

"Very good, sir. At once. Your honours."

He withdraws. The younger man makes a small grimace.

"Gird yourself, my friend. One last throwing of dust."

"I cannot leave our conversation here, sir."

"Be rid of him as soon as you civilly can."

The actor feels for his neck-stock, touches his hat and straightens his coat.

"Very well."

With a slight bow, he goes to the door. His hand is already on it when the younger man speaks one last time.

"And kindly ask our worthy landlord to send up more of his wretched tallow. I would read."

The actor silently bows again, and leaves the room. For a few moments the man by the fire stares at the floor. Then he goes and carries the small table near the window to beside the chair he has sat in; he fetches the candle-branch from the supper-table and sets it there in preparation. Next, feeling in the pocket of his knee-length waistcoat for a key, he goes and crouches and unlocks the brassbound chest by the door. It seems to contain nothing but books and loose manuscript papers. He rummages a little and finds a particular sheaf of the latter, takes them to his chair and begins to read.

In a few moments there is a knock on the door. An inn-maid comes in, carrying another lit branch on a tray. She is gestured to put it with the other on the table beside him; she does, then turns to clear the supper things. Mr Bartholomew does not look at her; as if he lived not two hundred and fifty years ago, but five centuries ahead, when all that is menial and irksome will be done by automata. Leaving with the dishes on the tray, she turns at the door, and curtsies awkwardly towards the oblivious figure in the armchair, absorbed in his reading. He does not look up; and awed, perhaps because reading belongs to the Devil, or perhaps secretly piqued by such indifference, since even in those days inn-maids were not hired for their plain looks, she silently goes.

In a much humbler room above, a garret beneath the roof, the young woman lies seemingly asleep beneath her brown riding-cloak, spread over her as blanket on a narrow truckle-bed. At the end of the unceiled room, by the one small gable-window, sits a single candle on a table, whose faint light barely reaches the far and inner end of the room where the girl lies; half on her stomach, her legs bent up beneath the cloak, and a crooked arm on the coarse pillow, on which she has spread the linen band that she used as a muffler. There is something childlike in her pose and in her face, with its slightly snub nose and closed eyelashes. Her left hand still holds the limp last of her violets. A mouse rustles as it runs here and there below the table, investigating and sniffing.

On the back of a chair beside the bed sits perched above the discarded chip hat something apparently precious and taken from the opened bundle on the floor; a flat white cambric hat, its fronts and sides goffered into little flutes, with hanging from the sides, to fall behind the wearer's ears, two foot-long white lappet-bands. It seems strangely ethereal, even faintly absurd and impertinent in that rough room. Such caps, without the lappets, were in history to become a mark of the housemaid and waitress, but they were then worn by all female fashionable society, mistresses and maids alike, as indeed were aprons on occasion. Male servants, the slaves of livery, were easily known; but female ones, as at least one contemporary male disapprovingly noted, and tried to prevent, were allowed considerable licence at this date. Many a gentleman entering a strange drawing-room had the mortification of bowing politely to what he supposed a lady intimate of his hostess, only to find he was wasting fine manners on a mere female domestic.

But the owner of this delicate and ambiguous little cap is not truly asleep. At the sound of steps on stairs outside, her eyes open. The feet stop at her door, there is a momentary pause, then two thumps, as its bottom-board is kicked. She throws aside the cloak and stands from the bed. She wears a dark green gown, fastened between her breasts, but with its edges folded back, as also just below her elbows, to reveal a yellow lining. Below she wears a full white apron, to the ground. The dress is stayed, to a narrow waist, and gives her upper body the unnatural and breastless shape of an inverted cone. She slips her stockinged feet into a pair of worn mules and goes and opens the door.

The manservant she has ridden with stands there, a large brass jug of warm water in one hand, an ochre-glazed earthenware bowl in the other. He is hardly visible in the darkness, his face in shadow. The sight of her seems to freeze him, but she stands back and points to the end of the narrow room, to the table. He goes past her and puts down the jug by the candle, then the bowl; but that done, he stands once more frozen, his back to her, his head hanging.

The young woman has turned to pick up her large bundle, then lay it on the bed. It reveals an assembly of clothes, ribbons, an embroidered cotton scarf; and wrapped in them another bundle, that holds an array of minute earthenware gallipots, whose lids are formed, rather like those on modern jam jars, of scraps of parchment bound with string. There are some small and corked blue glass bottles also; a comb, a brush, a hand-mirror. Suddenly she becomes aware of the man's stillness, and turns to look at him.

For a moment she does nothing. Then she goes towards him, takes his arm and urges him round. His face remains impassive; yet there is something both haggard and resentful in his stance, mute and tormented, a beast at bay, unbestially questioning why it should be so. Her look is steady. She shakes her head; at which his vacant blue eyes look away from her brown ones, past her head, at the far wall, though nothing else in his body moves. Now she looks down and lifts one of his hands, seems to examine it; touches and pats it with her other hand. They stand so for half a minute or more, in a strange immobility and silence, as two people waiting for something to happen. Finally she lets his hand fall and, walking back to the door, relatches it; turns and looks back at the man, whose eyes have followed her. Now she points to the floor beside where she stands, as one might to a pet dog — gently, yet not without a hint of firmness. The man moves back down the room, still searching her eyes. Once more she touches his hand, but this time only to press it briefly. She goes back herself to the table, begins untying the apron. Then, as if she has forgotten, she returns to the bed and, delving for a moment in the opened bundle, picks out one of the little pots, a small bottle and a square of worn huckaback, evidently a makeshift towel. With these she turns back to the table and stands there silent a moment, unfastening the cover of the pot in the candlelight.

She begins to undress. First the apron is removed, and hung on one of a row of primitive wooden pegs beside the window. Next the yellow-lined green gown, which reveals a quilted calamanco petticoat (a skirt in modern terms, the lower part of the dress opens upon it). It is of a plum colour, and strangely glazed, for satin is woven in its worsted cloth. She unties that at the waist, and hangs it on another hook; then her stays. Beneath them there remains only a smicket, or small white under-bodice, that one might have expected left on for modesty's sake. Yet this too is pulled over her close-drawn hair and hung beside the rest. She is naked now, above her swanskin and linen under-petticoats.

She does all this quickly and naturally, as if she is alone. The effect on the watching man is peculiar, since from the moment she has begun undressing, his feet have been cautiously shifting; but not towards her. He edges thus back against the inner wall of the room; only its beams and plaster can prevent him from retreating farther still.

Now she pours water and washes, having extracted a small wash-ball of gilliflower soap from the glass pot: her face and neck, the front of her body and her arms. Her movements make the candlelight in front of her tremble a little; occasionally some small twist of her body or arms causes a gleaming reflection on the wet skin, or shows a soft rim of its whiteness on the edge of the black-brown silhouette of her bare back. Among the rafters moves a sinister parody, in elongated and spiderlike shadows, of the simple domesticity of the ritual. It is sinister in both senses, for it is clear now she is left-handed by nature. Not once does she turn while this is going on, or while she is patting herself dry; and not once do the silent man's eyes move from her half-naked body.

Now she takes the blue bottle and moistens a corner of her huckaback towel in the liquid it contains, which she dabs here and there about her bared body; at the side of her neck, beside her armpits, and somewhere in front. A perfume of Hungary water creeps down the room.

She reaches sideways for her smicket and puts it on again; and now she does turn, and brings the candle to the bed, beside the man. She sits. Another little china pot is taken — the ball of soap has been carefully dried and replaced in its own container — and set beside the candle. It contains ceruse, a white cream or unguent made of lead carbonate, a universal cosmetic of her age, more properly seen as a lethal poison. She takes some on a forefinger and rubs it on her cheeks, then all over her face with little circular movements. The neck receives similar treatment; the tops of the shoulders. She reaches next back to the bundle and takes the mirror and one of the minuscule blue bottles, stoppered with a cork. She examines her face for a moment. The light on this improvised dressing-table is too far away; picking up the candlestick, she turns towards the man, indicating where she wants it held, closer.

He comes forward and takes it, and holds it slightly to one side, within a foot of the girl's face. She spreads the towel on her lap, carefully unlids the last small gallipot; it holds a safflower pomatum. A minute amount of this she touches across her lips, spreading the colouring first with her tongue, next, mirror in hand, with a fingertip; every so often she touches the fingertip against each cheekbone and rubs the colouring there as well, using it as a rouge as well as a lip-salve. At last, satisfied with the effect, she puts the mirror down and relids the gallipot. Having done that, she pushes the human candle-holder's wrist gently away and reaches for another blue bottle. That has a goose-quill in its cork when it is opened. To apply its colourless liquid she tilts her head back and allows one drop to fall into each opened eye. Perhaps it stings, for she blinks rapidly on each occasion. That bottle is recorked; and only then does she look up at the man.

The brilliance of her eyes, already dilating under the influence of the belladonna, the heightened colour of her mouth and cheeks — the scarlet seems not a natural red at all — make it clear that this is no maid, though the effect is far more doll-like than aphrodisiac. Only those tawny irises, with their enlarging pupils, remain of the simple young woman who dozed on the bed fifteen minutes before. The corners of her red lips curve just enough to hint at a smile; yet innocently, almost as if she is the staring man's sister, indulging some harmless foible in him. After a few moments she closes her eyes, without altering the upward angle of her face.

Another might have assumed it was an invitation to kiss, but this man's only reaction is to move the candle a little closer; to one side, to the other. He seems to search every inch of that faintly wax-like facial skin, every curve, every feature, as if somewhere among them lies a minute lost object, a hidden symptom, an answer; and his face grows mysterious in its intensity of concentration, its absence of emotion. The impression is of a profound innocence, such as congenital idiots sometimes display; of in some way seeing her more sustainedly, more wholly than normal intelligence could. Yet there is nothing of the idiot about his own face. Beneath its regularity, even handsomeness — the mouth is particularly strong and well shaped — there lurks a kind of imperturbable gravity, an otherness.

She bears this silent scrutiny for nearly a minute. His free hand rises, hesitates, gently touches her right temple. He traces the line of her face, down her cheek to the jawbone and chin, as if she is indeed not flesh, but wax, painted marble, a death-mask. The tracing continues, and she closes her eyes again: the forehead, the eyebrows, the eyelids, the nose, the mouth itself. Her lips do not move against the fingers that brush across them.

Suddenly the man falls to his knees, putting the candle upon the floor at her feet; and sinks his face into her lap, almost as if he cannot stand further sight of what he has caressed, and yet is at its mercy. She does not flinch or seem surprised at this; but stares down for a long moment at the back of the head buried against her; then reaches her left hand and strokes the bound hair. She whispers, so softly it seems to be to herself, not to him.

"Oh my poor Dick. Poor Dick."

He does not answer, seems once again frozen. She continues slowly to stroke his hair and pat it for a minute or more, in the silence. At last she gently pushes him away, and stands, though only to turn to her opened bundle and from it to unroll an oyster-pink gown and petticoat, which she smoothes out flat, as if preparing to put them on. Still he kneels, with his head bowed, it might seem in some kind of submission or supplication. The candle on the floor lights something that suggests neither, and at which he stares down, as hypnotized by it as he has been by her face; and that both his hands clutch, as a drowning man a branch, though they do not move. The top of his breeches has been torn aside, and what he clutches is no branch, but a large, naked and erect penis. The young woman shows no shock or outrage when she realizes this obscenity, though her hands are arrested in their smoothing. She goes quietly to the top of her truckle-bed, where the violets still lie strewn on the rough pillow; gathers them up, and returns to where he kneels, to toss them, it seems casually, almost mockingly under the down-turned face and across the hands and the monstrous blood-filled glans.

His face jerks up as in an agony at the painted one above, and they stare for a moment into each other's eyes. She steps round him and unlatches the door and stands holding it open, for poor Dick to leave; at which, clutching his opened breeches, he struggles clumsily to his feet and without looking at her, and still in obscene disarray, lurches through the open door. She steps into the doorway, it seems to give him light down the dark stairway to the landing below. Some draught threatens to extinguish the candle, and she draws back, shielding the guttering flame, like a figure from a Chardin painting, and closes the door with her back. She leans against it, and stares down at the pink brocaded clothes on the truckle-bed. There is no one to see she has tears in her eyes, besides the belladonna.

Dick had been, during his absence upstairs, briefly a subject of conversation at the long table in the inn kitchen. Such kitchens were once semi-public and as much the centre of the inn's life, for the humbler traveller or the servants of grander ones, as the equivalent room in the old farmhouse. If not finer, the food eaten there — and no doubt the company — was certainly warmer than in the more public parlours or private chambers. The inn servants welcomed the gossip, news and entertainment brought by strangers of their own approximate class and kind. The undisputed king of the Black Hart's kitchen, that evening, and from the moment he had stamped through the door from the stableyard, cutlass and cased blunderbuss under one arm, and managed, in one comprehensive removal of his hat and sweep of his eyes, to ogle kitchen-maids, cook and Dorcas the inn-maid, had been he of the scarlet coat, soon self-announced as Sergeant Farthing.

He was, it equally soon seemed, of that ancient type — as ancient as the human race, or certainly as human war — the Roman comedians dubbed the *miles gloriosus;* the military boaster, or eternal bag of bullshit. Even to be a modest soldier was no recommendation in eighteenth-century England. The monarchs and their ministers might argue the need for a standing army; to everyone else soldiers seemed an accursed nuisance (and insult, when they were foreign mercenaries), an intolerable expense both upon the nation and whatever particular and unfortunate place they were quartered in. Farthing appeared oblivious to this, and immoderately confident of his own credentials: how he was (despite his present dress) an ex-sergeant of marines, how as a drummer boy he had been on Byng's flagship during the glorious engagement of Cape Passaro in '18, where the Spaniards were given such a drubbing; had been commended for his courage by Admiral Byng himself (not the one to be filled with Portsmouth lead in 1757 to encourage the others, but his father), though "no bigger than that lad" . . . the potboy. He had a way of fixing attention; and not letting it go, once it was fixed. There was certainly no one in that kitchen to challenge such a self-proclaimed man of war, and of the outer world. He had in addition a bold eye for his female listeners, since like all his kind he knew very well that half the trick of getting an audience into the palm of one's hand is flattering them. He also ate and drank copiously, and praised each drop and mouthful; perhaps the most truthful sentence he spoke was when he said he knew good cider when he tasted it.

Of course he was questioned in return, as to the present journey. The younger gentleman and his uncle were riding, it seemed, to pay court to a lady who was respectively an aunt and a sister; a lady as rich as a supercargo, old and ailing besides, who lived at Bideford or thereabout; who had never married, but inherited lands and property fit for a duchess. Various winks and nose-taps glossed this already sufficiently explicit information: the young gentleman, it was hinted, had not always in the past been a model of assiduity, and lay even now in debt. The wench upstairs was a

London lady's maid, destined for the aunt's service, while he, Timothy Farthing, had come as a service to the uncle, with whom he had been long acquainted and who was of nervous disposition as regards highwaymen, footpads and almost any other human face met more than a mile from St Paul's. Though he said it himself, they had travelled thus far under his vigilant eye as safe as with a company of foot.

And this uncle? He was a man of means, a substantial merchant in the City of London, however with children of his own to provide for. His brother, the younger gentleman's father, had died improvidently some years before, and the uncle stood as his nephew's effective guardian and mentor.

Only once had he broken off during all this discourse or quasi-monologue; and that was when Dick had come from the stables and stood, as if lost; uncomprehending, unsmiling, in the doorway. Farthing had bunched fingers to his mouth and pointed to an empty place on the far side of the table, then winked at Puddicombe, the landlord.

"Hears naught, says naught. Born deaf and mute, Master Thomas. And simple into the bargain. But a good fellow. My younger gentleman's servant, despite his clothes. Sit you down, Dick. Eat your share, we've met none so good as this on our way. Now where was I?"

"How as you came on the Spainer's tail," ventured the potboy.

Now and again, while the silent servant ate, Farthing did appeal to him. "Isn't that so, Dick?" Or, "Ecod, Dick could tell more if he had a tongue — or a mind to wield it."

It was not that these appeals were answered, indeed Dick seemed oblivious to them, even when his vacant blue eyes were on Farthing and he was being addressed; yet his companion seemingly wanted to show avuncularity among all his other virtues. The eyes of the maids, however, did wander the deaf-mute's way more and more frequently; perhaps it was curiosity, perhaps it was a kind of wistfulness that so well-proportioned and fundamentally attractive a young male face, for all its expressionlessness and lack of humour, should belong to such a pitiful creature mentally.

There had been one other interruption: the "wench upstairs"

had appeared in the inner doorway towards the end of the supper, bearing a tray with the remains of her own, and beckoned to the inn-maid Dorcas, who rose to speak there with her. Some low words were exchanged between them, and Dorcas looked round at the deaf-mute. Farthing would have had the newcomer join them, but she declined, and pertly.

"I have heard all your bloodthirsty tales, I thank you."

The little curtsey she gave as she retreated was almost as much a snub as her words. The ex-sergeant touched up his right moustache and sought sympathy from the landlord.

"There's London for you, Master Thomas. I'll warrant you that girl was as pleasant and fresh of face as yon Dorcas a few years ago. Now the chit's all Frenchified airs, like her name, that I'll warrant she never was born with. She'd be all pale civility, nice as a nun's hen, as the saying goes." He puts on an affected voice. " 'Would the man I love best were here, that I might treat him like a dog.' So's her kind. I tell you, you'd have ten times more a better treating from her mistress than a maid like Louise. Louise, what name is that for an Englishwoman, I ask you, sir. Isn't it so, Dick?"

Dick stared and said nothing.

"Poor Dick. He has her mincing manners up with him all day long. Don't you, lad?" He went through a pantomime, cocking his thumb towards the door through which the mincing manners had just departed, then mimicking by means of forked fingers two people riding together. Finally he pushed up his nose and once more cocked his thumb at the door. The deaf-mute still stared blankly back at him. Farthing winked at the landlord. "I' faith, I know blocks of wood with more wit."

However, a little later, when he saw Dorcas filling the brass jug from the copper in which it had heated, since that had evidently been the matter discussed with the girl upstairs, the deaf-mute stood and waited to take it; and again at the door, where the maid handed him an earthenware bowl from a dresser. He even nodded, in some token of thanks for her help; but she turned to Farthing as if in doubt.

"Do 'er know where to take 'un, then?"

"Aye. Let him be." He closed an eye, and tapped it with a finger. "Eyes like a falcon, has Dick. Why, he sees through walls."

"Never."

"He must, my love. Leastways I never met a man so fond of staring at 'em." And he winked again, to make clear he was joking.

Mr Puddicombe advanced the opinion that this was a strange case for a gentleman's servant — how could a master use one who understood so little? How command, and make him fetch?

Farthing glanced towards the door and leant forward confidentially.

"I'll tell you this, Master Thomas. The master's a match for his man. I never met a gentleman spoke less. 'Tis his humour, his uncle warned me thus. So be it, I take no offence." He pointed a finger at the landlord's face. "But mark my words, he'll speak with Dick."

"How so?"

"By ciphers, sir."

"And what might they be?"

Farthing leant back, then tapped his chest with a finger and raised a clenched fist. His audience stared, as blankly as the deaf-mute. The gestures were repeated, then glossed.

"Bring me . . . punch."

Dorcas put her hand over her mouth. Farthing tapped his own shoulder, then raised one open hand and the forefinger of the other. Again he waited, then deciphered.

"Wake me, six of the clock prompt."

Now he extended a palm and put his other hand, clenched, upon it; touched himself; cupped his hands against his breasts; then raised four fingers. The same fascinated faces waited for an explanation.

"Wait — a play upon words, do you not take it, a weight in a balance — wait on me at the lady's house at four o'clock."

Puddicombe nodded a shade uncertainly. "I grasp it."

"I could give you ten times more. A hundred times. Our Dick is not the fool he looks. I'll tell you something more, sir. Between ourselves." Once again he looked to the door, and dropped his voice. "This yesternight I must needs share a bed with him at

33

Taunton, we could find no better place. I wake, I know not why, in the middle of the night. I find my bed-partner gone, slipped away as I slept. I think not too much on that, he must to the vaults, the more room for me, and would sleep again. Whereupon I heard a sound, Master Thomas, as of one talking in his sleep. No words, but a hum in the throat. So." And he hummed as he had described, paused, then hummed again. "I look. And there I see the fellow in his shirt, and on his knees, as it might be praying, by the window. But not as a Christian, to our Lord. Nay. To the moon, sir, that shone bright on where he was. And he stood, sir, and pressed to the glass, still making his sounds, as if he would fly up to where he gazed. And I thought, Tim, thou'st faced the Spanish cannon, thou'st given the ruff of the drum, thou'st seen death and desperate men more times than thou canst tell, but rat or rot me, none like this. 'Twas clear as day he was in a lunatic fit, and might at any moment turn and spring and tear me limb from limb." He paused, for effect, and surveyed the table. "I tell you, my good people, no jest, I would not pass another hour like that for a hundred pound. Ecod, no, nor for a thousand."

"Could you not seize him?"

Farthing allowed a knowing smile to cross his features.

"I take it you were never at Bedlam, sir. Why, I've seen one there, a fellow you'd spit upon for a starving beggar in his quiet hours, throw off ten stout lads in his passions. Your lunatic's a tiger when the moon is on him, Master Thomas. 'Sdeath, he'll out-hector Hector himself, as the saying is. Finds the rage and strength of twenty. And mark Dick's no weakling, even in his settled mind."

"What did you then?"

"I lay as dead, sir, with this hand on the hilt of my blade beside my bed. A weaker spirit might have cried for help. But I gave myself the credit of keeping my head, Master Thomas. I braved it out."

"And what happened?"

"Why, the fit passed, sir. He comes once more to the bed, gets in. He starts snoring. But not I, oh no, 'fore George not I. Tim Farthing knows his duty. Ne'er a wink all night, my blade at the ready, sat in a chair where I could swash him down if the fit came on again or worse. I tell you no lie, my friends, had he but woke a second, he should have been carbonadoed in a trice, by Heaven he should. I reported all to Mr Brown next morning. And he said he would speak to his nephew. Who seemed not troubled, and said Dick was strange, but would do no harm, I was to take no account." He leant back, and touched his moustache. "I keep my own counsel on that, Master Thomas."

"I should think so, verily."

"And my blunderbush to hand." His eyes sought Dorcas's face. "No need to fright yourself, my dear. Farthing's on watch. He'll do no harm here." The girl's eyes lifted involuntarily towards the ceiling. "Nor up there, neither."

" 'Tis only three stairs."

Farthing folded his arms, then put his tongue in his cheek. "By hap she finds him work to do?"

The girl was puzzled. "What work would that be then?"

"Work no man finds work, my innocent." He leered, and the girl, at last understanding what he would say, raised a hand to her mouth. Farthing transferred his eyes to the landlord. "I tell you, London's an evil place, Master Thomas. The maid but apes the mistress there. Ne'er rests content, the hussy, till she's decked out in her shameless sacks and trollopees. If my lady has her lusty lackey, why shouldn't I, says she. Spurn the poor brute by day, and have him to my bed each night."

"Prithee no more, Mr Farthing. If my good wife were here . . ."

"Amen, sir. I should not speak of it, were the fellow not lecherous as a Barbary ape. Let your maids be warned. He came on one in the stable on our road here . . . happily I passed and prevented the rogue. But enough's enough. He knows no better, he thinks all women as lascivious as Eve, God forgive him. As eager to raise their petticoats as he to unbreech."

"I wonder his master don't give him a good flogging."

"And well you may, sir. Well you may. No more of it. A word to the wise, as the saying goes."

They passed then to other matters; but when, some ten minutes later, the deaf-mute reappeared, it was as if a draught of cold air had entered the room. He seemed as expressionless as ever, looked at no one, regained his place. One by one all there covertly glanced at him, as if searching for some flush, some outward sign of his sin. However, he stared down with his blue eyes at the old table just beyond his plate, blankly awaiting some further humiliation.

"Well powdered, I trust?"

"His flock, his lodgings, his vestry, his churchwardens, I have had damnation on them all, anathema singular and plural. You are invited to dine tomorrow to hear the recitation over again. I ventured to decline on your behalf."

"And no enquiry?"

"Beyond civility, and barely that. The gentleman has only one profound object of interest in life. It does not comprehend the affairs of others."

"You have had a poor last audience for your talents. My apologies." The actor, who stood planted on the opposite side of the fire from where Mr Bartholomew sat with his papers, stared heavily at him, as if not to be fobbed off by this lighter mood. "Come, my dear Lacy. My word to you stands. I mean no evil, I do no evil. No one shall, or could, blame you for your part."

"But your purpose is not what you led me to believe, Mr Bartholomew. Is it not so? No, I must speak now. I have no doubt you mean well to me in all your concealings. But I must doubt whether you mean well to yourself."

"Do we say a poet lies when he speaks of meeting the Muses?"

"We know what he intends to convey by that figure."

"But do we say he lies?"

"No."

"Then in that sense I have not lied to you. I go to meet one I desire to know, and respect, as much as I would a bride — or my Muse indeed, were I a poet. Before whom I am as Dick before myself, if not more ignorant still. And whom I have been hitherto prevented from seeing as much as by a jealous guardian. I may have deceived you in the letter. But not in the spirit."

The actor's eyes glanced at the papers.

"I am bound to ask why a meeting with a learned stranger has to be conducted in such very great secrecy, and in this remote place. If the purpose be wholly innocent."

Mr Bartholomew leant back in his chair, this time with a distinctly sardonic smile.

"Perhaps I am one of those seditious northern Jacks? Another Bolingbroke? These papers here are all in cipher. If not in plain French or Spanish. I go to plot with some emissary of James Stuart."

For a moment the actor seemed confused, as if his secret thought had been read. "My blood chills, sir."

"Look. They are indeed in a cipher of a kind."

He held out the sheet of paper he had been reading, which Lacy took. After a few moments the actor looked up.

"I can make nothing of it."

"Necromantical, think you not? I am here to creep into the woods and meet some disciple of the Witch of Endor. To exchange my eternal soul against the secrets of the other world. How does that cap fit?"

The actor passed the paper back to him.

"You choose to be playful, I think this not the moment."

"Then let us talk no more nonsense. I bring no harm to king or country, nor to any person thereof. I place neither body nor soul in danger. My mind perhaps, but a man's mind is his own business. What I am upon may be a wild goose chase, a foolish dream. Whom I wish to meet may — " but he broke off, then put the paper with the others on the table beside his chair. "No matter."

"This person is in hiding?"

Mr Bartholomew stared at him for a moment.

"No more, Lacy. I beg you."

"I must still ask why I should be deceived, sir."

"My friend, that question sits strangely in your mouth. Have you not spent your own life deceiving?" Lacy seemed set back a moment by such a charge. The man in the chair stood and went to the fire, his back to the actor. "But I will tell you. I am born with a fixed destiny. All I told you of my supposed father I might have said of my true one — and much worse, for he is an old fool; and hath given birth to another, that is my elder brother. I am, as you might be, offered a part in a history, and I am not forgiven for refusing to play it. Mark, the case between us is not exact. If you will not play, you lose but your money. I lose ... more than you may imagine." He turned. "I have no liberty, Lacy, unless I steal it first. If I go where I will, as now, I must go as a thief from those who would have me do as they want. That is all. And now truly, I would say no more."

The actor looked down, with a little shrug and nod, as if confessing himself baffled; and the speaker went on in a more even tone, and watching him.

"Tomorrow we leave together. In a very few miles we shall come to where we must part. The road you and your man shall take joins that to Crediton and Exeter, which city I would have you gain with all speed. Once there, you may return to London as you please and when you please. The only thing I desire of you to conceal is all that concerns me and the manner of our coming to this place. As we agreed at the beginning."

"Does the maid not come with us?"

"No."

"I must tell you something." He left a little pause. "Jones, that is Farthing, believes he has seen her before."

Mr Bartholomew turned away to the fire again. There was a small silence.

"Where?"

The actor eyed his back. "Entering a bagnio, sir. Where he was told she was employed."

"And what said you to that?"

"I would not believe him."

"You were right. He is mistaken."

"But nor is she now a lady's maid, sir, by your own admittance. I think you must know your man is smitten. Farthing tells me, for good reason. He is not spurned." He hesitated. "He has gone to where she lies, at night."

Mr Bartholomew gave him a long look, as if the actor now grew impertinent; but then he showed a distinctly sarcastic smile.

"May a man not lie with his own wife?"

The actor was once again caught unawares. He stared a moment at Mr Bartholomew, then down.

"So be it. I have said what I must."

"And I do not impugn the regard that inspired it. We will settle our business and bid our formal adieux tomorrow, but permit me now to thank you for your assistance and patience. I have had little commerce with your profession. If they are all like you, I perceive I have lost by my ignorance. Though you cannot credit me in so much else, you will, I hope, credit me in that. I most sincerely wish we might have met in more open circumstances."

The actor gave him a dryly rueful smile. "And I wish that we still may, sir. You have raised a devilish curiosity in me, beside my apprehensions."

"The first you must quell. For the second you may rest easy. It is truly like a tale, why, one of your play-pieces. I think you would not let an audience have the final act before the first, for all your love of fixed tomorrows? No? Then leave me my mysteries also."

"The final act of my plays will be told, sir. I am not to have that privilege."

"And nor can I give it, for it is not yet written. There is the true difference." He smiled. "Lacy, I bid you goodnight."

The actor gave him one last searching, yet uncertain, look, as if he would still say more; then bowed and turned away. But on opening the door to leave, he stopped in surprise, and looked back.

"Your man waits here."

"Send him in."

The actor hesitated, cast one more look at the silent man in the shadows outside, passed him with a curt gesture, and disappeared.

꧁꧂

The deaf-mute servant comes into the room, and closes the door. He stands by it, staring at his master by the fireplace, who looks back. Such a fixed, mutual, interlocked regard would have been strange if it had lasted only a second or two, for the servant has made no sign of respect. In fact the stare lasts much longer, beyond all semblance of a natural happening, almost as if they speak, though their mouths do not move. It is such a look as a husband and wife, or siblings, might give, in a room where there are other people, and they cannot say what they truly feel; yet prolonged far beyond that casual kind of exchange of secret feeling, and quite devoid even of its carefully hidden hints of expression. It is like turning a page in a printed book — and where one expects dialogue, or at least a description of movements and gestures, there is nothing: a *Shandy*-like blank page, or a gross error in binding, no page at all. The two men stand in their silence, in each other's looking, as in a mirror.

At last both move, and simultaneously, as a stopped film begins again. Dick turns to the box beside which he stands by the door. Mr Bartholomew goes back to his chair and sits, and watches his servant lift the box and carry it to the hearth before the fire. There he begins immediately to feed the sheafs of written paper inside the box to the red embers; without a look at his master, and as if they were no more than old newspapers. They catch almost at once, and now Dick kneels and starts disposing similarly of the leatherbound books. One by one he takes them out, demi-folios and large quartos, some smaller, and many stamped in gilt with a coat of arms, and drops them opened with their pages down, into the mounting flames. One or two he tears apart by main force, but most he simply lets drop, and does no more than push them to a heap where they have fallen loose, or with the primitive poker splays those that are slow to burn from the packed density of their pages.

Mr Bartholomew stands and picks up the sheaf of papers on the table, and throws them to blaze with the rest; then stands behind the crouched servant, who now reaches beside the huge hearth, where more logs stand piled, to set five or six transversely across the incandescent pile of paper; then resumes once more his watching pose. Both men now stare at this small holocaust as they had earlier stared at each other. Intense shadows dart and shiver about the bare room, since the hearth flames are far brighter than the candle-branches. Mr Bartholomew makes a step to look down into the chest beside the hearth, to be sure that it has been properly emptied. It seems it has, for he bends and closes its lid; then returns to his chair and sits again, waiting for this incomprehensible sacrifice to be concluded; each fallen scrap, each leaf and page, burnt to ashes.

Several minutes later, when it is near complete, Dick looks across at Mr Bartholomew; and now there is the ghost of a smile on his face, the smile of someone who knows why this is done, and is glad. It is not a servant's smile, so much as an old friend's, even a collusive fellow-criminal's. There, it is done, is it not better so? As mysterious a smile meets his, and for a few seconds there begins another stare between the two. This time it is brought to an end by Mr Bartholomew. He raises his left hand, making a circle of the thumb and forefinger; then he stiffens his other forefinger and firmly pierces the circle, just once.

Dick rises and goes to the foot of the bed, where the bench-stool lies; lifts it and comes back with the long piece of furniture and sets it facing the still lively fire, some ten feet from it. Then, returning to the bed, he opens its curtains. Without another look at his master he leaves.

Mr Bartholomew watches the fire, seemingly lost in thought. He remains so until the door opens again. The young woman from upstairs, with her painted face, stands on the threshold. She curtsies, unsmiling, comes into the room a few paces. Dick appears behind her and closes the door, then waits by it. Mr Bartholomew goes back to watching the fire, almost as if he resents this interruption; at last looks coldly at the standing girl. He examines her as he would an animal: the matching grey-pink brocaded gown and petticoat, the lace wing-cuffs on the three-quarter sleeves, the inverted cone of her tight-laced bust, the cherry and ivory stomacher, the highly unnatural colour of the face, the pert white head-cap with its two hanging side-bands. She wears now also a small throat-necklace of cornelians, the colour of dried blood. The net result is perhaps not aesthetically unattractive; yet it seems pathetically out-of-place, something plain and pleasant turned artificial and pretentious. The new clothes do not improve appearance, they ruin it.

"Shall I send thee back to Claiborne, Fanny? And bid her whip thee for thy sullenness?" The girl neither moves nor speaks; nor seems surprised to be called by a name different from the one that Farthing gave her, of Louise. "Did I not hire thee out to have my pleasure?"

"Yes, sir."

"French, Italian, all thy lewd tricks." Again the girl says nothing. "Modesty sits on thee like silk on dung. How many different men have cleft thee this last six month?"

"I don't know, sir."

"Nor how many ways. Claiborne told me all of thee before we struck our bargain. Even the pox is afraid to touch thy morphewed carcase." He watches her. "Thou hast played boy to every Bulgar in London. Why, even worn men's clothes to please their lust." He stares at her. "Answer. Yea or nay?"

"I have worn men's clothes, sir."

"For which thou shalt roast in hell."

"I shan't be alone, sir."

"But double roasted, since thou art the cause. Think'st thou God makes no distinction in His wrath between those that fall and those that make them fall? Between Adam's weakness and Eve's wickedness?"

"I cannot tell, sir."

"I tell thee. And I tell thee I'll have my money's-worth of thee, whether thou wilt or not. Didst ever hear a public hackney tell its master how to ride?"

"I have done your will, sir."

"In shadow. Thy insolence has showed as naked as thy breasts. Dost think me so blind I did not catch that look of thine at the ford?"

"It was but a look, sir."

"And that tuft of flowers beneath thy nose but violets?"

"Yes, sir."

"Thou lying jade."

"No, sir."

"I say yes, sir. I saw thy glance and what it spake: what stench in the nostrils thy damned violets were for."

"I wore them for themselves, sir. I meant no else."

"And swear to it?"

"Yes, sir."

"Then get thee to thy knees. Here." He points to a place in front of him, beside the bench. The girl hesitates, then comes forward and kneels, her head still bowed. "And let me see thy eyes." The grey ones stare down into the uplifted brown. "Say this: I am a public whore."

"I am a public whore."

"Hired for your use."

"Hired for your use."

"To please you in all."

"To please you in all."

"I am issued of Eve, with all her sins."

"I am issued of Eve."

"With all her sins."

"With all her sins."

"And guilty of insolence."

"Guilty of insolence."

"Which henceforward I do renounce."

"Which henceforward I do renounce."

"And so I swear."

"So I swear."

"Or may I be damned in Hell."

"Damned in Hell."

Mr Bartholomew stares down into her eyes a long moment. There seems something demonic now in that face beneath the bald head; demonic not in its anger or emotion, but in its coldness, its indifference to this female thing before him. It speaks of a hitherto hidden trait in his character: a sadism before Sade, still four years unborn in the dark labyrinths of real time; and as unnatural as the singeing smell of burnt leather and paper that pervades the room. Had one to represent in a face the very antithesis of human feeling, it is here, and frighteningly so.

"Thou art shriven. Now bare thy putrid body."

The girl looks down a moment at the floor, then rises to her feet and begins to unlace her dress. Mr Bartholomew still sits implacably in the chair where he has read. The girl turns her back slightly to him as her undressing proceeds. At the conclusion of it she sits on the far end of the bench-stool, beside the garments she has removed, and peels off her clocked stockings. At last she sits naked, but for the necklace of cornelians and the cap, with her hands in her lap, her head once more bowed. Her body is not truly to the masculine taste of its time: it is slim and small-breasted, and more white than rosy, although it shows not a sign of the morphew it has just been accused of.

"Shall he serve thee?" The girl says nothing. "Answer."

"My inclination is to you, sir. But you won't have it."

"No, to him. And his cockpiece."

"It was your will."

"To see you sport and couple. Not strut your attachment like turtling doves. Art not ashamed, to have had acquaintance with the finest, and now fall so low?" Once more she says nothing. "Answer."

Seemingly driven at last beyond timidity, she does not. Mr Bartholomew stares at her, with her mutely mutinous bowed head, then across at Dick by the door; and again they regard each other, as before she came, in some mysterious blank page. Yet not for long; although with no apparent sign from Mr Bartholomew, Dick turns abruptly and leaves. The girl glances quickly round at the door, as if surprised at this going; but will not look at Mr Bartholomew for explanation.

Now they are alone, he stands and goes to the fire. There he stoops and takes the poker and carefully pushes some last scraps of page and paper that have escaped burning towards the now flaming logs that were added. He straightens and looks down at what he has done, his back to her. Slowly her head comes up to watch him. Some kind of speculation, or calculation, clouds those brown eyes. She hesitates, then stands and goes softly on her bare feet behind that impassive back. She murmurs something in a low voice, inaudible across the room. The offer made is not difficult to guess, since her hands rise in a cautious yet practised fashion and come to rest on the sides of his damask coat, while her naked body moves to press lightly against his back, as a pillion-passenger's might.

The hands are immediately caught; not angrily, but merely prevented from slipping forward; and unexpectedly his voice is less scathing and bitter.

"Thou art a fool and a liar, Fanny. I heard thy pantings when last he rammed thee."

" 'Twas only feigning, sir."

"What thou'dst fain have."

"No, sir. 'Tis you I desire to please."

He says nothing, and her hands attempt to escape his and insinuate themselves forward. Now they are firmly removed.

"Then dress. And I'll tell thee how."

Still she solicits. "With all my heart, sir. I'll make you stand tall as a beadle's staff, that then you may use on me."

"Thou hast no heart. Cover thy shamelessness. Away."

He remains at the fire with his back turned while she dresses, in a seeming brown study. When she is ready, she sits again on the bench and waits; so long that in the end she speaks.

"I am dressed, sir."

He glances half round, as if indeed from some reverie, then resumes his staring down at the fire.

"When wert thou first debauched?"

Something in that voice from the hidden face, some unexpected spark of curiosity, makes her slow to answer.

"At sixteen, sir."

"In a bagnio?"

"No, sir. A son of the house where I was maid."

"In London?"

"In Bristol. Where I was born."

"He got thee with child?"

"No, sir. But his mother discovered us one day."

"And gave thee thy wages?"

"If a broom-handle be wages."

"How cam'st thou to London?"

"By starving."

"God gave thee no parents?"

"They would not have me back, sir. They are Friends."

"How friends?"

"What people call Quakers, sir. My master and mistress too."

He turns, and stands astride, his hands behind his back.

"What next?"

"The young man gave me a ring, before we were discovered. It was stole from his mother's box, sir. And I knew when 'twas found out, I should be accused, for she would not hear wrong of him. So I sold it where I could and came to London, and found a place, and thought myself fortunate. But I was not, for the husband my master came to lust after me; and I must let him have his way, fear of my place. Which my new mistress discovered, and then was I out again upon the street. Where I must come in the end to begging, because I could find no honest work. There was that in my face seemed not to please mistresses, and 'tis they who do the hiring." After a moment she adds, "I was carried to it by need, sir. 'Tis so with most of us."

"Most in need do not turn strumpet."

"I know, sir."

"Therefore the corruption lies in thy wanton nature?"

"Yes, sir."

"And thy parents were right to reprobate, for all their false doctrine?"

"For what I did, sir. But I was blamed for all. My mistress made out I had bewitched her son. Not true, he forced the first kiss, he stole the ring without my asking, and all that followed. My father and mother would not hear, for they said I had denied the inner light. That I was Satan's child, not theirs, and would poison my sisters."

"What inner light is that?"

"The light of Christ. 'Tis the manner of their faith, sir."

"And not thine, since that day?"

"No, sir."

"No belief in Christ?"

"No belief that I shall meet Him in this world, sir. Nor the next."

"Thou hast belief in a next world?"

"Yes, sir."

"Which must be Hell, must it not, for such as thee?"

"I pray not, sir."

"Is it not as sure as that this wood will burn to ashes?" The girl's head bows deeper, and she does not reply. He goes on in the same even voice. "Or as sure as the hell that awaits thee here on earth, when thou'rt become too stale for the bagnio. Thou'lt end a common bawd, Fanny, or a crone in the poorhouse. If the pox has not already claimed thee. Or think'st thou to multiply thy sins and swell to another Claiborne in thy after-years? That will not save thee." He waits, but the girl does not speak. "What stops thy tongue?"

"I would not be what I am, sir. Far less Mistress Claiborne."

"The virtuous wife, no doubt. With mewling brats at thy skirts."

"I am barren, sir."

"Then thou art a prize pigeon indeed, Fanny."

Slowly her head rises and she meets his eyes; it seems more in puzzlement than in outrage at being taunted so, as if she were trying to read on his face what she could not comprehend in his words. His next action is even more incomprehensible, for of a sudden that arctic face smiles — it is hardly an unmistakably human smile, yet neither is it a cynical or sneering one. Most singularly, it is nearest to an understanding one. Greater strangeness still follows, for he takes three or four steps, plants himself in front of her; bends and takes her right hand and raises it briefly to his lips. Having done which, he does not release the hand, but holds it, staring down at her face, and still not without a smile. For a moment they are, Mr Bartholomew with his bald head, Fanny with her painted face, like pantaloon figures from some *fête galante* by Watteau, despite the very different environment. Abruptly he drops the hand and turns away to his original chair, where he sits, leaving her to stare in shock after him.

"Why did you that, sir?"

"Know you not why gentlemen kiss a woman's hand?" That final surprise, in his change of person of address to her, is too much. She lowers her head, and shakes it. "For what you are about to give me, dear lamb."

Her lost eyes seek his again.

"What shall I give, sir?"

"We are come near those waters I spake of, that shall cure me.

Tomorrow we shall meet those who keep them, and who have it in their power to advance my most cherished hopes. I would bring them a present, a token of my esteem. Not of money, nor jewels, they care not for such things. It shall be of you, Fanny." He contemplates her. "What say you to that?"

"What I must, sir. That I am bound to Mistress Claiborne, and sworn to return."

"A bond with the Devil's no bond."

"That may be, sir. But she's worse than the Devil to those that forsake her. She must, or we should all run loose."

"Have you not said, but a minute past, that you wish you were not what you are?"

Her voice is almost inaudible.

"I would not be worse still."

"Did she not say when we engaged that you must please me in all?"

"Yes, sir. But not that I must please others also."

"I purchased you for three weeks, did I not?"

"Yes, sir."

"Then I have two weeks' use of you yet. And in that use that I have purchased, and dearly, I command this. You shall tomorrow essay to please those we hope to meet."

She bows her head, as if in reluctant submission, and he continues.

"I would have you mark my every word, Fanny. You must not mistake the manner and appearance of those who keep these waters. They are but late arrived from their native country. It is most far from this of ours, and they do not speak our tongue."

"I know some little French, of Dutch some words also."

"Nor that neither. With them you must converse as you have learnt with Dick." He is silent, staring at her still bowed head. "You have shown well enough there, Fanny. My displeasure was semblance, to test you for this my real intent. But listen well. In their country there are no women like you. You have a faculty of playing the prudish virgin. Such I would have you be tomorrow. No paint, no finery, no London manners. No knowing looks, no sign of what you truly are. Demure in all, a young woman brought up in country modesty, one innocent of men. They we meet would see respect in you, not your practised lust, not such as you showed me but this half-hour gone, and have showed a thousand others besides. Is that understood?"

"So be it they would have me to their beds, I must?"

"What they shall plainly want, that you must do."

"Whether I would or not?"

"I tell you you shall do their will, that is mine. Doth Claiborne let you pick and choose, so you were fine lady?"

She bows her head again, and there is silence. Mr Bartholomew surveys her. His expression now is without cynicism or sarcasm, or the former cruelty. If anything it shows a strange patience, or calm; from anachronistic skinhead he seems now become something even more improbable: Buddhist monk, praeternaturally equable and contained, drowned in what he is and does. Yet there is a hint of something else in his eyes, that is more unexpected still. Nothing in his seeming behaviour until now has predicted this: a contentment, a satisfaction of the kind his servant Dick had momentarily shown when the papers were burnt. Nearly a minute passes, and then he speaks again.

"Go to the window, Fanny."

She looks up at him, and her side of the silence at least is explained. Her eyes are wet with tears again, the small tears of one who knows herself without choice. Her time has little power of seeing people other than they are in outward; which applies even to how they see themselves, labelled and categorised by circumstance and fate. To us such a world would seem abominably prescribed, with personal destiny fixed to an intolerable degree, totalitarian in its essence; while to its chained humans our present lives would seem incredibly fluid, mobile, rich in free will (if not indeed Midas-rich, less to be envied than to be pitied our lack of absolutes and of social certainty); and above all anarchically, if not insanely, driven by self-esteem and self-interest. Fanny does not weep with frustrated rage, from a modern sense of self, because life obliges it to suffer this kind of humiliation, but much more with a dumb animal's sadness. Such humiliation is as inseparable from life as mud from winter roads, or as child-death from child-birth (of the 2,710 deaths registered in England in the by no means unusual month previous to this day, very nearly half were of infants below the age of five). The conditions of such past worlds were more inexorably fixed than we can imagine; and as little worth expecting sympathy from as seems proven by Mr Bartholomew's impassive face.

He says quietly, "Do as I say."

She still hesitates, but then abruptly stands and goes to it.

"Now open the shutter and look out." He waits till he hears, for he does not turn in his chair to look, the shutter open. "Do you see the Redeemer on His throne in the heavens, beside His Father?"

She looks back to where he sits. "You know not, sir."

"Then what instead?"

"Nothing. The night."

"And in that night?"

She glances quickly out of the window. "Nothing but the stars. The sky is come clear."

"Do the beams of the brightest shake?"

Again she looks. "Yes, sir."

"Do you know why?"

"No, sir."

"I will tell you. They shake with laughter, Fanny, for they mock you. They have mocked you since your day of birth. They will mock you to your day of death. You are but a painted shadow to them, and all your world. It matters not to them whether you have faith in Christ or not. Are sinner or saint, drab or duchess. Man or woman, young or old, it is all one. Whether Hell or Heaven awaits you, good fortune or bad, pain or bliss, to them it is equal. You are born for their amusement, as you are bought for mine. Beneath their light you are but brute, as deaf and dumb as Dick, as blind as Fate itself. They care not one whit what may become of you, no more for the courses of your miserable existence than those on a high hill who watch a battle in the plain below, indifferent to all but its spectacle. You are nothing to them, Fanny. Shall I tell thee why they scorn?" She is silent. "Because thou dost not scorn them back."

The girl stares across the room at the oblivious back of his head.

"How should I scorn stars, sir?"

"How do you scorn a man?"

She is slow to answer.

"I turn away, or flout his desire."

"But say that man a justice, who would have you whipped and clapped in the stocks without fair cause?"

"I should protest I was innocent."

"And if he doth not hear?" She is silent. "Then you must needs sit in the stocks."

"Yes, sir."

"Is such, true justice?"

"No."

"Now say the justice who gives you such justice is no man, but you yourself, and the stocks you sit in made not of iron and wood, but of your blindness for the one part and your folly for the other? What then?"

"I am bemused, sir. I know not what you would have of me."

He stands and walks to the hearth.

"What I should have of far more than thee, Fanny."

"Sir?"

"No more. Get thee to where thou must lie, until thou wak'st."

She does not move for a moment or two, then starts to cross the room towards the door; but stops behind the stool, and looks obliquely at him.

"My lord, I beg you, what would you have?"

But the only answer she receives is his raised left arm and hand, that point towards the door. He turns his back upon her, in final dismissal. She gives Mr Bartholomew one last look, and an unseen curtsey, and leaves.

For some time in the silence he remains standing and staring at the now dying fire. At last he turns and looks at the stool; and a little later goes to the window. There he looks out and up as she had done, almost as if he wishes to assure himself that there are indeed stars alone in the sky. It is impossible to read by his face what he is thinking, although there appears on it now a last paradoxical metamorphosis. If anything it seems a translation, in terms of his own sex and features, of the meekness the girl's face has shown him during their one-sided conversation. In the end he quietly latches the shutter close again. He walks towards the bed, unbuttoning his long waistcoat. As he comes to it, he sinks to his knees on the broad-planks and buries his bald head against its side, as a man seeking undeserved forgiveness or the oblivion of infancy might, against a mother's skirt.

Historical Chronicle, 1736.

APRIL.

Extract of a Letter from Savannah in Georgia, dated Feb. 14, 1735-6.

E arrived here the 5th Inst. which for § Time is incredibly improved; there are about 200 Houses regularly built, some of which lett at 30l. Sterling a Year: Mr *Oglethorpe* went next Day, tho' very wet Weather, to see the adjacent Settlements, in which there are several *English*-like regular Townships, viz. *Beuzez*, *Thunderbolt*, *Fartargile*, *Westbrook*, &c. in a flourishing Condition, beyond any Colony ever known in so short a Time. Tho' we had a long and very stormy Passage, yet we arrived without the Loss of a Soul out of any of our Ships, which were six in Number and very large; Mr *Oglethorpe*, during the Passage, was extremely careful both of the Souls and Bodies under his Care; but what surprizes me beyond Expression is his abstemious and hard Living, for, tho' even Dainties are plentiful, he makes the least Use of them, and goes thro' the Woods, wet or dry, as actively as any *Indian*: his Humanity so gains upon all here, that I have not Words to express their Regard and Esteem for him: He goes To-morrow about 80 Miles farther into the Country, where he is to settle a Town, near which, upon the River *Altamaha*, a Fort with four Bastions is to be built, that is design'd for the Barrier. The Country abounds with Fish, excellent Fruit, and Venison.

Sunday, 4.

Mr *Andrew Pitt*, an Eminent Quaker, &c. waited on the Pr. of *Wales*, to sollicit his Favour in Relation to the Quakers Tythe Bill, whom his Royal H. answer'd to this Effect.——'As I am a Friend to Liberty in General, and to Toleration in particular, I wish you may meet with all proper Favour, but for myself I never gave my Vote in Parliament, and to Influence my Friends, or Direct my Servants in theirs, does not become my Station. To leave them entirely to their own Conscience and Understanding, is a Rule I have hitherto prescrib'd to myself, and purpos'd throughout my whole Life to observe.' Mr *Pitt* overcome with this Conduct, reply'd,——May it Please the Pr. of *Wales*,——I am greatly Affected with your Excellent Notions of Liberty; and am more

'Pleased with the Answer you have given us, 'than if you had granted our Request.'

Tuesday, 6.

Bryan Benson, Esq; was chosen Governor, *Thomas Cooke,* Esq; Deputy Governor of the Bank of *England.* And

Wednesday, 7.

The following Gentlemen were chose Directors for the Year 1736.

Robt Alsop, Esq;	Robt Atwood, Esq;
Sir Edw. Bellamy, Kt.	Wm Snelling, Esq;
John Bance, Esq;	Sir John Thompson, Kt
Sir Gerard Conyers, Kt.	Mr Robt Thornton
Delil'ers Carbonnel Esq;	Stamp Brooksbank, Esq;
Mr Jn Enton Dodsworth	Wm Fawkener, Esq;
Nathaniel Gould, Esq;	Fred. Frankland, Esq;
Samuel Hollen, Esq;	Mr James Gualtier
Mr Benj. Longuet	Henry Neal, Esq;
Mr Joseph Paice.	Charles Savage, Esq;
John Rudge, Esq;	James Spilman, Esq;
Moses Raper, Esq;	Mr Samuel Trench.

The Directors of the *East India* Company.

Robt Adams, Esq;	Samuel Feake, Esq;
Abra. Addams, Esq;	Harry Gough, Esq;
Miles Barne, Esq;	Mr Samuel Hyde
Dodding Braddyll, Esq;	Michael Impey, Esq;
Sir Wm Billers, Kt	Edw. Lovibond, Esq;
Stephen Bisse, Esq;	Baltzar Lyell, Esq;
Mr Rich. Blount	Wm Pomeroy, Esq;
Capt. Rich. Boulton	Jones Raymond, Esq;
Christ. Barrow, Esq;	Wm Rouse, Esq;
Charles Colburne, Esq;	Sir John Salter, Kt
Dr Caleb Cotesworth	St Quin. Thompson, Esq;
Mr John Emmerson.	Josi. Wordsworth jun.

Friday, 9.

Wm Bithell and *Wm Morgan*, were Hang'd at *Worcester* for cutting down, in Company with other Rioters, *Ledbury* Turnpikes. *Morgan* died a Papist. The Turnpike Levellers having been very Tumultuous at the Trial, a Party of Soldiers attended the Execution; on which it pass'd without Disturbance.

Tuesday, 13.

Dr. *Shaw*, a learned Physician at *Scarborough*, was sent for to Court, on Account of the surprizing Cure performed by him on General *Sutton*, and was introduced to his Royal Highness the Prince of *Wales*, the Duke and the Princess; by whom he was very graciously received, and had the Honour of kissing their Hands, as he had before done of their Majesties.

G g

Wednes

Wednesday, 14.

Seven Prisoners in *Newgate*, under Sentence of Transportation, found means to get down the Common Sewer, and 4 of 'em got up a Vault into a House in *Fleet Lane*, 3 of A whom went thro' the Shop and made their Escape, a 4th was secur'd and carried back to *Newgate*. Search was made after the other 3.

Thursday, 15.

One *Wilson* was hang'd at Edinburgh for robbing Collector *Stark*. He having made an Attempt to break Prison, and his Comrade B having actually got off, the Magistrates had the City Guards and the *Welsh* Fusiliers under Arms during Execution, which was perform'd without Disturbance; but on the Hangman's cutting down the Corpse (the Magistrates being withdrawn) the Boys threw, as usual, some Dirt and Stones, which falling among the City Guard, Capt. *Porteous* fired, and C order'd his Men to fire; whereupon above 20 Persons were wounded, 6 or 7 kill'd, one shot thro' the Head at a Window up two Pair of Stairs. The Capt. and several of his Men were after committed to Prison.

Saturday, 17.

An Experiment was tried before several of the Commissioners of the Victualling Office, relating to the Salting of Beef. (*viz.*) A Bullock was Blooded in the two Jugulars almost to Death, knock'd on the Head and ripp'd up, the Guts taken out, and before Cold a Tube was put into one of the Arteries near the Back into which a strong Brine, being pour'd; it circulated thro' all the Vessels, so that it was Salted all over equally alike; for E a Piece of the Leg and Lip being cut off, the Brine issued out. Some of this Beef was put up and sent to Sea, to try how it will keep.

Thursday, 22.

A Fire broke out in Upper *Shadwell*, which burn'd down three Houses. one Mr. *Stringer*'s, whose Aunt, aged 79, was entirely consum'd except a Leg; Mr. *Stringer's* House was F burn'd down a Year ago, by a Fire which happen'd at the same Place.

Sunday, 25.

The Princess of *Saxe-Gotha*, arrived at *Greenwich*. Her Highness, attended by the Lord *Delawar*, and several Ladies of her Brother's Court, and her own Retinue, set out from *Gotha* the 17th, and lay that Night at *Cassel*, G the next at *Paderborn*, on Tuesday at *Munster*, reach'd *Utrecht* on *Thursday*, was Conducted in one of the States Yachts to the *Hague* on *Friday*, where she receiv'd the Complements of the Prince and Princess of *Orange*, by one of their chief Officers, also of the Grand Pensionary. On *Saturday* Morning about 10 reach'd *Helvoetsluys*, and without any Stay H embarked on Board the *William* and *Mary* Yacht, when a fresh Gale blew up, and lasted as long as the Occasion. (*See Bargain with the E. Wind, p. 176.*) This Day about 2, her H. landed at the Hospital, and was conducted in

one of his Majesties Coaches, to the Queen's House in the Park, amidst the Acclamations of Thousands of Spectators. Her Highness seem'd highly Delighted with the Joy the People express'd at her Arrival, and had the Goodness to shew her self for above half an Hour from the Gallery towards the Park. The Prince of *Wales*, came to pay her a Visit, and their Majesties, the Duke, and Princesses sent their Compliments.

Monday, 26.

The Prince of Wales din'd with her Highness at Greenwich, in one of the Rooms towards the Park, the Windows being thrown open, to oblige the Curiosity of the People: His R. H. afterwards gave her the Diversion of passing on the Water, as far as the Tower and back again in his Barge finely adorn'd, and preceded by a Concert of Music. The Ships saluted their Highnesses all the way they pass'd, and hung out their Streamers and Colours, and the River was cover'd with Boats. Their Highnesses afterwards supp'd in public.

Tuesday, 27.

Her Highness came in his Majesty's Coach from Greenwich to Lambeth, cross'd the Water at Lambeth, and was brought from Whitehall to St. James's in the Queen's Chair, where was a numerous and splendid Court, beyond Expression. The Prince of Wales receiv'd her at the Garden Door, and upon her sinking on her Knee to kiss his Hand, he affectionately rais'd her up, and twice saluted her. His Royal Highness led her up Stairs to their Majesties Apartments, where presenting her to the King, her Highness fell on her Knee to kiss his Hand, but was gently taken up and saluted by him. Her Highness was then presented to the Queen in like manner, and afterwards to the Duke and Princesses, who congratulated her Arrival. Her Highness din'd with the Prince of Wales, and the Princesses. At Eight the Procession began to the Chapel, and the joining of Hands was proclaim'd to the People by firing of Guns. Her Highness was in her Hair, wearing a Crown with one Bar as Princess of Wales, set all over with Diamonds; her Robe likewise, as Princess of Wales, being of Crimson Velvet turn'd back with several Rows of Ermin, and having her Train supported by Lady Caroline Lenox, Daughter to his Grace the Duke of Richmond; Lady Caroline Fitzroy, Daughter to his Grace the Duke of Grafton; Lady Caroline Cavendish, Daughter to his Grace the Duke of Devonshire; and Lady Sophia Farmer, Daughter to the Earl of Pomfret, all of whom were in Virgin Habits of Silver like the Princess, and adorn'd with Diamonds, not less in Value than from 20 to 30000l. each. Her Highness was led by his Royal Highness the Duke, and conducted by his Grace the Duke of Grafton, Lord Chamberlain of the Houshold; and the Lord Harvey, Vice-Chamberlain; and attended

Barnstaple, THURSDAY, JUNE 17TH. The Discovery six Weeks since, in a Wood of a Parish some 10 Miles from this Place, of a Stranger hang'd by his own Hand, or so adjudg'd by the Coroner, whose first Inquiries could find no Name to this *Felon de se* nor Cause for so ghastly a Deed, now raises upon fresh-found Informations Alarm of a far greater Crime. It is now learn'd he was Manservant, tho' deaf and dumb, to a Gentleman named Bartholomew that pass'd for *Bideford*, with three others, in April last, but not heard of, nor his Companions, since that Time. 'Tis thought the mute Servant may have kill'd all, and hid their Corses, in a fit of lunatick Madness; then overcome by Remorse, or Fear of Justice, ended his wretched Days; but the more to be wonder'd, that to this Present no Inquiry is made by Mr Bartholomew's Friends.

The Western Gazette, 1736

The Examination and Deposition of
THOMAS PUDDICOMBE
the which doth attest upon his sworn
oath, this one and thirtieth day
of July in the tenth year of the
reign of our sovereign Lord George the
second, by the grace of God King of Great
Britain and of England, &c.

I am three score years and six of age. I am landlord of the Black Hart Inn. I have been so nigh upon these forty years and my father before me. I am capital burgess of this town. I have been thrice its mayor, and justice also, in that office.

⌘

Q. Now, Master Puddicombe, I would have you first affirm that this portrait in miniature I have shown and now show you again is that of the younger of the two gentlemen that stayed in this your inn some three months past.

A. To the best of my belief, sir. 'Tis very like. I will swear thus far. Though he was dressed less fine.

Q. Look upon his face. The dress matters not.

A. So I judge it. 'Tis he.

Q. Very well. When came they?

A. The last day of April past. I remember it well, I shall never forget it.

Q. At what hour?

A. The man came first, a three hours before sunset, to command chambers and victuals. For he said they had dined ill, and had empty bellies.

Q. His name?

A.   Farthing. Then rode back to conduct them, and they came as he promised, a little after six of the clock, or thereabout.

Q.   Five in all?

A.   The uncle and nephew. The two men and the maid.

Q.   Mr Brown and Mr Bartholomew, they so gave themselves?

A.   That they did, sir.

Q.   Marked you whatsoever untoward in their manner?

A.   Not at that time. Until what ye know of was discovered.

Q.   But on this night they stayed?

A.   Why, sir, they seemed in all what they said, that is, journeying for Bideford. I spake very little with either gentleman. The younger went straight to his chamber on the coming and did not show his face outside until he left. I know no more of him than one I might pass in the street. He supped, he slept, woke up and brake his fast. 'Twas all within these four walls. And then he went.

Q.   And the uncle?

A.   I can tell ye little else, sir. But that he took chay after supper with Mr Beckford and —

Q.   Who is this?

A.   Our curate. For he came with his compliments to the gentlemen.

Q.   He knew them?

A.   I think not, sir. When I told them he was below, they seemed not to know him.

Q.   How soon was this upon their coming?

A.   An hour, sir. Mayhap more. They had supped.

Q.   But they did speak with him?

A.   Mr Brown came down, sir, in a few minutes. And sat with Mr Beckford in the private parlour.

Q.   That is the uncle? The nephew was not present?

A.   But the uncle, sir.

Q.   How long?

A.   Not an hour, sir. I think less.

Q.   Did you hear the subject of their conversation?

A.   No, sir.

Q. Not a word?

A. No, sir. My maid Dorcas served them. She said —

Q. I will hear that from her. Tell what you know of your own eyes and ears.

A. I took Mr Brown to where Mr Beckford was in wait. They bowed and sat, there was manners and compliments, but I did not mark them, I went to see for their chay.

Q. Met they as strangers — or as men who had fore-acquaintance?

A. As strangers, sir. Mr Beckford does often thus.

Q. How so?

A. Why, with quality who pass here. They who have letters and Latin.

Q. In sum, two gentlemen encountered by chance?

A. So I thought to it, sir.

Q. Did Mr Beckford speak to you afterwards of this meeting? Of what passed?

A. No, sir. Save as he went, he said I should see the two gentlemen well served and lodged. That the uncle was a worthy person of London, on Christian business. He said that, sir. Christian business.

Q. To wit?

A. He did not say, sir. But the man Farthing had spake in the kitchen of why they travelled. Of the young gentleman's a-coming to court his aunt, at Bideford. A rich lady, he said, sister to Mr Brown. Rich as a sultaness, so 'twas said. And the maid carried from London to serve her and dress her hair, the like.

Q. But there is none such at Bideford?

A. No, for they have lately enquired. And when I said I knew her not, this Farthing said 'twas not to be wondered, for she lived much retired, and not in Bideford town itself, but near. But he lied, the rogue, they have asked all about, and there is none such lady of that name.

Q. What said Farthing of Mr Brown's profession?

A. That he was London merchant, and alderman of that city, and had children of his own, but was left guardian of the nephew on his parents' decease. For he was child to another sister, who was dead, and her husband also.

Q.   And he had inherited no fortune of his own, this nephew?

A.   All spent and wasted. So I took the man to mean. But he lied in all.

Q.   Was aught said of Mr Bartholomew's dead parents?

A.   No, sir. But that their son had grown above himself.

Q.   Very well. I would have your closer remembrance of the servants.

A.   One is easy said, sir. The nephew's man, he that was found, him I might make nothing of.

Q.   His name?

A.   They called him Dick, no other name, sir. Farthing told tales of him, of a kind I would not have had my maids hear. I had a scolding for that, when Mistress Puddicombe came home. She was away to Molton for our youngest daughter's lying-in, who bore a —

Q.   Yes, yes, Master Puddicombe. What tales?

A.   Why, that he was moon-struck, and a lecher into the bargain. But I put no credence in Farthing. He was Welsh. They are not to be believed.

Q.   You are sure he was Welsh?

A.   As I am of my own name, sir. By his voice, first. Then his bluster and bragging, for that he was ancient sergeant of marines, or so would have us believe. He was one who would seem to know much, to be wiser than us. He boasted but to make favour with my maids. And as for the lechery, it turned out he could have better charged himself than him they called Dick.

Q.   Why?

A.   I did not hear till they was gone, sir, the girl was afraid to tell till then. My maid Dorcas, sir. He would have made free of her in the night. He offered her a shilling for it. Though she is a good girl, and promised, and gave no encouragement.

Q.   What else did he speak of?

A.   Much on military matters, and his past prowess therein.

Then he would have us believe him better than he was. Thus always he spake of my friend Mr Brown when 'twas clear he was servant to the gentleman. He made more noise than a company of dragoons. I counted him an idle fellow, sir, and well named. As hollow as brass, and as bold. And then his going off before sunrise, there was more to that than met the eye.

Q. What was this?

A. Why, sir, he was saddled and gone before dawn, and ne'er a word of warning.

Q. He was sent ahead for some purpose?

A. He was gone when we rose. 'Tis all I know.

Q. You would say, without his master's knowledge?

A. I know not, sir.

Q. Did Mr Brown show surprise that Farthing was gone?

A. No, sir.

Q. Nor any of the others?

A. No, sir. 'Twas not spoke of.

A. And yet you say there was more in it than meets the eye?

A. That he said nothing of it when us supped.

Q. What age was he?

A. He did say he was drummer boy in a battle of '18, by which I did have him to be born, a year or two given, these thirty years past; to which also he might answer, by his present looks.

Q. And as to those — had he especial that you marked?

A. Unless his mustachios, that he wore quilled, like the false Turk he was. For the general, did show more tall than short, and carried more lard than meat besides, of which my table and cellar did bear the proving. For he did so eat and drink that my cook did call him, tho' then in jest, Sergeant Cut and Come-again.

Q. But a well-built fellow, in appearance?

A. More in the eye than in truth, sir, or my name is not Puddicombe.

Q. What colour were his eyes?

A. Dark and quick, not as an honest man's.

Q. And he bore no scars, ancient wounds, I know not, that you saw?

A. No, sir.

Q. Nor was halt, or limped in his gait?

A. No, sir. Us doubts us now he had fought an inch, outside of taverns or in his cups.

Q. Very well. And the other fellow, this Dick? What of him?

A. Said not a word, sir. Since he could not. But I saw somewhat in his eye that Farthing was no more in his books than mine. For which I blame him not one whit, seeing he must dure that Farthing would use him for a Jack-a-Lent. For the rest, brisk to his work, so far as I could tell.

Q. And no lunatick?

A. He seemed simple, sir. Able for nothing beyond the doing of his duties. But rather a poor dog of a man than aught else. Poor dog for his wits, that is. A strapping fellow for his body, I would I had one such in my service. I think he meant no harm. For all they say now.

Q. Nor lecher, neither?

A. Farthing told tattle when he took water to the maid upstairs and was slow to come down again. Which us did credit a little then.

Q. He made no advances to your maids?

A. No, sir.

Q. And this maid they brought — what name had she?

A. A strange one, sir, that is after the king of France, God rot him. Louise 'twas said, or some such.

Q. She was French?

A. No, sir, or not by her voice, that sounded of Bristow or thereabout. Though in manner, she was fine enough to be of France, such as I have heard tell. But Farthing said, 'twas these times the mode in London for such as she, that are lady's maids, to ape their betters.

Q. She came from London?

A. So 'twas given, sir.

Q. But she did speak as one born in Bristol, you say?

A. Yes, sir, and would sup in her room, like a lady, and not share it neither. Which we found strange. Farthing spoke great ill of her and her fine airs. In contrary my girl Dorcas said she spake kind, and made no great pretence of being other than she was. And said she would not sup below because she had the megrims, would rest, so asked to be excused. I fancy 'twas Farthing she could not abide, not us.

Q. What manner of looks had she?

A. Fair enough, sir, fair enough. A trifle pale and city sickly, but well featured, tho' small in flesh. I do not forget her eyes, that were brown and grave as hind or hare's — aye, that spake doubt of all. I mind not to have seen her once smile.

Q. What mean you by doubt of all, Master Puddicombe?

A. Why, sir, doubt of why she was come among us; as trout before oven, so say us here.

Q. She said little?

A. No, sir, except it be to Dorcas.

Q. Might she have been no maid, but a person of breeding in disguise?

A. Well, sir, some now think her such, some lady upon an adventure.

Q. An elopement, you would say?

A. I say nothing, sir. 'Tis Betty the cook and Mistress Puddicombe will have it so. And I can't decide, sir.

Q. Very well. Now I have an important question. Did what this rogue Farthing say of Mr Bartholomew fit his demeanour? Seemed he to be such, one who had lived above his fortune and was now come, albeit against his will, to grovel at his aunt's feet?

A. I could not say, sir. He seemed one used to command, impatient in his manner. But no more than many young gentlemen are in these times.

Q. But did he seem truly a greater gentleman than you was led to believe, one who came from a finer world than his merchant uncle?

A. Why, he had the air and manner of a gentleman, sir. I can't say more. Unless it be they seeming spake no common voice. Mr Brown as of London, like enow; but he his nephew, what little he said, it did sound of more northern parts, somewhat as to your own, sir.

Q. He appeared to respect his uncle?

A. More in the seeming than the heart, sir. He took my best and largest chamber to himself, which I also counted strange at the time. I would look to Mr Brown for instructions, but it was his nephew that gave 'em. His uncle would see Mr Beckford, not he. And suchlike. Tho' 'twas done with politeness.

Q. Did he take much wine?

A. Neither, sir. A sneaker of punch when they came, a pint of burnt claret, a flask of best Canary with their supper. But that last still not empty when they left.

Q. Let us come to that. At what hour did they leave?

A. I would say soon after seven of the clock, sir. Us were much occupied, it being May Day. I did not mark it in the particular.

Q. Who paid you the lodging?

A. Mr Brown.

Q. Handsomely?

A. Well enough. I bear no complaint there.

Q. And they took the Bideford road?

A. They did, sir. Leastways asked they my ostler Ezekiel directions for the leaving of the town thither.

Q. And you heard no more of them that day?

A. Only from some that had met them on their road here for the maying. Who did ask their business of me, supposing they had lodged by my roof.

Q. Out of mere curiosity?

A. Yes, sir.

Q. But no other news of their journeying that day?

A. No sir, not a word. Until that of the violet man, a sennight later.

Q. The which, what is he?

A. 'Tis how they named him, poor Dick, seeing they knew none other for him. But first, sir, I must say the mare. Of which I heard, without knowing what I heard. 'Twas late on the morrow, the second of May. One Barnecott of Fremington, that is badger and that I do know well of his trade these many years, did come by upon his business, and did speak of a loose horse on his way hither. He said 'twas wild, would not be caught, and the hour pressing for him. So he gave up.

Q.   What manner of horse?

A.   An old bay pad-mare, sir. She wore no harness, no bridle nor saddle. He but said it idly in passing, thinking it run from its field. 'Tis nothing unaccustomed, our horses here are much mixed with the moorland kind, and such no more like being crimped in the one meadow than an Egyptian.

Q.   This was the packhorse?

A.   As I know now, sir. But I took no account of it till the man Dick was found.

Q.   How heard you of that?

A.   From one who passed at Daccombe when his corse was brought on a hurdle.

Q.   How far is Daccombe from here?

A.   A good league, sir.

A.   And how and where was the body found?

A.   By a shepherd-boy. In a great wood we call Cleave Wood, that stretches to the moor and is more steep than ne'er a man may walk in many places, more cleave than combe. He might have hung there seven years and not been found. If God had not willed it otherwise. 'Tis place fitter for polecats than human mortals.

Q.   This is near where the horse was seen?

A.   A mile above the road, sir, where it was seen.

Q.   And this tale of violets?

A.   Is true, sir. 'Twas all said at the inquisition. I have spaken with one who went to cut the corse down and carry it back before 'twas staked and buried at Daccombe Cross. He said 'twas a tuft torn up by its roots, stuffed in the poor man's mouth before he took his last leap, and still bloomed as green as on a bank. 'Twas taken as witchcraft, sir, by many. But the more learned say the plant took sustenance from the flesh, finding it soil at heart, as us must all come to. Yet 'twas as

strange a sight as ever he saw, my man said, to see such
sweetness in a blackened face.

Q. You took here no suspicion as to who it was?

A. No, sir. Nor then, nor when the Crowner's man first came.
For it was a full week gone, ye must understand, since they
had passed. And Daccombe, 'tis not our parish. With that my
guests were five, I had no thought of one alone come to such
an end, without enquiry made of the gentlemen his masters.

Q. And next?

A. Next was the finding of the brassbound chest, sir, close by the
road where Cleave Wood runs and the old mare was seen.
Then at last I waked, and prompt advised my friend Mr
Tucker, who is mayor, of my reasonings. And then did Mr
Tucker and myself, with Mr Acland the apothecary, that is
clerk to our town, for he do know somewhat also of the law,
and Digory Skinner, that is sergeant at mace and our constable, and others beside, ride out upon *Posse comitatus,* that us
might enquire and make report.

Q. When was this?

A. The first week of June, sir. Us rode to where they had took
the chest. And I knew at once 'twas the same as the gentleman's, Mr Bartholomew's. My ostler Ezekiel has likewise
since seen it, who helped rope it on with their other baggages
that very morning they left. Then I would see the horse, 'twas
haltered by then and kept in a farm nearby. And I took a suspicion that that too was the same, sir, and sat down and
bethought me, and would hear more of the violet man's
looks. Which he I spoke of that had seen him, told me. That
he was fair of hair, and had blue eyes. And then it was plain,
and all was writ by Mr Acland to Barnstaple, to the Crowner.

Q. Have you no coroner here?

A. By charter, sir. But none to fill the place. 'Tis lapsed. So he of
Barnstaple was called.

Q. Dr Pettigrew?

A. Yes, sir.

Q. This chest had been hidden?

A. 'Twas thrown in a goyal of thick bushes, four hundred paces from the road. But he who found it saw a glint of the brass, amid the leaves.

Q. A goyal, what is that?

A. A combelet, sir. A narrow sunken place.

A. And this place lies also below where the body was found?

A. Yes.

Q. The chest was empty?

A. As your glass, sir. And there is a tale there, that Dorcas must tell. For some say now 'twas full of gold, but she saw when 'twas open, and that it was not.

Q. I shall ask her. Now, had they not other baggage?

A. Yes, sir. A great leather portmantee, and else. But 'tis not found, not a smallest piece, nor the seam beside.

Q. It was searched for well?

A. Ten men, sir. And the constables. And they were much afeared they should come upon other corses, that all was waylaid and murthered. Some think 'tis so still, if we but knew where to look.

Q. Then why was the fellow Dick's not hidden also?

A. I know not, sir. 'Tis all riddle. Some say he murthered and hid, and ended his life in despair. Others would have it he was in league with the murtherers, but repented, and so they must silence him and made it seem like self-murther, they being in too much haste to bury him.

Q. You are troubled with such here?

A. Not this twenty years past, sir, thank the Lord.

Q. Then I think not much to your second explanation, Master Puddicombe.

A. Nor I, sir. I say no more than what is said. But certain 'tis that some foul deed was done, about the place where the mare ran loose and the chest was found. And I'll tell ye why, sir. If they had gone further, they must have passed by Daccombe. And being May Day, with many in the streets, it would have been marked.

Q. They were seen by none there?

A. Not one eye, sir. They passed not.

Q. There are no other roads?

A. Not that wise travellers take, nor cumbered as they were. Nor would they know them, sir, being strangers. Nor even if they did, take them if they were truly for Bideford.

Q. They were asked of there?

A. Yes, sir. But the scent was cold. For it is a busy town, and full enough of strange faces. Those Dr Pettigrew sent had no gain for their pains. 'Twas said as much at the second inquisition.

Q. That night they passed beneath this roof, heard you no quarrels? High words?

A. No, sir.

Q. None came to speak to them, apart from Mr Beckford? No messenger, no strange person?

A. No, sir.

Q. Mr Brown, may you describe his looks?

A. Why, sir, more fierce in face than manner.

Q. How, fierce?

A. Rather I would say grave. Such as a learned doctor, as us say here.

Q. Then unlike to his supposed occupation? Was he not said a merchant?

A. I cannot tell, sir. I know not London. But they be great men there, 'tis said.

Q. Was he fat or thin? How tall?

A. Why, middling in all, sir. A sound carriage.

Q. Of what age?

A. Near fifty, sir, I can say no more. Perhaps more.

Q. No other thing that bears upon my enquiry?

A. Not that I can think of at this present, sir. Naught of importance, ye may be sure.

Q. Very well, Master Puddicombe. I thank you. And at your pain to keep my commission secret, as I warned.

A. I have sworn, sir. My word is my bond, I assure ye. King and true church, I am no fanatick nor meeting man. Ask any here.

> Jurat tricesimo uno die Jul.
> anno Domini 1736 coram me
> Henry Ayscough

Historical Chronicle, 1736.

MAY.

Saturday, May 1.

General Court of the *Charitable Corporation,* order'd the Prosecution against their late Directors to be carried on with the utmost Vigour.

The Ld Mayor, and Court of Aldermen of *London,* were entertain'd at Dinner by Ld *Baltimore* in *Grosvenor-Square,* on the Part of his R. Highness the Prince of *Wales,* who invited them when they presented their Congratulations; which He received with such Marks of Condescension and Goodness as are peculiar to himself: Among other obliging Th ngs, told them, That he was sorry the Princess was not so well versed in the *English* Language, as to return an Answer to them in it; but that he would be answerable for her, that she should soon learn it; and enquir'd of Sir *John Bernard,* if he understood *French,* to speak to her Royal Highness in that Tongue. Sir *John* handsomely excusing himself, referr'd to Alderman *Godshall* who, with Alderman *Lequesne,* made short and agreeable Compliments to the Princess, and received gracious Answers from her.

At One this Morning, and at Noon the preceeding Day, was a terrible Earthquake along the *Ochil-Hills* in *Scotland,* which rent several Houses, and put the People to flight, it was accompanied with a great Noise under Ground.

Monday, 3.

Notwithstanding the Example made last Month, *(See p. 229. E.)* the People of *Herefordshire* cut down the Turnpikes again

Tuesday, 4.

At a Court of Aldermen held at *Guildhall, Denn Hammond,* Esq; an eminent Attorney in *Nicholas Lane,* was sworn Comptroller of this City, purchasing the Place for 3,600 l.

Wednesday, 5.

His Majesty went to the House of Peers, and gave the Royal Assent to the Bill for Exhibiting a Bill for Naturalizing the Princess of *Wales.*—To the Geneva Bill.—To a Bill for better enlightening the City of *London.*—To several Road Bills,—And other private Bills, to the Number of 41.

A Cause was try'd in the Mashalsea-Court, *Southwark,* wherein *Wm. Berkins,* Joyner, was Plaintiff, and the noted *Julian Brown,*

alias *Gueliano Bruno,* an *Italian,* (on whose sole Evidence, *Wreathock, Bird, Ruffet, Campbell* and *Chamberlain,* were found guilty for robbing Dr. *Lancaster*) was Defendant, for *Joyner*'s Work in fitting up a Chandler's Shop, &c. for the said *Brown* in *Bloomsbury* : The Work was admitted; but *Brown,* in order to prove Payment of it, set up a Receipt in full given to him by *Berkins* for Work done in 1731, hav.ng altered the Date to 1734; but the Fraud appear'd so plainly to the Court, that a Verdict was given for the Plaintiff; and the Receipt detained, in order to have the said *Brown* prosecuted thereon, to the great Satisfaction of all Persons then present.

Thursday, 6.

His Majesty in Council order'd, that at Morning and Evening Prayer, in the Litany, and all other Parts of the publick Service, as well in occasional Offices, as in the Book of Common Prayer, where the Royal Family is particularly appointed to be pra ed for, that the following Form be observ'd, *viz.*

For his most sacred Majesty King *George,* our gracious Queen *Caroline,* their Royal Highnesses *Fredrick* Prince of *Wales,* the Princess of *Wales,* the Duke, the Princesses, and all the Royal Family.

Friday, 7.

Several Merchants of *Dublin* met at the *Tholsel,* to consider of Means to prevent any Alterations in the Coin, and afterwards went in a Body to wait on the D. of *Dorset,* Lord Lieutenant. The Rev. *Dean Swift,* and their two Representatives in Parliament, were with them, and the Dean set forth the ill Consequence it would be to that Kingdom, if the Coin should be reduced.——Notwithstanding this Zeal of the *Irish* Merchants, a Writer in the *Daily Advertiser, May* 10, charges it on them not only as an Error, their raising our Guineas to 23 s. Moidores to 30 s. and our Shilling to 13 d. but says, it is very obvious, that their Intent was to make it profitable to carry Money to *Ireland,* and a Loss to bring it back to *Great Britain* ; and as it was done without Authority, is unwarrantable, and has not had any good Effect. That they have raised the Gold Coin much too high, and thereby have been drained of almost all their Silver. Tho' he allows the Guinea ought to be raised (but by Authority, and in both Kingdoms)

P p

doms) to 21 *s.* 6 *d.* and the Shilling to 13 *d.* that his Majesty's Subjects may trade on equal footing with one another, and with their Neighbour, the neglecting of which he reckons a prodigious Loss to *Great Britain.*

Saturday. 8.

Henry Justice, of the *Middle Temple,* Esq; was tried at the *Old Baily,* for stealing Books out of *Trinity College* Library in *Cambridge,* He pleaded, that in the Year 1734. he was admitted Fellow Commoner of the said College, whereby he became a Member of that Corporation, and had a Property in the Books, and therefore could not be guilty of Felony, and read several Clauses of their Charter and Statutes to prove it. But after several Hours Debate, it appear'd he was only a Boarder or Lodger, by the Words of the Charter granted by *Hen.* 8, and Q. *Eliz.* So the Jury brought him in guilty of the Indictment, which is Felony within Benefit of the Clergy, so Transportation.

Monday. 10.

Mr *Justice* was brought to the Bar to receive Sentence, and mov'd, that as the Court had a discretionary Power, he might be burnt in the Hand and not sent abroad ; First, for the Sake of his Family, as it would be an Injury to his Children, and to his Clients, with several of whom he had great Concerns, which could not be settled in that Time ; 2dly, for the Sake of the University, for he had Numbers of Books belonging to them, some in Friends Hands, and some sent to *Holland,* and if he was transported he cou'd not make Restitution. As to himself, considering his Circumstances, he had rather go abroad, having liv'd in Credit till this unhappy Mistake, as he call'd it, and hop'd the University wou'd intercede for him. The Deputy Recorder commiserated his Case, told him how greatly his Crime was aggravated by his Education and Profession, and then pronounc'd, that *he must be transported to some of his Majesty's Plantations in America for seven Years.*

Receiv'd Sentence of Death, *Stephen Collard* for stealing a silver Watch, *George Ward,* for robbing Mr *Gibson* a Baker at *Islington, Tho. Tarlton* for Horse stealing, *Daniel Malden* for stealing a Silver Tankard, *Jos. Glanwin* for stealing 12 Handkerchiefs, *Chris. Freeman* for stealing wet Linnen, *Fra. Owen* for setting Fire to the Bell-Inn in *Warwick Lane.* *Collard* and *Glanwin* were repriev'd for Transportation.

Thursday. 13.

A Gentleman unknown, gave 1000 *l.* to the Society for propagating the Gospel in Foreign Parts ; 1000 *l.* to the Corporation of the Sons of the Clergy, for poor Widows; and 500 *l.* for the Propagation of Christian Knowledge.

The Gen. Assembly of the Scotch Church met at *Edinburgh,* and chose Mr *Lauchlan Mac Intosh* their Moderator ; they had a Debate about their Answer to the King's Letter,

but at last agreed to insert these Words, *hoping from his Majesty's Goodness, that this Church shall yet be reliev'd from the Grievance of Patronages.*

Monday, 17.

One Hundred *Felons Convicts* walk'd from *Newgate* to *Black-fryars,* and thence went in a close Lighter on Board a Ship at *Blackwall.* But *Wreatbock* the Attorney, Mess. *Ruffhead, Vaughan* and *Bird,* went to *Blackwall* in a Hackney Coaches, and *Hen. Justice,* Esq; Barrister at Law in another, attended by *Jonathan Forward,* Esq; These 5 Gentlemen of Distinction were accomodated with the Captain's Cabbin, which they stor'd with *Plenty of Provisions,* &c. for their Voyage and Travels.

Thursday. 20.

His Majesty went to the House of Peers, and gave the Royal Assent to An Act to enable his Majesty to borrow 600,000 *l.* and to pay off one Million of *S. wth-Sea* Annuities. An Act for Naturalizing her Royal Highness the Princess of *Wales.*—For building a Bridge cross the *Thames* at *Westminster.*—For continuing the Duties upon Stamped Parchments, Paper, &c.—To render the Laws more effectual for the preventing the Importation of Fish by Foreigners, and for the better Preservation of the Fry of Lobsters on the Coast of *Scotland.*—To explain so much of an Act to prevent Bribery and Corruption in Elections, as relates to Prosecutions grounded upon the said Act ; which are not to take Effect, unless some Process is already begun for that Purpose.—For encouraging the Manufacture of *British* Sail Cloth.—To prevent lifting his Majesty's Subjects into Foreign Service.—To indemnify Persons, who have been guilty of Offences against the Laws made for securing the Revenues of Customs and Excise ; and for enforcing the Laws for the future. After which his Majesty made a most gracious Speech, which (See p. 236) and then prorogu'd the Parliament to the 29th of *July.*

A Fire broke out of a Malt Kiln in *Stony Stratford, Northamptonshire,* and burnt down above 50 Houses.

Saturday. 22.

Mr *Pickering* who had been committed to *Newgate* for riotously entering, with others, the *Sardinian* Ambassador's Chapel, &c. was admitted to bail in the Court of King's Bench, and it has been since propos'd to regulate the foreign Ambassadors Chapels by an Act of Q. *Eliz.* for that Purpose, which allows them no more Privileges here, than what is granted to *English* Ambassadors.

The University of *Oxford* in full Convocation conferr'd the Degree of Dr of Laws upon *John Ivory Talbot,* Esq; Kt of the Shire for *Wilts ;* Sr *Wm Carew* Bt. Kt of the Shire for *Cornwal,* and *Tho. Masters,* Esq; Member for for *Cirencester ;* as an Acknowledgment for their Service in Opposition to the *Quakers Tythe* and *Mortmain Bills.*

About

The Examination and Deposition of
DORCAS HELLYER
the which doth attest upon her sworn
oath, this one and thirtieth day
of July in the tenth year of the
reign of our sovereign Lord George the
second, by the grace of God King of Great
Britain and of England, &c.

I am seventeen years of age, born of this place, spinster. I am maid of all work to Master and Mistress Puddicombe.

❧

Q. Your master has told you of my purpose here?

A. Yes, sir.

Q. And that you stand upon oath as in a court of law?

A. Yes, sir.

Q. So speak truth, for this person will write down all you say.

A. Book truth, sir.

Q. Very well. Now I would have you look upon this portrait again. Is he the gentleman you attended in this very chamber on the last of April past?

A. Yes, sir. I believe 'tis he.

Q. You are sure? Thou must say if thou art not, girl. No harm will come to thee for that.

A. I be sure.

Q. Very well. You served the two gentlemen their supper?

A. Yes, sir. Their supper and all else.

Q. Is it not a more usual case that travelling gentlemen, such as lodge here, are served by their own servants?

A. 'Tis as they please, sir. Few do pass.

Q. No remark on this was made?

A. No, sir.

Q. Did they speak together as you served?

A. No, sir. Not that us heard.

Q. You stayed as they ate?

A. I would, sir. But they told I to leave, once 'twas brought ready.

Q. They would serve themselves?

A. Yes, sir.

Q. Marked you naught in their manner?

A. What should us mark, sir?

Q. I but ask thee. Recollect. Seemed they troubled, or impatient to be left alone?

A. Not beyond the having rid far, sir. And 'twas said, poorly dined.

Q. And wishing to sup without further ado?

A. Yes, sir.

Q. What ate they?

A. Collops and eggs and a mess of dry pease and onion with brook-sallet beside, and a bowl of whitepot after.

Q. They ate well of these?

A. Yes, sir. Passing well.

Q. Seemed they friendly the one to the other? Not angry, as if they had quarrelled?

A. No, sir.

Q. Which gentleman gave you their commands?

A. The older gentleman, sir.

Q. And later you brought tea to the same and Mr Beckford? [*Non comprendit.*] Chay, girl. Bohea. China leaf.

A. Yes, sir. 'Twas below.

Q. What did they speak that you heard?

A. Mr Beckford spake of himself, that I do remember.

Q. What of himself?

A. Of his family, sir. For he come from Wiltshire. I heard he to tell of a lady his sister, who is new-married in Salisbury city.

Q. And nothing else?

A. No, sir.

Q. Have you seen Mr Beckford converse thus with strangers before?

A. Yes, sir. For where he lodges, 'tis close across the square, no more than there where you may turn and see, sir. And he may see all from his window.

Q. He enjoys genteel company?

A. None else, sir. Or so it be said.

Q. Now, Dorcas, what saw you in either gentleman's bedchamber, among their belongings, that you thought strange?

A. Nothing, sir. Unless 'twas the chest and papers.

Q. What papers are these?

A. The younger gentleman, sir, in a chest he had carried up. Some was spread upon the table there, where that gentleman writes, when us brought him more light. The older gentleman did ask for it to go up when he came down to Mr Beckford.

Q. He was reading?

A. Yes, sir. He wished more light.

Q. What manner of papers?

A. I could not tell, sir. I has no alphabet.

Q. You would say letters? Had these papers superscription — address?

A. Us can't read, sir.

Q. Yes, yes. But you have seen letters — saw you seal, or folds, or close writing?

A. No, sir. 'Twas more like counting papers.

Q. What are they?

A. As Master writes in his bills of lodging, sir, for those who want such.

Q. You mean there were numbers written thereon?

A. Yes, sir. Numbers and signs that were no alphabet letters, for I knows their look.

Q. And fell these numbers in lines and columns, as upon a bill or accompt?

A. No, sir. Among figures.

Q. What figures?

A. Us saw one, 'twas a great circle, and another with three sides, and marks like the moon.

Q. How, like the moon?

A. Like a cheese-rind, sir, or the black in the old moon.

Q. Upon a curve?

A. Yes, sir.

Q. With counting numbers beside?

A. Yes, sir.

Q. Upon that table you saw how many papers such as bore figures and numbers?

A. Many, sir. A dozen or more, like enough.

Q. And the size of each paper?

A. As the gentleman write on now. And one twice as large.

Q. Put folio and demi-folio. They were written in ink, by hand?

A. Yes, sir.

Q. Not as letters are printed in a book — they were not pages taken from a book?

A. No, sir.

Q. Did the gentleman write?

A. No, sir. Not that us saw.

Q. Saw you the means — an inkstand, pen or quill?

A. No, sir.

Q. And the chest was full of other such papers?

A. Some, sir. And books, and among them a great clock of brass, without its case.

Q. A clock — you are sure?

A. 'Twas so big, sir, like unto the workings of Mistress Puddicombe's mantel-clock, when 'tis seen through its backgate.

Q. Saw you a dial, hands to mark the hour?

A. No, sir, for it lay the face down. But us saw a mizmaze of wheels, as in our clock.

Q. And these books — where were they?

A. The chest was by the door, sir, with her lid thrown back. 'Twas in shadow, but us peeped in as us passed.

Q. You saw books therein?

A. Yes, sir. They say now 'twas all gold, 'tis why they were murthered.

Q. But you know that was not true?

A. Yes, sir. But they will not believe I.

Q. No matter. I believe thee, Dorcas. Now I come to Louise, the maid. I would hear what prattle passed between you.

A. Us spoke a little when I took her to her room, sir. But that was all.

Q. Of what?

A. Of how far they had rid, sir. Of where they went. Such things.

Q. And nothing of herself?

A. Yes, sir, for I asked. And she said she was brought for maid to a lady to Bideford town, the gentlemen's relation. And as how her old mistress to London was gone abroad, and would not take her. Then she asked if us knew Bideford and I said us had been there but once with my father, which is truth, and it is a large town enough, and fine market.

Q. Did she give her past mistress's name?

A. She said a name, sir, but us don't mind it now.

Q. An English name?

A. Yes, sir.

Q. A lady of title?

A. No, sir, plain mistress. Us be forgot.

A. Did you not ask this Louise whence she came, where she was born?

A. She said of Bristow city, sir, by her birth. But she had been long in London, maid all her grown life, for her parents were dead. Could sew and dress hair, and how there were good wages for such as she there.

Q. She asked you nothing of yourself?

A. Yes, sir. If I liked Mistress, and was happy at my work.

Q. What else?

A. Us did not talk long, sir, us was called for. And she said she knew us was busy, and would be no burden. That she was very weary, and would sup alone, but us need not care, for he called Dick should bring it above.

Q.   She said nothing of the two gentlemen?

A.   That she had not set eyes on them till ten days before, but her past mistress had spake well of the older.

A.   What said she of the two menservants?

Q.   She said nothing of Farthing, sir. And of the other, Dick, who was deaf and dumb, that he meant no harm and us was not to be afeard of his looks and ways.

Q.   I would have thee search thy mind, my child. Seemed she truly a lady's maid, as she would have the world believe, or one for some purpose but feigning to be so?

A.   She had London ways, sir. She was well-spoke, and very comely, such eyes a man might die for.

Q.   More like a lady than a maid? Too fair for her station?

A.   I cannot say, sir. But she did say her words somewhat as they do from Bristow.

Q.   You would say, without the airs and manners of a lady?

A.   Yes, sir. And she did not go to bed after she supped, as she said. For when us came to bed an hour or more later, us passed by the younger gentleman's chamber. And she was within.

Q.   You heard her voice?

A.   Yes, sir.

Q.   Did you stop and listen?

A.   Yes, sir, begging your pardon. A moment or two, for us was a-wonder to hear her there, when us thought her asleep.

Q.   Could you hear what was said?

A.   The door is thick and they spake low, sir.

Q.   Who spoke most?

A.   The gentleman, sir.

Q.   What made you of this?

A.   That he gave her instructions to please her new mistress, sir.

Q.   You heard such? Thou must tell me what passed.

A.   On my oath, sir. I tried, but I could not.

Q.   Why should he give such instructions at such an hour?

A.   Us don't know, sir.

Q.   I ask again. Did you not think: this is no lady's maid?

A.   Us thought it strange they should speak so long, sir.

Q.   How do you know it was long — did you not say you tarried but a moment or two?

A.   So us did, sir. But her chamber was next to I's and Betty's, sir. And us heard her creep in and close the latch before us slept, which was half an hour or more after.

Q.   Did you not think her service might be more to the young gentleman's pleasure than her new mistress at Bideford?

A.   I dursn't say, sir.

Q.   Come, Dorcas, thou art seventeen, brisk and and pretty. I'll wager thou hast ten sweethearts already.

A.   Yes, sir. I have one, that I shall marry.

Q.   Then spare me thy blushes. Saw you no evidence the next morning that the conversation had been carnal?

A.   Us don't know carnal, sir.

Q.   That they had lain between the sheets.

A.   No, sir. For the bed was not slept in.

Q.   Not slept in — you are sure?

A.   Yes, sir. It had been lain upon, but the clothes not taken back, nor nothing.

Q.   And heard you no other person enter this young woman's chamber next to yours?

A.   No, sir.

Q.   Nor her leave in the night?

A.   No, sir.

Q.   Nor voice nor sound there?

A.   No sir. Us sleeps deep, and Betty the same.

Q.   Seemed she one of ill virtue, a trollop, a harlot?

A.   No, sir.

Q.   Did she not perchance tell you that with handsome looks like yours she could find you a far better place and richer vails in London?

A.   No, sir.

Q.   Or perchance a tale of woe, of being crossed in love?

A.   Nor that neither, sir.

Q.   Seemed she sad or happy with her lot?

A.   I don't know, sir. 'Twas like she had better stayed where she was than come so far among strangers.

Q.   She said as much?

A.   'Twas her look that said, sir.

Q.   She smiled not?

A.   But once or twice, sir. Then she seemed else.

Q.   How else? You would say, more skittish and gay?

A.   No, sir. Us don't know how to say.

Q.   Come, girl. I shan't eat thee.

A.   When they had gone, us found a flowered kerchief upon her pillow, like 'twas there for I to find, to please I.

Q.   Where is this cloth now?

A.   My mother made us burn it, sir. When the murthers were known, and the violet man. For she said 'twould bring I ill luck.

Q.   It was of costly stuff?

A.   Yes, sir. Indian cotton, the like, close-worked with blooms and strange small fowl.

Q.   More than a maid might buy?

A.   'Twas such the Tiverton higgler showed last fairtide, that he said new made in London town, and wouldn't sell ever below three shilling; and said good as the Indian, tho' not, nor against the king's law to wear.

Q.   The next morning did you not ask her what she had been about in the younger gentleman's chamber so long?

A.   No, sir, for us spoke only to say goodbye. 'Twas May Day, and much to do, work for three.

Q.   I am told the man Farthing took liberties with thee, Dorcas.

A.   He would, but I would not 'bide 'em, not I.

Q.   He took you aside?

A.   He came after where I had need to go in the still-room, sir, when us had supped, and tried to embrace I. But when us would not suffer it, he said us should come later where he slept above the stable, and promised I a shilling if I would, and suchlike.

Q.   And you would have none of him?

A.   No, sir. He was much in drink, and I did not care for the mommet, and knew he be liar.

Q.   How so?

A.   That he did speak evil of the other man called Dick, at supper, for that he was half beast and would have his wicked way with us if he had his chance. When he was as bad, or worse. And when us would not take his shilling, he then would come to where us sleep, he said to protect I, but I believed him not.

Q.   And he came not, in the night?

A.   No, sir. Tho' I wish he mought, and had our Betty kiss his head with her cudgel.

Q.   Did he tell you he should leave early, before dawn, as I hear?

A.   No, sir, not a word.

Q.   I see thou art an honest maid, Dorcas. Thou art constant at church?

A.   Yes, sir.

Q.   Be always so, And here's the shilling for thee, that thy honesty lost.

Jurat die et anno
supradicto coram
Henry Ayscough

Historical Chronicle, 1736.
JUNE.

THE Beginning of this Year some Noblemen and Gentlemen, to the Number of 102, formed a Society for the En- couragement of Learn- ing. The Deposit on En- trance is 10 Guineas, & Yearly Subscription is 2 Guineas. The Duke of *Richmond* is President; and *Brian Fairfax*, Esq; Vice-President; Sir *Hugh Smithson* and Sir *Thomas Robinson*, Bts. theTrustees for this Year; and the Committee of Managers are,

Earl of *Hartford*,	*Charles Frederic*,
Earl of *Abercorn*,	*James West*,
Earl of *Oxford*,	Major *Edwards*,
Earl *Stanhope*,	*Benjamin Martyn*,
Lord *Percival*.	*George Lewis Scott*,
Sir *Brownlow Sherard*,	*Paul Whitehead*,Esqrs;
Bart.	Mr *John Ward*, Pro-
The Hon. *Wm Talbot*,	fessor at Gr. Coll.
Dr *Richard Mead*,	*James Thompson*,Esq;
Dr *Alexander Stuart*,	*Samuel Strutt*, Esq;
Dr *Robert Barker*,	*Dan. Mackercher*,Esq;
Dr *Addison Hutton*,	*George Sale*, Esq;
The Rev. Mr *Thomas*	The Rev. Mr *George*
Birch,	*Watts*.

By their *Statutes*, which are dated *May* 27, 1736, their General Meetings are to be the first *Thursdays* in *August*, *November*, *February*, and *May*. The Committee meet every Week, and such Work as they shall direct, are to be printed at the Expence, or by the Assistance of the Society; who are to settle the Price of Books so printed; but the Authors are to make over their Properties in the same, and their Interest in the whole Impressions to the Treasurer, in Trust for the Society; or give such farther Security for reimbursing the Charges of Printing and Publishing, as shall be judged proper by the Committee; on Re- payment of which Charges the Security to be delivered up; 8 of the 24 Managers are to be changed every Year, and not re-elected till after 3 Years. All future Members are to be proposed at a Meeting of the Committee of Managers, remain proposed 8 Days, and not to be admitted but by a Majority of two thirds of the Committee then present, on a Ballot. No Member of the Society (as such) to re- ceive any Profit or Advantage from the same. The Managers are not to expend above 200 l. on any Work without Consent of a General Meeting. The Treasurer to pay no Sum but by Order of 5 of the Managers; and if the Sum be above 10 l. he is to draw on the Tru-

stees for it, and they on the *Bank*. The Ac- counts to be audited every 8 Months. The present Auditors are the Hon. *John Talbot*, *Henry Talbot*, *Henry Kensall*, *Edw. Stephen- son*, and *Wm Newland*, Esqrs;

Tuesday, June 1.

One *Anne Boynton* of *Old Henstrige* in *So- mersetsh*. was delivered of 3 Daughters and one Son; one of the Daughters div'd, the rest like to live. The Woman has been married but 4 Years, and lain in 3 Times, at first she had a Female Children, at the second 2 Male, the third 4 as above.

Thursday, 3.

The Sum of 600,000 l. to be rais'd by Annu- ities of 3 per Cent. payable out of the Sinking Fund, was subscribed at the Auditor's Office in the Exchequer, by several Persons, to be paid the 10th of *July*.

Saturday, 5.

14 new Serjeants, viz. Tho *Parker*, Tho. *Hussey*, Abr *Gapper*, Robt *Price*, Michael *Foster*, Tho. *Burnet*, Wm *Wynne*, Jn *Agar*, Rich *Draper*, Robt *Johnson Kettleby*, Wm *Hayward*, Sam. *Prime*, Tho *Barnardiston*, Edw *Bootle*, Esqrs; were call'd to the Bar of the Common Pleas *Westminster* with the usual Formality. The Motto to the Rings distributed on the Occa- sion was *Nunquam Libertas gratiæ*. This Call gave Birth to the following Lines;

Dame *Law*, to maintain a more flourishing state, Having happily compact the *Mortmain* of late; As first she call'd over her Word-selling Crew, Cries, 'The Harvest is great, but the Lab'rers
are few:

Then Courage, my Sons! here is Work for you all!

And fourteen new Serjeants stept out at the Call.

Monday, 7.

The Grand Jury for the County of *Middle- sex* found a Bill of Indictment against *James Bayley* and *Tho. Reynolds*, on the *Black Act*, for going arm'd and disguis'd, and cutting down *Ledbury* Turnpike. See p. 229, E.

The Demurrer to a Bill filed by a Society of Weavers in *Spittle-fields*, against Mr *Sutton*, Landlord of the House where their Club was kept, for a Sum of 30 l. lent him out of the Box, was argued before the Barons of the Exchequer, when the Court were of Opini- on, that they were not a legal Society, and therefore could neither sue nor be sued.

Tuesday, 8.

A remarkable Cause was try'd before Ld *Hardwicke*, between 2 Merchants, on a *Scire Facias* upon a Recognizance of 320 l. to prosecute a Writ of Error in Case the Judgment should be affirm'd. wherein the Defendant was bound for a Person who since absconded. The Defendant pleaded, That the Transaction was 11 Months before the Commission of Bankruptcy was awarded, that he had obtain'd his Certificate, and was discharg'd from all Debts &c. by Act of Parliament. But the Council insisting, that this was a Debt of such a Nature, that the Plaintiff could not have Relief under the Commission; and that the Cause of Action arose by Contingency, since the issuing out of such Commission, the Jury brought in a Verdict for the Plaintiff.

Wednesday, 9.

Was held a Court of Common-Council at *Guild-hall*, when the Affair about building a Mansion House for the Ld Mayor, and that for the better lighting the City came under Consideration, and were referr'd back to the proper Committee. Mr *Eston* mov'd for an Enquiry into the Great Delay of Causes in the Law Courts of the City, how they have been occasion'd, and how they may be prevented for the future; which was carried *Nemine contradicente*, and a Committee was chosen accordingly.—Order'd, That the Recorder be desir'd to be present at the next Common-Council, and give his Reasons why he did not attend the Ld Mayor and Common-Council, when they waited on his Majesty with their Address on the P. of *Wales's* Marriage.

Thursday, 10.

Came on a Trial before Ld Chief-Justice *Hardwicke*, on an Action brought by Mrs *Elizabeth Barker* against Sir *Woolston Dixie*, Bart for 5000 l. for false Imprisonment, and a charge of Robbery, for which she was tried at the Old Bailey, and acquitted; after a Hearing of about seven Hours, the Jury, which was a Special one, brought a Verdict of Five Shillings for the Plaintiff: upon which his Lordship sent them out again, but in about half an Hour they returned without altering their Verdict. (See Vol. V. p. 735 D)

Saturday, 12.

The Sessions ended at the *Old Bailey*, when 35 Prisoners were try'd, of which 28 cast for Transportation, 1 burnt in the Hand, and *George Watson* condemned for the Murder of a Watchman, and 3 acquitted.

Monday, 14.

Daniel Malden broke (a second time) out of *Newgate*, by sawing his Chains near the Staple, by which they were fix'd to the Floor of the Condemn'd Hold, and getting thro' the Brickwork dropt into the Common Sewer; several Persons were employ'd to search after him, but to no Purpose, tho' the Chains about him weigh'd near 100 Pounds: They found the Bodies of two Persons, who trying to escape had been smother'd. (See p. 230, A.)

Thursday, 17.

Capt. *Porteous*, of the City-Guard, *Edinburg*, received a Copy of his Indictment in which he is charged with the Murder of 6 Persons, and wounding 11; *see Apr. p. 239 B*

Thursday, 21.

Her Majesty issued out her Royal Proclamation, prohibiting any of his Majesty's Subjects from furnishing Assistance to the Inhabitants of *Corsica*, and at the Request of the Senate of *Genoa*, gave Orders for seizing the Captain of the Ship which carried over *Baron Neuhoff*, and for calling to account the *English* Consul at *Tunis*, for permitting a *British* Vessel to be employed on such an Occasion.

Mr *Wm Russ*, Citizen and Salter, and Mr *Benj Rawlins*, Citizen and Apothecary, were elected Sheriffs of the City of *London* and County of *Middlesex*; the following Gentlemen having paid the usual Sums of Money as Fines, to be excused serving that Office, *viz*, Mr *Laurence Victorin*, Ironmonger, Mr *Sam. Swinson*, Fishmonger, Mr *Jos Barrash*, Weaver, Mr *Robt Bergusson*, Glass-Seller, Mr *Tho. Diggles*, Woolman, and Mr *Jos. Shaw*, Draper.

Monday, 28.

The Court of King's-Bench granted an Information against a Clergyman of Northamptonshire, for hiring a Man to set Fire to the Earl of Northampton's House.

Tuesday, 29.

Mr *David Boyce*, who had been confined in the Fleet-Prison several Years, at his Majesty's Suit for some thousand pounds, for Smuggling, was had before the Barons of the Exchequer, and discharged, he having by Council previously moved the Court, in pursuance of the late Act, which makes it Death to those who take the Benefit of it, and are afterwards found guilty of Smuggling, or of receiving or concealing run Goods.

Wednesday, 30.

A Receipt for a New DRAM *and a New* PUNCH, *far more wholesome and pleasant than any with distill'd Liquors.*

SQueeze 4 *Sevil* Oranges (or 2 Oranges and 2 Lemons as you like best) into a Quart of fair Water, sweeten it with fine Sugar to your Liking, and then put to it a Pint of *Sack*, to be drank as *Punch*, or bottled and us'd as a Dram. And a most delicate, fine, pleasant and wholesome Liquor it is.—The Reason why *Sack* is best for this *new Punch* and *Dram*, is, because of all *Wines*, none contains more *Spirit* than *Sack*; more Ounces of a high exalted Spirit being by Chymistry drawn from only a small Quantity of *Sack*, than from any other *Wine*, and this it is that makes *Sack* or *Canary Wine*, the only next (undistill'd) Liquor that can supply *Spirituous Liquors* in Punch.

This New *Punch* is not only vastly pleasant, but is far more *wholesome* than *Punch* made of any distill'd inflaming Liquors, which by their *Heat* parch and shrivel up the Coats of the

The Examination and Deposition of
MR SAMPSON BECKFORD
the which doth attest upon his sworn
oath, this one and thirtieth day
of July in the tenth year of the
reign of our sovereign Lord George the
second, by the grace of God King of Great
Britain and of England, &c.

My name is SAMPSON BECKFORD. *I am clerk, of Wadham College, Oxon., and curate of this parish since Michaelmas two years past. My age is twenty-seven years, I am not married.*

❧

Q.   I thank you for attending me, sir. I shall take little of your time.

A.   Take all you will, sir. I am at your service.

Q.   I thank you, Mr Beckford. I take it you had never set eyes on Mr Brown or Mr Bartholomew before this 30th of April last?

A.   Most unequivocally not, sir.

Q.   Nor had any expectation, forewarning by letter, I know not what, of their coming here?

A.   Nor that, sir. My calling was inspired by civility. I chanced to see them ride up, I took them for persons of education. *Rarissimæ aves,* Mr Ayscough, in this unhappy town.

Q.   You have my sympathies, sir.

A.   I thought to assure them that they had not arrived in wildest Muscovy, as I doubt not they might well have supposed at the appearance of the place — to show we are not quite without *politesse,* for all our exile from speakable society.

Q.   You did not meet the younger gentleman?

A.   I did not, sir. His uncle, Mr Brown, told me he was much fatigued, and made his excuses.

Q.   And this uncle — he told you the purpose of their journey was to visit his sister at Bideford?

A.   His allusions were veiled, but I understood him to intimate that his nephew had hitherto foolishly neglected certain expectations of property, since the lady had no descent of her own.

Q.   Did he particularise the nephew's foolishness — of what nature was it?

A.   I can't say that he did, sir. I meant to say that such neglect is always foolish. He made some hint of a life too much given to pleasure, of living above one's means. I recall he used that very phrase.

Q.   That the nephew had outrun his means?

A.   Just so.

Q.   He was reproving of his nephew?

A.   How shall I put it to you, sir? I saw as I thought an uncle and guardian who has led a sober, industrious and Christian life and finds himself obliged to look upon the tares of folly in his own close kin. Though I noted he blamed London in part, and its temptations. I recall he spoke particularly against the licence of the theatres and coffee-houses, and would have had them all closed down.

Q.   He spake of himself?

A.   That he was a London merchant. I presumed of some wealth, since he adverted in passing to one of his ships. And at another time to a friend, alderman of the City.

Q.   But named neither?

A.   Not that I recall.

Q.   Did he declare himself likewise City alderman?

A.   No, sir.

Q.   Now did you not find it strange, Mr Beckford, that this London merchant — I know them well, sir, they are a close breed — should tell you of delicate family business, upon so short an acquaintance?

A.   He ventured no detail, sir. I took it as a compliment to my cloth. That he owed me as a gentleman some small explanation of their presence here.

Q.   But he was gentleman by wealth rather than breeding?

A.   Exactly so, sir. My own impression. A worthy man, but not of true refinement. He asked me of my cure here, which was civil. But when, by way of modestly alluding to my sense that my merits are somewhat wasted in this place, I ventured an apt line or two of the poet Ovid, I think he was taken somewhat at a loss.

Q.   He knew more of counting-houses than of classical tongues?

A.   I deemed it so.

Q.   But what think you now, Mr Beckford? You know search was lately made for this lady his sister, and none found?

A.   I do, and am entirely at a loss. Why a man of such seeming substance and honesty should go to such prevaricating lengths to mislead me — suffice it to say I have thought much on it. His real purpose was evidently not one that could be told strangers. I fear me, because it was evil.

Q.   Others here marked that on occasion it was the feigned repentant nephew who gave instructions and took precedence, while the uncle stood by. What say you to that?

A.   I have heard it since, sir. And I must tell you that when I watched them from my window as they came first to this inn, and speculated as to their business here, I confess but idly, yet be that as it may — I did not then suppose them by their manner uncle and nephew.

Q.   But what?

A.   I could not say, sir. I put no clear name to it. I thought rather a young gentleman and an older one of your own honourable profession, it may be on some affair of legal aspect. Perhaps a tutor. I truly could not say, save that the conjecture of a blood relationship did not enter my mind. I fancy I was somewhat surprised to learn it when I waited upon them.

Q.   What manner of speaking had Mr Brown?

A.   A grave, plain manner, without flowers or figures. Well enough.

Q. You had no suspicion that something illicit or unseemly was afoot?

A. I confess not, sir. I took him at his word. The circumstances were not such as to provoke my incredulity. The case is common enough.

Q. Spake you both, in this conversation, more of his affairs or of your own?

A. Your question is well asked, sir. I have thought on that, also. I believe he may have led me to speak more of myself than either my natural inclination wished or strict politeness allows.

Q. If I may put it thus bluntly, you were somewhat his gull in this?

A. He would know of my hopes and disappointments, then of the state of religion in this godless place. I have the misfortune to be a youngest son, Mr Ayscough. We are afflicted with schism here, to a most wicked degree, and it is much on my mind. I confess that if invited by a sympathetic listener, I do not stint the expression of my loyal abhorrences. I fear it was so that evening.

Q. He sympathised with your views — would hear more of them?

A. He did, sir, and even did me the honour of wishing there were more who held them as strongly. And regretted he could not stay to hear a sermon I was to preach that coming Sunday, in which I do myself the justice to say that I handsomely refuted the pernicious arguments of those who would deprive us of our tithes. You would perhaps care to peruse a copy of it I chance to have retained?

Q. I should esteem that honour, sir.

A. I will have my man bring it, as soon as I return home.

Q. I thank you. But now, Mr Beckford, I must sow a seed of doubt in your mind. Do you not know that the City is Whig to a man? That most would never embrace what I understand to be your worthy sentiments upon religion? That respect of ancient principle, save that of their own secular right, holds little place among them? That many have room for only one god in their world, and that is Mammon, to wit, their own profit; and will flout all that doth threaten to hobble or trammel it. Did you not find it strange that this merchant should show such sympathy for your own views?

A.   I must confess myself his dupe, sir. Alas, I know indeed of these matters, and how such would tolerate our nonconformists and schismaticks to a most reprehensible degree; but here I believed I had stumbled upon a happy exception to this general rule.

Q.   Might not this merchant uncle have been in truth a man of law — since we have some skill in directing a train of discourse? I pray you, think, sir. Does this bear root in your recollection?

A.   He had not your manner, sir. With respect.

Q.   But allowing for the circumstance that he was or might have been, for some reason unknown, obliged to conceal his ordinary manner and that you were shown but a plausible screen, not what truly lay behind?

A.   By such hypothesis it is possible, sir. Yes, it is possible he but played a part. I can say no more.

Q.   *Id est,* he was one trained to deceive, and even a gentleman so perspicuous and educated as yourself, sir? He spake, would you say, in a natural fashion — not as one who has affairs to hide, in a low voice, or such?

A.   As I say, sir. With some gravity, yet I thought openly. As one accustomed to speak his mind on public matters in public places.

Q.   I would have you describe him to me.

A.   Of middling height, somewhat stout in the belly. A fair complexion for his age, though somewhat pale. The gaze penetrating, as if he were a fair judge of men. Heavy brows.

Q.   Now, sir, if you would be so kind as to guess upon his age.

A.   Forty-five years are certain. I would guess a lustrum more.

Q.   No other distinguishing characters?

A.   I marked a wart to one side of his nose. Here.

Q.   Put the right nostril. No rings?

A.   A wedding band.

Q. Gold?

A. Yes. And plain, if memory serves.

Q. His dress?

A. Of good cloth, but I noticed somewhat worn, as it might be his travelling suit. The wig somewhat in the old style.

Q. The linen clean?

A. Indeed, sir. All as one might expect in a person of such a kind.

Q. I felicitate you on your memory, sir. Now no other peculiarities, no manners you marked especially?

A. He took snuff, sir, and too frequently to my taste. I found it little elegant.

Q. Mr Beckford, you have heard nothing subsequent to the events that is pertinent to them — I should add, beyond what is common knowledge?

A. I have heard idle gossip, it is everywhere. The benighted clowns hereabouts are much given to it.

Q. But nothing from other gentlemen or their families in this neighbourhood?

A. In this parish there is alas only Mr Henry Devereux to whom I may grant the appellation. He was not then here.

Q. He is here now?

A. He is returned a fortnight since to Bath.

Q. But you spoke to him of the matter?

A. I did my best to satisfy his curiosity, sir.

Q. And he seemed as ignorant as one might expect?

A. Quite so.

Q. Gentlemen of your own cloth?

A. I live in a desart, sir, though it pains me to say it. No person of refinement would happily inhabit such a region as this, were he not, as I am, forced to it by circumstance. I regret to say that my fellow in the cloth on one side is far more a professor of the hunting of the fox than of his faith. He would sooner have his bells rung for a good main than for divine service. On the other, at Daccombe, is a gentleman who devotes his life to his garden and his glebe and allows his church to look after itself.

Q.   Mr Devereux is your patron?

A.   No, sir. That is Canon Bullock of Exeter. He holds the preb-
end, and is my vicar in title.

Q.   Of the Chapter?

A.   Just so. He visits but once a year, for the tithes. He is old,
near seventy years now.

Q.   This is a family borough, is it not? Mr Fane and Colonel
Mitchell are the members?

A.   They are, sir. But they have not honoured us since the last
election.

Q.   Since two years ago, in short? They were entered unopposed?

A.   Indeed, sir.

Q.   And they have made no enquiries, concerning the events in
question?

A.   Neither to me nor to any, that I have knowledge of.

Q.   Very well. Enough of that. You had no communication with
the three servants?

A.   None whatsoever.

Q.   Have you knowledge of other travellers in these parts being
robbed or murdered — either since or previous to your coming hither?

A.   Not in this parish or its neighbours. I have heard tales of a
gang of footpads near Minehead some five years past. But I
understand all are long since caught and hanged. They came
not this far afield.

Q.   No highwaymen?

A.   There is not rich enough custom for them here. There are
scoundrels and pickpockets enough at Bideford, who prey
upon the quays. And travelling Irish that are little better. But
we are strict on such here who have no passes. They are soon
whipped out of the parish.

Q.   Have you formed any opinion as to what happened on the
first of May?

A.   Only that divine retribution was exacted upon gross deceit.

Q.   You would say, they were all murdered?

A.   I have heard it proposed that the two servants were in league
and did murder their masters, then fell out over the booty

95

and the maid, whom the victor took, and then escaped by taking devious ways.

Q. But why should they have waited thus far from London to do the deed? And why should your victor, if he was so cunning as to conceal the first two bodies beyond finding, not conceal the third the same?

A. I cannot tell, sir. Unless it were in the awful haste of his guilt.

Q. You mistake your comprehensive rogue, Mr Beckford. I have had dealings with too many of that brotherhood not to know they are far more concerned for their mortal skins than their eternal souls. A man who should have waited thus long to premeditate his crime . . . no hothead, sir. He would not have acted thus.

A. I must bow to your greater experience. I can advance no further possibility.

Q. Never mind, sir. You have assisted me more than you may know. As I informed you in our preliminaries, I am not at liberty to reveal the name of the person at whose behest I prosecute these enquiries. But I will tell you, in the confidence that I may rely on your utmost discretion, that it is the fate of he who called himself Mr Bartholomew that is my concern.

A. I am most sensible of your trust, sir. If I do not violate delicacy, may I ask if the younger gentleman was not of noble family?

Q. I can say no more, Mr Beckford. I act upon the strictest instructions. So far as the world is concerned the person in question is engaged upon a voyage in France and Italy. Such indeed was his declared intention before his departure from London.

A. I must beg leave to admire that you know so little of his companion.

Q. Because with one exception, sir, *videlicet* the dead man, those who came with him here were not those he had engaged for his supposed voyage. Where he found these, we do not know. Since he was secret in all and hid his own true name, we must suppose he also had them to hide theirs. It is to this that you

owe the tedious imposition of my questions. You perceive my
task is no small one.

A.   I do indeed, Mr Ayscough.

Q.   I leave tomorrow to pursue my quarry elsewhere. But I shall
greatly esteem it, should you chance to hear of any further
information in the affair, that you will at once communicate
it to me at Lincoln's Inn. Rest assured that I will see to it that
your good offices do not go unnoticed.

A.   There is nothing, sir, I would not do to oblige a deceived parent, and especially were he of noble birth.

Q.   I shall find the bottom to this, Mr Beckford. I work slow, but
I sift small. What heresy is to gentlemen of your cloth, subterfuge and deceit are to those of mine. I will not suffer them
in my parish, sir. I'll not rest till all's laid bare.

A.   Amen to that, sir. May Heaven concur in granting us both
our prayers.

> Jurat die tricesimo et uno Jul.
> anno supradicto coram me
> Henry Ayscough

Barnstaple, the 4th Augt.

Your Grace,

Would that it were not my unhappy duty to inform Your Grace that my journey west has met with success in the least, but defeat in the greatest matter. *Non est inventus.* But since it was Yr Grace's most express command that he should be spared nothing of what I might find, I must obey.

The testimonies I enclose for Your Grace's perusal will I doubt not lead him to conclude that of the true person of Mr Bartholomew there can be no room for mistake; and most particularly when it is grounded not solely (which Yr Grace may consider sufficient in itself) upon the portrait entrusted to me, but the particular circumstance of a servant without speech or hearing, moreover according in all other report of appearance and manner. I have not troubled Yr Grace with some several further testimonies I have sought and undertaken, since they but largely repeat what is here sent. Dr Pettigrew, the Coroner, has affirmed all within his cognizance and recollection; and I have spoken also with his clerk, who rode out upon the first report, the doctor (who is aged) being indisposed when it fell.

I must beseech Your Grace (and his august consort, to whom I beg leave to present my humblest compliments) not to take the discovery of Thurlow's end at *prima facie* seeming, that is, as certain proof of some far greater tragedy. Those who would place such burden upon it are ignorant, fearful people, more apt (*omne ignotum pro magnifico est*) for the most part to see the Devil's hand in all than to weigh with reason. Their hypothesis requires a body, and here we have none; neither the noble person of such interest to Yr Graces, nor those of his three unknown companions on his journey.

More to the purpose I have had searched by two dozen sharp-eyed fellows, well-versed *in loco* and under promise of good reward, all that place where the chest was found. Not a bush, not an inch, was not searched again, and over a much wider extent; *idem*, where Thurlow was found, and all about, and as closely. I may assure Yr Grace that *auspicium melioris aevi* a blank covert was drawn in every quarter. In all of this Yr Grace may likewise be assured that the discretion he enjoined has been most scrupulously observed. When need hath driven, I have declared myself Mercury to Jupiter, steward to one who reaches far; and given no clew whatsoever as to his most eminent rank. To Dr Pettigrew alone I have told near truth, that this is no common case of a disappearance; he is a worthy gentleman, of strictest principle, and may be trusted.

Yr Grace once did me the honour of saying he placed as great trust upon my nose as upon that of his favourite hound; if he will still credit that oracular appendage, it tells me that he whom I search both lives and breathes, and shall be found; tho' I cannot deny the purpose of his presence in this county is most difficult to unfold, and I have yet, lacking all scent to it, no opinion thereon. The pretext given, 'tis clear, was *ad captandum vulgum*, powder to blind other eyes; yet neither can I conceive what might have drawn his Lordship, so contrary to all his tastes and proclivities, into this dull and barbarous western land. There where his footsteps were last seen is not unlike some of Yr Grace's ruder and more bosky dales, tho' less elevated in their heights, and more tree'd than be-moored (save where 'tis pasture for sheep), and unless it be upon a great filthy barren hill named Ex-moor, whence the river Exe takes its source, that lies some few miles to the north. All here is at this present the more displeasing for this last month's continued rains, that is said out of living memory, and hath done much damage to hay and growing corn alike, and buildings beside. ('Tis said in sad jest that it matters not so many mills be ruined, for there will be no corn for grindstones, smut and the mildew being in league to take all first.)

The common people are more secret than ours, their language most obscure and uncouth. They know not the pronominal nor its conjugation, speaking of he and she indifferently as her (*aitchum non amant*), of we as us, all f's grow v's: 'tis a most foul-ravelled Boeotian, the which my clerk hath largely endeavoured to spare Yr Grace the expression of, for his quicker comprehension. Nor is there person of education at the miserable place where last his Lordship lodged, beyond Mr Beckford. I doubt not, that gentleman would be as high a Tory as ever Sacheverell was, were not all bishops Whigs. He'd turn Mahometan tomorrow, to gain a better living.

I trust Yr Grace will accept my belief that little remains to be discovered in these parts. My further inquisitions both at Bideford and in this town whence I have the honour to address Yr Grace have met no more success than those of Dr Pettigrew. Yet must I now deem it certain his Lordship was here, upon ends unknown. There is none of his Lordship's acquaintance that I enquired upon before proceeding here to account for the pretended uncle and his man. Nor, as Yr Grace will recall, did I then discover suspicion or noise of any clandestine and illicit attachment on his Lordship's part, that might explain the maid. Even were it so, and her outward seeming mask upon a lady, I cannot suppose that the scandal of such an elopement would not by now have been cried about; nor, *non obstante* such being the case, understand why their flight should not have been straight to Dover or some place more contiguous for France, rather than to these most disconvenient (for the purpose) parts.

In truth I remain at a loss to suggest to Yr Grace what need his Lordship had for these three superadded persons in his train. It is to be presumed that to travel alone with his man had best suited the secrecy of his intent. I can but surmise that he deemed a party of five, in which he played a subordinate part to the supposed uncle, more favourable to throw off pursuit, if such for some reason were feared. 'Tis possible this coming to Devon is no more than a hare's double, if Yr Grace will pardon the expression. Both Bideford and Barnstaple have frequent trade with Wales and Ireland, some also with France, Portugal and Cadiz, this last grown greater since the new peace. I have enquired and no French-bound ship sailed (though several for Newfoundland and New England, for this is the favoured season) from either place in the first two weeks of May. Yet must I count such round-about to refuge little probable.

Your Grace knows better than I the attachment between his Lordship and Thurlow. I have considered much on this, that is, on the great improbability of such a fond master provoking the ghastly deed; or at the least, it once done, not making enquiry upon the loss. I can account for it but by supposing his Lordship obliged for some reason to turn Thurlow off and to continue his travels alone, and that (it may be) the man in his natural deficiencies imperfectly understood his Lordship's reasons, and so took his life in despair, after his Lordship had departed from him. But I will weary Yr Grace no further with such conjecture.

Your Grace will doubtless mark the testimony of the serving-girl. 'Tis evident that his Lordship brought papers and an instrument of his favoured study upon his journey, an encumbrance little consonant with an elopement or sentimental assignation. I thought therefore also to inquire whether any *curiosi* of the mathematick or astronomick sciences resided in this neighbourhood. Through Dr Pettigrew's good offices I attended on one such at Barnstaple, Mr Samuel Day, a gentleman of private fortune, and amateur of the natural sciences, concerning which he has communicated with the Royal Society and Sir H. Sloane, among others. But to my particular enquiries he could answer nothing of import; nor could think of any study only to be satisfied by observation in this neighbourhood; nor knew, closer than Bristol, of any other such as he that a London virtuoso might wish to seek out. I fear that there too Yr Grace's servant found himself left *in tenebris*. Even should such a matter be the *primum mobile* of his Lordship's journey, I own I cannot conceive why it should, with so harmless a purpose, have been thus conducted.

I did also, likewise upon advice of Dr Pettigrew, call but yesterday upon one Mr Robert Luck, that is master of the grammar school here and accounted a learned scholar, and good gossip besides. 'Twas he who taught the late Mr Gay his letters, of which he remains inordinate proud, and inordinate blind to all that is seditious in this his ancient pupil's work. He did press upon me a copy of Gay's eclogues, that were imprinted these twenty years past under the title of the Shepherd's Week, and that Mr. L. doth maintain to be a most truthful portrait of this northern part of Devon; and likewise was pressed upon me by this rhyming pedagogue a copy of some verses by himself, that is new published by Cave and he says has been noticed in his magazine; both which volumes I dispatch with this for Yr Grace's eyes, should he deign to bend them to such paltry stuff. As to my enquiry, Mr Luck proved ill luck; like in all else, he could say nothing to the point.

Tomorrow I shall for Taunton, and there take coach without delay for London, to prosecute a suspicion I have gained. Yr Grace will, I trust, forgive me for not here and now expatiating upon it, since I am in haste not to delay the expedition of this packet, which I might wish a veritable winged Mercury to bear to Yr Grace's hands, for I know with what expectation it is attended; nor would my respect for Yr Grace dare risk raising hopes upon too small a ground. Should such ground prove larger, it shall at once be communicated. Yr Grace knows me well enough, I trust, to believe that *quo fata trahunt, sequamur* and with that every diligence which Yr Grace's past favours have lain as a hallowed duty upon ever his most humble and obedient servant,

Henry Ayscough

Post-scriptum. Mr Luck did impart to me news fresh arrived from London of the most disgraceful verdict at Edinburgh against Captain Porteous, and the riotings of the mob but a week since at Shoreditch, the both which I know will alarm Yr Grace. 'Tis thought here the mobility is consequent upon the Gin Act, that all resent. H.A.

Historical Chronicle, 1736.

JULY.

Thursday, July 1.

THE Court of King's Bench after many learned Arguments by Sir *Woolston Dixie*'s Council, refused to grant a new Tryal, which had been mov'd for by Mrs *Elizabeth Burker.*
(See p. 354. F)

One *Ereskin* a Quaker made a 2d solemn Progress thro' *Edinburg,* crying, *The great and terrible Day of the Lord is coming!*

Saturday. 3.

The *Godolphin,* Capt. *Steward,* arriv'd at *Spithead* from the *East-Indies,* and brought Advice that the Purser and Surgeon of the said Ship being walking near *Bengal,* a Tyger seiz'd and carry'd off the latter, Mr *Sedgwick:* And §§ *Anselme* Capt. *Derby,* of 30 Guns and 90 Men, going from *Bombay* to *Tellicherry* in a Calm, was attack'd by a Number of Grabs, Row-Boats, and 800 Men belonging to *Angria* the *Indian* Pyrate; and after a desperate Fight, wherein she lost 30 Hands and spent all her Powder, she was boarded and carry'd off, having some Ladies and Gentlemen Passengers on Board, and a Quantity of Silver.

Monday, 5.

George Watson a Smuggler was hang'd at *Tyburn,* (See p. 354. G.) and dyed without shewing any Concern.

From the beginning of the Month, we had such continued Rain, the like not known in ye Memory of Man; Insomuch that all the low Meadows in ye Kingdom were about this Time floated, and the Hay, Corn, and Grass thereon carry'd away, or spoil'd. Some Bridges and Mills gave way, and the Damage done almost incredible. In the Parish of *Tingwick, Oxfordshire,* a large Tract of Earth computed at about 6,000 Loads, with a Hedge and several large Trees thereon, was carry'd by the Violence of the Torrent a-cross the Channel of the River, by which Means the Current was entirely stopp'd, and the Meadows floated for many Miles.

Tuesday. 13.

Came on before Ld *Hardwicke* at *Guild-Hall,* a Tryal on a Case of Usury and Extortion. The Plaintiff alledg'd, that in *August* 1733, he borrow'd 400 l. of the Defendant

on Bond, for which he was obliged to pay 100 l. Interest till *July* 1735, which being prov'd, the Jury brought in a Verdict for the Plaintiff of 1200 l.

Wednesday, 14.

A large Paper Parcel was discovered under the Seat of the Counsellors in the Court of Chancery, *Westminster-hall,* then sitting, which being kick'd down the Steps, it blew up, and put all present in the utmost Confusion. A large Quantity of printed Bills was by the Explosion scatter'd about the Hall, giving Notice, that this Day, being the last Day of the Term, the 5 following Acts (*impudently and treasonably call'd Libels*) would be burnt in *Westminster-hall,* at the *Royal-Exchange,* and on St *Margaret's-Hill, Southwark,* between the Hours of 12 and 2. The *Gin Act* was call'd, an *Act to prevent the Sale of distill'd Liquors.* The *Mortmain Act* (*the Act for taking away the little remains of Charity.*) The *Westminster-Bridge Act;* (*the Act to prevent People passing over London-Bridge.*) The *Smugglers Act;* (*the Act to prevent innocent Gentlemen travelling armed.*) And the Act for *borrowing 600,000l.* on the Sinking Fund, had the last Words chang'd into the *Sacred Fund,* and ye Expression *Foreign Prince* added.

The Ld Chancellor committed two Gentlewomen of considerable Fortune to the Fleet Prison; they were brought by Habeas Corpus from *Chester* Gaol, where they had been confin'd 13 Months for Contempt, in not putting in an Answer to a Bill fil'd in the said Court.

Came on at the King's-Bench, *Westminster,* a Cause concerning a Bastard Child, when the Power of Justices in relation to the Parents of illegitimate Children was debated; and the Court was of Opinion, that no Justice of Peace had Power to commit any Person to Gaol in such a Case, but only to oblige them to find Security for their Appearance at the next Quarter-Sessions.

Thursday. 15.

Her Majesty in Council order'd the Parliament to be farther prorog'd to the 14th of *October.*

At a Court of Common-Council at *Guild-Hall,* a Report of the Committee of City Lands was read, setting forth what Money had been expended in filling up Fleet Ditch, &c. also shewing what farther was necessary for erecting ng the New intended Market, which in all amounted to 10,265 *l.* 17 *s.* 10 *d.* half-penny. In this Market is to be a Recess, capable of containing 100 Country Carts, 218 Shops and Stalls, and a large Market House 252 Feet in Length, and 44 in Breadth.

Saturday, 17.

A Proclamation by the Queen and Council, was publish'd offering a Reward of 200 *l.* to any Person who should discover the Author, Printer or Publisher, of the scandalous Libel dispers'd in *Westminster-Hall,* and charging all his Majesty's Judges, Justices, &c. to put the Laws in Execution, especially those good ones made last Session, which were so scandalously misrepresented and reflected on.

Tuesday, 20.

The Jury at *Edinburgh* found Capt *Porteous* guilty of Murder, whereupon the Lords sentenc'd him to be executed in the *Grass-Market* upon the 8th of *Sept.* next. (See p. 544, A. and p. 230. B, C.) The Verdict was as follows; *viz.* ' That the said *John Porteous,* ' fired a Gun among the People assembled at ' the Place of Execution and Time libelled; as ' also, that he gave Orders to the Soldiers un-' der his Command to fire, and upon his and ' their so firing, the Persons mentioned in the ' Indictment were killed and wounded. And ' find it proven, that He and his Guard were ' attacked and beat by several Stones of a con-' siderable Bigness, thrown among them by ' the Multitude, whereby several of the Soldi-' ers were bruised and wounded.'

Wednesday, 21.

Was held a General Court at the *South-Sea House,* when a half Years Dividend of one and a half was agreed to. The Sub-Governor reported, that by a Letter from Mr *Keene,* the Court of *Spain* was not yet come to a Resolution when the Galleons wou'd sail, and nothing could be fix'd with regard to the Schedula. Mr *Woodford* complain'd of the Hardships the Company suffer'd in Defiance of the *Assiento* and several Treaties; and mov'd the Court might be adjourn'd to Thursday fortnight, by which time they might hear again from Mr *Keene,* which was agreed to. Mr *Gaswall* said it was evident that the Company had lost 10,000 *l.* by the Non-acceptance of a Proposal made 3 Years ago to the Directors, for farming the Introduction of Negroes to *New Spain,* which with an additional Advantage-offer'd wou'd bring in 6000 *l. per An.* That as former Experiments had not answer'd, it seem'd the Opinion of the Proprietors, that a certain Profit to the Company was superior to any Calculation; He then instanc'd Mr *Read's* Calculation concerning the Introduction of 200 Negroes annually to *La Vera Cruz,* en which the Company wou'd clear exclusive of the *Indults* 11,000 *l. per Ann.* whereas their Factor Mr *Hayes,* who had a fair Character, sold but 70.

Thursday, 22.

The Sessions ended at the Old-Bailey,

where 54 Prisoners were tried, of whom 14 were cast for Transportation, 23 acquitted, and 7 Capitally convicted, *viz. Tho Mills,* for stealing a Horse value 12 *l. Jn Mackworth,* alias *Perry,* alias *Parliament Jack,* for Housebreaking; *Thomas Ricketts,* for stealing a Silver hilted Sword; *Jn Kelsey,* for robbing the *Cirencester* Coach at *Hyde-Park Corner; Stephen Philips,* for Horse stealing; *Tho Morris,* and *Jn Pritchard,* for House breaking.

Monday, 26.

One *Reynolds,* a Turnpike Leveller, condemn'd with *Bayley* on the 10th (See p. 353.) (on the Act against going arm'd and disguised) was hang'd at *Tyburn.* He was cut down by the Executioner as usual, but as the Coffin was fast'ning he thrust back the Lid, upon which the Executioner would have tyed him up again, but the Mob prevented it, and carried him to a House where he vomited three Pints of Blood, but on giving him a Glass of Wine, he died. *Bayley* was repriev'd.

This and 2 or 3 following Nights, a great Mob rose in *Shoreditch* and *Spittlefields,* occasioned by some *Irish* Labourers and Weavers working at under Rates. They cry'd, *Down down with the Irishmen,* broke the Windows where they lodged, and almost demolish'd two publick Houses kept by *Irishmen;* one in *Brick-lane,* in Defence of which some Fire-Arms were discharg'd, which killed a young Man and wounded 7 or 8. The Justices, Constables, and Train'd Bands not being able to quell 'em, a Party of Horse and Foot Soldiers were call'd in, on which and the committing 6 or 7 to Prison, they became quiet.—A like Tumult happen'd a few Days before, at *Dartford* in *Kent,* on the same Occasion, which could not be appeased till the *Irish* Labourers were discharged, and some of the Rioters who had been apprehended, were released.

Saturday, 31.

In the *Daily Advertiser, July* 28, *Joshua Ward,* Esq; having the Queen's Leave, recites 7 extraordinary Cases of Persons which were cured by him, and examined before her Majesty *June* 7. Objections to which had been made, in the *Grub-Street Journal, June* 14. But the Attention of the Publick has been a little taken off from the Wonder-working Mr *Ward,* to a strolling Woman, now at *Epsom,* who calls her self *Crazy Sally;* and had perform'd Cures in Bone-setting to Admiration, and occasion'd so great a Resort, that the Town offer'd her 100 Guineas to continue there a Year.

A LIST *of* BIRTHS *July* 1736.

10. THE Lady of *George Venables Vernon,* Esq; Member for *Litchfield,* was DELIVERED of a Daughter.

26. The Countess of *Deloraine,* Wife to *Wm Wyndham,* Esq;—of a Son.

30. The Lady of *Tho. Archer,* Esq; Member for *Warwick,*—of a Son.

THE MAN IN THE DOVE-GREY SUIT and discreetly flowered waistcoat stretched over an incipient belly, with the heavy brows, the wart on the side of his nose, the rather too studiedly imposing carriage, stands with his walking-cane in the doorway of the wood-panelled chamber in Lincoln's Inn. One wall of it is mostly taken up with cased tomes of precedent, rolls and parchments; before the cases stands a tall writing-desk and stool, a sheaf of paper and writing materials neatly laid ready upon it. Opposite gleams a marble mantelpiece on which sits a bust of Cicero. This is flanked by silver candlesticks, not in present use; nor is the fire-grate below. A morning sunlight shafts the room's warm peace from its south-facing windows ... which give, at a little distance, upon a wall of still green leaves. From somewhere outside, since an upper sash is down, there sounds the faint yet melodious voice of a woman crying (for it is their season) first pearmains; but in the room, silence.

The very small, frail and bewigged man in black, who reads behind a round table in a far corner of the room, does not look up from whatever he reads. The man in the doorway glances round; but whoever conducted him to this point has mysteriously disappeared. He therefore clears his throat, in the practised manner of one who has no phlegm to lose, but a laggard attention to draw. At last the figure at the table looks up. He is evidently a few years his visitor's senior, although physically his marked inferior, of the puny build of a Pope or a Voltaire. The man in the door raises his hat with a hint of a polite flourish, and slightly inclines.

"I have the honour to address Mr Ayscough? Mr Francis Lacy at your command, sir."

Most strangely the little lawyer does not offer any courtesy in exchange, but merely lays down his papers and leans back a little in his armed and highbacked chair, which almost dwarfs him, and folds his arms; then slightly tilts his head, like a robin alert to prey. There is a quizzical, almost glistening fixity in the gaze of his grey eyes. Mr Francis Lacy shows himself somewhat at a loss at this reception. He assumes a forgetfulness in the man of law, a temporary inability to place, and speaks again.

"The Thespian, sir. I attend to meet your client, as requested."

At last the lawyer speaks. "Be seated."

"Sir."

And the actor advances towards a chair on the opposite side of the table, with regained aplomb. Before he reaches and can sit on it, the sound of the door behind being firmly closed makes him turn. A tall and silent clerk, also in black, like a heron turned crow, stands with his back to the door, a leatherbound quarto book in one hand. His stare is as intent as his master's, though markedly more sardonic. Lacy looks back down at the diminutive lawyer, who repeats his previous phrase.

"Be seated."

Lacy parts his coat-tails and sits. There is a silence, and still the lawyer will not leave the actor with his eyes. Ill at ease, the latter feels in his waistcoat pocket and produces a silver snuff-box. He opens, then extends it.

"Do you partake, sir? It is best Devizes." Ayscough shakes his head. "Then by your leave."

Lacy places two pinches on the snuff cushion of his left hand and sniffs them in; then snaps close and replaces the box in his pocket; at the same time extracting a lace handkerchief, with which he dabs his nostrils.

"Your client has a dramatic effusion upon which he seeks my advice?"

"He does."

"He has chosen well, sir, though I say it with modesty. Few can rival my experience, even my critics do me the honour of granting that." He waits for some polite agreement, but the cue is not taken. "May I ask if his Muse is laughing Thalia, or rather grave Melpomene?"

"His Muse is Terpsichore."

"Sir?"

"Is she not the Muse of dance?"

"I am no dancing-master, sir. I fear you mistake. For the pantomime you must seek my friend, Mr. Rich."

"No mistake."

Lacy draws himself up a little. "I am an actor, sir. My talents are familiar to all the cognoscenti of this city."

The lawyer, who has not unfolded his arms, shows a humourless smile.

"And shall soon be as familiar to the cognoscenti of Tyburn. My client has written a piece for you, my friend. It is called The Steps and the String, or Twang-dang-dillo-dee. In which you shall jig upon the scaffold, at the end of Jack Ketch's rope."

There is a moment's shock on Lacy's face, then he sits bolt upright, his cane held to one side.

"Is this an impertinent jest, sir?"

The little lawyer stands, his hands on the table, and leans a fraction towards his victim.

"No jest ... Mr *Brown*. By Heavens, no jest, you impudent rogue."

The actor stares back at the fierce eyes, as if he cannot credit their sudden sternness, or his own ears.

"My name is —"

"Four months since in the county of Devon you passed as Brown. Do you dare to deny it?"

The actor looks abruptly away.

"You extravagate, sir. I take my leave."

He stands and turns to march towards the door. The clerk, who still waits there, and no longer has any smile, does not shift. He simply lifts the book he holds in front of him, against his breast,

A MAGGOT

holding it there with both hands, and exhibiting the cross stamped on its leather cover. The lawyer's voice speaks sharply.

"You are smoked out, sirrah!" Lacy glances back, and draws himself up. "And do not try your hollow airs upon me. It is not so long since that your kind were publicly flogged for their pains. I advise you to put your buskins by. This is a chamber of the law. No playhouse, where you can strut in a tawdry crown and awe a crowd of gaping dolts with your rodomontadoes. Do I make myself plain?"

Once again the actor looks away from those eyes, through the nearest window and at the green leaves, as if he wished himself among them. There is a small silence. At last his eyes turn back.

"I would have your authority to address me thus."

The lawyer extends a small hand and, not leaving the actor's eyes, begins counting his authority on his fingers.

"Item, I have enquired and you were not in London at the time in question. Item, I have been where you were, I have marched in your mendacious footsteps. Item, I have sworn affidavits as to your exact appearance, down to that very growth I perceive upon your right nostril. Item, my clerk behind you has spoken with one who called on some matter at your lodging at the said time and was told you was upon private business in the West Country. And by whom, pray? None other than your wife, forsooth. Would you have her so great a liar as yourself?"

"I will not deny I chanced to be in Exeter."

"You lie!"

"It may be proven no lie. Ask at the Ship, beside the Cathedral, where I lay."

"On what business?"

"Upon promise of an engagement . . . which came to nothing."

"I'll not discuss with you, Lacy. I have not done with other items. For servant you had one Farthing, a Welsh fellow not worth his name. You also carried with you one who passed as a maidservant, one Louise. Well may you cast your eyes down, sir. For there is worse yet. You had one other with you, a servant both deaf and dumb, to your supposed nephew, Mr Bartholomew. That servant is not disappeared, sir. But found dead, under great suspicion of further foul murder done by persons hitherto unknown — but now known, sir, and here before me!"

At the word "dead" the actor has looked up, and for the first time without semblance of artifice.

"How . . . dead?"

The lawyer slowly sits back down in his chair. He is silent a moment, sizing his man. Then he poises his fingertips together and speaks in a less peremptory voice.

"Well, sir. And what's that to you? Were you not in Exeter at the time — upon promise of an engagement?" The actor stands silent. "Did you not play a main part in an impudent new satire, this last March and April, until the non-week? A piece called *Pasquin* by an arrant rogue, one Fielding, at the Haymarket little theatre?"

"It is well known. All London saw it."

"You were Fustian, were you not — a large part?"

"Yes."

"A great success, I am told, like everything else in these sacrilegious times that has the effrontery to mock the constitution. How long had it run, when the Easter week came — April the seventeenth, was it not, that you stopped?"

"Some thirty performances. I forget."

"No, sir. Thirty-five. The longest run since its equal in impertinence, *The Beggar's Opera,* was it not?"

"It is possible."

"What, you don't know? Were you not also in that piece, these seven or eight years past?"

"I took a small part, to please Mr Gay. We were friends, I had that honour."

"Honour, indeed! Is that honour, to take a part that made a footpad and felon of the most eminent commoner in this nation, its chief minister besides? Were you not that most wicked and scurrilous travesty of Sir Robert Walpole, named Robin of Bagshot? And your wife no better — was she not in that same piece Dolly Trull, a shameless trollop, that I doubt she found it trouble to impersonate?"

"Sir, I most indignantly protest your last aspersion. My wife —"

"A fig for your wife. I know you, sir, and far better than you suppose. As I know what happened when they return to resume with *Pasquin* on the twenty-sixth of April last. You are mysteriously not there, sir, your fine part is played by some one else, one Topham, is it not so? And I know the lying excuse you gave, sir, I have witnesses to it, for breaking your engagement. Am I to believe that you forsook the triumph of the season, in which you had a handsome share, to go to Exeter upon promise of an engagement? You were bought away, Lacy, and I know by whom."

The actor has stood at an oblique angle, listening to this, his head slightly down. Now he looks back at the lawyer, a simpler man, without pretence.

"I have committed no crime, I know nothing of . . . what you tell me. I will swear to that."

"You will not deny you were bought to accompany a person called Mr Bartholomew on his journey west, in the last week of this April past?"

"I have a right to know what bears upon my answer to that."

The little lawyer is silent for a moment. "I will tell you your right. Deny me still and I will have you straight from this room to Newgate, then in chains to Devon, for the next assize. Admit you are who I say, tell all under oath, and we may see. He for whom I proceed shall decide." He raises a stern finger. "But I warn you, I'll have all — not one tittle omitted. Or he and I will have you broken into as many shards as a china pot. He has but to nod, and you are dust. You shall curse the day that you were born."

The actor returns to his chair and sits heavily. He shakes his head, and looks to the floor.

"Well, sir?"

"I was deceived, sir, grossly deceived. I believed it a harmless subterfuge in pursuit of a worthy and pitiable end." He looks up. "You will not credit me, but you see an honest man before you. That I was guilty of credulity, foolishness in what happened, alas, I cannot deny. But not of evil intent or action. I must pray you to believe that."

"Plea me no pleas, sir. I give no credit, except upon facts."

"To the estimable Mrs Lacy you are unjust. She had no part whatsoever in this."

"I shall determine that."

"You may ask of me, sir. I am well known in my profession. I knew Mr Gay well, his friend the Duchess of Queensberry too, and her most august husband. I had the honour of General Charles Churchill's friendship, I met him most often at Grosvenor Street, before Mrs Oldfield died. I know Mr Rich of Goodman's Fields. Mr Cibber the poet laureate, Mr Quin, the virtuous Mrs Bracegirdle. All will speak for me, that I am no Thomas Walker, no shame to my profession." The lawyer says nothing, watching him. "I have offended some great person?" Still the lawyer says nothing, his gaze intent. "I feared it might be so. If I had known at the beginning what I came to know finally . . ." Again he is not answered. "What am I to do?"

"Make oath and tell, without omission. And from the beginning."

Hiſtorical Chronicle, 1736.

AUGUST.

Sunday, 1.

MOBS aroſe in *Southwark*, *Lambeth* and *Tyburn-Road*, and took upon 'em to interrogate People whether they were for the *Engliſh* or *Iriſh*? but committed no Violence; ſeveral Parties of Horſe Grenadiers diſperſ'd the Mobs which were gathering in *Ratcliff-highway*, to demoliſh the Houſes of the *Iriſh*.

Monday, 2.

The firſt Stone was laid of a new Building at St *Bartholomew's* Hoſpital, which is to contain 12 Wards; it is to be of the ſame Dimenſions as the firſt Side already built of *Bath* Stone, and 2 more are to be added on the Eaſt and Weſt. The Workmen found at the Depth of 20 Feet, 60 or 70 Pieces of old ſilver Coin, the Bigneſs of Three-pences.

A very extraordinary Cauſe was try'd at *Hertford* Aſſizes, on an Action brought againſt the Defendant for debauching the Plaintiff's Daughter, (both Perſons of Fortune,) and having a Child by her under Marriage Promiſes. A ſpecial Jury gave her 150 l. Damages, and directed her to bring an Action in her own Right upon a Marriage Contract.

Thurſday, 5.

A great Cauſe was tried at *Chelmsford*, *Eſſex*, between Sir *John Eyles*, Bart. Plaintiff, and *John Smart*, Gamekeeper to the Hon. *Edward Carteret*, Eſq; Defendant. The Action was brought for ſhooting 3 Hunting-Dogs. The Defendant juſtified, that the Dogs being in purſuit of the Deer in his Maſter's Park, and very near killing ſome of them; he did not malicouſly but for the Preſervation of the ſaid Deer ſhoot the Dogs; which the Judge ſeem'd to admit as lawful; but the Jury (being Gentlemen) in regard to the Game Laws brought in a Verdict for the Plaintiff, and a Guinea and half Damages. The Judge declared, that if a new Tryal was moved for, he would certify in Behalf of the Defendant.

Monday, 7.

Came on a Hearing before the Ld Chancellor at *Lincoln's-Inn-Hall*, of the great Cauſe between the *South-Sea* Company and one of their Super-cargoes, which his Lordſhip determin'd intirely in Favour of the Company.

Wedneſday, 10.

Was held a General Court of the *South Sea* Company, when the Sub-Governor told the Court; that the Directors had receiv'd no farther Proposals relating to the Negro Trade, Farming the nor any further Anſwer from the Court of *Madrid*, Then Debates ariſing, it was reſolv'd, that the Directors be impower'd to put in Execution ſuch Proposals, as have or may be offer'd within two Months to Advantage of the Company, for the Diſpoſal of § Negro Trade.—And that all Matters relating to the Demand of the King of *Spain* for a Quarter of the Profits ariſing by the annual Ship, and for ſettling the Value of Dollars, be referr'd to the Conſideration of the Court of Directors, and then adjourn'd.

Four Malefactors were hang'd at *Tyburn*, *viz.* Tho. *Mills* and S. *Phillips*, for Horſe ſtealing.; *John Maxworth* alias *Parliament Jack* for Buglary; *John Kolſey* for robbing the *Cirenceſter* Coach. *Mills* declar'd juſt before he was turn'd off, that he was not guilty of the Fact. *Rickets, Morris* and *Pritchard*, (See p. 422 A.) were repriev'd for 14 years transportation.

Thurſday, 11.

A Fire broke out at *Peaſmore, Berkſhire*, which in a few Hours conſum'd the whole Street leading from the Church to *Market Iſley*; the Damage is computed at ſeveral thouſand Pounds.

Monday, 16.

Mr *Nixon*, a Nonjuring Clergyman of the County of *Norfolk*, was committed to *Newgate* by the Secretaries of State, on a Charge on Oath of his being Author of a ſcandalous Libel fix'd up at the *Royal Exchange*. We ſee this further Account in one of the Publick Papers, *viz.* Doctor *Gaylard*, a Printer, one of *Rayner's*

Journeymen, and formerly a Prisoner on Account of *Mist*'s Journal, hath made Oath, That he, together with one *Clark*, another Printer not yet taken, did compose from a manuscript Copy, written by Mr *Nixon*, the Libel dispersed in *Westminster-Hall*, the 14th of *July* last, at the House of the said Mr *Nixon* in *Hatton-Garden*, and the said original Copy has been found by the Messengers. 'Tis believed, Mr *Nixon* had a Premium given him by a private Collection; but however it be, 'twill cost him dear."

Thursday. 17.

At *Hereford* Assizes a Cause was try'd concerning the Power of the Bayliff of *Cardiff* to make Burgesses, which was very strenuously argued by Council on both sides, but the Jury without going out of the Court gave a Verdict in favour of the Bayliff.

Thursday. 19.

At the Assizes at *Bristol*, one *Vernon* who was indicted for House breaking with two more, insisting on his Right to be admitted as an Evidence, refus'd to plead; but being remanded back to the Press, thought good to stand Tryal; and immediately after Sentence was pass'd on him, said D——n it, I don't value my Life of a Halfpenny.

Friday 20.

The Bakers at *Dublin* not liking the Assize of Bread made by the Lord Mayor, which was above 14 *lb.* Houshold Bread for 1*s.* refused to bake 2 or 3 Days; whereupon the poor People in that City were in great Distress, some had Recourse to Potatoes, and some bought Flower to bake themselves, and found their Account in it, tho' the Bakers thought their Profit too small, but the Church Wardens threatned to present them as having no regular Visible Way of Living, on which they went to baking again.

Monday 23.

The Church of *Boudham* near *Larlingford* in *Norfolk*, was burnt down to the Ground.

Tuesday 24.

A fatter Boar was hardly ever seen than one staken up this Day, coming out of Fleet Ditch into the Thames: It prov'd to be a Butcher's, near *Smithfield Bars*, who had mist him 5 Months, all which Time, it seems, he had been in the common Sewer, and was improv'd in Price from 10*s.* to 2 Guineas.

Wednesday, 25.

Came on 2 remarkable Trials at *Rochester*, one of a Fellow for ravishing a Wo-

man upwards of 60: The other of a Soldier who pretended to cure a Boy of an Ague, and thinking to fright it away, by firing his Piece over the Boy's Head, levell'd it too low, and shot his Brains out. The Ravisher was cast, the Soldier acquitted.

Thursday. 26.

On the humble Petition of several Magistrates and Citizens of *Edinburgh*, her Majesty was pleas'd to reprieve Captain *Porteous* for 6 Weeks.   (See p.422.

Tuesday 31.

The Cures performed by the Woman Bonesetter of *Epsom*, (see p. 442) are too many too be enumerated: Her Bandages are extraordinary Neat, and her Dexterity in reducing Dislocations and setting of fractured Bones wonderful. She has cured Persons who have been above 20 Years disabled, and has given incredible Relief in the most difficult Cases. The Lame came daily to her, and she got a great deal of Money, Persons of Quality who attended her Operations making her Presents. Her Father it seems is one *Wallin* a Bonesetter in *Wilts*. The Money she got procured her a Husband; but he did not stay with her above a Fortnight, and then went off with 100 Guineas.

This Month the Parliament of *Paris* adjudg'd an Estate to *Madamoiselle de Vigny*, who had liv'd 50 Years without knowing who were her Parents. This was the Case. M. *Ferrand* President of one of the Chambers of Justice in *Paris*, had been many Years married, & had no Issue; at length his Wife was with Child, on which the old Gentleman was uneasy, and pretended to be certain he was not Father of it. The Moment it was born he ordered it to be taken out of his House: The Midwife carried it to a Church to be christen'd; but a Dispute arising about the proper Name it should be registred by, M. *Ferrand* enter'd a Protest against calling it by his, and there remain'd a Blank in the Book to the Time of the Trial. The Girl was put to a common Nurse, and now and then relieved but never visited by the Mother, nor at all made acquainted with her Parents, till the Midwife found her out, and by her personal Evidence prov'd the above Circumstances.

They also decided a great Cause between the Duke *de Richlieu* and the Count *de Vertus*, for an Estate of 50,000 Crowns *per Annum* which had been 82 Years depending.

The Examination and Deposition of
FRANCIS LACY
the which doth attest upon his sworn
oath, this three and twentieth day
of August in the tenth year of the
reign of our sovereign Lord George the
second, by the grace of God King of Great
Britain and of England, &c.

My name is FRANCIS LACY. *I dwell at Hart Street near the Garden, two houses above the Flying Angel. I am fifty-one years of age. I was born in London, in the parish of St Giles. I am an actor, grandson to John Lacy, whom King Charles favoured.*

Q. Before all else you shall answer me this. Knew you Mr Bartholomew was under false name?

A. I did.

Q. Knew you who he truly was?

A. I did not, and do not, to this day.

Q. On what occasion did you last see him?

A. The first of May last.

Q. Do you know where he is now?

A. I do not.

Q. You are upon oath.

A. So do I speak, sir.

Q. You swear that since that first day of May you have neither seen, nor held communication with him, nor had news whatsoever of him through any other party?

A. I most solemnly swear. Would to God that I did know.

Q. Now I ask the same of your other two companions — your man and the maid. What of them?

A. I know no more of them, since that same day. I beg you to believe, sir, the circumstances are so embroiled, if I might explain —

Q. You shall explain. But in good time. For now, you also swear you do not know where these two may be found?

A. I do, and also that until this day I knew nothing of the death of the servant. May I ask —

Q. You may not. And Heaven help you if you lie.

A. May Heaven strike me down upon the instant, sir, when I shall.

Q. Very well. But I remind you that ignorance of consequence is no plea in court. You remain accessary to the crime. Now I will hear all, and from the beginning.

A. It is a strange tale, sir. I must seem foolish in it. In my own defence I must tell as I took matters at the time. Not as I later learnt them to be.

Q. On that we may agree. Commence.

A. It was in the middle of April last. As you know, I played Fustian in young Mr Fielding's *Pasquin,* a part in which, I flatter myself —

Q. Never mind your flattery. To the point.

A. I deem it to the point, sir, that the piece was most favourably received and my playing noticed. A day or two before it was to close for Easter, the man Dick came one forenoon to my house in Hart Street, with a letter for me from his master, who signed himself not by name, but as Philocomœdia. There was a packet within, containing five guineas. The letter asked me to accept them as a token of esteem for my performance, on which the writer paid me some more particular compliments.

Q. You have this epistle still?

A. At my house. I remember its terms. It is little germane.

Q. Continue.

A. The writer claimed he had seen the piece three times, solely for the pleasure of studying my talents, such as they are.

Then that he would be greatly favoured if I would meet him, as he had a matter of mutual benefit to broach. A time and place were proposed, tho' he held himself ready to suit my convenience.

Q. What time and place?

A. Trevelyan's coffee-house, the morrow morning.

Q. And you said yes?

A. I did sir. I won't deny I found the present handsome.

Q. And smelt more guineas to come.

A. Honest guineas, sir. My profession is less richly rewarded than yours.

Q. Were you not surprised? Are not the females in your calling the more customary recipients of such golden requests for assignations?

A. I was not, sir. Not all have your poor opinion of the stage. Many gentlemen take pleasure in conversing upon the dramatic and histrionic arts, and by no means spurn our company. Others aspire themselves to the bays, and are not above seeking our advice and support in seeing their effusions mounted. I ventured to presume that this was one such. It would not have been the first I have had such commerce with, I may assure you. I have myself Englished from the French, and with success. My *The Cit Grown Beau* from Molière was —

Q. Yes, yes. Roscius sallied out to earn his fee. What next?

A. His man, this mute fellow Dick, was at the door of Trevelyan's, in wait for me. I was conducted to a private room. There I met Mr Bartholomew.

Q. Under this name?

A. Yes. He so presented himself.

Q. Alone?

A. Alone, sir. We sat, he renewed the compliments of his letter, he asked me of myself and other parts I had played.

Q. Seemed he one of your cognoscenti?

A. He made no pretence there, sir. Confessed himself a stranger in London and to the theatre till recently, and hitherto taken up with other interests.

Q.   Arrived from where?

A.   From the North, sir. He was not more precise, but from his voice I judged him from the North-east. So do they speak from Yorkshire north.

Q.   And these other interests?

A.   The natural sciences. He claimed he had much neglected the arts since leaving university.

Q.   And of his supposed family?

A.   I come to that. I made a polite enquiry there, having spoken overlong of my own history. Thereupon he said, with I thought a somewhat embarrassed face, that he was younger son of a country gentleman, but wished to disclose no more, for we now touched upon the more serious matter of our meeting. I must tell you that all that followed was proven false.

Q.   Tell as you were told.

A.   I would not waste your —

Q.   I will judge of my time. Tell.

A.   He began in hypothetick vein, sir. Which I came to discern was a frequent thing in all his conversation, as you shall hear. He asked me what I should say, were I suitably rewarded, to playing a part for him alone. I requested to know what kind of part. He replied, One I should give you. I thought we had come then to the nub of it, that he had written some piece he would hear me declaim for him, so said I was sure I should be pleased to serve him in such a thing. Very well, he says, but say it should not be here and now, Mr Lacy, neither for one performing, but for several days, perchance more; and I must ask it for this end of month, for I am desperate pressed; yet that may be to your advantage, for I know you are engaged at the Little Theatre, and I must make it worth your while to leave. So said he. I confess I was somewhat taken aback, and the more when he went on to ask how much I took for my part at the Haymarket. I explained our way of dividing receipts and put it at a mean for my share of five guineas the week. Very well, he says, let me put my part at five guineas the day, whatever the receipts. Should you consider that worthy of your powers? I was the so dumbfounded at such prodigious handsomeness, I might hardly credit my ears, and thought him at first to jest. But he was not, very far from it. For as I hesitated, he further declared that since I must travel to play the part, and suffer other inconvenience, that might take a fortnight in all, he would happily offer another thirty guineas for my acceptance, thus making a round hundred for my service to him. Mr Ayscough, I am not so well circumstanced that I could lightly turn up my nose at such an untoward offer. Here was I offered to gain in a fortnight what I should not despise for a six-month of endeavour. I must tell you further I knew *Pasquin* was very nigh played out, as we say, for our receipt was falling, and the season likewise near its end. My friend Mr Topham had taken my part for two days earlier when I was indisposed, and not without some plaudit, tho' —

Q.   Enough. Very well, sir, you were tempted. To the point.

A.   I thought in addition that I conceived what he would be at — some surprise, some entertainment he intended to gratify his neighbours and family with in his native province. I was soon undeceived, however. I prayed him to be more particular. I remember his reply *verbatim,* sir. I have need of one, Mr Lacy, he said, to go with me on a journey. A grave and creditable person, he said, as I perceive it would take you no trouble to act, since you are thus by nature. I thanked him for the compliment, but declared myself at a loss to guess why he should need such a companion. Once again he appeared confused and would not answer. He stood and went to a window, as if cast deep in thought. There at last he turned upon me, as one obliged to take a new course, and asked me to forgive him, he was driven to subterfuge against his nature, and unused to not dealing frankly with all he met. Then he said, I have someone I must see, my life depends on it, and there are those who would prevent me, therefore I must make my journey under some colour of false circumstance. To which he added most vehemently that there was nothing of discredit or dishonour in what he wished. He said, I am a victim of unjust and unkind fate, which I would try to remedy. I give it you word by word, sir.

Q. And next?

A. I was somewhat astonished, as you may suppose. I said I presumed we spoke of a lady, of a sentimental attachment. He smiled sadly at that. No mere attachment, Lacy, he said. I am in love and half dead of it. He told me then of a stern and obstinate father and of an alliance designed for him, upon which his father had set his heart, for the lady was rich and had lands settled on her that his father coveted, they lay adjacent to his own estate. However, she was ten years older than Mr Bartholomew. In his very own words, the ugliest old maid for fifty miles about. Thereupon he informed me that even had she been the most beautiful, he still could not have obeyed his parent, for in London, that previous October, he had formed an ardent interest in a young lady then in town with her uncle and guardian, and his family.

Q. Her name?

A. None was ever mentioned. Her plight was this. The young lady was orphan, and had estate in title, upon majority. Alas, her uncle and guardian had a marriageable son; you perceive the case.

Q. I do.

A. Mr Bartholomew informed me that his interest had been discovered, and what was far worse, the otherwise happy circumstance that his attentions had been warmly reciprocated. Upon which the young lady was promptly removed to Cornwall, where her guardian's estate lies.

Q. And placed in bond?

A. Precisely so. However, they had been able to maintain a surreptitious correspondence by means of a maid, and confidante of the young lady's feelings. Absence makes the heart grow fonder, their common ardours were increased. Eventually in despair Mr Bartholomew revealed the matter to his own parent, to solicit his assistance and approval. Sentiment proved no match for paternal ambition. It came to high words, his father not being one to brook denial. I put it to you as it was put to me, Mr Ayscough, though I omit some colour and minor circumstance.

Q. Proceed.

A. In short, then, Mr Bartholomew, still refusing the other alliance, was commanded out of paternal house and home, and told not to return until he had cooled his temper and learnt his filial duty. With the further threat that should he pursue the course he was on, all his future prospects would be forfeit. He then came to London and fired by both love and a sense of injustice, since the lady of his heart, though not so rich as she of his father's choice, was neither without sufficient wealth nor breeding, and infinitely surpassed her in other charms, he attempted to force the matter by going to the West.

Q. When was this?

A. But a month before. He confessed he did it without forethought, almost without knowing why he went beyond his most violent need to see his loved one again and assure her of his abomination of this other proposed marriage, that she should never be expunged from his heart and —

Q. Spare me the tender protestations.

A. Sir. He arrived to find he had been forestalled. He knew not how, perhaps some letter had been intercepted. He admitted he had foolishly spoken on the matter in London with friends, and perhaps some noise of it had reached ears hostile to his interests. Then too he had travelled under his own name, and the greater part by public coach, and now suspected advice of his coming may have travelled ahead. However it may be, when he arrived the house was empty, nor would any there tell him where the family had gone, except that they had left in great haste the day previous. He waited a week in vain. All his enquiries were to no avail, for it seems the uncle rules all in those parts. He thus retreated back to London. There, sir, a letter awaited him, in which the young lady stated very plain that their removal had been against her every desire, that her uncle was in a great fury with her and daily using all means in his power to impel the marriage to his son, her cousin. That her one present hope lay in this cousin, who, though he loved her well enough, would not force the issue as his father wanted. Yet she feared he could not hold out much longer in this small mercy, since both his own natural affection and his father's wishes inclined to the same end. To which was added that the maid who had served in their previous correspondence had been dismissed, that she her mistress was now without friend or confidante, and in despair.

Q. I see the pretext. Now come to the business.

A. Mr Bartholomew declared that he knew they were now gone back to the estate, and was determined to return there. This time he would conceal his coming. For that reason he had pretended to the same intimates as before that he had given up all hope of the young lady and was now reconciled to obeying his father. Yet he greatly feared some rumour of this supposed change of heart would come to the uncle and thence to the young lady, who might take it as truth. Therefore he must act with celerity, and travel under a false name, not alone and — in brief, as you seemingly know, sir. As if for some other purpose. That is the kernel of it.

Q. *Facile credimus quod volumus.* You swallowed this cock-and-bull whole, it seems?

A. I confess I was flattered by his confidences. They conveyed to my ears the accent of truth. If he had seemed to me some young deceiver, some practised rake . . . I assure you he did not, sir.

Q. Very well. Go on.

A. I told Mr Bartholomew he had my sympathy, but not all the treasure in Spain would induce me to stoop to a criminal undertaking. And that I foresaw very unpleasant consequences, should he be successful in his enterprise.

Q. What said he to that?

A. For his father, that he felt sure he could be brought to forgiveness in time, since their relations had been affectionate enough before this rupture. For the uncle, that his cruelties to his niece, and his intentions, were too gross to have escaped notice, and he must know what public disclosure might show of his own conduct and selfish aim. That he might huff and puff if his niece fled his roof, but would not dare prosecute the matter.

Q.   He won you to his cause?

A.   I still had scruples, Mr Ayscough. He assured me he wished no future blame attributable to any save himself. He had thought on the matter, and proposed that my part should extend no farther than to within a day's ride of his destination. He would then proceed alone with his man. Upon his most solemn word he would not ask me to take any direct part in an elopement. I was merely, as he put it, to safe-conduct him to the threshold. What passed thereafter was not my affair.

Q.   Had he some plan of elopement?

A.   He intended to ride out the storm in France, then to return, his wife's majority once attained, and to throw himself with his bride at his father's feet.

Q.   What next?

A.   I requested a night to reflect on his proposal, sir. I wished to discuss it with Mrs Lacy, as is my habit in all that appertains to my life. I have learnt to value her opinion. If she considers an engagement below me, I will not take it. Mrs Lacy's parents no more approved my profession than you do, Mr Ayscough. When Mr Bartholomew spoke of his troubles, I thought of my own greener years. Not to put too fine a point on it, Mrs Lacy and I also did not wait upon parental blessing. It may be a sin by the book, but its fruits have been a Christian and most happy marriage. I say this not in excuse, sir. I cannot deny my heart and ancient memory somewhat blinded my eyes.

Q.   She approved?

A.   After she had helped me examine my sentiments concerning Mr Bartholomew — I would say, of his sincerity in his cause.

Q.   Let us hear these sentiments.

A.   That he was a serious young man, even somewhat grave for his years. I cannot say he spoke in general with much outward feeling of his attachment, yet I formed the impression that it was deep and virtuous in intent. I say this, tho' I know now I was being duped and gulled. And even when the veil was lifted from my eyes . . . well, sir, I found another and even darker veil remained. I will come to that.

Q. You met on the morrow?

A. At Trevelyan's again, in the same room, by which time I had spoken with Mr Topham also, concerning the playing my part. I put on some semblance of uncertainty at first.

Q. To raise the fee, no doubt?

A. You persist in misjudging me, sir.

Q. Then do you not persist in suggesting you were not a hired instrument in a criminal offence. Cupid is one thing, Lacy, a duly appointed guardian is another. To say nothing of a father's right to bestow his son's hand where he pleases. Enough. Proceed.

A. I wished to know more of Mr Bartholomew and his circumstances. He politely refused this, maintaining that it was not only for his own protection, but mine. That the less I knew, the less harm might come of it, if the matter became public. That I might claim ignorance of his real purpose, *et cœtera*.

Q. Did you not ask his true name?

A. I forgot to say, sir, that he had early confessed the one given me was false, for the reason just stated. I took it favourably that he did not attempt to impose on me in this.

Q. Did you never find his manner disconsonant with that of younger son of a mere country gentleman?

A. Am I to guess that —

Q. You are to guess nothing. Answer my question.

A. Then, sir, not at this time. He seemed little used to London ways, as he claimed.

Q. You were of different opinion later?

A. I had doubts, sir. He could not hide a certain assurance, and an impatience with his part. I knew him more than a country squire's son, even though I could not guess what he was, behind what he would seem.

Q. Very well. To your story.

A. I requested his repeated assurance that my obligations to him would cease at the point he proposed. That furthermore, whatever his plans might be beyond this point, violence formed no part of them.

Q.   Which assurance he gave?

A.   Most earnestly. He offered to swear it upon the Bible, should I wish.

Q.   Come to the practice.

A.   He wished we should set out a week thence, that is, the Monday next, the twenty-sixth of April, which you will doubtless recall was the day before his Highness the Prince of Wales was to join hands with the Princess of Saxe-Gotha; and which Mr Bartholomew did think would cause great stir, and make our leaving the less likely to be marked. My guise would be that of a London merchant, his of my nephew, under the same name of Mr Bartholomew, our ostensible purpose the visiting of —

Q.   I know of that. The supposed aunt at Bideford?

A.   Just so.

Q.   Now, did he lead you to believe that he was watched, that there were spies set upon him?

A.   He gave no evidence, yet implied as much: that there were those who would spare no pains to thwart his attachment and his intention therein.

Q.   You did understand, those of his own family, or those of the young lady's, her guardian?

A.   I conjectured the former, sir. For he did speak once of an elder brother, that did think as their father in all, and with whom Mr Bartholomew said he was scarce on speaking terms, so estranged had they become.

Q.   They had become estranged for the reason that this elder brother dutifully obeyed his father's wishes?

A.   That like his father he placed the acquiring of a fortune and handsome estate above the satisfaction of natural affection.

Q.   You have said nothing of the man Farthing or the maid.

A.   There was question of a servant for me. Mr Bartholomew asked if I knew of a person I could trust, someone of quick wits, able to play a part and also be of service on the roads, to guard us down against highwaymen and the like. One such occurred to me.

Q. His name?

A. He is even more innocent than I am, at least in this.

Q. Why say you, at least in this?

A. I first knew him when he was doorkeeper at Drury Lane, but he was dismissed that post for negligence. His failing is strong drink, it is common in our profession, alas.

Q. He is an actor too?

A. He would have been so once, I believe. On occasion he has taken small clowning or menial parts, he has some skills at the droll. He is Welsh by origin, he played me the porter in Shakespeare's *Macbeth* one day when we were in straits through sickness and could find none better. He was passably received, we thought to employ him further. But he never got his lines well enough, even when sober, for any but smallest parts.

Q. His name?

A. David Jones.

Q. And you say, you have not seen him since the first of May?

A. I have not, sir. Not since the day previous, if you would have me exact. For he ran away in the night, without our knowledge.

Q. He did not go on, either with you or Mr Bartholomew?

A. He did not.

Q. Let us come to that in place. You have not seen him since? Nor heard of or from him?

A. Upon my word. I met a man in the street but ten days since, who knows him well, and I asked. And he too had not seen or heard news of him, these four months past.

Q. Know you where he lived?

A. Only a punch-house he frequented in Berwick Street, where I have also several times enquired since I returned. He has not been seen.

Q. We talk of Farthing?

A. Yes. When he ran off, he said in a note to me that it was to see his mother in Wales. At Swansea. He told me once she was keeper of a wretched alehouse, but I know not if this is truth, nor if he be there. I can help you no more.

Q. You engaged him?

A. I brought him to meet Mr Bartholomew, who approved him. He is a well-built fellow, can carry arms and look bold, is skilled with horses, and so was taken. He had played me once also the part of a blustering braggart, a drunken sergeant in Mr Farquhar's *The Recruiting Officer,* where he gained no small applause, though he did not merit it, for in truth he was so drunk before we commenced he needed not to act his part; nor could have done, had he even the powers. But it was decided he should play something of that part again, to accomplish this our present design.

Q. At what fee?

A. Ten guineas for the whole, which I was to pay him at the end, save one for earnest, to keep him sober. And his living.

Q. But you have never paid him?

A. I have not, sir. Or only a small part, as I will tell. And that is not the least mystery of the affair, that he took to his heels when it was well-nigh earned.

Q. He was told all?

A. That our purpose was to effect a secret journey, under false names. That an affair of the heart was involved.

Q. He made no objection?

A. None. He took my word that there was nothing heinous in the venture. He owed me services.

Q. And what services had you done him?

A. I had employed him as I say. I obtained him a post when he was dismissed his office at Drury Lane. I have lent him small sums of money on occasion. He is more shiftless than rogue.

Q. What post?

A. Coachman to the late Mrs Oldfield, the actress. But she was obliged to give him his wages, he was too often drunk. Since then he has lived from hand to mouth. He was scrivener's clerk for a time, window-polisher, more newly chairman, I know not what else. His hat covers all his household.

Q. He sounds rogue enough to me.

A.   He met the part, sir, as we say. He is a great boaster among
his equals. A glib tongue is second nature with him. Since Mr
Bartholomew's man was mute, we thought a fellow like Jones
might allay suspicion where we lodged. For he knows how to
keep a close mouth, whatever his appearance and even in his
cups. He is no fool at heart, nor more dishonest than the next.

Q.   Very well. Now what of the maid?

A.   I forgot to tell, Mr Bartholomew had advised me of her coming with us. But I saw her not, till we came to Staines. He informed me she was that very maid he had spoke of, the young
lady's confidante, who had been dismissed for her pains.
Upon which he had had her brought to London and placed
under his protection, and now carried to rejoin her mistress. I
took little notice of her at the first meeting. She seemed like
enough to be a lady's maid.

Q.   Her name was given as Louise? You never heard her called
other?

A.   It was, sir. And I did not.

Q.   You did not find her over-delicate and haughty for her station?

A.   No, sir. Silent and demure in her outward.

Q.   But a handsome wench?

A.   Fine eyes, sir, and her face did not want elsewhere. Well
enough spoken withal, when she did venture. I might call her
modest beauty, had she not been to my taste too slight and
thin of figure. Yet I must tell you also there is great mystery
concerning her part; and that of his man likewise.

Q.   What of that last?

A.   Why, sir, beside his natural deficiencies, he was like no manservant else I have ever seen. Had he not worn a blue livery
waistcoat when first he came to my door, I doubt I should
have recognized him as such. He had the eyes of an idiot, nor
any of the accustomed manners of his station; as he had never
been in polite society, nor knew to respect those above him.
Nor wore he livery at all when we travelled, but looked like
some simple country fellow, more Irish vagrant than gentle-

man's servant, and surly to all but his master and the maid.
This is not the half of it, sir, there is stranger still.

Q. In proper time. Let us come to your journey. Mr B. was manager in all?

A. As to our itinerarium, yes. He said he feared the Bristol road,
since it is much frequented, and he thought it likely the uncle
had a man posted to watch it, at Marlborough or Bristol itself, so he might have warning. Therefore we took that to the
south, as if for Exeter, upon the pretext we had business there
before my visit to the supposed sister in Bideford.

Q. He had told you so much before you started — that Bideford
was where he tended?

A. Yes. But requested us to advise him in the subterfuge, saying
it was the first time in his life he had put on such a pretence,
and we must know better how to carry off such matters. So
we advised him, as I say.

Q. Where met you first?

A. It was decided Jones and I should proceed alone by coach to
Hounslow the day previous, and lodge at the Bull there.

Q. This is the twenty-fifth of April?

A. Yes. And there we should find horses waiting for us, and then
set out at first sunrise that next morning, upon the Staines
road, where we should meet him and his man, and the maid.
And so it passed. We came upon them a mile before Staines.

Q. Where had they come from?

A. I don't know, sir. 'Twas not said. Unless they had lodged at
Staines, and rid back. Yet we passed that place without stopping when we came to it.

Q. Nothing passed at this meeting?

A. No, sir. I confess we set out not without some spirit of expectation, as upon a happy venture of sorts.

Q. Was payment made to you before you started?

A. An advance upon my agreed fee, and likewise that of Jones,
though the latter was paid to me. I had some outlay to make
on necessaries.

Q. How much?

A. Ten guineas to me, one to Jones. In gold.

Q. And the remainder?

A. Was given me when we parted, that last morning, upon a bill. I have encashed it.

Q. Drawn upon whom?

A. Mr Barrow of Lombard Street.

Q. The Russia merchant?

A. Yes.

Q. Let us set off. Spare me the petty circumstance. I wish all that pertains to your discovery that Mr B. was other than he claimed.

A. Suspicion did not tarry, sir, I may tell you that. We had ridden but an hour when my trust was first shaken. I had fallen a little behind with Jones, who led the packhorse, whereupon he said he must tell me something, but if he spoke out of place, I was to bid him hold his tongue. I said he should speak. At that he looked ahead to where the maid rode, sat sideways behind Dick, and said, Mr Lacy, I believe I have seen that young woman before, and she is no lady's maid, far from it. He then said he had seen her some two or three months since entering a bagnio behind St James, Mother Claiborne's, as it is vulgarly called. The acquaintance he was with told him that she was — if you will forgive the expression — one of the choicest pieces who worked there. I was shocked, as you may think, sir, and pressed him to say he was sure. Thereupon he admitted he had but seen her briefly, and by linklight, and could not swear, yet found the resemblance striking close, if he were mistaken. I confess I was left at a loss, Mr Ayscough. I know what such creatures and their mistresses may earn by their trade, and tho' I have heard that such as Claiborne will furnish flesh out for a night to the favoured libertine, I could not believe she would do it for such a journey as ours. Nor saw I reason why. I was loath to believe Mr B. had so grossly deceived me, nor could I conceive that a notorious whore, if such she were, should let herself be hired out as a maid. In short, sir, I told Jones he must certainly be mistaken; but that if he had opportune chance, he should speak to the wench, to see if he could discover more.

Q.   Could Jones put no name upon her of the bagnio?

A.   No proper nor Christian name, sir. But that she was known by those who frequented the house as the Quaker Maid.

Q.   What is that to mean?

A.   That she would play modesty, the better to whet the appetite of the debauched.

Q.   She would dress as such?

A.   I fear so.

Q.   And did he speak with her, as you counselled him?

A.   He did, sir, later that day. He told me she would say little. Only that she was Bristol born, and looked forward to seeing her young mistress again.

Q.   Then she appeared privy to the false pretext?

A.   Yes, but would say nothing when Jones would lead her to gossip. For she said Mr B. had commanded her to silence. He said she seemed more timid than aught else. Spoke very soft, and answered most often with a yes or no or mere nod. Jones was less certain now, he confessed as much himself, thinking such as he first credited her could not be so modest and he must be wrong. In brief, sir, our suspicions was lulled and abated for then.

Q.   Did you speak of this to Mr B.?

A.   I did not, sir. Not to the end, as I will tell.

Q.   Did he speak apart to the girl — give any sign of covert collusion?

A.   Not then, sir, nor indeed ever in my own sight and hearing. As we travelled he seemed the rather indifferent to her, as if she were no more than box and baggage. I must tell you he rode most often alone during our journey. He asked me more than once to forgive him, it was little courteous in him to play the sour hermit, as he put it, but I should understand his thoughts lay all ahead, and not in the dull present. I thought it of no account then, indeed natural in a hopeful lover.

Q.   It was to spare himself the pains of pretence?

A.   I now so believe.

Q.   Then in general you had little converse with him?

A.   Some, for he would ride with me on occasion. I think none of moment on that first day. We but spoke of what we passed, our horses and the road, such matters. Not of what we were engaged upon. He asked me more of my life and seemed ready to hear such tales as I told him, of myself and of my grandfather and the king, though I deemed it more politeness than true interest. In general, the more westward, the more silent he grew. Beside, in manner direct, I was prevented by our agreement. I gained a little of him, by chance. It is true, Mr Ayscough, that the part I played in *The Beggar's Opera* did mock Sir Robert Walpole, but I beg you to believe we actors must always be two persons, one upon the boards and another off them. Why, that very first day we must pass those heaths of Bagshot and Camberley, and I was no Robin there, I may assure you, for I rode most alarmed that a real such as I had played should appear — which he did not, I thank the Lord.

Q.   Yes, yes, Lacy, this is nothing to the point.

A.   I must contradict, sir, with respect. What I tell you, I told Mr B.; and went on to speak well of this present government's policy of *quieta non movere,* at which he did give me a look, so to say that he did not agree. And when I did press him to declare his views, he said that as to Sir Robert he must concede he was good manager and man of business for the nation's affairs — that he who could contrive to please both the country squire and the city merchant must be no fool; but that yet he believed that the great founding principle of his administration of which I had spoken must be wrong. For how might a better world come, he said, if this one may not change? And asked me if I did not think that of the Creator's divine purposes this at least was most clear: that His giving us freedom to move and choose, as a ship upon the vast ocean of time, could not mean that we had always best stay moored in that port where we were first built and launched. Then that merchants and their interest should soon rule this world, that already we saw it in statesmen, for he said, A statesman may be honest for a fortnight, but it will not do for a month; and such is mercantile philosophy, from the most wretched niggler and tradesman up. Then did he give me a sad smile, and added, Though I durst not tell my father such things. To that I replied that I feared fathers would ever have their sons in their own close image. To which he answered, And nothing change to the end of time — alas, I know it, Lacy. If in this a son doth not bow to every paternal Test and Corporation Act, he is damned, he hath no being.

Q.   He said nothing else of his father?

A.   Not that I recall, sir. Beyond what was said at the first, that he was too strict; and on one other occasion, when he said he was an old fool, and his elder brother the same. On this aforesaid occasion he did end by confessing that he was in general indifferent to politics; and did cite me the view of one Saunderson, that professes mathematicks at the university of Cambridge, and that it seems did teach him while he was there; whom he had heard once say, upon a similar question being put to him, that all politics was as clouds before the sun; that is, more necessary nuisance than truth.

Q.   And with which he concurred?

A.   So I took him to mean. For on another occasion I remember he said, We should be well quit of three parts of this world; so to intimate, it was superfluous, or he judged it thus. But now he spoke more of the learned gentleman, that is blind, yet hath by his intelligence largely conquered that deficiency; and it seems is much loved and revered by his pupils.

Q.   Spake Mr B. of religion, of the Church?

A.   But once, sir, upon a later occasion. We met a reverend gentleman upon the road, or rather sitting beside it, for he was too drunk to ride his horse, which his man held beside him till he was fit enough to mount again. At which Mr B. showed some disgust and said it was too common a case and that it was little wonder the flock strayed, with such shepherds. In our further conversation he declared himself a hater of hypocrisy. That God placed most worthy and necessary veils upon His mystery, but His ministers too often used them to blindfold their charges and lead them into ignorance and baseless prejudice. That he believed a man was finally judged, and his soul saved, by his deeds, not his outward show of beliefs; that no established church would ever give ground to such plain reason, for thereby it would deny its own inheritance and all its earthly powers.

Q. Those are free-thinking tenets. Did you not hold them reprehensible?

A. No, sir. I held them good sense.

Q. To scorn the established church?

A. To scorn the hypocrite, Mr Ayscough. We who tread the boards are not the only players of parts in this world. Such is my view, sir, with respect.

Q. Your view leads to sedition, Lacy. Spurn the holder, spurn the office. But enough of this, it is idle. Where stayed you that night?

A. At the Angel, Basingstoke. Thence early to Andover and Amesbury; in which place we lodged the next.

Q. You were in no great haste, then?

A. No, and even less that second day, for as we came to Amesbury he said he would view the famous heathen temple nearby, at Stonehenge. And we should rest at Amesbury, though we might have gone farther, and I had expected to.

Q. Were you not surprised?

A. I was, sir.

Q. We will stop now. My clerk shall take you to dine, and we shall resume at three of the clock prompt.

A. Mrs Lacy expects me to dine at home, sir.

Q. Then she must wait in vain.

A. May I not send to say I am detained?

Q. You may not.

The same further deposeth upon oath, die annoque praedicto.

Q. Did nothing pass the previous night at Basingstoke, before you came to Amesbury?

A.   No, sir, all passed as was intended. Mr B. played my nephew, would have me take the best chamber at the Angel, and showed me all deference in public. We supped in my chamber, for he would not go into the public rooms, wherever we lodged. Nor would he linger, sir, the eating once done, but retire to his own chamber and leave me to my own devices, which he called no discourtesy, but a favour to me, since he was such a dullard. I saw him not again.

Q.   You do not know how he occupied himself?

A.   No, sir. Unless it was with his books. For he brought a small chest with him, that he did call his *bibliotheca viatica,* as I saw opened two or three times. The one inn, it was at Taunton, we had no choice but to share the one room. And there he read papers from his chest when he had eaten.

Q.   This chest held books or papers?

A.   Both. He told me all were mathematick, his travelling library, as I said, and that such study diverted his mind from more troubling thoughts.

Q.   Was he ever more particular, as to their nature?

A.   No, sir.

Q.   Did you not enquire?

A.   No, sir. I am not formed to judge of such matters.

Q.   Saw you ever a title to any of the books?

A.   I remarked a work by Sir Isaac Newton, that was in Latin, I do not recall the title. Mr B. spoke of him with a greater respect than I heard him use of any other, that he said he had first gained of his tutor at Cambridge, the gentleman I named earlier, Mr Saunderson. He did essay one day as we rode to explain Sir Isaac's doctrine of fluxions and fluents. There, sir, I must confess myself lost; and had politely to inform him that he wasted his breath. Again, it was when we did come to Taunton Deane, he talked of a learned monk of many centuries ago, who did hit upon a way of multiplying numbers. That in itself I might understand, for it was simple, but the adding of each last two figures to make the next. To wit, one, two, three, five, eight, thirteen, one and twenty, and thus forward as you may will. Mr B. averred that he himself did believe these numbers appeared, though secretly, in many places in nature, as it were a divine cipher that all living things must copy, for that the ratio between its successive numbers was that also of a secret of the Greeks, who did discover a perfect proportion, I believe he said it to be of one to one and six tenths. He pointed to all that chanced about us, and said that these numbers might be read therein; and cited other examples, that I forget now except that many accorded with the order of petals and leaves in trees and herbs, I know not what.

Q. He made much of this matter of ciphering?

A. No, sir. As one might speak of a curiosity.

Q. He would claim to have penetrated some secret of nature, is it not so?

A. I would not say that, Mr Ayscough; rather that he had glimpsed such a secret, yet had not fully explored it.

Q. Did you not think it odd that he should follow these pursuits, and bring this travelling library, if the journey was for the purpose alleged?

A. A trifle, sir. The more we travelled, the more I perceived he was not as ordinary men, let alone as ordinary lovers. I supposed him more serious in his scientific pursuits than he cared openly to allow, and intended not to deprive himself of them in the exile consequent on an elopement.

Q. I have one last question here. Did you see in this chest an instrument, that had appearance as of a clock, with many wheels, and was made of brass?

A. No, sir.

Q. Yet you saw this chest open, you say?

A. Always full, and with loose papers scattered on top. I was never enabled to see all it held.

Q. Nor saw such an instrument being used?

A. No, sir.

Q. Let us come to Amesbury.

A. I should remark something else first, that passed at Basingstoke.

Q. Very well.

A. It concerned the maid Louise. Jones told me that she too would have a chamber of her own, and not sleep with the inn-maids, as is the custom. Nor would she dine at their table, like the rest, she must have her victuals taken upstairs to her by the mute. Furthermore, that he saw the man was deep smitten by her, which he found strange. We discussed upon it, yet could come to no conclusion then.

Q. Seemed she smitten in return?

A. That he could not determine, sir, except that she did not openly rebuff him. There is more to tell on this. I but mention it as it came.

Q. Did she always thus — sleep and eat apart?

A. She did, sir, where such a chamber was to be found. For in one, it was Wincanton, there was some dispute upon such an unaccustomed demand, such as that Mr B.'s authority was sought, and he said she should have as she demanded. I saw this not, Jones told me of it after.

Q. To Amesbury.

A. As I told, before we came there Mr B. said we should stay there, though we might have ridden farther. That he wished to see the temple and after we had dined I might if I wished ride out with him over the downs to view it. The day was fine, the distance small, I had some curiosity to see the place, though I confess I found it less imposing and ruder than I had imagined. You have visited it, sir?

Q. I have seen it graved. Your servants came with you?

A. Only Dick. Mr B. and I dismounted and walked among the stones. To my surprise he seemed familiar with the place, though he had said he had no more seen it before than I.

Q. How is that?

A. Why, sir, he began to expatiate upon what it was conjectured its barbarous religion had been, the purpose of its entabled pillars, how it would have appeared were it not half ruined, I know not what else. I asked him with some astonishment how he had come to this knowledge, whereat he smiled and said, Not by the black arts, I assure you, Lacy. And he said he had met the Reverend Mr Stukeley of Stamford, the antiquary, and seen his drawings and chorographies, and discussed with him. He spoke of other books and discourses upon the monument that he had read, yet that he found Mr Stukeley's notions more just and worthy of attention.

Q.   He found his tongue there then?

A.   Indeed, sir. He did speak like a true virtuoso. I confess I was the more struck by his learning than by the place itself. He asked me, as it were in passing, if I gave credit to the belief of the ancients in auspicious days. I said I had not thought on the matter. Very well, he said, then by contrary: should you happily open a new piece upon a Friday that was also thirteenth of the month? I confessed I should rather not, though I hold such things superstition. And he said, As do most men, but it may be they are wrong. He then took me a step or two aside and pointed to a great stone some fifty paces off, and informed me that upon Midsummer's Day the sun would rise upon that stone, from the temple's centre where we stood. Some other learned writer, whose name I do not recall, had found it so; that the temple was so set upon its ground that it must always match this one day, which could not be by chance. Then he said, I will tell you this, Lacy, these ancients knew a secret I should give all I possess to secure. They knew their life's meridian, and I still search mine. In all else they lived in darkness, he said, yet this great light they had; while I live in light, and stumble after phantoms. I remarked that I apprehended the charming object of our journey, from what he had vouchsafed, was no phantom. At which he seemed somewhat set back, sir, but then smiled and said, You are right, I am wandered into dark pastures. We walked some paces in silence, then he resumed. Yet is it not strange, he said, that these rude savages may have entered a place where we still fear to tread, and have known what we can bare begin to comprehend? Why, to which even that great philosopher, Sir Isaac Newton, was but a helpless child? I said I did not understand what arcane knowledge this might be, Mr Ayscough. To which his answer was: Why, that God is eternal motion, Lacy. This is his first orrery. Know you the true name for this pile? Chorum Giganteum, the dance of the Gogs and Magogs. The country people say it will not dance again until the Day of Judgement. But it spins and dances now, Lacy, if we had only eyes to see it.

Q. What made you of this?

A. 'Twas said lightly, sir, as if he mocked me for my ignorance. Which, albeit in the same light spirit, I charged him with. He assured me not, he meant no railing, there was truth in what he said. For we mortals are locked as at Newgate, he said, within the chains and bars of our senses and our brief allotted span, and as such are blind; that for God all time is as one, eternally now, whereas we must see it as past, present, future, as in a history. Then he gestured about us, at the stones, and said, Do you not admire that, perhaps before Rome, before Christ Himself, these savages who set these stones knew something even our Newtons and Leibnitzes cannot reach? Then he likened mankind to an audience in a playhouse, who knew not of actors, and had no notion that they acted to fixed and written lines, and even less that behind the actors lay an author and a manager. To which I demurred, sir, for I said we most certainly knew there was an Author behind all, and likewise His sacred text. At which he smiled again and said he did not deny the existence of such an Author, yet must beg leave to doubt our present notions of Him; for he said it would be juster to say we were like the personages in a tale or novel, that had no knowledge they were such; and thought ourselves most real, not seeing we were made of imperfect words and ideas, and to serve other ends, far different from what we supposed. We might imagine this great Author of all as such and such, in our own image, sometimes cruel, sometimes merciful, as we do our kings. Notwithstanding in truth we knew no more of Him and His ends than of what lay in the moon, or the next world. Well, Mr Ayscough, I would argue upon this, for it seemed he spoke in contempt of established religion now. Then of a sudden, as if he would talk on such matters no more, he beckoned to his servant who waited nearby; and told me he must make some measurements, upon Mr Stukeley's request. That they would be tedious, and he would not presume upon my patience to wait while they were taken.

Q. You were given your congé?

A. So I took it to be, sir. As a man might say to himself, I talk overmuch, it is better I find an excuse to be silent now.

Q. What took you him to mean by this great secret we cannot reach?

A. I must leap ahead, sir, to answer that.

Q. Then leap.

A. I must tell you I saw not Mr B. further that day. The morrow I seized my opportunity as we rode past the monument on our way west and would have him speak further of his views concerning the ancients and in what their secret lay; to which he answered, They knew they knew nothing. Then he said, I answer you in riddles, is it not so? To which I agreed, sir, to make him expatiate the further. And he said, We moderns are corrupted by our past, our learning, our historians; and the more we know of what happened, the less we know of what will happen; for as I say, we are like the personages of a tale, fixed it must seem by another intention, to be good or evil, happy or unhappy, as it falls. Yet they who set and dressed those stones lived before the tale began, Lacy, in a present that had no past, such as we may hardly imagine to ourselves. And next he spake of Mr Stukeley's belief, that it was they called the Druids who had built this monument and that they came hence first from the Holy Land, bearing within them the first seed of Christianity; that for himself, however, he believed they had pierced some part of the mystery of time. For the Roman historians, tho' their enemies, had said as much, that is that they could see into the future by reading the flight of birds and the form of livers, yet he believed them far more subtle than that, as their monument showed, if one could contrive to read it right, in mathematick

terms. Which is why he took his measurements. And he said,
I believe they knew the book and story of this world, to the
very last page, as you may know your Milton — for I carried
his great work in my pocket, Mr Ayscough, and Mr B. had
enquired of what I read.

Q.   What said you to that?

A.   I did admire, if they could read the future, that they had
been conquered by the Romans, and disappeared from this
world. To which he said, They were a nation of seers and innocent philosophers, no match for the Romans in war; and
then he said, Was Christ Himself not crucified?

Q.   Did he not say earlier to you that man is able to choose and
so change his course — now the very opposite, that his history is predestined, if it may be read in days to come, and we
are no more free than the fixed characters of a play or book
already written?

A.   Mr Ayscough, your observation occurred to me also, and I
remarked upon it. To which he answered, that we may
choose in many small things as I may choose how I play a
part, how dress for it, how gesture, and the rest; but yet must
at the end, in greater matters, obey that part and portray its
greater fate, as its author creates. And he said although he
might believe in a general providence, he might not in a
particular one, that God was in each; for he would not believe that God was in the most vicious and depraved as He
was in the good and worthy, nor that He would allow those
He inspired, who were innocent, to suffer the pain and
misery that they most often did, such as we must see all
around us.

Q.   All this is most dangerous doctrine.

A.   I must agree, sir. I tell you as it was put to me.

Q.   Very well. We left you riding back to Amesbury.

A.   I there came upon Jones, who was fishing for roach in the
stream, and sat with him an hour or more, the evening being
fine. When we returned to where we lodged, I found a note
from Mr B. in my room, to ask me to excuse his presence at

supper, as he felt greatly fatigued, and would straight to bed.

Q. What made you of that?

A. Nothing at that time, sir. I have not finished. I was tired myself and was to bed early, and slept deep. Which I should not have, had I known Jones shall come to me early that next morning, with a most strange tale. He had slept in the same place as Dick. Just before midnight, for he said the bells sounded not a quarter after, he was awake and heard Dick quit the chamber. He thought, to answer nature. But no, just as the bells strike, he hears sounds below in the yard. Whereat he goes to the window, and makes out three figures; there was no moon, yet light enough for this. One is Dick, who leads two horses with stifled hooves upon the cobbles. Another is his master. The third, the maid. He was sure, these only. I questioned him closely.

Q. They rode out?

A. They did, sir. He thought to rouse me, but saw they took no baggage, and resolved to watch for their return. He was waking for an hour, then Morpheus conquered him. At cockcrow he wakes, and finds Dick asleep, as if nothing had passed.

Q. Did he not dream it?

A. I think not, sir. In company he will boast and tell tales enough; I am certain not to me, on such an occasion. Besides, he was alarmed for us both, for a suspicion had come upon him. I must tell you, Mr Ayscough, that I had watched the maid more close during that previous day, as we rode. Now, I did not believe Jones' story of seeing her at the bagnio. We perforce come to know such women only too well in the theatre. She had none of their airs and impudence. Yet I found something knowing in her, for all her modesty of manner. I perceived also Jones was right concerning Dick: there was that in his eyes would have devoured her alive, had he dared. Now I found it strange she was not offended, no, seemed even kind to this attention, would smile at him on occasion. It seemed against nature to me, sir, as if she played a part, to mislead us.

Q. And Jones' suspicion?

A. Now supposing, Mr Lacy, he said, all is true about Mr Bartholomew and the young lady except this: that she and her uncle are in the West. Supposing that until a day or two ago she was indeed kept his prisoner, yet not where we think; but in London, where Mr B. told you he first met her. And therefore — you take his drift, sir.

Q. You were assisting an elopement *post facto?*

A. I was shocked, Mr Ayscough. The more I reflected on what I had observed of her myself, the more I saw colour in it — were it not for her kindness in Dick's regard, yet I saw that might have been to deceive us. Jones proposed that the going out in the night had been to solemnize a clandestine wedding; which did explain why we should have delayed at Amesbury, upon so trifling an outward reason. The only good I could discern in it was that had Mr B. accomplished such an end, he should not need our service further; and that we must soon know. I will not repeat all we conjectured, sir. I had almost feared to find Mr B. already decamped with his bride when I came down.

Q. But he was not?

A. He was not, sir; nor indeed seemed changed in any way. So we must set out, and myself to feel gravely at a loss to know how to broach the matter with him. However, before with Jones I agreed he should find opportunity to speak aside with the girl, to hint playfully he had wind of her night adventure; in short to see what might be teased out of her.

Q. Did he succeed?

A. No, sir, though he found an opportunity to charge her. He said she seemed at first in some confusion, when he pressed his hints; would not admit them and grew angry when he persisted, till she would not answer at all.

Q. She denied she had left the inn?

A. She did, sir.

Q. Tell me this now. Subsequent to that day were you informed what purpose this nocturnal adventure had?

A. No, sir, I was not. It is a mystery, like so much else, alas.

Q. Very well. I can no more today, Lacy, I have other business. You will attend here tomorrow morning, eight o'clock prompt. Is it understood? Without fail, sir. You are not clear yet.

A. My own conscience shall bring me, Mr Ayscough. You need not fear.

The Examination and Deposition of
HANNAH CLAIBORNE
the which doth attest upon her sworn
oath, this four and twentieth day
of August in the tenth year of the
reign of our sovereign Lord George the
second, by the grace of God King of Great
Britain and of England, &c.

My name is HANNAH CLAIBORNE. *I am forty-eight years of age, and widow. I am keeper of the St James house, that is in German Street.*

❧

Q. Now, woman, we will not beat about the bush. You know him I search after.

A. To my cost.

Q. And even more to your cost, if you do not speak truth.

A. I know which side the butter lies.

Q. I would hear first of this creature of yours. Know you her true name?

A. Rebecca Hocknell. But we called her Fanny.

Q. You never heard her called by French name, Louise?

A. No.

Q. And whence hailed she?

A. Bristol, or so she said.

Q. Has she family there?

A. For all I know.

Q. Meaning you do not?

A. She never spake of them.

Q. When came she first to your house?

A. Three years past.

Q. How old was she then?

A. Near twenty.

Q. How came she in your claws?

A. By one I know.

Q. Claiborne, thou art one of this town's most notorious whore-mongers. None of thy laconic insolence with me.

A. By a woman I sent out.

Q. To spy out the innocent and corrupt 'em?

A. She was already corrupted.

Q. Already a whore?

A. She lost her honour where she was maid, to a son of the house, at Bristol where she came from. And was dismissed. Or so she said.

Q. She was by child?

A. No, she is barren naturally.

Q. Unnaturally. Now, was she sought after at your stews?

A. More for her tricks than her flesh.

Q. What tricks?

A. That she knew to tame men to her fancy. She had as well been actress as whore.

Q. How encompassed she this taming?

A. That she was no ordinary piece of flesh, but pure as Hampstead water, and must be treated so. 'Twas miracle her custom stood for it, and came back for more.

Q. She played the lady?

A. She played innocence, when she was not one jot, as cold-wanton a trollop as ever I knew.

Q. What innocence?

A. Prude, modest sister, Miss Fresh-from-the-country, Miss Timid Don't-tempt-me, Miss Simple — would you have more? A novel of her tricks would make a book. She was innocent as a nest of vipers, the cunning hussy. None better at whipping, when she wanted.

Q. Explain yourself, woman.

A. Such as old Mr Justice P———, doubtless you know him well, sir, that cannot spend till first he be well thrashed and striped. With him she'd be disdainful as an infanta and cruel as a tartar, all in the same bout. Which he craved, beside. But no matter.

Q. Where learnt she these powers of simulation?

A. Not from me, from the Devil. 'Twas born in her nature.

Q. Was she not famed for her lewd skill in one part?

A. What is that?

Q. I would have thee look at this printed paper, Claiborne. I am told it went out at thy expense.

A. I deny it.

Q. Have you seen it?

A. I may have seen it.

Q. I will read you a choice passage. "For an amorous Encounter with the Quaker Maid, Reader, thou had'st best count thy Gold first. This is no silver Quean, despite her modest Appellation, nor no modest One, neither, despite her first Appearance. Thou must know nothing pleases your true Debauchee better than to be obliged to force, and such is this cunning Nymph's Device — to blush, to flee, to cry for Shame, until at last she's brought to Bay. But thereafter 'tis a most curious and commodious Hind, who neither fights for Life nor swoons of Fear; but sweetly bares her pretty Heart to the fortunate Huntsman's Dagger; though 'tis whispered she requires such Stabbing there as more often leaves Sir Nimrod dead than she." Well, madam?

A. Well, sir.

Q. Is it she?

A. Yes, I suppose. What if it is? I did not write nor publish it.

Q. That shall bring thee no mercy on Judgement Day. He whose name I forbid you to utter, when came he first into this?

A. At the beginning of April last.

Q.. You had seen him before?

A. No, and would I had not seen him then. He came with a gentleman I know well, my Lord B———, who presented him to me and said he would meet Fanny, whom his Lordship had commended. But of this I knew before.

Q. How?

A. Lord B——— had already taken her, by note of hand, a four

days before; though he said not for who it was, 'cept one of
his friends.

Q. This is frequent, that your wenches are taken, ahead of their
vile employment?

A. If they are prize pieces.

Q. And this one was one such?

A. Yes, curse her.

Q. Lord B——— introduced his friend under his true name?

A. No name was said. But Lord B——— told me in private afterward.

Q. And what passed?

A. He went with Fanny. And two or three times more, in the
week that followed.

Q. Seemed he to know houses like yours?

A. A gosling.

Q. What are they?

A. That are over-lavish in their gifts, that will have one wench
or one pleasure and no other, that would hide their names
and be secret in their coming and going. They are our gos-
lings.

Q. And your geese the hardened rakes?

A. Yes.

Q. And he we speak of was still in down?

A. He would have none but Fanny, and first hid his name, or
would hide it from me. He made presents above what was
due.

Q. To you or the girl?

A. To both.

Q. Presents of money?

A. Yes.

Q. And what led to her going from you?

A. He came to me one day and said he had matter to discuss
that he hoped would be to both our advantages.

Q. When was this?

A. Toward the middle of the month. He said he was invited to a
party of pleasure in Oxfordshire, at a friend's estate, where
there was to be other rakes, and a prize given him who had

brought the finest whore, when all had tasted all. That with that and other entertainments, 'twas to be a fortnight's folly. Which with the travelling there and back, must mean three weeks. In the end that he would hire Fanny from me for this time, if I would allow and name a price for my discommodation by loss of her.

Q.   He said where this estate was?

A.   He would not. They would cause no scandal, all was secret.

Q.   How answered you?

A.   I said I had never done such a thing. He said he had been told I did. I said I might now and then send out upon terms to gentlemen I well knew, to suppers and the like in town. That I did not know him well, not even his true name.

Q.   There was a false one he bore?

A.   He called himself Mr Smith. Tho' now he said me his true one that I knew already of Lord B———. Then that he had spoken of the diversion with Fanny, who was on her mettle and willing to the sport; howsoever she told him all lay with me. I said I would think on it, I could not decide on such a proposal at so short notice.

Q.   How took he that?

A.   He said that I knew now he lacked neither rank nor wealth, and I must give that consideration. On which he went away.

Q.   You came not to mention of terms?

A.   Not then. He came again to Fanny a day or two later, and after to me, by which time I had spoke to Lord B——— and asked if he knew of this party of pleasure. Which he said he did, he was himself invited to it, tho' prevented by other business he could not put off. That he was surprised I had no wind of it. That I should be foolish to offend someone so great as a duke's son. That there was butter in it for me, for I might name what price I liked for the favour. And other matters.

Q.   What other matters, woman?

A.   That once done, gossip would spread news of the folly, and fame attach to all who had a part in it. That Mistress Wishbourne had promised two of her girls to it, and should steal a march upon me.

Q. Who is Wishbourne?

A. An upstart keeper of the new Covent Garden house.

Q. You were persuaded?

A. I was his fool. The more fool me.

Q. Did you speak with the girl?

A. She said she was passing indifferent, she would do as I pleased. But the cunning slut lied.

Q. How lied?

A. She was privy to all. She was practised in the meek face, I was deceived by it. She was already bought to it.

Q. You have proof?

A. She has never come back, that's proof enough for me. I have suffered great loss by her.

Q. Small loss to decency. I desire to know what the flesh-rent was.

A. I put it upon three weeks' loss of her employment in my house.

Q. How much?

A. Three hundred guineas.

Q. Did he baulk?

A. Why should he? He pays me that, and steals ten thousand.

Q. Watch thy impudent tongue, woman!

A. It is true. For all her faults she was a delicate good whore, barren, only three years' use.

Q. I say enough. What part of this was hers?

A. I dress, feed, find linen, all. And pay the 'pothecary, when they have the Barnwell ague.

Q. A fig for thy economy. I will know her share.

A. One fifth, beside what presents she might gain for herself.

Q. Sixty guineas?

A. More than she deserved.

Q. Which you gave her?

A. I gave her nothing, till she returned.

Q. To oblige her to return?

A. Yes.

Q. And you hold it still for her?

A. I hold more than that for her.

Q.   You have had no word from her since she left?

A.   No, not one, and I wish her in hell fire.

Q.   Where you shall both meet. And when she did not return as she should?

A.   I spoke to my Lord B——— and complained. And he said he would enquire, so came to me a two days later and said there was some mystery afoot, that it was rumoured the person was now gone to France, not to the party of pleasure at all, for he had spoken with one that was there, who had sworn neither the person nor Fanny was present. That I must be patient, there was to be no scandal let abroad about it, or I should know the cost and lose far more than what I did by her going-off.

Q.   Did you believe him?

A.   I did not, and I forgive him not, for I found in the meantime that none had left Wishbourne's, and likewise none knew of this folly. 'Twas all lies, to blind me.

Q.   Did you charge him with this?

A.   I know which side my bread is buttered. He brings many to my house. What I must bear, I bear. Tho' I wish him —

Q.   We'll hear no more of that.

A.   And pay him in kind for it, as all London knows.

Q.   Enough. Now I would know what the girl said of he I enquire upon to you or your other strumpets.

A.   That he was green, but promised well, was quick set to the task, then spent fast; which is the easier work for 'em.

Q.   Seemed he especially taken with her?

A.   Yes, for he would not try any other, though they offered and would woo him away.

Q.   Or she with him?

A.   She would not say, even if she was. She knew well enough what rules I make, on that score. I allow no secret attachments, nor unpaid favours.

Q.   She had been obedient to your rules, till this occasion?

A.   Yes. 'Twas her plan.

Q.   What plan?

A.   Why, to cozen me. She was no fool, for all her country-maid

airs. She knew it served her best with me, as it did with most
her men.

Q. How with men?

A. Why, when she played the innocent at heart, that has never
known a man before, and must be treated gently and won,
not taken at the gallop. Which many who went with her
liked, for they found her prudish guiles more lickorish than
the usual kind, and thought they had made a conquest when
she let them at last to cockadillo between her legs. She would
not have culls except by the night, which I allowed her, seeing we gained as much so as by shorter hire. I could have sold
the slut six times over a same night, more than once. Most
often she was full taken a week ahead.

Q. How many such women do you keep?

A. Some ten, that is regular.

Q. She was your choicest flesh on offer, your most costly?

A. Choicest is freshest. That was no virgin, for all her airs. More
fools men, if they pay more for well-trodden goods.

Q. Your other jades were surprised, when she came not back?

A. Yes.

Q. And what have you told them?

A. That she is gone, and good riddance.

A. And that you and your ruffians have seen to it that she'll
whore no more, is it not so?

A. I will not answer that. It is a lie. I have a right to recover
what is mine.

Q. And what have you done to that purpose?

A. What should I do, now she's gone abroad?

Q. Have your rogues and spies watch for her coming back,
which I doubt not is done. Now I warn thee solemnly, Claiborne. That wench is mine, now. If one of your vile instru-
ments should find out where she is, and you come not upon
the instant to tell me, you'll never again drive geese and gos-
lings. By Heaven you shan't, I'll end your traffick once and
for all. Do I make myself plain?

A. As one of my ruffians, sir.

Q.   I won't be provoked by such as thee. I repeat, dost understand me plain?

A.   Yes.

Q.   So be it. Now take thy putrid painted cheeks out of my sight, madam.

> Jurat die quattuor et vicesimo Aug.
> anno domini 1736 coram me
> Henry Ayscough

The further examination and deposition
of MR FRANCIS LACY, upon oath renewed,
the four and twentieth day of August,
anno praedicto.

Q.   Now, sir, I would go back in one or two particulars upon yesterday. When Mr Bartholomew spoke of his interests; or in
what he said at your viewing of the Amesbury temple, as you
report, or on any other occasion, seemed it to you that here
was a man who mentioned these things out of no more than
politeness to you, to pass the time? Or seemed it out of some
closer interest — I would say preponderant interest, rather?
Did you not begin to think, Here is a strange lover — more
eager and eloquent before a heap of stones than before the
prospect of the lady he purports to adore? Content to delay
and pursue his studies when most young men would resent
each wasted hour upon the road? Are they not strange companions — a headstrong passion and a box of learned tomes?

A.   Certainly I thought that. As to whether it were a crotchet of
Mr Bartholomew's character so to occupy himself, or a
greater interest, I could not then have said.

A.   You could say now?

A.   I could say Mr Bartholomew told me at the last that there
was no young lady in Cornwall. It was all pretext. The true
purpose of our journey, I still do not know, sir. As you will
discover.

Q. What took you him to mean by searching for his life's meridian?

A. Why, sir, no more than is conveyed by any such obscure and fanciful metaphor. It may be, some certainty of belief or faith. I fear he found little consolation in religion as we see it practised in this land.

Q. You have said nothing further of his servant — what made you of him upon the road?

A. At first, little, beyond what I stated yesterday. Later, I saw more in him I liked not. How shall I say, Mr Ayscough — why, suspicion he was as much hired as Farthing and I, no servant in reality. I mean not in what he did, for in that he did, if not with grace, with due attention. Yet something in his manner, I cannot say an insolence, but yet . . . I am hard put to describe it, sir. I saw looks he gave his master, behind his back, as if he were himself the master, knew as much as he. I detected a secret resentment, I might even put it at a jealousy, such as I have known in my profession between a famed actor and another inferior, despite their smiling faces and compliments in public. Why, says the lesser to himself, I'm as good as you, you applauded rogue, and one day I'll show the world I'm a great deal better.

Q. Spoke you of this to Mr Bartholomew?

A. Not directly, sir. Tho' one day as we supped, 'twas at Wincanton, I asked of Dick in a sidelong manner, that I found it strange he should choose to employ such a lacking man. Whereon he told me they had far longer acquaintance than I might suppose. How Dick was born on his father's estates, his mother was his own — I would say Mr Bartholomew's — nurse, they were suckled at the same breast, therefore foster-brothers. He said, Indeed by some strange humour of the stars we first breathed on the very same hour of the very same autumn day. Then how Dick was the constant companion of his childhood, his servant from the time he was given one. He said to me, All he knows I have taught him — his speech by signs, his duties, his scantling manners, his everything. Without me he would be a wild creature, no better than a beast, the butt of the village clowns — if they had not long before now stoned him to death. Well, sir, I did then venture to say that I liked not looks I had seen him give . . . as I said before.

Q. And how answered Mr Bartholomew?

A. He laughed, sir — or as near as he ever came to laughing, as if to say I mistook. Then went on to say, I know those looks of his, I've seen them all my life. They come from anger against the fate that has made him what he is. Where they light is the chance of the moment. It might as well be you as I, or the nearest passer-by. A tree, a house, a chair. It makes no odds. He is not like us, Lacy. He cannot dissemble what he feels, he is like a musket. Wherever he points, when he curses fate, he must seem to discharge. Then he said that he and Dick were one mind, one will, one appetite. What suits my taste suits his, what I covet he covets, what I do he would do also. If I should see Venus in a lady's face, why, so will he. If I dressed like a Hottentot, so would he. If I declared the most nauseous offal fit for the gods, he would greedily devour it. He told me I judged Dick as I judged other men, with all their faculties. He said he had several times tried to instil some sense of the Divine Being in the man, had shown him Christ's effigy, God enthroned in Heaven. In vain, he said, for I know whose effigy he persists in seeing as the only true divinity in his life. I could stab him to death and he would not raise an arm to defend himself. Flay him alive, what you will, and he would submit. I am his animating principle, Lacy, without me he's no more than a root, a stone. If I die, he dies the next instant. He knows this as well as I. I do not say by reason. It is in his every vein and every bone, as a horse knows its true master from other riders.

Q. What thought you to all this?

A. I must take him at his word, sir. For he said finally, albeit Dick was ignorant in so many things, he had in recompense a kind of wisdom, and for which Mr Bartholomew had respect, and even a kind of envy in return. That he had the senses of an animal, and could see things we cannot, thus he could brush aside the specious veils of speech, of manners and dress and the like, to the reality of a man; and had found him more than once right in his judgement of a person, where he himself was wrong. And he remarked, when I showed some surprise at that, that Dick was his lodestone in more matters than I might suppose, that he put great value on this his unthinking power of judgement.

Q. Now, Lacy, I must venture on delicate ground. I would ask this. Saw you in any occurrence or at any point upon your journey, in it may be no more than a covert look, a gesture, an exchange of signs, evidence that this attachment between Mr Bartholomew and his man had roots in an affection that was not natural?

A. In what way, not natural, sir?

Q. Very well, I'll not beat about the bush. That there was evidence, however small, of a most abhorrent and unspeakable vice, anciently practised in the cities of Sodom and Gomorrah? Why answer you not?

A. I am shocked, sir. No thought of such a thing had crossed my mind.

Q. And now that it has?

A. I cannot believe it. I received not the slightest suspicion of such. Besides that it was clear the servant's interest was bound fast to the maid.

Q. Might that not have been but a trick, to throw off suspicion?

Q. It was no trick, sir. I have not told all there yet.

Q. Very well. Let us return to the journey. Where passed you that following night?

A. At Wincanton. Nothing of particular import happened there, that I marked myself. But as we rode on the next morning, Jones told me that Dick had left the bed they shared and gone to a room adjoining, where by chance that night the maid Louise lay, and he saw him not till that next morning.

Q. What thought you to that?

A. That she must indeed be what she maintained, and our previous suspicions false.

Q. She could be neither proud whore nor a lady in disguise?

A. That is so.

Q.   You said nothing to Mr Bartholomew?

A.   No. I confess I thought it best to keep my own advice, since I knew our journey must be near done.

Q.   You said the more westward, the more silent he became?

A.   Yes. Not only we spoke less as we rode, as if he had indeed only one object in mind, but when we supped together I found myself obliged to do most of the talking, and finally as little as he. I fancied there was some fresh doubt or melancholy in his mind. He made some effort to conceal it from me, yet I took that impression.

Q.   Doubt of his enterprise?

A.   I so supposed.

Q.   You did not try to rally him?

A.   I had learnt my lesson by then, Mr Ayscough. I must presume you know Mr Bartholomew far better than I. There is that in his manner that is not easily turned from what preoccupies him. That can make the most innocent intentions of sympathy and interest seem to risk impertinence.

Q.   And neither you nor Jones learnt more? Nothing else passed at Taunton?

A.   No, sir, beyond our being obliged to share the one chamber, as I said. When Mr B. craved my pardon, he would read his papers, once we had supped. He read still, when I retired to rest. I was not used to such travelling.

Q.   This road from Taunton was your last together?

A.   It was, sir.

A.   And nothing pertinent, that day?

A.   Unless it be that towards the end on two separate occasions Mr Bartholomew rode aside with Dick and the maid, as if to view the prospect ahead.

Q.   This had not been done before?

A.   No, sir. On both occasions they rode apart with him to an eminence, where it chanced our road passed. I saw the man Dick point, as if to some distant hill or place.

Q.   Did Mr Bartholomew make no remark upon it to you?

A.   Yes, he said they searched the most favourable road. And I asked if we were near our destination. To which he replied,

We are on the threshold I spoke of, Lacy; and then, Your kind service is near done. Which was as Jones and I had already surmised, by this stopping to look ahead.

Q. Were you not near where Mr Bartholomew and his man had been but six weeks earlier? And where the maid had lived? Why should they need to search their road?

A. We admired ourselves, sir. But not being privy to their plans and intentions, supposed they sought the most secret way, since they neared where they must be most in danger.

Q. And this was your first advice of this parting on the morrow?

A. Yes, sir. Tho' 'twas plain we must be close, with Bideford scarce a day's ride forward. I cannot call myself surprised.

Q. Now I would know all that passed at the Black Hart.

A. Much as before, sir, until we had supped. Were it not that he requested me for once to yield him the best chamber, where before, when we had choice, I had always taken it. He doubted he would sleep that night, and would have a room he might pace about, as he said. The second-best was small.

Q. Saw you no other purpose?

A. Except that it looked out upon the square, and where I slept but upon the garden and back parts. Beside its greater largeness I saw no advantage.

Q. Proceed. What was said when you had supped?

A. He began by thanking me for bearing with him, and what he called his *vacua,* his silences, and said he feared he had been tedious company, to one such as I. That never the less I had played my part well, and he was grateful. To which I returned that I might have played it better, had I known better how all was to end. Once more he made some obscure allusions, which I took to signify that he was by no means confident of success in his venture. I did rally him a little then. I said that even if he failed once more on this occasion, he might surely try again. He answered, One cannot cross the Rubicon twice, it is this time or never, or some such words. I told him he took too despondent a view. And now he struck out upon one of his fancies, Mr Ayscough, and in a manner that alarmed me. For I had said he was not in some fixed story, as it were in a tragedy, where all is antecedently doomed. To which he replied that perhaps his story had neither Romeo and Juliet, and asked what I should do before one that had pierced the secrets of the future.

Q. How is this — how pierced them?

A. He did not say, sir. He put it as a parable, so as to say this hypothetick person truly knew what was to happen in time to come, and not by superstitious or magical means, but by learning and study. And how, if I granted him that, it were better such knowledge were not told. Which I took to be his way of saying, It is better I do not tell you of my real purpose. I confess I did not take it kindly, sir. For now I thought he had as good as admitted he deceived me, and broken his word. I said as much. Whereupon he most earnestly begged me to believe that what he hid from me was for my own good. That I had his word that it was not criminal. He then added what he had told me was true inasmuch as he wished to meet someone, and as much as any man might his mistress — or his Muse, I recall he put it so — and yet had been hitherto prevented.

Q. In what manner prevented?

A. He did not say.

Q. Who was this person?

A. Mr Ayscough, I cannot tell you. He would not be pressed. I asked if it were not some affair of honour. He smiled sadly at that, and said he would hardly ride so far to do what might be as well done in Hyde Park, nor without a friend to second him. Things had gone thus far when I was unfortunately called away. A Mr Beckford who is curate there —

Q. I know of him, I have spoken with him. You knew him not before that day?

A. I did not.

Q. Then no more of him. You spoke with Mr Bartholomew again, when he had gone?

A. Yes, but found him changed. As if he had reflected in my absence, and found he had said too much in our first conversation. I will not say he was discourteous. Yet he was more impatient with my doubts. He had papers from his box spread on a table before him when I returned, I saw they were mostly figures and with what I took to be geometrick or astronomick, I know not what, other signs. He handed me one to look at, and asked if I did not think they might not be seditious writings in cipher to James Stuart.

Q. By way of sarcasm, you would say?

A. Yes. Likewise that he had perhaps come to practise the black arts with some local witch. By which he meant also to mock my fears. Thereafter he grew more serious, and spoke again of this person he would meet; that before him he stood, in respect of powers of understanding and wisdom, as the mute man Dick before himself. Then that what he was about might be a foolish dream, but it did not put his soul in danger. You take his drift, Mr Ayscough. He confounded all in riddles, I assure you. He might seem to inform me, yet told me nothing.

Q. Some scholar, some learned recluse?

A. I must presume. By chance I had asked Mr Beckford if such there were, at least persons of taste and learning, in the neighbourhood, and he replied, there are none, that he dwelt in a desert. His very words.

Q. Mr B. gave no indication of how close this person lay or lived?

A. No, sir. Tho' one must suppose, within that next day's ride, and towards Bideford, where I left him on the morrow.

Q. It is implied, is it not, that this person now lives there or near there; that he knows Mr B. seeks this meeting, which he eschews, or is indifferent to; nay, that he will flee if he has foreknowledge of his coming in his own person and has his agents, spies, I know not what, posted to prevent him . . . whence all the elaborate subterfuge of which you were part? Is that not the case? I do not believe it, Lacy. I can sooner swallow the heiress. Did you not think, why does he mar a plausible tale, albeit a false one, with a far less credible account?

A. I did, sir. I saw no reason why I should be so newly misled, at this very last stage of our adventure. If I give you a reason for it, that came to me later, I fear you will call me a fool.

Q. Never mind, sir. I'll take you now for an honest fool, at least.

A. Then I flatter myself Mr B. had gained some respect for me, even were it no more than you have just suggested. When I look back, I apprehend he wished to suggest a greater and and more serious purpose than he had led me to believe. He wished me to know he sought something beyond the seeming of our parts till then. As if to say, I have deceived you, but it is in a great and worthy cause, though beyond what I can reveal.

Q. Can you not be more exact as to what was written on the papers?

A. I know little of the learned sciences, sir. There were many numbers on the sheet he passed to me, in columns. With some two or three parts scratched loosely out, as if they had been found in error. And another on the table showed a geometrick figure, a circle cut by many lines that passed the circle's centre, against which were writ, at the lines' ends, words of Greek, tho' abbreviate; if I do not mistake, rather as astrologers make their casts. I could not discern more closely.

Q. Did Mr B. ever speak of such — of astrology, or belief or interest in it?

A. Unless at that observation at the temple, concerning his searching his life's meridian, no.

Q. In sum, he gave you to understand, tho' obscurely, that what had brought him there was not what he had hitherto given you to believe?

A. Yes, of that I am sure.

Q. And you presume, from this conversation, and those others that preceded it, that his true design was in some way pertinent to these his hints and allusions as to a piercing of the secrets of time to come.

A. Sir, to this day I know not what to presume. I sometimes think I must believe as he hinted; and at others, that all is riddle, that he would in all play the jack with me and never discoursed of these matters but to deceive; yet again, as I say, that though he must perforce deceive me, he did regret it sincerely.

Q. You had no more converse that night?

A. Upon one matter only, Mr Ayscough. For his admitting that he was here upon other business than had been pretended did raise a further enigma: why we had brought the maid. I confess I was piqued, sir, that I had been hitherto trusted so little; and so I did tell Mr B. of what Jones had believed her to be.

Q. What said he to that?

A. Whether I did believe it so; and I replied, easily I could not, yet, that we suspected his man was privy to her bed. At which he did put a last confusion upon me, for he said, May a man not sleep with his wife, Lacy?

Q. What was your answer?

A. None, sir. I was the too discomfited. Jones and I had aired much in our speculations, but never that.

Q. Why should they have hidden that they were married?

A. It is beyond my conceiving. Nor why a comely, well-spoken young woman such as she should join her fate to such a deficient creature as Dick, without hope or prospect.

Q. This concluded your dealing on that evening?

A. Beyond that he did assure me of his esteem for me.

Q. Your agreed reward, how was that settled?

A. I forget, he said it should be done the next morning. As it was indeed. When he gave me the bill in settlement, and also begged me to keep or sell the horse, as I wished. Which I thought handsome of him.

Q. And it is sold?

A. Yes, when I came to Exeter.

Q. Now let us come to Jones, and his going off.

A. I was not a party to it, Mr Ayscough. He gave me no warning, not the least.

Q. Spake you to him, after you came to the Black Hart?

A. Unless some few words upon trivial matters.

Q. You had told him your task was near ended?

A. Yes, to be sure. As I said, we had divined it should be so before we came to the Black Hart; and when I retired, after being informed by Mr B. of our instructions, as to proceeding forthwith to Exeter, I did call Jones up from the kitchen and told him what had befallen.

Q. Seemed he set aback?

A. Not in the least, sir. He said he would be glad to be done with it.

Q. You did not discuss further?

A. Why, he might have done so, sir, for he was a little in his cups. But I sought my bed, and forbade it. I believe I said we should have time enough after to think upon all that had happened.

Q. When did you discover he had gone?

A. Not till I woke, that next morning, when as I dressed I remarked a note lying inside the door, as if pushed there. I have brought it, I fear it is poorly written.

Q. Read it, if you please.

A. "Worthy Mr Lacy, I hope you shall not take it too ill thanks for your past kindness that I will be gone when you read this, I would not have it so, but as you well know I have an aged parent at my place of birth in Wales, as well a brother and sister I have not seen these seven years past. Sir, it has been much on my mind in this coming west that I have sore neglected my duty as a son and being here so close, I asked our landlord of passage across the channel to Wales, and he said there was weekly ships in culm and coals to Bideford and Barnstaple and I found on asking there was one such sails by chance on the flood this coming day as I write, I mean from Barnstaple, which I must take, tho' rest assured I will tell any who ask I ride ahead for you to Bideford to warn of your coming, and for the horse I will leave it at the Crown Inn, which is on Barnstaple Quay, for you or Mr B. to take up when and where you please, the blunderbush I leave beneath the bed, I would steal nothing. Pray believe it is my mother, sir, who I know is ailing, it is respect of her and if I should not take this chance when that I am come so close, but forty miles' sail, and our own journey done. Please assure Mr B. I shall keep my mouth closed tight as a" — I can't read it, sir — "and I beg with all my heart nor he nor you will think me failing on my side of the bargain other than by this one small day and if he is so kind as to forgive your humble servant and friend I beg you hold safe my part owed unto my return to London, which shall not be long hence, I trust, and now begging once more your sincere pardon, I must end, for time presses." That is all, Mr Ayscough.

Q. He put his name to it?

A. His initials.

Q. You had no suspicion or forewarning of this whatsoever?

A. Not a particle, sir. It may be if I had had my wits more about me — I confess there was a circumstance at Taunton. Jones came to me there, and told some tale of having used most of his earnest money to settle a debt in London, so that he now found himself too little provided, and asked me to advance a sum upon the rest of his wages for the journey. Which I did, and noted in a pocket-book I keep for such purposes.

Q. How much?

A. A guinea.

Q. You were not surprised he should need such a sum?

A. I know him too well, sir. Where he can't impose by his bragging, he will impose by treating.

Q. Now, Mr Lacy, what credence do you put upon this letter?

A. I was angry, most angry that he should betray me so. Yet I thought it true, sir, at that time. I knew he came from Swansea or thereabout, and had heard him speak of a mother still living there.

Q. Who kept an alehouse?

A. Yes, so I believe he once told me.

Q. You say at that time — why not now?

A. Because he has not come for the rest of his money.

Q. Might he not have found work at Swansea?

A. Then he would have written. I know the man.

Q. Enquired you at the inn as to this — that there was truly a ship for Swansea that day? That Jones had sought such knowledge?

A.   I did not, sir, upon Mr Bartholomew's instructions. For I had hardly read it when the man Dick came to bring me to Mr B., who knew Jones had gone, Dick having told him. And thought it might be by my instruction. To which I was obliged to tell him not, and the truth of the matter.

Q.   You showed him the note?

A.   At once.

Q.   It alarmed him?

A.   Less than I feared. He was kind to my embarrassment, though he had hired Jones upon my recommendations. He questioned me a little, as to what belief we might give the letter. I replied as to you and that I was sure he need have no alarm for his own purposes, since Jones knew even less of them than I. That if he had had some evil intent, he would not have written his note, nor left it so late to act upon it.

Q.   Jones knew you were commanded to return by Exeter, you say?

A.   Yes. I had told him that.

Q.   What instructions did Mr Bartholomew give as to this new turn of events?

A.   That we must show no sign that what Jones had done was without our knowledge, but pretend it was at our instruction. That is, leave together, then go our separate ways and proceed as before. I confess I did not relish the prospect of riding alone in such a wild and sparse-peopled country, but I held my tongue. I felt myself most to blame for the loss of my intended companion, such as he was.

Q.   Have you thought on what might prevent the fellow from claiming his due of you?

A.   I have, and have no answer. It is most unlike.

Q.   It would not be his guilt at leaving you in the lurch?

A.   No. He's too poor to be tender on that point; or not to try.

Q.   He was not married?

A.   He never spoke of a wife. I did not know him as I might a friend, Mr Ayscough. I have seen him put on a pretence of fine manners, but not such as would pass him for a gentleman, however humble, or that I should impose upon Mrs

Lacy. He came once or twice to my house, but never past the door. There were a dozen others such as he that I truly know no worse or better, and might have recommended to Mr Bartholomew. It so fell I had met Jones a day or two previous in the street and spoken with him, and knew he had no work.

Q. Very well. We come to your parting with Mr Bartholomew.

A. I could not tell you the name of the place. In two miles or a little more we came to a fork, where there stood a gallows. Mr Bartholomew stopped and said it was the place, that in some few miles my road should come to the highway from Barnstaple to Exeter and I had but to follow that, and should with any luck find other travellers to journey with. That I might sleep at Crediton or straight to Exeter, as I chose.

Q. Said he no more?

A. Yes, we must wait a minute or two while the fellow Dick took my baggage from the packhorse and tied it to the beast I rode. And I forget, Mr Bartholomew had insisted most solicitiously that I take Jones' blunderbuss with me, tho' I doubt I should have brought myself to discharge it, except under most desperate need; but fortune was with me, none arose. As to our parting, Mr B. and I dismounted and walked a few steps away. Once again he thanked me and begged my excuses for the doubts he had occasioned in me, and prayed I would ride on with no shadow in my soul, as he assured me I should, or would, had he been able to divulge the entire truth.

Q. Still he gave no more precise indication of where he went, or whom he hoped to meet?

A. No, sir.

Q. Seemed he more confident in his demeanour?

A. I would rather say resigned, as if the die were cast. I remarked that the sun at least smiled on his enterprise, since the day was a true old May Day, not a cloud to be seen. And he said, Yes, I try to find that good augury, Lacy. When I then hoped he would encompass this interview he so desired, he merely bowed and said, I shall soon know. He added nothing else.

Q.   The maid and the man — they seemed not surprised that
      you left their company?

A.   No doubt they had been told that here my part ended, as in-
      deed it did. I shook hands with Mr Bartholomew, we
      mounted, they went their way and I went mine. Sir, I have
      told you all that I know. I am sorry to disappoint where you
      would most have me say more. I think I did warn you it must
      come to this.

Q.   Now I would put a case to you. Supposing Jones had known
      himself right in his first suspicion, that the maid was no maid,
      but a whore; that he had more forcefully charged her with it
      than he led you to believe, and demanded money for his si-
      lence, and received it, either from her or Mr B. himself. That
      is, say he was suborned from your interest, and well paid to
      remove himself for fear that he might tell you what he knew,
      once you had parted as planned from Mr B. Is this not more
      likely, and why he hath foregone his agreed wages? May he
      not already have received them there in Devon, and no doubt
      more than was bargained in the beginning?

A.   I cannot credit he would trick me so.

Q.   I may tell you his suspicion was right, Lacy. Your modest
      maid was neither modest nor maid, but hired fresh out of
      Claiborne's stews.

A.   I am dumbfounded, sir.

Q.   You were too fond, my friend. I know Jones' kind. Their
      honesty is ever where their interest lies. A lifetime's trust is
      nothing to a few guineas' profit.

A.   But why was such a creature as she brought with us?

Q.   There, I have still to determine. One would presume, for Mr
      B.'s pleasure. You assure me there was no sign of that?

A.   None that I saw.

Q.   And for the fellow Dick being taken to her bed, you have
      none but Jones' word?

A.   And their manner together, Mr Ayscough. In him it was
      naked he lusted after her. She was more discreet, yet I smelt a
      closeness there.

Q.   Let us return to your parting. You rode thence as directed, to Exeter?

A.   I soon fell in upon the high road with a packhorse train, and two stout fellows to guard it, and did not bid them farewell until we were inside the city gate at Exeter; where I stayed two days to repose myself, and sold my horse; then took coach to London, on the third.

Q.   And to the enquiries of your fellow-travellers?

A.   I dare say the most disagreeable old crab they have ever coached with. They gained nothing.

Q.   You have told Mrs Lacy of your adventures?

A.   I have, sir. She is discretion itself, I assure you. Not all ladies in my profession are as that shameless hoyden, Mrs Charke, that has brought such distress through her malicious conduct and ill repute upon her worthy father, Mr Cibber; far from it, sir. She is the exception, not the rule. No one who knew Mrs Lacy could impute to her loose morals or the least indiscretion in private matters.

Q.   Then you have a rare pearl in her sex. None the less, Lacy, I trust you will, having presented my compliments, request her to continue in that most estimable quality.

A.   You may be confident, Mr Ayscough. Now we are done, I feel my conscience much relieved. Would that my apprehensions were in the same case. May I venture now to ask, what you informed me of Mr B.'s servant — I cannot forget that?

Q.   He was found hanged, Lacy, not three miles from where you saw him last. Whether by his own hand, as it seemed, or by some other evil person, and made to appear as self-murder, is as undetermined as so much else.

A.   And of his master there is no news?

Q.   Not one whit, nor of the whore. You may think yourself lucky that you took the Exeter road.

A.   I now know it, sir. I would I had taken no part.

Q.   No doubt he would have found another to aid him. Your part was small matter. He was set upon something such as this, long before he sent his servant to your door.

A.   Upon disobedience?

Q. What would you say of a young man in your own calling, who having shown talents and powers far beyond the ordinary, having in addition as rich expectations in his private life as upon the public stage, sets his face, upon principles he does not deign to declare, against all that Providence most plainly designs for him? To say nothing of spurning all the reasonable hopes and counsels of his family and friends? That is not disobedience alone, Lacy. The common people of the county of my birth have a proverb of a child grown to a troublesome man. They say the Devil rocked his cradle. By which they would say, he is not so much to blame for his perversity as some malign accident of nature. Mr B. was given all, except contentment with his seeming most fortunate lot. He you knew was no hobbledehoy son of a gentleman nobody, that much you will have now divined, I doubt not. But enough, I begin to say too much. Lacy, I thank you for your evidence, and hope we part on better terms than we began. You will allow we must both be actors on occasion, though it is for different ends.

> Jurat die annoque praedicto coram me
> Henry Ayscough

Lincoln's Inn, the 27th August

Your Grace,

What Yr Grace will here read attached speaks for itself, and I proceed now as Yr Grace may guess. My men are already upon the road to Wales. If the rogue Jones be in his native place, they shall find him more soon than late, I doubt not. My nose tells me Lacy is no liar, and may be credited, tho' he credited far too much himself. He is a child at heart, behind his airs, like all his kind, and would be seen better bred and more important than he is; Yr Grace may judge him a fool, but not a perjuring villain. The bawd Claiborne should have her back flogged to the bone, were there justice in this world, and spend the rest of her shameless life in the colonies. Plain hanging is too kind for such as her.

I waited upon Lord B——— this forenoon and showed him Yr Grace's letter and my authority, and then laid such facts as was needful before him. He declared he was innocent of all knowledge of them until this day; had supposed his Lordship abroad; confessed he was a party to the matter at the bagnio, and thought the wench gone likewise abroad for his Lordship's pleasure. I asked Lord B——— if he had at any time suspected that his Lordship's intentions were not what he publickly pretended. He replied that his Lordship had talked much of his tour of Europe and he had believed him.

Upon my further questions Lord B——— vouchsafed that tho' he had seen his Lordship but infrequently since their Cambridge days, he counted him an honoured friend and was always pleased to renew their old intimacy, when he was in town; that he found himself somewhat surprised, on this last occasion, when his Lordship pressed to be introduced to Claiborne's bagnio, since he had always supposed his Lordship insusceptible to the temptations of the flesh and indeed seeming indifferent to womankind in general, since he had never yet married; but that his Lordship now appeared determined (*ipsissima verba*) to make up for lost time. (I spare Yr Grace some more particular expressions of this determination that Lord B——— described, since I believe them but said to add colour to a supposed debauchery and cloak his Lordship's true purpose.)

Lord B——— further said that he himself had first proposed that his Lordship should seek the favours of the woman in question; that he himself had been their recipient and had vouched for her skills and charms. Lord B——— then used a blasphemous figure I dare not repeat to Your Grace, but so as to say there was no better at her lewd traffick in London. I requested to know in what these charms consisted, beyond the carnal. Lord B——— replied that it was part in a seeming modesty, the more striking for being found in a world of brass; that it lay not in any particular faculty of wit or speech, since she spoke little, and then simply; that he knew of more than one who had gone in boldly to her, not believing report, yet had come out tamed; that since to the accustomed rake the most prized flesh is the newest, some now counted her stale meat, but he knew of none better for such as his Lordship, who took their first step in the Cyprian rites, which is why he proposed her to him; that in some licentious imitation of Tacitus he had lately read she was described *meretricum regina initiarum lenis,* which he deemed just.

I asked then if subsequent upon this first visit his Lordship had spoken to Lord B——— of her, and in what terms. He said that he had, and that very next day, and seemed much pleased; and to Lord B———'s recollection said that were he seeking a wench for his private use and satisfaction, yet with whom he need form no closer attachment, then this was such a one; that on some further occasion Lord B——— had of speaking with his Lordship, to his best memory some six or seven days later, his Lordship now broached the matter of bribing the woman away from Claiborne's to amuse him during his stay in Paris, and how it might be managed, and at what cost, *et cœtera;* that he (Lord B———) had declared he thought it could be done, but his Lordship must not delay his departure for France, as Claiborne might cry scandal and make trouble if she knew her whore still in London.

Furthermore that (it might be three or four days later still) his Lordship had called on Lord B——— and told him a difficulty lay with the whore, who was not unwilling to suit, but greatly feared her mistress's anger if she were discovered, which fear neither the money his Lordship offered to procure her running away nor assurances of his protection would stifle; that Claiborne kept too close a watch and was notorious cruel on any that dared quit her service in such a manner; and in fine that if his Lordship could hire her away, openly with Claiborne, upon a pretext (some other than to accompany him to France, which she would never allow), she would come, but otherwise feared it was more than her life was worth to accede to his Lordship's wishes.

Lord B——— said he thereupon advised his Lordship, if his mind was set on having her, to proceed as the girl advised, though it might seem the more expensive way; because that there lay some justice behind her fear for herself, since it is common knowledge no pandaress may afford to let one of her whores escape unpunished, lest the others should follow her example; and that the arrangement had this to be said for it: that if, the time elapsed, his Lordship had grown tired of the wench, then he had but to send her back, and no one the wiser as to what was first intended.

Upon my closer questioning Lord B——— admitted that he had helped devise the pretext his Lordship employed to deceive Claiborne, and had done as the creature accuses as to the substantiation of it, when called upon; but considered it no sin to practise upon such as she, who live by evil practice.

I am confident Your Grace knows sufficient of Lord B————'s character to know what worth to set upon his unsworn evidence, but will permit me to add that I took no suspicion in our interview of matters being hid, tho' it is sadly plain the noble lord played no noble part in all that transpired.

I thought finally to ask Lord B———— whether his Lordship had declared his private feelings to him, as regards the severity, eminently just and merited though it was, that he had provoked in his most noble father. I pray Yr Grace will remember, in what I repeat of what Lord B———— replied, that it was his command that I should attempt to ascertain this. Lord B———— said that though he had heard, before they met anew, that his Lordship was most angry with his parent, he was at first surprised to find him seemingly the rather resigned to his fate than determined not to submit to it. Yet that on a later and more intimate occasion his Lordship stated that he did not believe himself Yr Grace's son, for he could not countenance such a person as his father; and did say he would rather lose the strawberry leaves than believe Yr Grace was so. Lord B———— said he then made use of other most opprobrious epithets, the more so for being uttered not when he was inebriated or in a rage, but in his apparent senses, and most icy cold in manner, as if Yr Grace were some Turkish bashaw or other Oriental despot into whose cruel hands he had fallen. Lord B———— said further that he did conclude his Lordship's new will to play the rake might be placed upon this malevolent resentment in him for so sacred a figure as a father should be; but added in some small extenuation of his Lordship that these things were said to him alone (on an occasion when they strolled apart together in the Mall) and he never heard his Lordship to express himself thus in more publick company; and in extenuation of himself that he had suggested to his Lordship (as Yr Grace will know, Lord B———— was on ill terms with his own father, before that noble gentleman's late decease) that in his experience it was best to stifle one's resentments and to leave time as arbiter, that must in the nature of things be upon a son's side; and that after all, Heaven agreeing, his Lordship and he should one day themselves be fathers also. To that his Lordship appeared to acquiesce, and no more was said on the matter.

I am asked to convey to Yr Grace Lord B————'s profoundest regrets that matters have taken this unforeseen turn and his assurances that he remains as ignorant as Yr Grace's self as to his Lordship's real intentions and present whereabouts; and respectfully to suggest to Yr Grace that bearing in mind the notorious risk of infection from French whores and seeing that his Lordship's mind seemed fixed on its course of pleasure, he could not advise against what he was led (falsely) to believe were his plans, but on the contrary saw good reasons for seconding them; that he had given his Lordship his word that he would keep the matter entirely secret and also that he would find means to silence Claiborne's resentment if need arose, which he has done and will continue to do; and finally begs to insist that if he can be of any further assistance to Yr Grace in the affair, Your Grace will not hesitate to call upon him.

Yr Grace's ever most humble and obedient servant,

Henry Ayscough

ꕥ

The Eighth of September, Lincoln's Inn

Your Grace,

I write late and in great haste, so as not to delay the news my clerk Tudor has this minute brought. Jones is found, with an ease I had scarce hoped, and brought to London. They arrived but two hours since, and he is safe lodged. I shall begin upon the rogue to-morrow morning.

He was found by the greatest fortune at Cardiff, as they passed for Swansea; for my man says Jones was drinking in the very inn where they chanced to lodge; and that they might most easily not have remarked him, had not another spake his name, that they heard; and then watched close and listened, and so knew their good fortune. At first he would deny, but my clerk soon had him well sifted; then would run off, but to no avail; then cried he was false arrested, but changed his tune most swiftly when he was offered by my clerk to be brought before the justices of Cardiff to plead his innocence. They have since kept silence with him, nor let him speak as he would, and my man says he is much dejected and alarmed — in his words, well hung for the roasting, the which Yr Grace will believe me he shall have.

Yr Grace will, I pray, permit me at this present not to remark upon the justly outraged paternal sentiments he deigned to vouchsafe in his last letter. I am persuaded he knows that they are most respectfully shared. Like Yr Grace, I am confounded in all my understandings and expectations, as regards his L'dship. *Quantum mutatus ab illo!* Nothing shall be undone that may cast light upon this most unhappy affair.

Yr Grace's most humble and diligent servant,

Henry Ayscough

Post-scriptum. I do adjoin a copy of the letter that I have received of Mr Saunderson of Cambridge, that Yr Grace may see how his younger son's talents was esteemed by academy. Of Mr Whiston Yr Grace knows, I doubt not; he is quarrelsome dissenter and dangerous-mouthed, *ter-veneficus,* that did lose him that place at Cambridge that Mr Saunderson now fills, these twenty-five years past; and is grown more poisonous violent and turbulent since, for I hear now he waits upon that gentleman's decease, that he may once more put forward and take again the place he so deservedly was ejected from. H.A.

the 4 of 9er, *Christ's College, Cambridge.*

Sir,

I am in sad receipt of your letter of the 27 August, to which I hasten to reply, albeit deficiency doth oblige me to dictate to an amanuensis. I fear, sir, I can be of no assistance in the most pressing of what you request. I have not had the pleasure of meeting his Lordship in these two years past; I had last that pleasure at the time of the election, that is, in the April of '34. His Lordship then did me the honour of visiting me here, when he was in this town. Some letters we have exchanged since that meeting; all have been confined to matters mathematick and algebraical. The last such I received was of the 24th March last, that wished me well of the coming year, and did announce that his Lordship intended soon to be in town, and designed a summer tour to France and Italy; yet hoped before he left, when the weather was more clement, that he might make an excursion to Cambridge to call upon me, for he sought my advice on whom he might visit during his tour. Alas, since then I have had no further letter nor other news of him, and had presumed him gone. I am as perplexed as I am dismayed by this news of a disappearance. The letter of March contained naught, beyond the above-mentioned, of more personal import.

Of his Lordship I may most sincerely state that I have had few pupils to equal him, and none to surpass. You may know, sir, that I am fourth Lucasian professor at this university, and have been so since the year 1711; and thus in commending him so highly I lack not grounds for comparison. Did not his rank preclude him, I consider his talents such as would have most usefully adorned this University; I cannot say the like of many others, far his inferior, that have been elected fellows this last twenty years.

I am alas the more accustomed, with young gentlemen of his rank, to find that whatever interest and assiduity in study they may show when here is swift to disappear when they go out upon the world. It has not been so with his Lordship; he has most pertinaciously continued his studies in the mathematick science and in all to which it pertains. I have found him always well read, and a most excellent practiser. For this it is not only I who vouch; this has been also the opinion of my eminent predecessor, Mr Whiston, whose religious views one may deplore, but not his mathematick ability, and of a far greater still, my most illuminate ante-predecessor *in cathedrâ Lucasianâ*, Sir Isaac Newton. To the attention of both have I more than once brought propositions or solutions advanced by his

Lordship; and though they did, before Sir Isaac's lamented death, fall out with each other, in this they concurred: that here was a young philosopher worthy their attention.

I would not bore you, sir, yet I may add that I have myself these several years been engaged upon a method by board for the easier computation of great numbers; that in this design I have several times discussed with his Lordship the problems of method that I have encountered; and that I have found him by no means the least skilled in assisting me to surmount them. His talents here are not common ones; for the common mind in such matters will attempt to solve by small refinement and improvement of the proposed method; whereas his Lordship did proceed by most close examination of the principles of the method; and more than once he hath hit upon a better and more advantageous one. I count myself fortunate to have had such a noble coadjutor.

If I am to find fault in him, it is that he was sometimes seized by beliefs or theories of this physical world that I must term more phantasies than probable or experimental truths. The one that you require me to explain is such, in my view. The series of numbers to which you allude appears first in the *Liber Abaci* of one Leonardo da Pisa, a learned Italian. He did devise it, but, upon his own admission, for no more than to calculate the multiplication of conies in a warren. Yet his Lordship would find this rate of proportion (which doth stay the same however superfetatiously its parts be added) everywhere in nature besides, indeed even discernible in the motions of the planets and the arrangement of stars in the heavens; and saw it likewise in all plants, in the disposition of their leaves, for which ordering he would make a name, that is, from the Greek, *phyllotaxis*. And he did believe also that this same most elementary sequence might be traced in the history of this world, both past and to come; and thus that were it fully understood, the chronology of the future might be prophesied as well that of the past explained.

There, sir, I believe he put far too much upon some trifling coincidences in the base phenomena of physical nature; and must believe also that in this he did suffer, though through no fault of his own, from his aristocratic place in society, *viz.*, that he lacked the daily commerce of a world of common learning and discussion upon it; and thus suffered from what may be called a *dementia in exsilio,* if you will forgive me. Or as it is said here, *In delitescentia non est scientia,* those who lie hidden, or live far, from knowledge, may never fully have it.

Now, sir, in matters of my science I am accustomed to speak my mind; and when his Lordship did first put his notions on this matter before me, I was somewhat strict upon them, and found them ill-grounded. This happened some five years ago, and did at the first occasion a coldness between his Lordship and myself, that I did venture to criticise many of the too extravagant deductions he would make upon his premises. Yet am I happy to say we have made truce since then, upon terms proposed by his Lordship himself: that he valued his relation with me far too highly to lose it for a dispute over a matter that he conceded he could not prove (this was in allusion to his chimerick notion that a chronology of the future might be established from the aforesaid sequence). He proposed then that we should, as *amici amicitiae* (so he put it), ban this bone of contention from our conversation. And so since has it been, sir; and I had believed it no longer his study, for he has been good to his word in all our subsequent meetings and in all correspondence.

As I say, sir, I am perplexed as to where his Lordship now might be, and cannot advise you; and must pray one I have the honour to count as a most worthy, talented, amiable and noble friend shall soon be found.

Your obedient servant,

Nicholas Saunderson A.M.
Regalis Societatis Socius

Written by me, Anne Saunderson, daughter.

O N the 28th past, a Man passing the Bridge over the *Savock* near *Preston, Lancashire*, saw two large Flights of Birds meet with such Rapidity, that 18o of them fell to the Ground, were taken up by him, and sold in *Preston*-Market the same Day.

Friday 3.

Joshua Harding, and *John Vernham*, condemn'd for House-breaking, were hang'd at *Bristol*, when cut down, and put in Coffins, they came both to life; but the latter, tho' he had been blooded, dy'd about 11 at Night; and *Harding* continuing alive, was put in *Bridewell*, where great Numbers of People resorted to see him: He said, he only remember'd his being at the Gallows, and knew nothing of *Vernham*'s being with him; having been always defective in his Intellects, he was not to be hang'd, but to be taken care of in a Charity-House.

Monday, 6.

The Bills of Indictment presented to the Grand Jury at *Hicks's-Hall* against two of the *Spittle-fields* Rioters were return'd Ignoramus. *See 425.*

Tuesday, 7.

Betwixt 9 and 10 at Night, a Body of Men, (See p. 522 H) enter'd the West Port of *Edinburgh*, seized the Drum, beat to Arms, and calling out, *Here! All those who aare avenge innocent Blood!* were instantly attended by a numerous Crowd. Then they seized and shut up the City Gates, and posted Guards at each, to prevent Surprize by the King's Forces, while another Detachment disarm'd the City Guards, and advanced immediately to the Tolbooth or Prison, where not being able to break the Door with hammers, &c. they set it on Fire, but at the same Time provided Water to keep the Flame within due Bounds. Before the outer Door was near burnt down several ruin'd thro' the Flames and oblig'd the Keeper to open the inner Door and going into Capt. *Portens* Apartment, call'd, *where is the Baggar Porteous?* who said I'm here, what is it you are to do

with me? To which he was answered, we are to carry you to the Place where you shed so much innocent Blood and Hang you. He made some Resistance, but was soon overcome, for while some set the whole Prisoners at Liberty, others caught him by the Legs and dragged him down Stairs, and then led him to the *Grass Market*, where they agreed to Hang him without further Ceremony; accordingly, taking a Coil of Rope from a Shop, they put one End of it about his Neck, and flung the other End over a Dyers Cross Post or Gallows, and drew him up; but having got his Hands to the Rope, they let him down and tyed them, and draw'd him up again, but observing what an indecent Sight he was without any Covering over his Face, they let him down a second Time, and pulled off one of the two Shirts he had on and wrapped it about his Head, and hal'd him up a third Time with loud Huzza and a Ruff of the Drum. After he had hung till suppos'd to be dead, they nail'd the Rope to the Post, then formally saluting one another, grounded their Arms, and on t'other Ruff of the Drum retir'd out of Town. Nothing of this Kind was ever so boldly Attempted, or so successfully Executed, all in the Space of two Hours, after which every Thing was quiet The Magistrates endeavoured to prevent their Design, but were attack'd and driven away. Next Morning at 4 when the Captain was taken down, his Neck was broke, his Arm wounded, and his Back and Head bruised.

In what we mention'd last Month, with relation to the obtaining this unfortunate Man's Reprieve, there was a small Mistake; several Persons of Quality and Distinction, did apply to her Majesty, in favour of the Captain, but we are assur'd the Magistrates of *Edinburgh* did not in the least Interest themselves in that Matter; and no doubt they had their Reasons; since this is not the only Instance of the Populace of that City, putting into Action, the brave but unforgiving Principle, couch'd under the Motto of their Nation, *Nemo me imvune Lacessit*. To mention one: In the beginning of Q. *Anne*'s Reign, when the Earl *Seasfeld* was Chancellor, one *Green* was condemn'd for the Murder of Capt. *Middleton*, and the Council in *Edinburgh* order'd him to be reprieved, which the Mob hearing, when the Earl came out of the Council, they broke, and overturn'd his Coach, and greatly insulted the Earl, and oblig'd him to go back

Aaaa to

to the Council and get the Reprieve chang'd into an Order for his Execution, and he was executed accordingly.

About 14 Persons were taken into Custody the next Day on Account of this Riot, but no Evidence appearing against them, 11 were soon discharg'd, and the others not long after.

Friday, 10.

A Fire broke out in upper *Shadwell*, by which 42 Houses, 6 Warehouses, and 8 Sheds were burnt to the Ground, and 18 damaged.

Wednesday, 15.

At the Sessions at the *Old-Bailey* 77 Prisoners were tried, 6 of whom receiv'd Sentence of Death, (viz.) *Edward Bonner*, a Butcher in *Newgate-Market*, *Tho. Dwyer*, and *James Oneal*, for robbing on the Highway; *Edward Rowe* for shooting and robbing Mr *Gibson*, the Baker at *Islington*; *John Thomas* for Shoplifting; and *Tho. Hornbrook* for Horsestealing. 26 order'd for Transportation, one burnt in the Hand; and one (viz.) *Joseph Cady*, to stand in the Pillory for Perjury; and 62 acquitted. Mr *Nixon* the Nonjuring Clergyman was admitted to Bail. *See p.* 420D. Three Men and one Woman were committed for Perjury on *Bonner's* Trial.

Nine Persons in Custody on occasion of the late Riots in Spital-fields were brought to the Bar, indicted for Misdemeanours; but their Trials not coming on, they were, with the Approbation of his Majesty's Attorney General, referred to Bail, each to find Sureties to be bound in 50 *l.* Recognizance.

Thursday, 16.

At a Gen. Court of the Bank of *England*, a Dividend of Two 3 qrs per Cent. was agreed to for Interest and Profits for the Half Year ending at *Michaelmas* next; and the Warrants made payable *October* the 13th.

Friday, 17.

The Court of Common Council, *London*, order'd that the 1st Collection of the Tax for lighting the Streets, pursuant to a late Act, should be for 3 Quarters of a Year ending at *Christmas*, after the following Rates (viz.) Every House under 10 *l.* per Ann. 3 s. 6 d. from 10 to 20 *l.* 7 s. 6 d. from 20 to 30 *l.* 8 s. from 30 to 40 *l.* 9 s. 6 d. all above 12 s.———Every Freeman of *London* liable to pay the said Rate, neglecting or refusing to pay, or desiring to be excused paying, shall be under the same Incapacity of Voting at all Elections in the City, as other Persons now are, who do not pay Scot and Lot.

The *Glasgow* Mail with several Bags and an *Irish* Mail therein, were carry'd

off by two Rogues, who stabb'd the Post-man in the Thigh.

Wednesday, 22.

One *Cadwal*, a Deserter, got Change for a 20 *l.* Bill at *Coupar* in *Fife*, when paid, it was discover'd to have been taken out of the *Glasgow* Mail above-said, whereupon the Person who paid it, rode after him, and got his Money; but let the man go off, yet kept the Note.

At a Court of Common Council at *Guild-hall*, it was agreed to complete *Fleet-Ditch* for a Market, and that the Committee of City-Lands do immediately advertise to receive Proposals for building a Market-House, Shops, Stalls, &c.

Friday, 24.

At a General Court of the *East-India* Company it was resolved to reduce the Interest of all the Bonds that bore a higher Price, to 3 per Cent.

Turshay, 25.

A Proclamation was publish'd, offering a Reward of 200 *l.* and his Majesty's Pardon, to the Discoverers of any Person concern'd in the Murder of Capt. *Porteous*, and for every Person so discover'd, and convicted, 200 *l.*

Sunday, 26.

Daniel Malden having been retaken at *Canterbury*, upon a Quarrel with his Wife, was brought under a strong Guard to *Newgate*, and cha n'd down in the Hold. *See* p. 291 A 354 H.

Monday, 27.

Bonner Rowe, Dwyer, and *O Neal,* were hang'd at *Tyburn;* but *Hornbrook* and *Thomas* were repriev'd.

Tuesday, 28.

Wm Rous and *Benjamin Rawlings* Esqs; were sworn into the Office of Sheriffs of this City and County of *Middlesex.*

The Time approaching for putting a Stop to the Retailing of distill'd Spirituous Liquors in small Quantities, the Persons who kept Shop for that purpose began to make a Parade of mock Ceremonies for Madam *Geneva's* Lying-inState, which created a Mob about their Shops, and the Justices thought proper to commit some of the chief Mourners to Prison. The Signs also of Punch-Houses were put in mourning; and lest others should express the Bitterness of their Hearts by committing Violences, the Horse and Foot-Guards and Train'd-Bands were order'd to be properly station'd. But many of the Distillers, instead of spending their Time in empty Lamentations betook themselves to other Branches of Industry; some to the

The Examination and Deposition of
DAVID JONES
the which doth attest upon his sworn
oath, this ninth day of September in
the tenth year of the reign
of our sovereign Lord George the
second, by the grace of God King of
Great Britain and of England, &c.

My name is DAVID JONES. *I am Swansea born, as old as the century, thirty-six years. I am not married. I am at this present ship-chandler's clerk at Cardiff.*

⟞⟎⟝

Q. Jones, I have been at great cost to find you.
A. I know it, sir, and am most sorry.
Q. You have read this summary of Mr Francis Lacy's deposition?
A. I have, sir.
Q. You do not deny you are he Mr Lacy speaks of?
A. No, sir. I cannot.
Q. But you denied it to him I sent to fetch you hither?
A. I knew him not, sir. He said at first nothing of Mr Lacy, and I consider myself with respect that worthy gentleman's friend, and bound in honour to protect him if I could. For I knew him as innocent as Jones, sir, in what passed last April. One must look for one's friends, as the saying goes.
Q. My man says you still denied, when he spoke of Mr Lacy; that you swore on your oath you knew no such person.
A. It was but to prove him, sir, to see if he knew as much as he claimed. And when I was satisfied he did, I lied no more.

Q.   And shall lie no more, Jones.

A.   I shall not, sir. Indeed I shan't.

Q.   Be it so. We will come to what happened subsequent to your setting forth from London. I first desire to know whether there are any matters in Mr Lacy's deposition, or such of it as you have read, that you know are false.

A.   Not one, sir.

Q.   Or inexact?

A.   No, sir. 'Twas all as he says, that I know.

Q.   Or deficient in any substantial way — were there matters of import you discovered that you did not tell him?

A.   No, sir. 'Twas my duty to tell him all I saw and marked. And so I did.

Q.   There is nothing you can add?

A.   Upon my oath, there is not, sir.

Q.   Do you deny that you ran away, as Mr Lacy tells, without his permission?

A.   No, sir. 'Twas as I did write him, sir. I would see my old mother, God rest her soul, and I knew but the Bristol Channel between us, and thought I should not have better opportunity. Near is my petticoat, but nearer's my smock, as the saying goes. I was wrong, sir, I know it. But I have been a bad son, see you, and wished to mend.

Q.   Was not your employment with Mr Bartholomew at an end, that very next day? Why should you not ask Mr Lacy if you might go then?

A.   I judged he would say no, sir.

Q.   Why?

A.   Because he's a fearful gentleman, sir, and I knew would not want to ride alone in those parts.

Q.   Had he not been a good friend to you — on this as well as past occasions? Found employment for you?

A.   Well, sir, I won't deny it, and so was I deep ashamed to treat him so, yet see you my conscience as a son and Christian said I ought, and must. So I did.

Q.   And hoped you would find his forgiveness when you returned to London?

A. I hoped, sir. He is soft of heart too, God bless him. And Christian likewise.

Q. I would have you tell me what you made of Mr Bartholomew's servant Dick.

A. I made nothing of him, sir. Jones knew him no better at the end than at the beginning.

Q. You found nothing strange in him?

A. What was plain to any, sir. That 'twas beyond an Irishman's belief, a gentleman thinking to employ him for what he was. He was strong enough, well set, for a good lackey, but naught else, see you.

Q. Not a gentleman's servant, you would say?

A. He did what he was bid, sir, well enough. And I'll allow his master's secrets was safe enough with him. And his belongings. He would not even let me touch the little chest we had upon the packhorse, that weighed so heavy. Our first day out I would help him carry it up, he pushed me off; and so for the rest. He was more jealous cur than serving-man in that.

Q. Marked you nothing else peculiar in him?

A. That he would not laugh, nor even smile, not even when the company was merry as cup and can. There was a maid at Basingstoke one morning at the well, where Dick and I and others was standing by, and would dowse the stableboy for some impertinence, and ran after him with the bucket but fell, and dowsed herself, which a dead man would have laughed to see how droll it was. But not he. He stood always at the coffin's side, as the saying goes. Ever found sixpence, and lost a shilling.

Q. A melancholy fellow?

A. Simple, sir. As if he had dropped from the moon. He was more figure of wood than human flesh. Except with the girl. I could tell your worship a tale there.

Q. Seemed he frightened of his master?

A. No, sir. Quick to his command, but no more than is natural. Attentive when they spoke by their signs — which I learned to read a little, and tried to speak to Dick by what I could make out of 'em, but 'twas wasted time.

Q. Why?

A. I cannot say, sir. In simple things, such as help me tie that, give a hand to lift this, he would understand. Tried I to ask something of him, of what he thought, no more than in common friendship at an idle moment, he would not. I should as well have spoken my mother's Welsh.

Q. So was he not less simple than he seemed?

A. It may be, sir. Some might say that.

Q. I have a deposition of Master Puddicombe, of the Black Hart Inn. He says you told there of a lunatick fit one night upon the road.

Q. I told tales wherever we went, sir. Mirrors for larks, as they say.

Q. It was false?

A. Sir, I did in that as I was bid by Mr Lacy and the gentleman.

Q. That you should spread word the fellow was moon-ridden?

A. Not in the particular, sir. Since Dick must seem so close, that I should play the loose-tongued companion, free with his tittle-tattle, and so put off suspicion.

Q. And did you not say the maidservants should watch to their dealings with him?

A. I may have, sir. And if I did, 'twas nearer the mark.

Q. In what way?

A. That was no Italian eunuch, sir, no Faribelly. For all he lacked elsewhere.

Q. You speak of the maid Louise?

A. I do, sir.

Q. And of other females, upon your road?

A. He had eyes only for her, sir. The other was no more than spice. To tickle the young women in Puddicombe's house.

Q. And did you not tickle one such in a grosser manner, Jones?

A. In play, sir. No more, upon my word. I tried for a buss.

Q. And her bed, sir?

A. Well, I am still young, sir. Begging your worship's respect I have my natural vigours, like any man. I had had the goose's simpers at supper, see you. She was but a country malkin.

Q. Very well. Let us pass to Louise. What think you now of what

you first told Mr Lacy, to wit, that you had seen her at Claiborne's house one day?

A.   It was night, sir, and by linklight, no more than a passing
quick as she went in. I did not swear to it. I do not doubt I
was mistook. The eye is a shrew, it will look for the worst.
'Twas a resembling, not her.

Q.   You tell me, you are now positive you was mistaken?

A.   Yes, sir. Was I not?

Q.   Why ask you?

A.   That you should seem to doubt it, sir. 'Twas whist, whist, I
smell a bird's nest. A fancy I took, that was wrong.

Q.   You are positive she was not what you thought?

A.   I took Mr Bartholomew's word, sir. Or rather, Mr Lacy's
taking of his word as to who she was. 'Twas well for him,
'twas well for me.

Q.   Did you speak much with her?

A.   Little, sir. She made it plain at setting-out she was nice,
would keep herself to herself. Why, nice as a nun's hen,
hoity-toity she cared not to look on me, if we sat at table or
had to pass; and had better things than to talk, when we were
on the road. 'Twas fit her name was French.

Q.   Was this her niceness not excessive in a purported maid?

A.   So in these times are most of her kind, sir. Odsocks, they'd all
have you believe 'em their mistresses.

Q.   No vulgar oaths in this room.

A.   I beg your worship's pardon.

Q.   You did not know her by any other name?

A.   No, sir, how should I?

Q.   Know you the name of she you saw to enter Claiborne's?

A.   No, sir, nor he I was with that pointed her out. Save that he
knew she was a prize piece in the house, that was called the
Quaker Maid. And we thought the gentleman we had
brought might be come to go with her. That was the Marquis
of L———, sir.

Q.   You were there as chairman, is it so?

A.   Yes, sir, as I was by occasion, when I had no better for my
bread.

Q.   You went often as chairman to this house?

A.   Sometimes, sir. As it fell.

Q.   And had never learnt the names of its strumpets?

A.   No, sir. Only that it was said to hold the best flesh in London, for that half the richest culls — begging your pardon, sir, I would say the greatest gentlemen of London, did go through its doors.

Q.   And you are certain, she you travelled with was not this whore?

A.   I am now, sir.

Q.   Did you not ask this Louise whence she came, and such things?

A.   I did, sir, and more times than once before we came to Amesbury. Such as how long she had been in service, and where. 'Twas charity to a miser, she had a manner of saying little to tell you nothing. That was no clack-patten tongue.

Q.   And when you asked her of the going out in the night at Amesbury?

A.   She denied it flat, sir, and grew angry, in a fluster, then sour as verjuice, and I knew she lied, as to that.

Q.   Now, before you knew Dick was privy to her bed, had you marked any understanding between them?

A.   'Twas plain enough in him, sir, that he was besotted, to one who watched close if she were by. He'd scarce take his eyes off her; and once he'd served his master, he'd serve her.

Q.   How so?

A.   Why, carry her victuals, carry her bundle, what he could. 'Twas like the old rhyme: He that loves glass without G, Take away L, and that is he.

Q.   But she was more modest in showing affection?

A.   More sly, sir. You would take him more her pet dog than her lover, by the outward of it. But after Amesbury, when 'twas out, she hid less. She would sleep riding, I see her now, sat forward there between his arms, head turned to rest against his breast, so a child would or a wife.

Q.   And this, despite she was so nice?

A.   'Tis as the proverb says, sir. Know Eve, know all.

Q.   Rode she most often there, or behind?

A.   Why to begin, behind, sir, as is most common, like to mackaw or cockatoon upon a perch. Then took the third day to sitting forward between his arms, she did say it was more soft, there upon the withers; which she might the better have said it was softer between the lusty fellow's legs, begging your worship's pardon.

Q.   Did you not ask her more of him, if they was not to marry?

A.   I did not, sir. For Mr Lacy had told me privily not to pry further, fear it would seem I was spying on Mr Bartholomew for him, which he would not have. So I held my tongue and thought kinder of her, that perhaps at first she feared I might mock her for her fancy for such a fellow as Dick, and had been short with me for my own good.

Q.   How is that?

A.   Why, sir, she was a handsome wench. Love will creep if it can't go. I dare say my eyes soon told her as much.

Q.   You played the gallant?

A.   I might have, sir, if she'd let. But 'twas half to see if she knew what gallantry was. And whether my thinking her one of Mother Claiborne's lambs was true.

Q.   You can tell me nothing more of her?

A.   No, sir.

Q.   And you have seen or heard nothing of her, or of Dick, or his master, since the last day of April?

A.   No, sir.

Q.   Or read report, in newspaper or gazette?

A.   No, sir, on my word.

Q.   And your belief has been that Mr Bartholomew succeeded in his plan of elopement, without any crime committed in which you are blamable?

A.   Yes, sir, until this present. Where I might be alarmed, were I not innocent, and see your worship's most just and merciful. I have no fear, my part was nothing, no more than porter at the door, see you.

Q.   Why have you stayed in Wales, and not returned to London for the money Mr Lacy holds for you?

A.   I wrote Mr Lacy my reasons, sir, this three months gone.

Q.   He knows naught of this.

A.   No, sir, and I will take your liberty to inform you why. First when I was landed where I was born, I did have news that made me weep, your worship, weep as a child, for I found my poor old mother, God rest her soul, was no more, but in her grave, and had been the like these three years past; and a sister likewise, that I had loved, but six months gone. And now I had no more than a brother left, that is poorer even than Jones, true Welsh beside, which is brother most to his own misery. Well, sir, with him I did lodge most wretched for a month and help as I might. Then says I, Jones, says I, 'tis time you were returned to London. 'Tis a miserable small Welsh place, your Swansea, sir. While money and Jones is like the clocks of London, sir, we are never long together. All I had brought was run down Gutter Lane. So I set out to walk to London, being short of means to a better way. And came to Cardiff, where I met a friend, who took me to his home and made me welcome; and by chance another man was there, who when he heard that I could write and cipher, and had been in the world, spoke of a place he knew where he worked himself, which was Mr Williams' where your man found me, sir. For see you his old clerk was but three days before struck sudden of an apoplexy, and given for dead, which now he is, and Mr Williams had such press of business upon him —

Q.   Yes, yes. Come to your letter.

A.   Why, sir, it was to tell of this post I had found and that I was happy as a fairday fowl in it, found apt and industrious by my new master, and so could not come to London. That I was very sorry for what I had done and hoped he would now consider to forgive me, which if he could, I should be grateful he might find some means to send me my accompt with him.

Q.   How sent you this letter?

A.   By one who had cause to Gloucester, sir, and who said he would see it sent further from there, for which I gave him a shilling. Which he assured me was done when he returned.

But I lost my expense and trouble, sir, I had no answer of it.

Q. Did you not write again?

A. I thought it not worth the trouble, sir. That Mr Lacy was angry, and serving me as I served him, as I dare say he had right.

Q. Too trifling a sum to be worth your trouble?

A. Yes, sir.

Q. How much, by your account?

A. I had already taken some of Mr Lacy, before we parted.

Q. How much?

A. Several guineas' worth, sir.

Q. Be exact.

A. A guinea the god's-penny before we left and else beside.

Q. How much else?

A. I asked some of Mr Lacy at Taunton, sir. I believe 'twas two or three guineas.

Q. Mr Lacy says one.

A. I have forgot, sir. I should have sworn it more.

Q. You are so mighty careless of money you confound one and three? [*Non respondet.*] You had taken two guineas, Jones. That left owed to you?

A. Eight, sir.

Q. How much does your present place pay per annum?

A. Ten pound a year, your worship, and I know what you would be at. But I thought it lost money, so counted it little.

Q. Near a year's wages, it is little?

A. I knew not how to claim it.

Q. Do not ships bring coals from Wales to London, and often?

A. It may be, sir.

Q. What, you work at a chandler's and are not sure?

A. Yes, I am sure, sir.

Q. Thought you not to send a letter by one of them, or take passage yourself, to recover your money?

A. Jones is no sailor, sir. I fear the sea, and the privateers.

Q. I say there is some other reason. You are lying.

A. No, sir.

Q. Yes, sir. You had found out something of this expedition into the West, that you saw fit not to tell Mr Lacy and that you knew might bring you and all who were associated with it into your present trouble. You would not run away and give up all your money, were there not some greater cause.

A.   I knew no more than we were told, sir. Upon my oath. Or found out for ourselves, that Mr Lacy has already said.

Q.   I have thee limed in thy own lime, man. Your first letter to Mr Lacy spoke of a ship to Swansea out of Barnstaple, that first of May. I have written to enquire. There was none such, nor for ten days after.

A.   No, sir, I was wrongly informed, as I found when I came there. So I thought it, when I wrote it down. At Barnstaple I was told I should do better at Bideford. Where I went, and found a collier three days thence. That is truth, sir, you may ask. Her name was the *Henrietta,* Master James Parry of Porthcawl, an excellent captain and well known.

Q.   How spent you those three days?

A.   I lay in Barnstaple that first day, sir, and the next to Bideford, where I enquired on the quay there and found Mr Parry and spoke with him for my passage. Which we took the day following and had a safe crossing, I thank the Lord.

Q.   Who told you wrongly of this ship at Barnstaple — who at the Black Hart?

A.   Why, sir, I forget now. One who was there.

Q.   You wrote Mr Lacy that it was Puddicombe.

A.   Then it was he, sir.

Q.   Jones, I warn thee. Thou reek'st of lies as thy country's breath doth stink of leeks.

A.   No, sir. As God is my witness.

Q.   I have thy letter here, which states plain that Master Puddicombe told thee. But he swears he did not, and he's no liar.

A.   Then I mistook, sir. It was writ in great haste.

Q.   And in great botch, like the rest of thy story. For I have written to the Crown, Jones, about the horse. Now, will you still say it was left there on the first of the month or at any day subsequent indeed? Why do you not answer?

A.   Sir, I am confused. I recollect now, I rode with it to Bideford and did leave it there, at the sign of the Barbadoes where I lodged, with money to keep till 'twas fetched, but did not forget to send message by boy to the Crown in t'other place, for if any should ask and think me thief of it. I swear, sir, you must forgive I am out of wits. I said the first day without thought, to be brief. I did not think it material.

Q.   Then I will tell thee why, thou rogue, and how near the gallows thou art. Dick is dead, upon strong suspicion of murder, his body found hanged not a day's ride from where thou slept; his master's chest found robbed, the box vanished; and since that day, no word of his master nor the maid. In which black mystery a strong presumption is that they lie murdered also — and a stronger still, that it is by thee. [Here the deponent exclaimed in the Welsh tongue.] What is this?

A.   Not true, not true. [Here more words in the Welsh tongue.]

Q.   What's not true?

A.   The woman lives. I have seen her after.

Q.   Well mayst thou hang thy head, Jones. Attempt me one more lie, and I'll have it hanged where it best belongs. I promise thee that.

A.   I have seen her after, I swear, your honour.

Q.   After what?

A.   There where they went that first of May.

Q.   How know you where they went? Did you not go to Barnstaple?

A.   No, sir. Oh dear God, would that I had. Dear God. [Again, Welsh words.]

Q.   Do you know where the maid presently is?

A.   On God's honour, no, sir. Unless it be at Bristol, as I will tell. And she was no maid.

Q.   And Mr Bartholomew?

A.   Dear God.

Q.   Why do you not answer?

A.   I know who he truly was. 'Twas thus I became entangled, curse the day, though I meant well. Your worship, I could not help it, it was told me without the asking, by a fellow that —

Q. Stop. Tell me the name you were told, no more and no less. Do not write his answer.

A. [*Respondet.*]

Q. Have you told or writ this name to any?

A. No, sir. Not one, on my mother's soul.

Q. You know then for whom I pursue, Jones? Why thou art here?

A. I may guess, sir. And most humbly crave his mercy, for I thought to act for him, sir, when I knew.

Q. We will come to that. Now I repeat, what know you of his Lordship, subsequent to the first of May? Have you spoken with him, had news of him, had any knowledge whatsoever of him?

A. I know not where he is, I swear, sir, nor whether he lives, nor of Dick and his dying. Your worship must believe me. Oh dear God, you must believe I hid all because I was so sore afraid, nothing else.

Q. Hid what, thou sniveller? Get off thy knees.

A. Yes, sir. I mean I knew later Dick was dead, sir, God rest his soul. But no more, I swear you on St David's grave.

Q. How came you by this?

A. By suspicion of it, sir, not certain information. When I had been two weeks or more in Swansea, I fell in with a mariner in a tavern there late come from Barnstaple, who told of a dead man found with violets stuffed in his mouth near that town. He gave no name, sir, he mentioned it in passing, as a strange matter, yet it gave me forebodings.

Q. And then?

A. By one I met after I removed to Cardiff, sir, in my master Mr Williams' house, that is, his place of business, who spoke of the same affair, for he landed that very morning from Bideford, and talked of new discoveries, and that Bideford was full of it and said 'twas now thought five travellers lay murdered two months past. He said no names neither, but I guessed by the number, and other circumstance he spake of, and have lived in great fear till this day and would have told you at once, sir, were it not for my poor mother and —

Q. Enough! When was this — the second report?

A. The last week of June, sir. To my best memory. Or worst, alas. I meant no harm.

Q. Why fear'st thou so much, if thou art innocent?

A. Sir, I have seen such things I'd not believe myself, were another to say them.

Q. Thou'lt say them to me, by Heaven, Jones. Or see thy own evil carcass hanged. I'll have thee swung for horse-stealer, if not for murderer.

A. Yes, sir. [More in the Welsh tongue.]

Q. And enough of thy barbarous gibberish.

A. Yes, sir. 'Tis but a prayer.

Q. Prayers will not save thee. Nothing but the truth entire.

A. You shall have it, sir. On my word. Where would you have me begin?

Q. Where you first lied. If that were not the cradle.

A. I have told you no lies till where we stayed when we left Amesbury, sir, which was at Wincanton. All passed as Mr Lacy told. Unless it be Louise.

Q. What of her?

A. I thought I was right in what I first told Mr Lacy, as to where I had seen her before.

Q. Entering Claiborne's — that she was whore?

A. Yes, sir. But he would not have it so. So I did not press it, yet believed what I believed, as the saying goes.

Q. That Mr Lacy had been deceived by his Lordship?

A. Tho' I knew not why, sir.

Q. Did you charge her with it?

A. No, sir, or not in manner direct. Mr Lacy said I maunt. I spoke some light words with her, by way of proving her, and half in sport. As I told, she would yield no ways, and spoke as a lady's maid might, no better nor no worse.

Q. You were less certain?

A. Yes, sir, and less again when I found she lay with Dick. I knew not what to think, unless they both laughed at their master behind his back. Yet still I thought her she I had seen, as was proved right, sir, you shall hear what fell at the end.

Q.   You are certain his Lordship showed her no special favours, nor met apart with her, or the like?

A.   Not that I saw, sir. He would bid her good day in the morning. He used once and again to ask if she were tired or sore, upon our riding, tho' no more than a gentleman should, passing civility to his inferiors.

Q.   She never to your knowledge went privily to his chamber, where you stayed?

A.   No, sir. I cannot truly tell, seeing I was seldom upstairs except to Mr Lacy. 'Tis most landlords' rule, no manservant shall lie where the maids lie, I mean in that same part of the house.

Q.   And wisely. So be it. Now let us come to what passed at Wincanton.

A.   One in a greatcoat came up to me, there at the sign of the Greyhound, who had seen us ride in and said, What's afoot? I said, Nothing's afoot, what mean you? Come, says he with a wink, I know who your Mr Bartholomew truly is, I was coachman till two years past to Sir Henry W———, and knew him there when he came to visit. I would know him and that mute man of his in a thousand, he said. He is — who I said you just now, sir.

Q.   He spoke the name?

A.   Yes, and his noble parent's as well. I was at a stumble, sir, I knew not what to answer, but thought it best to make no argument, so winked him back and said, Perhaps it may be, but hold your tongue, he'd not be known. To which he said, Very well, have no fear, but where goes he? I says, To hunt a young partridge in the West. Ah, he says, plump and pretty, I don't doubt. Then that he had guessed as much.

Q.   Who was this man?

A.   Coachman to an admiral, sir, who went with his lady to the Bath. His name was Taylor. A well enough fellow, he meant no harm beyond his curiosity, and was no trouble to turn aside, once we were started. I said Mr Lacy to be his Lordship's tutor, and our pretext that we made a tour, though it was truly to lay a siege, and the girl Louise at hand for when the young lady was captured. Then Dick came by and Taylor would greet him, and the fool near spoilt all by making out he knew him not, and going off. I said he was frightened, Taylor was to take no offense, he must know Dick had only half his wits. Then ten minutes later down comes Louise to fetch me. Farthing, she says, your master calls. So I went with her, and outside the door she says, 'Tis not Mr Brown, but Mr Bartholomew who wants you, I know not why. So I go to him, sir, and he says, Jones, I fear my disguise is pierced. I say, Yes, my lord, I fear it is, and explained how it came about, and what I had said to Taylor. Very well, he says, howsoever Mr Lacy knows nothing of this, and 'tis best we continue so.

Q. Gave he a reason?

A. That he esteemed Mr Lacy, sir, and would not cause him concern. To which I said I was his Lordship's to command. Then say nothing, he says, and give the fellow this to drink my health and hold his tongue, and here's a half-guinea for you also. Which I took, sir, and felt myself beholden.

Q. And never spoke of this to Mr Lacy?

A. No, sir. And later, when I drank with Taylor, he told me how he had heard his Lordship's noble father was in a great rage that he had refused a party proposed to him. I began then to be afraid, sir. Better a bed of nettles than a secret shared, as the saying goes. I saw an angered parent, sir, and one such I ought not dare offend. And thought of my Bible, and what is commanded in the fifth of Moses, honour thy father.

Q. Had you never thought that before? Did you not know the general case, what his Lordship was about, before you left London?

A. I saw it in new light, sir.

Q. To wit?

A. 'Twas my duty, sir, to see if I might find out more of what his Lordship intended.

Q. In plain, that it might serve thy pocket best to serve his father?

A.   That it was prudent, sir.

Q.   You begin to cant, Jones, like all your nation. You saw a smart profit, did you not?

A.   I hoped for some reward, sir. If the gracious gentleman saw fit.

Q.   That I'll believe. From Wincanton on you were full resolved to spy upon his Lordship. Was it not so?

A.   If I might, sir. I knew not then that I would. Those two days still of travelling were not in Gladherhat for Jones.

Q.   In what?

A.   'Tis how we Welsh say of Somerset, sir, a merry place, all cider and fat cattle.

Q.   Now thou'dst grant thyself scruples. I will not have it, thou art plain rogue. Why else didst thou call upon Mr Lacy at Taunton to advance thee more of thy money — thou wert resolved, and there's an end to it.

A.   Yes, sir.

Q.   And until you came to the Black Hart, you learnt no more what his Lordship purposed?

A.   No, sir.

Q.   Tell all, from the moment you waked on the first of May.

A.   Rogue I may be, sir, but I spent a poor night of it, I knew not what it was best to do. Yet in the end I rose and went quiet below and there found an end of candle and an inkhorn and wrote what you know of to Mr Lacy.

Q.   None of what I know of — pass to where they parted upon the Bideford road.

A.   'Twas two miles' riding, sir, a place where the road became two, a three-legged cross, and there I waited hid upon a well-bushed hill, on purpose to command the place, seeing I did not know which road they should take. 'Tis where the gibbet stands, you may know it without trouble. And I waited a two hours or more, and was pleased a fine clear sunshine day promised, fool that I was.

Q.   Did none others pass?

A.   A cart with some maids in, and young men beside it, who made a great laughing and singing. They went to the maying. Then others who came on foot soon after, for the same purpose.

Q. None came riding, as it might be messengers, upon pressing business?

A. No, sir. His Lordship's party alone came for Bideford, and stopped at the forking of the road, where the gibbet stands.

Q. I know of this. You heard nothing of what was said?

A. Not a word, sir. 'Twas four hundred paces to where I lay.

Q. Proceed.

A. Well, sir, I was sorry to see Mr Lacy go by himself in such a place. Soon he fell out of sight, for his road went down the penn, while theirs went rather up. I bided till they reached the first brow, and then came I down from where I was hid to the road, and after them; to get down from my horse at the brow, to see where they were and whether I might forward or must wait. And so, sir, it may be two miles more, by which time we was entered in great woods and the road with more close turns than a shipwright's awl, that I feared me greatly to come straight upon them, I could nowhere see far ahead. And so it fell, sir. For as I came round a bank, a great rock beside the road, I saw them not one hundred and fifty paces ahead. To my fortune their backs was turned. They was stopped at where a stream that fell from higher crosses the road, which happily made a rush, sir, or their ears must tell them I was behind. Off I jump from my horse, and lead him back in a trice and tie him out of sight, to come more cautious forward than before and peep. And wist, they are gone, tho' not upon the road, for I see a glimpse of Louise's back behind Dick, that climbs above it, upon the mountain.

Q. Know you the name of this place?

A. I do not, sir. I saw no farm nor house there, nor none near. You may tell it, 'tis not the first crossing of water in the woods, yet larger, and set well back. While the stream falls sharp on the left side of the road, with much noise.

Q. Next.

A. When I judged it safe I went to where they had stopped, beside the water, and saw 'twas a ford, mayhap some six paces across, not more, for it goes on a great flat bed of stone, and the road runs on behind it. And now I saw where they had gone, for the ground above was less steep than where I had been, and went uphill more in a cwm, as we call it, among the trees. Well, sir, I could see at first no path, and must cast about, until at last I came on where a way led up into the cwm, and could see where their horses had trod.

Q. A path often used, you would say?

A. Sir, I'll swear no other horses had been upon it that many a month. Further up, as I will tell, I saw signs 'twas a shepherds' path, to gain the summer grazing upon the mountain above. Branches plashed yesteryear, their beasts' dry turds, the like.

Q. What supposed you they were at?

A. Upon some secret way to where the young lady lived, sir, or to some meeting-place they had fixed apart. I could not say, see you I knew not where the great houses and fine estates lay in that country. Misery for me I did not turn back. But Jones, I thought, hung for the lamb, hung for the ewe, as the saying goes.

Q. Where led this path?

A. To a desert place, sir, narrow and steep and strewn with stones and great rocks among the trees. It lay on a curve, as a new moon, so, and ever upwards to the mountain. 'Twas melancholy, sir, despite the shining of the sun. I marked no birds that sang, as is their nature at that time, as if all had forsook it, which made me afeared, when I was already afeared enough for what I was at, and so twice in doubt of it.

Q. When came you up with them?

A. Not for near an hour, sir. 'Twas not so far, two miles, or hardly more. I must move very slow, with many halts, to listen, I could see nothing for the thorn-trees and bushes, and thought they must be in worse case than I, and slower still, their ears a-cock for such as I, and nothing but the tumble of the linn to hide me.

Q. Come to where you saw them first.

A. It was thus, sir. I came where the cwm made a trifle more narrow, yet ran on more straight, and where could I but find a vantage-point, I might see ahead. So I tied my horse, sir, and climbed afoot a little to one side, where I could look better. At first I saw nothing, tho' I saw the cwm's end. And thought, for all seemed bare up there, how shall I come close. 'Tis bad today, 'twill be worse tomorrow, as the saying goes. And I cursed myself then that I had thought such following was as easy as pissing abed. Then saw I a man that climbed the side, a half mile ahead, and knew it was Dick. I could not see his Lordship nor the wench, and supposed them still below, with the horses, where the stream ran. He stopped upon a shoulder and looked ahead to beyond my sight, see you the cwm's end was twain and forked like a serpent's tongue, and he sought into the part that lay atwist to one side from t'other.

Q. Seemed he cautious in his manner?

A. Not that I could see, sir. He stood not long, and walked on, out of my watching.

Q. And then?

A. I thought they must be come near their journey's end, and I must ride no more, sir. That if I did they might hear or see me from their better vantage. So I took me my horse to a thicket and tied him, the best I could hide in so buddled a place. Then made my way on foot beside the stream, where they had passed. Where after some little while I spy a white thing in the green, a hundred paces or more off, as of linen laid out to dry. So stop, then creep aside to where I can watch better, and find it is Louise, dressed out.

Q. How mean you, man, what dressed out?

A. As I say, sir. As a May queen upon that day, all in white linen, cambric, ribbands, I know not, as fine as fivepence.

Q. Jones, I will not be thy fool.

A. I swear it true, your worship. I lie not now.

Q. Saw you this dress earlier that day? Upon the road to this place?

A. No, sir, I am certain she wore it not, for at the gibbet she did go behind some bushes for her needs, begging your pardon, and I saw her green and yellowy dress then, her quilt Norwich petticoat, as always before.

Q. You maintain, she had changed garments at this waiting-place, while you crept up on them?

A. She must, sir, and not put back her cloak. There was no wind, and the day grew warm. You must believe me, sir. If I told some tale, I should make it more pleasing to your worship's will.

Q. And his Lordship?

A. Stood apart, sir, by the horses, which was tied higher, and watched up where Dick had gone.

A. And what the wench?

A. She sat upon her cloak, on a stone above the stream, sir, and made a chaplet of may-flower on her lap, paring the thorns with a pocket-knife Dick carried, that had brass ends, which I made out. And how as I watched she pricked her fingers more than once, and sucked upon them. And once looked back to where his Lordship stood, as if to complain she must suffer this for him.

Q. Against her will?

A. It might be, sir. I could not tell.

A. Was this dress simple or rich? Such as a lady, or more as village maid, might wear?

A. Rather the last, sir. Though there was rose ribbands at the hem and shoulder, and white stockings. The chaplet I found less strange, for she'd pick her nosegay, wherever we stopped. I rallied her once, I said I believed her no lady's maid, but crier of flowers about the streets.

Q. What said she to that?

A. That there were worse ways to earn a penny.

Q. She did not speak with his Lordship?

A. No, sir. She made her maying crown, and looked as innocent there amidst the green as a pail of milk. Faith, she'd have slain a blind man, as 'tis said. She was killing pretty dressed so, spite of all. I had not before seen her so sweet and handsome, sir, begging your pardon.

Q. As sweet as pitch. What next?

A. It stood so for a little while, sir. At the last I heard some
stones tumble, and there was Dick upon the far side of the
stream, back down whence he came, across from where his
Lordship was, and made a sign, and one that boded ill, sir,
for 'twas the Devil's horns.

Q. Show.

A. Like this, sir.

Q. Write, with little and forefinger cocked, and the two between
bended back by the thumb. You had never seen this sign
made before?

A. They say 'tis how witches greet, sir. So we believed when I
was a young lad. Tho' we used it among ourselves in scorn
and jest, as to say, to the Devil with you. Dick made no jest,
as I must tell.

Q. Then?

A. His Lordship came to where Louise sat and she rose, and they
spoke briefly, but I could not hear. Next went she with him to
where Dick stood, who leapt in the stream and carried her in
his arms across, that she wetted not her shoes. And his Lordship crossed after, and they made their way up the hill, that
Dick had already been.

Q. Seemed his Lordship pleased when Dick returned?

A. I could not see, sir. For his face was barred by a branch. He
made no sign. But when he came to fetch Louise, and spoke
with her, I thought him more brisk.

Q. He showed some eagerness?

A. Yes, sir. The like he would hearten her to what was doing.
And I marked, lifted her cloak from the stone and would hold
it for her to put on, tho' she would not have it, whereat he
carried it over his arm, as a servant might. Which I found
strange. But so 'twas.

Q. Did she wear her crown of may?

A. Not then, sir. But carried it in her hand.

Q. On.

A. Well, sir, once more I knew not what to do, for I knew they
must return, since the horses was left, and they could not be
gone far, and my own horse below, and not well enough hid,

which they might see in passing back, and would know, and guess all.

Q.   Yes, yes. You followed?

A.   I did, sir. Two hundred paces it was steep and rude, more clitter than path, but then smoother, though still rude.

Q.   Too steep for a horse?

A.   One of our Welsh ponies might, sir, not your full horse. Then came I to where I had seen Dick stand before, though I stood not myself for fear of being seen, and found I looked upon that other part of the cwm I spoke of, that lay to one side.

Q.   In which direction?

A.   Why, to west'd or north-west, sir. Leftward as I went. And I saw there was now no further of trees, be it not for some few poor twisted thorns, but sward and bracken above, rough leaze, than ran to somewhat of a basin, as so, like a Billings-gate fish-basket, sir, flat-bottomed to its sides, which were made of bare rock on the northern part, nigh to clift.

Q.   And those you followed?

A.   Plain enough to see, sir, they were above, some three or four hundred paces off, near upon this basin I speak of, so be it I could not see its bottom nor water from where I lay. But there, sir, I have not told the most. I marked they were alone no more.

Q.   How not alone?

A.   Why, I thought at first they had met with she we knew of, that his Lordship was covetous to marry. For a woman stood somewhat above them, that now they knelt before.

Q.   Knelt, do you say?

A.   Yes, sir, 'tis sure. They did kneel all, his Lordship foremost, hat in hand, and Dick and Louise a pace or two behind, as before a queen.

A.   How appeared she, this woman?

Q.   Your worship, it was far and I could but peep, for she did look to where I lay, I cannot be exact, save she was most strange dressed, as it seemed in silver, and more as man than woman, for she wore breeches and a blouse, no more; no cloak, no coat nor mantee, nor cap nor hat neither.

Q.   Saw you no horse, no attendant?

A.   No, sir. She alone.

Q.   In what manner stood she?

A.   As one who waits, sir.

Q.   She did not speak?

A.   Not that I spied.

Q.   How far apart were they?

A.   It might be thirty, forty paces, sir.

Q.   Was she fair in appearance?

A.   I could not tell, sir. 'Twas a good four hundred paces from where I watched. Of middle height and figure, and a dark hair that hung loose, it seemed not dressed nor curled, above a white face.

Q.   Seemed it as an expectant mistress might greet her long-awaited lover?

A.   No, sir, not one smatch, and 'twas mightily strange they made no movement.

Q.   Could you make out her expression? Did she smile, look joyous, I know not?

A.   'Twas too far, your worship.

Q.   You are sure she was woman?

A.   Yes, sir, and did then suppose her dressed as she was for some disguise of escape from where she lived, and the more easy mayhap to ride a horse, tho' I could see none. Yet as I say these clothes were not as a country clown or stable-boy might wear, but shining silver, as finest paduasoy or silk.

Q.   I would know this. Shall you tell me more of this lady that you later discovered?

A.   I shall, sir, and that she had best worn darkest night than what she did. .

Q.   Very well, in right time, as you did find upon that day. What next?

A.   I could not go closer forward, sir. There was no covert. If any turned, I must be seen. I minded if I went back a little I might find some way to the cwm's top, and there come unseen to some place above where they stood by the basin. So that I did, sir, though I tore my hands and clothes in the first part, and took longer than I wanted. 'Twas more place for your squirrel, see you, than mortal being. But I came over it in the end, and found it led out upon the open mountain, as I did hope. Where I began to run, with the cwm below me, though out of their sight. And when I came to where I judged they were, I first tore a piece of herbage to shield my face where I should watch. Then crouched and crawled upon my belly, sir, and found a good place among the whortles upon the brink, where I lay as in the gallery of Drury Lane, with all spread below me, like crow in gutter, or mouse in malt-heap.

Q.   Why do you stop?

A.   To pray you will give credit, sir, to what I have now to tell. Well I might speak of a theatre, nay, no piece was ever played more fantastickal, no, not half as much.

Q.   No credit before warranty. Speak on.

A.   I should have thought myself still abed dreaming, sir, had not the sun been hot on my back and my breath expiring from my running.

Q.   Devil take thy expiring. Get on with it, man.

Q.   Well, sir, I must do my best. Upon the far side of the basin, there was a scarp of stone, as high as a house, that fell to the plain. While at its foot, which I could not see from my first vantage, there was a black-mouthed cavern. I judged it used by shepherds, sir, for a broken hurdle lay on the ground to one side and I saw a place where they had lit a great fire before the entrance, the turf burnt dark. And closer to me there stood a little pool of water, made of a trieklet scooped out and barred across with an earthen bank, by human hand. Which at its brim had a tall stone, not so tall as they at Stonage, yet high as a man, set on end, as if to mark the place.

Q.   There were no sheep?

A.   No, sir, I doubt not it is as in my homeland, such pasture not fit till May is done, besides that they will not risk their flocks thus far till the lambs are strong.

Q.   Saw you his Lordship?

A.   I must, sir, and Dick as well. They stood beside the stone, with their backs to me, and stared at the cavern, which stood a hundred paces off, so they thought to see someone come forth.

Q. How far from where you spied?

A. Two hundred paces, sir. A good musket-shot.

Q. And the maid?

A. Knelt at the pool, sir, upon her cloak at the brink, and washed her face, then dried it upon an edge of the cloak. So rested there upon her knees and stared mope-eyed into the water, with her may-crown beside her.

A. And this fourth particular, she that you saw from below, that was dressed as a man?

A. I saw her not, sir. She was gone. I supposed entered inside the cavern, to change her costume, I knew not what. His Lordship turned and walked a few paces, and then did take his watch from his fob and opened its case, and I thought, Davy, the powder has failed the match. Something is amiss, he grows impatient. Yet he began pacing on, it seemed in thought. The turf was close, sir, and flat enough there for a bowling-green. And so for near another quarter-hour, with Dick still staring where the cavern was, and Louise sat upon the grass, like three who had never met nor spoken before, and all with different purposes.

Q. To the events.

A. At the end once more his Lordship looks to his fob-watch. Then 'tis as if the hour he waited is come, for he goes to Dick and lays a hand on his shoulder, so to say, as I say, the hour has come.

Q. Which was, by your computation?

A. Perhaps a half past ten of the clock, sir, I think not more. And now his Lordship goes to Louise where she sits apart and speaks to her and she bows her head, so she would not do what his Lordship wished. I could not hear, sir, or only their voices, not what was said, they spake low. 'Twas plain she had no heart for what he wanted, for shortly he took her arm, such as he had no patience with her hanging back, and made her walk to where Dick stood. And she would take her cloak, yet he snatched it from her hand and threw it down at the foot of the stone when they stood there; then found they had left the may-crown on the grass and made a sign to Dick to fetch it, which he did, and set it on her head when he came back. Whereupon Dick takes her hand, and makes her face the cavern, like as they are some man and bride before the church rails on their wedding-day. And they begin to walk across the turf to the cavern, sir, hand in hand, with his Lordship behind, such a strange procession as you never saw, there in the sun, with no reason for it. Then from strange it grew ill, sir. For all of a sudden she half falls, turns, and is on her knees looking up at his Lordship, as if she beseeches his mercy. And I thought she wept, sir, 'twas too far, I cannot be sure. But he would not hear, and quick as a trice draws his sword and points it down at the poor girl's breast, so to say, Your life is lost if you fail me now.

Q. You wretch, this is some cock-and-bull. You concoct it as you go.

A. God's honour 'twas so, sir. Would I venture what I know you would not believe?

Q. He drew his sword upon her, you assert that?

A. On my oath.

Q. Did he speak?

A. Not that I heard, sir. Dick made her stand again, and they went on, with his Lordship behind, still sword in hand, tho' he did drop the point; after a few paces, put it up again, so he feared no more she would disobey. Then come they upon the threshold of the cavern's mouth, and the strangest yet, sir. For just before they enter his Lordship raises his hand and sets his hat down against his breast, like to they entered some great person's presence, before whom his Lordship must uncover. Sir, I am sorry, you would have me tell all. And I must.

Q. You are sure, as if he would show reverence?

A. As sure as I see you now, sir.

Q. And then?

A. They passed inside, sir. I saw them no more. Until it might be the time to count twenty, when I heard a stifled sound, a woman's scream, from within. 'Twas stifled, yet I heard it.

Q. It was the wench?

A. Yes, sir. And it went to my marrow, for I thought murder was being done. Though I know now it was not.

Q. How large was this cavern?

A. It ran low on one side. To the other, large. A great laden wain might have entered, sir, and space withal.

Q. You could see within?

A. None, sir, beyond where the sunbeams smote. 'Twas black as midnight.

A. You saw no one there, no figure or motion?

A. No, sir. You may be sure I looked hard. Nor in all the long hours I waited. All lay in the silence, what I saw had never been. But yet knew I it had, for the cloak was there by the stone.

Q. Did you not go down, to look closer?

A. I dared not, sir, I was too much afeared. I saw some wickedness in his Lordship, some searching after evil knowledge, begging your pardon. For not a half-hour after they had gone in there came two great black crows, that they call ravens, with their young, and sat on the pentice slope above the clift where the cavern lay, and made a great noise, as of joy or mockery, I know not which. I know most they betide death, and naught else good besides, and are wise beyond other birds. Or so it passed in my homeland, your worship.

Q. Never mind your nonage and its tales. Nor your long hours, for the nonce. Came his Lordship out again?

A. I do not know, sir.

Q. You must!

A. No, sir. I waited all that day, and in the end first Dick, then she did come, but he not. You must believe me, sir. The last time Jones' eyes saw his Lordship was when he went in.

Q. Then the man and the wench, speak of them — when came they out?

A. Not till that evening, sir, an hour before the setting of the sun. All of which time I waited, not knowing what to do, for the sun burnt me and I had no water to quench my thirst, nor nothing to victual my camp, neither, my breakfast no more than a stale piece of loaf, and I had not thought to bring what was left of that and the piece of cheese I kept in my saddle-bag. And my poor Welsh soul needed food the more, dear God, I should have given my right arm for a piece of wormwood or the sweet angelick to protect me there.

Q. Omit thy pains, 'tis thy lying neck needs protection now. To their coming out.

A. I will, sir, I promise, but first must I say another strangeness I did not mark at once. Which was that a small smoke rose from a place above where this cavern lay, out of the green ground, as from a lime-kiln, tho' I could see no chimbly. Like to a fire inside, which found its way out by some hole or crack within and so to the pentice above the cliff, where the ravens had sat.

Q. You saw no flames?

A. No, sir, nor little smoke, and sometimes seeming none, but then issuing again. And I must tell from time to time I smelt it too, and liked not its stench, even though I lay far off and 'twas faint in my nostrils.

Q. It was not fire of wood?

A. I doubt not for part, sir, tho' with some foul substance mixed to it. I have smelt such in a tanner's yard, like of strange salts or oils. And I will add you more, sir. From time to time there came also a sound that crept to my ears from the cavern's mouth, which was much like to a swarm of bees, now seeming close, now so faint it might be gone. Yet I saw not a honey-bee where I lay, none but bumbards, and they but few, nor flowers to suck save small poor things.

Q. It came from the cavern, you say?

A. Yes. At loudest no more than murmur, yet I heard it well.

Q. What made you of these things?

A. I made nothing then, sir. I was bewitched, see you. I would go, I could not.

Q. Why say you, then?

A. As it happened, sir. I had not spake with Louise, as you shall hear.

Q.   Very well. First I have your word, you did not once leave your hiding-place that day?

A.   Two times, sir, and not five minutes apiece, to see if I could not find some water behind and to ease my legs, for I lay so still and the ground hard. I swear no more, and all as before when I came back to my post.

Q.   Is it not true you had slept little that night previous? Did you not then sleep there?

A.   No, sir. 'Twas no down bed, I assure you.

A.   Jones, I want the truth. You shall not be blamed for this, if you gave way to nature and circumstance, and slept. I will know.

A.   I may once or twice have fallen to a waking doze, sir, as one does riding. No full sleep, upon the Book.

Q.   You know what I drive at, man. Can you deny a person might have left the cavern without your seeing him?

A.   I cannot believe so, sir.

A.   You must. You admit you went twice away. And did you not doze?

A.   Yes, sir, tho' very little. And you have not heard what Louise was to tell me.

Q.   Come to that.

A.   Sir, as I told, the shadows grew long, and began to creep across the sward, and I lay with even greater shadows on my mind, my heart misgave me some most awful thing had happened, or they within should have come out by now; and knowing I must soon go, I would not for my life have stayed in darkness in that place. I first thought to ride back to where we had slept and tell all to the justices. Yet then, sir, I thought of the disgrace to his Lordship's noble parent should this become publick noise, and how I ought to find some way to tell him privily, that he might then do as he thought fit.

A.   To the point.

A.   Why, sir, as I lay there hollow as a kex, not knowing what to do, out comes Dick of a sudden, running, his face wild, such as truly a man in a fit, with the greatest fear upon him; and after a step or two he fell to his face as upon ice, then was up at once with a look of terror backward, so he saw what I could not, and close upon him, and his mouth opened as he would cry, tho' there came no sound; and then he ran on, as if all his thought was to escape from what was within. And run he did, your worship must believe me, so fast I must almost think I dreamed, why, he was gone before he was there, and back the way they had come. And I lying above, not knowing whether I should follow, or what was to be done. He went so fast I should ne'er have caught up with him. So I thought, Davy, thou'st let the first whiting leap, no matter, there's more yet, thou must wait; and then I thought mayhap Dick has gone only to fetch the horses, and will be back, and I would not for my life leave my place, sir, and risk the meeting of him, a desperate dangerous fellow and stronger than I. So I did nothing, see you, but lay as I was.

Q. He came not back?

A. No, sir, and I saw him not again. I doubt not he ran to hang himself. I must tell your worship he had such an air upon him, I see it now again, of one in Bedlam, who knew not what he did, unless to run away until he fell; like to the hounds of Hell were close upon his heels, or worse.

Q. Come to the wench.

A. Why, sir, I do. She came not so soon, for a half-hour or more passed, and once again I knew not what to do, and the sun crept close to the cavern's entrance, which when it should reach there I had made my hour-hand and time to withdraw. Then of a sudden, she came, yet as unlike Dick as could be, for she walked slow, like one who wandered in her sleep, or was turnsick, like those once I saw come from an explosion in a powder-mill, who could at first not speak nor tell nothing from the suddenness and great horror of it. Out upon the sward, your worship, so, in a daze, why, not able to leap a straw, as if she saw nothing, were blinded. And this, sir, she wore her white dress no more. She was naked as the day she was born.

Q. Not a stitch?

A. No, sir, not even shift, nor shoes and stockings, all as Eve before the Fall; bare breasts, bare arms and legs, bare all save
where no woman is bare, her black feathers, your worship's
pardon. Then stopped she and raised her arm to her eyes, I
doubt not she was dazzled by the light, though the sun stood
low. Next turned she toward the cavern's mouth and fell
upon her knees, so to give thanks to God for her deliverance.

Q. Her hands held in prayer?

A. No, sir, with her head bowed and her arms fallen by her side.
As a punished child, who asks forgiveness.

Q. Her person showed no wounds nor unnatural marks?

A. None that I could see, sir, that could see her white back and
buttocks as she prayed. None grave, you may be sure.

Q. Seemed she in pain?

A. More like one planet-struck, sir, as I say. All her movings
were most slow, I might believe she had drunk some potion.

Q. Seemed she not in fear of pursuit?

A. No, sir, which after Dick, I thought strange. For she rose, and
seemed more returned to her wits, and walked then less dazed
to the stone by the pool; and picked up her cloak that had
lain next it all the day; and covered her nakedness, I thought
gratefully, like one who was sore cold and needed its warmth,
tho' 'twas warm enough yet, for all the hour. And there she
did kneel by the pool again, sir, and scooped up a little water
in her hands and drank some, threw some on her face likewise. That was all, sir. For then she went her barefoot way, as
Dick, by that they had come in the morning.

Q. With what haste?

A. More quickly, sir, and she threw one look aside at the cavern's mouth, so to say being more woken herself, so was her
fear. Yet not running, as in true alarm.

Q. And you?

A. I waited a minute, sir, where I was, to see if his Lordship
should follow. But he came not, and you may blame me, your
worship, a bold hero might have gone to that cavern, and entered within. I am no such, sir, nor pretend to be. I durst not.

Q. Nor pretend to be, thou bag of boasting wind, nor pretend to be? In short, the Welsh coward thou art ran off after the wench, is it so? Truly thou art worthy thy nation. Didst catch her?

A.   I did, sir, and heard all. Which will not please your worship's ears, but you'd not have me say else than she said herself, I know. So I ask your pardon in advance.

Q.   But will get none, if I catch thee out. There, Jones, thou mayst dine on that, and chew it well. If all this be false, thou art dead. Now begone, my man shall take thee below, and bring thee back.

AYSCOUGH SIPS HIS MEDICINAL PURL (ale laced with the recently mentioned prophylactic against witches and the Devil, wormwood) and Jones eats where he belongs, below, in a silence that for once in his life he welcomes — and without benefit of alcohol, which he does not. The lawyer's crudely chauvinistic contempt for his witness is offensive, but it is stock, and really has little to do with poor Jones' Welshness. Above a certain line, and despite its ridiculous respect of, and obsequiousness before, title and rank, society was comparatively fluid at this time; with a touch of luck, and some talent, quite humbly born men could rise in the world and become distinguished churchmen, learned fellows at Oxford or Cambridge like Mr Saunderson, the son of an exciseman, successful merchants, lawyers such as Ayscough (youngest son of an obscure and very far from rich north-country vicar), poets (Pope was son of a linen-draper), philosophers, many other things. However, below this line, society was seen as static. It had no hope; in the eyes of those above, its fate was fixed from day of birth.

The thing then dearest to the heart of English society did not help relax the inexorable line in the least. It manifested itself as worship, if not idolatry, of property. A conventional Englishman of the time might have said the national palladium was the Anglican Church; but the country's true religion lay only outwardly within the walls of that sluggish institution. It was far more vested in a profound respect for right of property; this united all society but the lowest, and dictated much of its behaviour, its opinions, its thinking. Dissenters might be barred from all elected and official position (which they turned to advantage by frequently becoming masters of trade and commerce); their property was as sacrosanct as any other man's. Despite doctrine, many were increasingly prepared to tolerate the Church of England, given that it protected the right — and kept the infamous enemy of the other wing, the accursed papists and Jacobites, at bay also. What the nation agreed must be preserved at all costs was really far less the theology of the established church than the right to, and security of, ownership. This obtained from the single householder to the great estates of the Whig magnates who, in odd alliance with the City, the prosperous Dissenters and the bench of bishops, largely controlled the country — or far more than its king and his ministers did. Walpole might seem to hold power; he was rather more a generally shrewd gauger of what the national mood required of him.

Property also remained, despite the growing commercial prosperity of the century, a much more favoured investment than the early stocks and companies. The South Sea Bubble of 1721 had severely damaged confidence in that latter method of multiplying money. One might suppose that this general obsession with property would have swept away, through Parliament, the abominably antiquated laws concerning ownership and acquisition of it, as in the nightmarishly complex and dilatory Chancery system (whose law defeated even the greatest contemporary experts). But not a bit of it: here love of property clashed head on with the other great credo of eighteenth-century England.

This was the belief that change leads not to progress, but to anarchy and disaster. *Non progredi est regredi* runs the adage; early Georgian man omitted the *non*. That is why most called themselves Whigs at this time, but were Tories in the modern sense, that is, reactionaries. It was why the mob was feared almost universally, by Whig and Tory, conformist and dissenter, above the line. It threatened political upset and change; worst of all, it threatened property. The measure brought in to deal with it through magistrates and militia, the Riot Act of 1715, became almost holy in its status; while English criminal law remained barbaric in its brutality, its characteristically excessive punishments for anyone who infringed the sanctity of property in another way, by minor theft. "We hang men for trifles and banish them" (to the forerunner of convict Australia, convict America) "for things not worth naming," said Defoe in 1703. The criminal law had, however, one fortuitous saving grace. Lacking even a shadow of a police force to back it, its powers of detection of crime, even of arrest, were feeble in the extreme.

The legal profession itself, safely ensconced behind its labyrinth of elaborate special knowledge (*alias* verbiage), made fat by the endless delays and opportunities to charge costs inherent in the system, held an exceptionally powerful place. The smallest slip in a formal document, from deed to indictment, could in many courts lead to its being thrown out and disallowed. Exact performance of ritual procedure has its justifications; one might value such eighteenth-century punctiliousness higher if the performance had not also always pleased the lawyers' pockets. Many of Ayscough's time became effectively property dealers and estate managers, because of this ability to handle the requisite language and their knowledge of archaic procedures; to wangle (often by corruption) the *ex parte* or otherwise flagrantly biassed judgement. They could both get their hands on property, and keep the hands of others, who might in all rational justice have a perfect right, from it.

Ayscough indeed fell into that last category, as the man of affairs of a ducal master. He was also a barrister, a very different kettle of fish from the mere attorney, a species then generally hated and despised by the layman, who quite rightly saw them as far more concerned with stuffing their green bags full of money than in getting cases settled. Ayscough's father had been vicar of Croft, a small village near Darlington in North Yorkshire, whose squire had been Sir William Chaytor, an impoverished baronet obliged to spend the last twenty years of his life (he died in 1720) within the boundaries of the famous London debtors' prison, the Fleet. Sir William's endless family letters and papers were published only last year, and they are exceptionally vivid on this matter of the law. He had had to mortgage his entailed Yorkshire estate beyond hope of redemption. In the Fleet, like so many others, he became an even worse victim of pettifogging lawyers than of the law itself, a classic case of the misery they can cause. But he won the final case. His exasperation with the profession still sears down the centuries.

Such business as this present inquiry was indeed quite outside Ayscough's normal work, the purchase of property, the granting of leases and copyholds, foreclosing on defaulters, judging new petitioners for fields and farms; supervising repairing and insuring, dealing with heriot and farleu, thraves and cripplegaps, plowbote and wainbote, hedge-scouring and whin-drawing (and a hundred other obscure *casus belli* between landlord and tenant); besides the manipulation of boroughs to ensure the outcome of their parliamentary elections as his master willed; in short, fulfilling the functions of at least six separate professions today. He would not have got where he was, if he had not been an assiduous lawyer in his age's terms, a reasonably civilized man also; and a shrewd one in Claiborne's terms . . . seeing on which side the butter lay. I quoted Defoe just now, from his famous pamphlet, *The Shortest Way with the Dissenters*. It had been written a generation before, soon after William III had died, and Anne come to the throne. The administration then was Tory, and reactionary feeling ran high in the Church of England. Defoe played a practical joke, for (though of Dissenting background himself) he pretended to write as one of these "high-fliers" and proposed a very simple solution: hang all Dissenters or banish them to America. The joke misfired, because some of the Tories took his grotesquely draconian solution literally, and declared his pamphlet excellent. Defoe had to pay by being pilloried (amid cheering crowds, who drank his health) and imprisoned in Newgate; he had badly miscalculated the sense of humour of his real enemies, the Tory extremists in Church and Parliament. One of his victims then had been young Ayscough, who at the time had had Tory views. To be fair he had found the hanging too much, but had backed the idea of ridding England of seditious conventicles and meetings by depositing them all in the convenient dustbin of America. Circumstance and career had turned him outward Whig in the years since; but the memory of Defoe's trick to draw the beetles from the woodwork did not make him smile. It still rankled.

All ancient and established professions must be founded on tacit prejudices as strong as their written statutes and codes; and by those Ayscough is imprisoned as much as any debtor in the Fleet by law. Jones is and must be made to remain below the line; his "sentence," never to change, always to remain static. His movement from a Welsh nowhere (in which he was born to die) to a great English city is already an unspoken crime; if not, under the Poor Law, a definite one. The word *mob* was not fifty years old in the language at this date; a shortened slang version of *mobile vulgus*, the common rabble. Mobility or movement meant change; and change is evil.

Jones is a liar, a man who lives from hand to mouth, by what wits he has, not least by what creeping deference he can muster when faced with such real power as Ayscough holds. Pride he has not, nor can he afford it. Yet in many ways (and not only in that millions will copy him, later in the century, in deserting country and province for city) he is the future, and Ayscough the past; and both are like most of us, still today, equal victims in the debtors' prison of History, and equally unable to leave it.

The further deposition of
David Jones, *die annoque
p'dicto.*

Q. Jones, you rest upon oath.

A. Yes, sir.

Q. Come to the wench.

A. Well, your worship, I ran back the way I had come, see you, yet not so far, for I came down the slope before the trees began, in great fear I should be noticed if —

Q. Leave thy great fears, they are thy constant state. She was passed ahead?

A. She was, sir, but soon I came up with her, just where the path grew steep and went down to the stream, where all was now in shadow. I saw she hobbled, and knew not how to step, poor thing, with her bare feet upon the sharp clitter. And tho' I did try to tread softly, upon some noise my own foot made, she heard, then turned and faced me. Yet not as one who is surprised, more one who expects such pursuit, for as I came up to her I saw her eyes were closed and that she wept. She looked white as a clout, sick as a cushion, like shotten herring, so I were death upon her heels and she knew she could not escape. Well, sir, I stopped a pace or two off and said, 'Tis only I, my girl, what ails thee? Whereat she opens her eyes of a sudden and sees me, then in a second closes them again and swoons at my feet.

Q.   You would say, she expected some other she greatly feared,
     yet finding it you, was relieved?

A.   Just so, sir. I did what I might to recover her senses, in lack of
     salts or a better. When after a little I see her eyes flutter and
     she makes a small moan as of one in pain. So I say her name
     and that I come to help her. Then she says twice, the like still
     in her swoon, The maggot, the maggot.

Q.   What maggot!

A.   You speak my very words, your worship. What maggot, says
     I, what dost speak of? Whether 'twas the sound of my voice,
     sir, or what, suddenly she opens her eyes again and sees me
     full. How came you here, Farthing, she asks. I say, It matters
     not how, I have seen things today that pass my understand-
     ing. She says, What things? I say, I have seen all that passed
     up above. To which she says nothing. Then I say, What has
     happened to Mr Bartholomew? She says, They are gone. I
     say, How gone, I have watched the cavern's mouth all day
     and none has come out save thee thyself and Dick. Again she
     says, They are gone. I say, That cannot be. And a third time
     she says, They are gone. Then all of a sudden she sits away,
     for I held her supported till then, and says, Farthing, we are
     in danger, we must go from this place. I say, In what danger?
     She says, It is witchcraft. I say, What witchcraft? She says, I
     cannot tell thee, but if we are not gone by fall of night their
     powers will be upon us. And at that, sir, she stood to her feet
     and would set off again, more quickly, as if I had awoke her
     from her previous state, and she thought only now of her
     safety. Yet hobbled at once again, then said, Help me, Far-
     thing, I prithee carry me below. So it was, sir, I bore her in
     my arms down the steep, until we came to where 'twas grass
     again, by the stream, and she might walk. You may huff at
     me now for obeying her, sir. But I looked around me there in
     that lonely, desperate place, and saw no thing else save shad-
     ows and wilderness, and the coming of night. And bethought
     me of wild Dick besides, that I knew not where he was.

Q.   What of what she first said? This maggot?

A.   It shall come, sir. It shall be told.

Q.   The three horses were there below, and the baggage?

A.   They were, sir, and she went straight to where the seam lay, for I have forgot, the packhorse stood disburthened when I first came; and found her bundle and ordinary dress; then made me look aside, until she had put them on, and her buckled shoes that she was used to wear, and her cloak again. And tho' I asked questions, would not answer the while, till she was dressed, when she came to me with her bundle, and asked, Had I no horse? I told her, Yes, below, if 'tis not witched away. At which she said, Let us be gone. But I would not have it, sir, for I took her arm and said I must know first of his Lordship, and why Dick be run out as he did.

Q.   You spake so, saying his Lordship?

A.   No, sir, your pardon. Mr Bartholomew, as we had called him. Then she said, He is gone to the Devil, Farthing. He has brought me into a great sin by force, against my will. Then, I rue the day I ever set eyes on him and his man. Now, sir, I had thought me of a stratagem to explain my presence and that might oblige her to tell more. So I said, Not so fast, Louise, I must tell thee I am here secretly upon the orders of Mr Bartholomew's father, to watch his son and report what he does; and the father is a great person in this land and Mr Bartholomew likewise a much greater than he's pretended. She did give me a little stare askant then, and looked down, so as she knew not what to answer, but in such a manner that said also, This is no novels, I know it well. And then I say, For this reason thou must tell me what he's done, or look you, it shall be the worse for thee. She says, Then thou'dst best tell his Grace his son meddles in things that common people are hung for. Thus to the word, sir, except she said full out his Grace's name. I said, So thou know'st I do not lie. To which she answered, And much else besides, more shame to thy master, and the less said of it the better. I said, Brave words, but it is I who has to speak them to his face, and thou must tell me more that I can prove them. She looks troubled, then says, So I will, but we must be gone first. I say, What of this young lady, thy old mistress? Again she looks down, then

says, There was never a such. To which I say, Come, throw
again, I am not thy fool, I did see her plain as day when first
you came this morning. To which she answers, She was not
her; then, Would she had been. So now it is Jones who must
throw again and I say, If there be no young lady, then there
be no lady's maid. To that she speaks no word, and does
shake her head sadly, so to say she does not deny. Upon that I
say, I thought I had seen thee before when we first met, tho' I
have kept it to myself. Art thou not one of Mother Claiborne's lambs? She turns from me and says, Oh dear God, or
some such. I say I must know. Then she says, Yes, I have
greatly sinned and see where my folly has brought me, I wish
I had never left my parents' hearth. I say, What are we upon
if it is not an elopement? She says, We are upon wickedness,
madness, and I beg thee, Farthing, take no more advantage
of me now and let us be gone. I will tell thee all I know, but
let us be gone first. Very well, say I, save I must know when
his Lordship comes. Not this night, she says, nor till the
world's end, for all I care. I say, Speak plain. She says, He
stays above, he will not come. Then of a sudden, Thou must
set the horses free, they'll stay close. Well, your worship, I
said, No, I cannot. Now she casts her eyes on me, as one who
would make herself believed against all appearance, and says,
I have not been kind to thee, Farthing, I know I have seemed
to spurn thee and thy friendship, but I had my reasons, I
meant thee nothing if not good, no harm, and thou must
trust me now, I beg thee. I have enough on my conscience,
she says, without these poor beasts. Still I said no, sir, and
would ask more. Whereon she goes herself and begins to untie
the tether of the packhorse, until I come to her and say, Very
well, it is done upon thy head, not mine. To which she says,
So be it. And I did set the other two beasts free, and laid their
harness with the seam.

Q. You took nothing?

A. No, sir. I swear. And all with great misgiving, for it grew
dark, I feared Dick was about and watched us, and knew not
what else to do. And a thing else, sir, it near slipped my mind,

when she had put on her clothes, beside the seam, there where she had undid her bundle, was left strewn from it a fine pink gown and petticoat, else beside. And as I come close I see a small pot spilled upon the grass, and others likewise, and a Spanish comb, it seemed forgot, and so I tell her. She says, Leave them, I want them not. And I say, picking it up, What, a fine comb like this. And she says, Leave it, leave it, it is vanity. Well, sir, what's disowned may be owned, as the saying is; so I turned my back and slipped the comb in my shirt, and would have it still, needs I not to sell it in Swansea. And took five shillings and sixpence for it. She'd have none of it, I count that no theft.

Q. As I count thee an honest man. Next.

A. We walked to where I had left my horse, which I found secure, thank the Lord; and she mounted and I led her down toward the road, sir.

Q. Did you not press her to say more?

A. I did, sir, and more than once, you may be sure. Still she would not speak to any purpose, but again said she would speak all, once we were from that place. So I kept my counsel, sir, until we come close above the road. There I stop and turn and say I would know where we should go once below on the road. For see you I had bethought myself as we went, and saw I must persuade her to my purpose, which was that I should bring her to his Lordship's father. She answers, I must to Bristol as soon as I can. Why Bristol, say I; and she, Because my parents dwell there. Do they know what thou art, say I next. And she would not answer, 'cept she must see them. Then I said, I must know thy true name, and where thou be found there. And she says, Rebecca Hocknell, though some call me Fanny, and my father is Amos, he is joiner and carpenter, thou mayst find him at Mill Court near the sign of the Three Tuns in Queen Street, in St Mary Redcliff parish. I will tell you now, sir, I writ her so, this last June when I heard of Dick as I told, and have had no answer yet. 'Tis not sure, though I did believe her then.

Q. Very well. What followed?

A.   Why, just then as we spake we heard singing, sir, of some who came late home from the maying through the woods, I dare say six or seven, men and women, and more bawling than singing, for they had drank their fill. So we fell silent as they came, and took comfort to be among ordinary mortals, despite their cups and noise, after that place above.

Q.   It was not yet dark?

A.   Near, sir, the mogshade full upon us. The wooden shoes passed below, and on. Then of a sudden I heard Rebecca, so I will call her now, exclaim, I can no more, I must, I must; and before I may speak she is dismounted and runs off a little way, where she falls upon her knees, as if to give thanks once more for being delivered. Soon I hear she is weeping. So I tie the bridle to a bough, and go to her, and find her in a strange shaking, as she were in a great cold or fever, tho' the night was mild. And at each shaking she moans, oh, oh, oh, as if in pain. I take her shoulder, but 'twas like my hand scalded her, she twitches away, thus, sir, yet no other notice, nor spoke. Then of another sudden she falls in a seeming fit flat upon her face with her arms stretched out upon the ground, and there is more shaking and moaning. I will tell you, sir, Jones was as fearful then as of all else before. I thought they she spake so darkly of now played hot cockles with her soul; tormented her for her sins and took possession of her body. Dear God, her sobs and sighs was like one in hellfire. I have heard such from a woman's throat when brought to bed, as she labours, sir, if your worship will pardon. So 'twas, I swear. I drew back till the fit was finished and then she lay still a minute or more, though I heard her yet sob again and a while. At last I went close where she lay and asked, was she ill? Whereat, after a little pause, like one who speaks in sleep, she says, Never so well in all my life. Then, Christ is returned within me. I say, I thought thee possessed. And she: Yes, so I was, but as I should be, by Him alone, and have no fear; now I am saved. Next she sat and bowed her face upon her knees, yet soon looked up and said, I am famished with hunger, have you no bait? So I said, What's left of a penny brick and a morsel of cheese; and she replies, That will suffice. Which I fetched, sir, and brought to her, and she stood to take it from my hands, then went to sit in more ease upon a fallen tree that lay close by; and began to eat, but stopped, and asked if I was hungry too. I said I was, no matter, I had starved before. No, I won't have that, said she, thou hast comforted me in my hour of need, let us share. So I sat beside her and she brake me a piece of bread and the cheese, tho' no more than two or three mouthfuls each. And then I asked what she meant, that she was saved. She said, Why, the Lord is within me, and I pray it shall be as well with thee, Farthing. He will not forsake us now, and we may be forgiven what we have done and seen. Which I found strange words in a strumpet, sir, but said I hoped it so. And she replied, I was brought up a Friend, I have lost the light and all else these last five years; now the Lord has rekindled it in His mercy.

Q.   And believed you her cant, all this quaking and shaking?

A.   I must, sir. It seemed no pretence. No actress, no, none I have seen, could play it so well.

Q.   Ill. But proceed.

A.   Then said I 'twas very well speaking so, and of being saved and forgiven, still I must know what his Lordship had been about in that place, and where Dick could be gone. To which she answers, Why didst lie to me, Farthing? What lie, I say. She says, That his Lordship's father has set thee upon this. No lie, say I. Yes, she says, for else thou'dst have known for certain who I am, and not needed to put thy questions. Well, sir, I was caught, though I tried my best, but she would not have it, for she took my hand and pressed it, so to tell me I wasted my breath. Then said, Art thou afraid? Be no more afraid. Then, We are friends now, Farthing, and friends and lies don't walk together. I thought then to change my tack, since the first one brought me upon the rocks, and said, Very well, even so it can be truth if we wish, and we should together make it such; for it might bring us great reward at his Grace's hands, as well she knew. To which she said, Death is more like, I know the great of this world better than thee.

They would rather do murder than let live those who can bring scandal on their name. And scandal I have, such as they would never bear, nor believe belike even it were told. For who would take my word, or thine?

Q. She cozened thee, man; made thee play cony to a cunning whore.

A. She was much changed, sir. She had not spoke so kind before.

Q. Kind when she called you liar to your face? Why did you not answer your Christian duty lay in apprising his Grace?

A. I thought it best to let bide my plan, sir. For she seemed fixed, she said she had promised in her prayings she'd straight to her parents, she did know they lived; and I would have her speak of other things. So we came to what we should do that night. I was for riding with her behind me for Bristol, as she wanted. To which she said she feared to go back upon our road, it was best we went on for Bideford, and take ship.

Q. She gave no reason?

A. Yes, that she had given me credit at first for being his Grace's spy, for his Lordship had told her that such there were, who dogged his steps. And they might now be on our heels, and she should be recognised for certain if we met. And I thought then, sir, it made no odds. If she could take ship, so might I, and still come to Bristol together. And so 'twas, your worship, that we did make for Bideford.

Q. Come to her tale, upon the road.

A. Well, sir, I will tell all, tho' not as it came, for it came not all at once, but some upon the road that night and some when we were at Bideford, where we lodged two days, as I will tell. To begin she told me she first had met his Lordship at Claiborne's a month before, where he was brought by another lord who much frequented the place; and she said little better than pandar to it, sir, for all his rank. That she took his Lordship to her chamber for his pleasure, yet once there he'd have none of her, tho' he seemed forward enough in desire of her when in company below. That he placed five guineas upon her table and said he hoped it would buy her silence in what he had to propose. Which was that there was a great fault in his nature and alas he could not enjoy what she was hired to provide him with, for which he hoped she would the more pity than mock him. Notwithstanding which, he knew not how, it did afford him some pleasure to see the venereous act performed; that he had a willing manservant; and that if she could oblige him in so unnatural a thing he would see her 'ceeding well recompensed for it. He durst not for his fair name let wind of his disadvantage come to his friend's or Mother Claiborne's ears, nor for that reason risk to effect his desire in the house where they were. But to prevent that, if she agreed, he would first come to visit her there as a normal man might; then, having won her mistress's confidence, would propose to hire her out on some other pretext, when what he wished could take place. That he promised she should find the servant a lusty, handsome young fellow and perhaps more to her taste than many others she must take to her arms.

Q. I am to understand, that his Lordship never went to her bed?
A. So she said, sir. And how as on his next visit his Lordship pointed from her window down in the street, and showed her Dick there, who seemed as he said to her. And so, to be short, she consented, for she told me she then took some pity for his Lordship, who spoke to her with more courtesy and consideration than she was commonly used. On that or another visit she said he spoke of the unjust curse upon him and the embroils he was placed in by it, and in particular by his father, who was much vexed by his seeming disobedience as to a certain marriage and threatened him to stop him of his inheritance and I know not what else. And then he confessed that this he proposed was counselled him by a learned doctor in London, who claimed to have cured others in his Lordship's case by this method.

Q. He had not tried it before, as he first pretended?
A. 'Tis as Rebecca believed, sir.
Q. Had she known such cases, or had such requests, before?
A. She did not say, sir. But I have heard talk of such, with the debosht, sir, begging your worship's pardon. Such as old

men, who have lost their natural vigours. I forget, she said he told also he had tried more decent remedies, such as be found at the apothecary's, yet all to no avail.

Q. Come to the journey west — what told he concerning that?

A. That he would carry her upon a tour he proposed to make there, for he had heard of new waters, recent found, and reputed excellent for his failing, which he would also take, and thus try the both cures at once. That he would not have his father's spies upon his heels, watching all he did, so some pretext must be found.

Q. That of the elopement and the lady's maid?

A. Yes, sir.

Q. Did she speak of a party of pleasure, with other rakes?

A. No, sir.

Q. No matter. How did his Lordship account to her for your part in all this?

A. Well you may ask, sir. For I did myself, as we walked. And she said she was told we came as added colour to the pretext, and Mr Lacy as companion also to his Lordship. That she was to hold her distance, not question us, nor let herself be questioned.

Q. How came she to where you first met, by Staines?

A. I did not think to ask, sir. I don't doubt his Lordship had her in hiding, for she said she had done his wish with Dick, and he gave her money and thanked her, when 'twas done. Yet once we were set out, she found his Lordship soon altered, his former courtesy had been but a mask upon his real face. She must do as he wished before him that next night also. After which he seemed far less pleased, and upbraided her for showing so little of her bagnio arts, or what you may call 'em, sir; and how he would not hear blame for Dick's part in it, which came from a quickness in his passion that she could not prevent.

Q. We speak of the night at Basingstoke?

A. Yes, sir.

Q. What said she of Dick?

A. That the fellow seemed blind to his master's needs, so she were for himself to enjoy as he pleased. That he seemed not to know what she truly was, to believe she loved him because he had this use of her, tho' in such wicked circumstance.

Q.   She but feigned to show some favour for him, then?

A.   She said she felt some pity for him, sir, she could see his passion for her was real. That he knew no better, and having only half his wits, had no blame in that. She told me he came to her in the night, after his Lordship had dismissed them, to lie with her again. Which out of fear she had allowed.

Q.   You asked of what happened at Amesbury, when they rode out in the night?

A.   I did, sir, and 'tis such a tale you will not believe.

Q.   That may well be, but out with it.

A.   How upon our arrival, his Lordship called her apart to his room and said he was sorry for venting his impatience the previous night, she must not take it amiss that he had placed too great expectations upon being roused. Then that close by Amesbury there lay a place said to have special powers to restore such as he, and that night he would try it, and she must come with him. She must not be afraid, it was but a crotchet of his, he would prove superstition. He swore she would come to no harm, whatever befell.

Q.   He said this, he would prove superstition?

A.   Her very words, sir. And she told me, tho' his manner was kind again, she was much alarmed, for she felt some madness in his Lordship, some bias of the mind, and wished she had never come. Yet he made her further assurances, and promised reward, until she agreed.

Q.   In all this so far, seemed she truthful?

A.   As I could tell, sir. 'Twas dark, I could not see her face. She did seem to speak as one who would relieve her conscience, in plain sincerity, for all the sinfulness of what she had done.

Q.   On.

A.   Well, sir, they rode out, as I saw and told Mr Lacy, and to the heathen temple there on the hill, that they call Stonage. Where his Lordship had commanded Dick with their two horses apart, outside the place, then led her to its centre, where he pointed to a great stone that lay imbedded flat beside others that still stood and told her to lie upon it, for such was the superstition, or so he said, that a woman taken there might help a man regain his vigours. At first she would not, she was too afraid. Whereat she said he grew angry again and began cruelly to abuse her. At the end the poor woman must do as he bade, to still him, though she said she was froze with terror. So, sir, she lies on her back upon the stone as upon a bed.

Q. In her nakedness?

A. No, sir. But his Lordship said she should raise her petticoats and bare her merkin, begging your pardon, and place herself in the posture of love. Which she did, thinking his Lordship would now essay his prowess upon her, in this supposed auspicious place. Yet he did nothing, save to stand a little aside, between two great standing stones, the like to watch. Which she put down to a timidity in him, some fear he would still be disappointed in his hopes. And after a while she spake, saying, would he not try, she grew cold. He bade her hold her tongue, and lie still; and ever stood where he was, ten paces off. She knew not what time passed, yet it was many minutes, and she grew sore cold and discomforted upon her hard couch. That then there was all of a sudden a great rush or hurtle close in the night above, as of some great falcon that passed. And as a flash of lightning, so be it no thunderclap warned of its coming; and tho' but in this great flash, she did see a figure that stood above her on a stone pillar as a statue might, next above where she lay, that seemed of a great and dark-cloaked blackamoor, which did gaze most greedily down upon her, like he was that falcon whose wings she heard, his cloak still aflutter from his falling, and so he would in an instant spring down further upon her, as a bird upon its prey. Sir, she did say this most gashly and terrible vision was come and gone so quick she could not be sure it lay not in her imaginings; yet must she now believe it was no imagining, for what had happened after in the cavern, that very day we spake. And she said furthermore how, a moment or two after the lightning, there came a strange gust of air upon her, as from a furnace, yet one not near, that tho' it did not burn her skin, never the less did carry a most rank and foul stench as of roasted carrion upon it; which did by some mercy pass as quick as the other. And that then all was dark and cold as before.

Q. This figure did not pounce upon her? She felt nothing, no touch upon her, beside the warm air?

A. No, sir. I did ask, and she said not. She'd have said, if she had, for she feared as much again as she told me, she could not forget it.

Q. Who thought she this figure was, this buzzard blackamoor?

A. The King of Hell, sir, the Prince of Darkness.

Q. Satan himself, the Devil?

A. Yes, sir.

Q. Saw she horns, his tail?

A. No, sir, and said she was so beshocked by her alarm, she was not in her normal senses; and likewise all passed so swift, in two snaps of her fingers, so she put it, she had no time to think nor mark. And did most know this was he that she said, from what happened later; that I shall come to, your worship.

Q. What followed, there at the temple?

A. As strange again, though less supernatural, sir. For she said she lay in a swoon, she knows not how long, but woke to find his Lordship kneeling beside her, who took her hand, then made her rise and supported her, and of a sudden embraced her as she might be a sister or a wife, so she put it, and said, Thou art a brave girl, I am well content with thee. To which she said she was sore afeared, sir, as who would not be; and asks his Lordship what passed above. To which he says, Nothing, it can't harm thee. Then that they must go. Which they did, sir, she said he took her arm to help her and said again she had done most well; and how now he knew he had chosen one fit to his end.

Q. Where was Dick in all this?

A. I come to it, sir. They came on him there where he had been commanded to wait. And as with her, she saw his Lordship step forward and embrace him, and in no mere form, see you as one who gives heartfelt thanks to an equal, not as common master to man.

Q. Were signs made between them?

A. Not that she said, sir. She and Dick came back to the inn alone, for his Lordship stayed there beside the temple, and she knew not when he returned. When she and Dick crept back to their chambers, he would come and lie with her, so be it this time she would not have it. He did not force it upon her as at Basingstoke, she said, as if he knew she had been upon great fatigue and trial, and so left her. There, sir. I have told all exact, not one matter omitted.

Q. Did she make no other explanation of what had passed? Did you not press her?

A. That she was sure now his Lordship was bent on some great wickedness, and much afraid of what further might lie ahead. As she was now proven right to be, on that day we spoke.

Q. We will come to that. She spoke of nothing else of moment, before you came to the Black Hart?

A. No, sir, not till the eve of that day we were at. When she said his Lordship again spoke apart with her in his chamber, and behaved as without reason as ever before, first to revile her for some insolence that lay in his fancy, for she was sure she had given none in the flesh; then of her being so great a whore, she was certain for Hell, I know not what else. Which she said he spake in terms and language more like to one of her past Quaker ranters or an Anabaptist than a gentleman, like he would now see her punished for doing his very own command. And she said 'twas as if he was not one man, but two, when she looked back on all her dealings with him; that when she went to her bed, she wept for it, that he should be so cruel for so little seeming cause. And I asked her, What of his praise of thee at the temple? And she said, 'Tis ever so with those of rank, they be weathercocks, all turns with the wind of their fancy.

Q. Spoke the wench much in this vein — of disrespect for her betters?

A.   I fear she did, sir. I will come to it.

Q.   You shall. I ask this now. She did know, did she not, that something most wicked and terrible was afoot? She had known it since the night at the temple, three days before. Now why made she no attempt to escape, to seek the advice and protection of Mr Lacy, whatever else? Why went she for three whole days, as she were a lamb of a more innocent kind, to slaughter?

A.   Your worship, she did say she believed that Mr Lacy and I were a part of what went on, and of no avail. That she had thought, at Wincanton and Taunton both, of running into the night, she knew not where; but found herself so desperate alone in the world and, so she said, damned beyond hope of succour, that she found not the courage.

Q.   You believed this?

A.   That she was frightened out of normal wits, yes, sir, I did. One is no army, as the saying goes; and least of all when womanly weak.

Q.   Did his Lordship say whatever to her on the eve, at the Black Hart, of what should pass that coming day?

A.   No, sir. She thought it strange I was gone, when they set off, and she asked Mr Lacy, but he said only I was rid ahead. And so stranger still, when it came to the parting with Mr Lacy at the gibbet, of which she had no warning; and began greatly to apprehend, to find herself alone with her tormentors, for his Lordship rode ahead, and would not speak. Until they came to the ford by the cwm, where I watched them; and there at last she ventured to speak, and his Lordship said, We are come to where my waters spring; and that she too was to taste of them.

Q.   These are the waters of which he told her in London, that were reputed good for his case?

A.   Yes, sir.

Q.   Had you heard speak of them on your journey to Devon? Had Mr Lacy spoke of them?

A.   No, sir. Not one word.

Q.   Nor nothing said of them in that inn?

A.   Neither, sir. You will hear. His Lordship did speak in black jest. There be no waters.

Q.   Proceed.

A.   So, sir, she dared not ask more, for his Lordship and Dick seemed willed to one purpose, and she like mere baggage they carried with them to it, as they went in the cwm to where I found them, with Dick gone off. Where at the first, before I came up with them, she said his Lordship had had Dick unstrap the box and set it on the ground, and then opened it, and there laid on top was the May dress, new smicket and petticoat, and fair new stockings, the which she had never seen to this hour; and he commanded she put off what she wore, and wear this instead. And she would know why, 'tho in greater and greater fear at this further madness. But he would only say 'twas to please the keepers of the well. So she said, sir, and could make nothing of it, yet knew she must obey.

Q.   Keepers, you say?

A.   Yes, sir. It shall come what was meant, you will see. Then they went, as I told. And she said twice upon the way she asked what they did, and how his Lordship knew she had not bargained for this; and twice his Lordship told her once more to hold her tongue. And so they passed to where I first saw 'em, sir, as they waited upon their knees.

Q.   Before the woman in silver?

A.   Yes, sir. Which she said did stand of a sudden before them, as 'twere from magic, some fifty paces off; and that did seem of evil omen and baneful prodigy, most unnatural, not only in her manner of appearing, sir, in that wild place, but by her aspect also. That no sooner did she stand there, than his Lordship knelt and uncovered his head, and Dick also, and Rebecca must do as they. She said, 'twas as if they had met some great lady, a queen, sir. Tho' in all else she looked no earthly queen, no, most cruel and malevolent, that would do them untold harm if she were not obeyed in all. At first she did naught save stare down upon them, her hair was black and wild, her eyes blacker still. That she might have made some claim to beauty, did not something in her look stink of malice and evil, for at the end of a sudden she did smile upon them, yet was that smile, said Rebecca, a thousand times worse than her staring, 'twas as spider might smile upon a fly fallen in its web, see you, that licks its chops before a tidbit.

Q. How old was she?

A. Young, sir, of Rebecca's own age, though different in all else. So she said.

Q. She did not speak?

A. No, sir, stood there in silence, yet 'twas part as so they were expected. Which notion she took also from that neither his Lordship nor Dick did seem set aback at this most sinister spirit, more it were familiar.

Q. These clothes of silver — what of them?

A. None such as common woman had ever worn, not even such she had seen in masque and pantomime or the like of London; that she might, had she seen them in circumstance less awful, have mocked them for their shape and fashion, 'twas so fantastickal and unseemly.

Q. How did this encounter end?

A. Why, as it began, sir. Of a sudden she was not there, but disappeared into thin air.

Q. Had she so lost her tongue she did not ask his Lordship of whom this evil vision was?

A. I forget, sir. In truth she did and told me he answered, She thou art here to please, among others. And she would know more, but was told to ask no more, that soon she would see.

Q. What said his Lordship to her when she would not go into the cavern? You said they did speak.

A. More upbraidings, that she was sullen and rebellious and he would not stand for it from a whore already bought. And then when they came near the cavern, and she could no more, and turned to beg his mercy on her knees, and he drew, she said he said, Damn thee, my life's ambition lies inside that place, and I'll kill thee before I'm thwarted of it.

And she said his hand trembled like one in a fever, or crazed, sir, and she verily believed he'd have done as he said, had she not obeyed.

Q. He gave no hint of why she was so necessary to the fulfilment of this ambition?

A. Not one, sir. It shall come. Do I tell your worship now what lay within?

Q. Thou shalt, and all.

A. At first she could see nothing, all seemed black as night, sir. Still she must go forward, since she was pulled by Dick, until she made out a light upon a further wall, as of a fire, and smelt the burning of it. Then they came to a corner, for see you the cavern is shaped as the leg of a dog, a greater part opened where it bent back somewhat. And there, sir, she said, was opened such a scene as turned her poor mortal blood to ice.

Q. Why stop you, man?

A. Sir, you will not credit me.

Q. I'll credit thee the greatest flogging of your life, if thou dost not make haste.

A. And I fear the same when you hear, sir. But so I must. I tell as told, sir, I pray your worship remember that. There in the great inner chamber of the cavern she saw a fire and by it two hideous old women and a younger, who she knew at once for witches, for they stared most balefully, yet in seeming expectation, as if they awaited this. And how one was she they had met in their coming, the younger, tho' now was she garbed all in black, and did hold a bellows in her hand; and how another did sit with a great black cat and a raven at her sides, her familiars; while the other that was third span thread upon a wheel. And how behind these three stood one dressed in a dark cloak and masked, as it might be a hangman, sir, she said, but that the mask covered not his mouth, where he seemed as dark and his lips full-fleshed as a blackamoor's. And tho' she had seen but in a glimpse before, she knew upon the instant who he was and what dreadful plight she was now in. Satan, sir, plain as I see you, Bezzle Bob as the common say. And cried out loud in her horror, which I heard, as I told. She would run off, did Dick and his Lordship not hold her so tight; and make her go forward toward the fire. Where they stopped, and his Lordship spoke in a tongue she could not follow, it seemed with great respect, as one might speak to a great lord or king. Tho' Satan said not a word, yet seemed to stare upon her with eyes as red as fire behind his mask. And again she would escape, and could not, for Dick and his Lordship stood as ones tranced, yet did not loose their hold upon her. And she said she began to say the Lord's Prayer beneath her breath, but finished it not, for the youngest hag pointed a finger of accusation to her, to say she knew what Rebecca did, tho' 'twas without speaking. And how next the two older witches came to her and began to pinch and feel her as she were a trussed fowl, 'spite she began to weep and did beg for mercy. And she said they who held her had been pillars of flint for all they seemed to hear, holding her still for the hags to feel her, like they were hodmandod cannibals as well as witches. That did smell most vile, rank as goats. And the more she cried, the more the hags cackled and felt her body. The while of which, Satan came closer from where he stood, the better to view this sport.

Q. Stop. Now think, Jones, and tell me this. She was formal, this was Satan in person? That is, not one for some purpose dressed to impose upon her. Not some tricked-up semblance?

A. Sir, I asked her later that very question, and more than once. But she would not have it. As sure she was 'twas him in the flesh, as the horse we rode was horse. Her very words, sir.

Q. Very well. I will tell you now, this is beyond my belief, Jones. The strumpet was lying in her teeth.

A. Sir, it may be. I know not now what to believe, save I am certain that some most strange thing happened. She was much changed, sir. No more the Rebecca of old, see you.

Q. Proceed.

A. Next, sir, I blush to tell, but must. For she was forced back upon the ground, while the two hags went to their master and served as his tire-maids, until he stood naked, proud in his demon's lust and would come down upon her, tho' she still wept and cried, for she thought this her Day of Judgement, punishment upon her for all her past sins at Mother Claiborne's. So she said, sir, as he stood above her, black as Ham, to have his will. Of what happened next she could not tell, sir, for she said she swooned, and knew not how long she lay in her swoon, but that when she woke she found herself lying on one side, she must supposed dragged or carried there, and felt a great pain in her privities, as if her swooning had not spared her and some rude forcing had taken place. Then that she peeped open her eyes and saw what she could scarce believe, sir, for the young hag and his Lordship stood naked before the Devil like man and bride, and he married them, or made out to do so in blasphemous mock, sir, and blessed them in evil jest, gave them his nether parts to kiss, which they did; and that this black wedding, 'twas no sooner done in such wicked form than done in the flesh, and all about the fire fell likewise to practising lecherous abominations among themselves, as 'tis said witches do in their covens.

Q. Do you say, his Lordship also?

A. Yes, sir, the Devil and his handmaids, Dick and his master. All. And you must forgive me, sir, his Lordship was cured of his previous state and seemed most eager in the lewdness, to vie with the Devil himself. So she said; and how she had seen somewhat in this guise at Claiborne's, yet none like this. Why, even the raven stood upon the cat, as though to cover her.

Q. Now I ask this, but first I make warning. What is said here between us thou shalt not repeat. Shouldst thou speak and I hear, it is thy doom soon after. Is that most clear?

A. Most clear, sir. I swear I shall not.

Q. And had better not, Jones, or by Heavens thou art dead. This is my question. Said she that among these lecherous abominations that she saw there was one practised between his Lordship and his man alone?

A.   Sir, save the black wedding she did not tell what she saw, no more than that it took place.

Q.   She spake not of such a vile act in the particular?

A.   No, sir.

Q.   Saw you no sign, it matters not when or where upon your journey, of such an unnatural relationship between his Lord-ship and Dick?

A.   No, sir, upon my life.

Q.   You are certain, Jones?

A.   Certain, sir.

Q.   Very well. Now tell on as she told.

A.   That in some interval in these foul diversions one of the hags came and shook her by the shoulder where she lay, as if to see whether she waked yet. Rebecca made pretence of being still swooned. Whereupon the hag went off and fetched some po-tion and forced her to take some in her mouth. 'Twas nau-seous and bitter, said Rebecca, as of aloes or venomed toadstools. Its effect drowsing, for soon she fell asleep; yet she had no relief in it, as your worship might think, for she had a dream that seemed not a dream, so real it seemed, and like waking. In it she walked down a passage-hall, or gallery, as in some noble house, that was hung with great tapestries as far as she could see. And the Devil beside her, in a black suit, who now treated her with a seeming courtesy, so a gentleman might show a lady his estate and its possessions, tho' he said nothing. So be it when she chanced to look more closely on his face, it was not he she had seen in the cavern, no, more like his Lordship's, tho' swart of skin; yet somehow she knew they were both the one, despite this strangeness.

Q.   They spake no word?

A.   No, for she said in that it seemed truly as in a dream. That while they walked he would touch her arm and show her this of that of the hangings, as he might point to a picture by some great master of the brush or pencil, sir. And I forget, she said all was in a poor light, sometimes shadowed and hard to discern, yet even that light seemed most diabolick, for there

were no windows, no lustres, no flambeaux, no, not even the
smallest candle. And moreover, as they walked this dark gallery, she saw these hangings lay not still. They moved, they
swole and fell, as if touched by some wind or air behind
them. Yet she felt none upon her face.

Q. What showed they, these hangings?

A. Why, sir, she said all kind of most monstrous horror and cruelty of man against man, such as waking she could not have
borne to see but did seem now obliged to study. For Satan
had only to point, and willy-nilly her gaze must follow. And
the more horror still because the figures and nature therein
stood not fixed, as in your true pictured hanging, yet moving
as in life, tho' silent. And so lifelike, said she, there appeared
no stitches nor threads, why, the very scene they would represent seemed acted again, as on a stage for one who stood close
by in the pit. And yet she must look at all, as commanded,
like as she had no lids to close her eyes against such inhuman
cruelty. How there was death in all, sir. And the Devil himself in all, sometimes taking a main part, the bespeaker, at
others standing aloof, with a malignant smile, so to say, My
work is done for me, see what good helpers I have in this
world. And as she looked the furthest scenes would seem of a
sudden brought close. How one moment she might view as if
from a hill a city below being pillaged by soldiers, and the
next as from ten paces poor innocent children being put to
the sword or their mother ravished before their eyes. A torture chamber, through a window; then stood she above the
victim's face in his agony. So, sir. You must believe me.

Q. And how did this dream end?

A. She felt a great thirst, or so she put it, sir, she did mean it in
her soul, a need for our Redeemer Christ. And began to look
in these hangings for some sign of Him, a cross, a crucifix, yet
could find none; till at last they came to a place where this
Devil's gallery seemed to end, for she saw a wall that closed it
and upon it a hanging that seemed to shine with a greater
light, though she could not yet make out what it showed.
Some little hope began to spring in her breast that Christ lay

there, as we all hope at the end of our travails in this world. And she would hasten to it, but still was made to stop and unwillingly to look where she had already seen more than enough. Then, sir, she could bear it no more, and broke away and raised her petticoats and ran to where she thought her thirst should be quenched. 'Twas the greatest deceiving of all, sir. For as she came close she saw it was no Christ portrayed, 'twas a barefoot beggar-girl in rags, who wept like Rebecca herself and seemed to raise her arms towards her as a child to its mother. And behind, sir, she said all was fire, endless fire under an endless night, as far as she could see, and whence came this greater light; and tho' 'twas in her seeing, she could feel no heat herself, yet could see the little beggar-girl that reached to her did so feel it, and most terribly, and was stricken with pity and sorrow for her. And would reach to save her, sir, but could not, however much she tried, for she said when it seemed they might touch 'twas as if a pane of glass lay between them, tho' none to be seen. And I must not forget, she said as she told it me, sir, there came to her as she tried in vain to touch and save the child a belief she had known her before, that they had once lain close in love and affection, as sisters might; albeit now, upon reflection, she said she believed it her own self, as she was before her coming to London; how for some reason, perhaps the child's clothes (tho' she had been poor, sir, she was never a beggar) she did not in her dream know herself.

Q.   Conclude.

A.   I am near, sir. And must offend belief again, sir.

Q.   Offend. Thou hast me well used by now.

A.   How the flames gained upon the beggar-girl, and she burnt not as flesh does, but more as wax will, or fat too nigh a fire. For her features seemed to melt, sir, if you may picture it, and to drip down and fall, and drain to a pool of grease, which only then the flames did eat and made a blackened smoke thereof, that was all that was left. This passed sooner than I can speak it, sir, she said, as happens in dreams before sleeping eyes. And now she felt a great despair and rage, for this burning of the beggar-girl seemed to her the most cruel and unjust of all she had seen. And thus she turned to face Satan, who she took must be behind. She knew not what to do, yet must let him see her anger at the least. Now, as she told, she stopped. And I asked, Was he not there? And she said, He was not there. On which she was silent a moment, then added, Thou must not mock me. I said I should not. Next she said, All that had been there as I came was gone. For I seemed to stand upon a Bristol quay, one I once knew well. And on it stood my parents, who watched me sadly, to say they too knew who was the beggar-girl lost in hellfire. Beside them stood another, a carpenter by his apron, like my father, tho' younger and most sweet of face. And I began to weep again, for I had known him well, too, when I was younger. Dost understand? I said, You would say Our Lord? And she said Yea, though in an evil dream, and though not a word was spoke; but yea, a thousand times yea, Our Lord Jesus Christ. Well, sir, I knew not what to say, so I said, And how looked He at thee? And she said, As I had looked at the little beggar-girl, Farthing. But yet there stood no ice-cold pane between us, and I knew I might still be saved. There, sir. I have told all I can save her very voice and the circumstance.

Q. And is this the gloss she put upon such a farrago? She is brought to sainthood by hobnobbing and coupling with Lucifer himself? Why, man, you should have pitched her off your horse into the nearest ditch. He deserves to be hanged who would believe a word of this; or boiled in wax himself.

A. It seemed best policy to believe her then, sir. That lay behind.

Q. To her waking.

A. Yes, sir. For she said in her dream she would fain run on her Bristol quay to fall to her knees before the Lord and her parents, but waked before it could take place; and found herself as before, in the cavern, to her great relief alone, though naked and bitter cold. For now the fire was embers, and all the others vanished. And so she left, sir, as I have told before.

Q. And how did these others vanish, did she suppose? Upon a broomstick?

A.   Sir, I asked the same, saying they had not left, or only Dick, to my eyes. She could tell no better than I.

Q.   Saw she no passage or way farther into this cavern than she went herself?

A.   No, sir, yet said there must be, or they might have turned themselves to other creatures I had not marked, thinking them natural, such as the ravens I spake of.

Q.   Old women may credit that. Not I.

A.   No, sir. Then the cavern must have its inner parts. And it may be it ran under its hill and out upon another side.

Q.   Seemed the land apt to provide it?

A.   It may be, sir. I could not know how it lay, see you, there behind the clift.

Q.   This smoke you saw — was there not an issue above?

A.   Why, yes, sir, plainly. I doubt such a one five persons might have passed from, without my seeing.

Q.   This humming you spake of also — enquired you concerning that?

A.   I did, sir. And Rebecca said it came from the great spinning wheel I spake of, that one of the hags had beside her, that circled more swift than eye could follow, at her smallest touch.

Q.   What, in a close cavern, and you two or three hundred paces off? 'Tis not to be believed.

A.   No, sir.

Q.   You are certain she intended you to believe that Satan had lain with her? Seemed she in pain as she rode?

A.   No, sir.

A.   Showed she no great abhorrence or horror, in thinking that she must have his seed in her womb? I do not mean at the telling, Jones; but after. Did she not speak of it again?

A.   No, sir, but much of the great mercy of her escape, and finding Christ again. Or the light, as she said.

Q.   What said she of Dick's running out, as if sore afraid?

A.   Naught, sir, beyond the supposing the fellow driven at the end out of his wits, the while she lay drugged, by what had passed.

Q. And this speaking of a maggot, when first you came upon her?

A. She said it was from one of the hangings in her dream, sir, in the Devil's gallery. For there she saw a fair corse of a young lady being gnawed by a seethe of maggots as it lay, unburied; and one of which was monstrous large, she could not forget it.

Q. If all she said were true, how comes it to pass that she is let escape to tell all? That Satan in person may come and claim his own; well, we'll not go into that. That he should come and not claim, I do not conceive. Why lay she not murdered or spirited away with the rest?

A. We spake of that, sir. And she believed it was because she prayed as she lay there and begged God's mercy on her sins, and swore with all her heart she would never do such again, if He would succour her now in her extremity. That she heard no answer there, as she lay. Yet felt she was answered, in her dream. And when she did wake, and found herself rid of her persecutors, all gone, felt more sure still. And more and more full of the divine presence, the light as she called it, when she met me, that she called the good Samaritan, and we came down safely, so that in the end she must thank the Lord and solemnly renew the promise she had made. Which she did, sir, in the manner of her religion, with the shaking and sobbing I told of.

Q. Now consider this, Jones. You fall on the wench, when she least expects and desires. Least of all does she wish to go with you to his Lordship's father. She is no fool. She knows her men, and thee and thy failings, and the tale thou art most like to swallow. So she cooks thee a fine repast, admixed of superstition and quack conversion, and plays the repentant fallen woman in need of thy protection. And moreover warns thee that what passed was so loathsome and terrible a commerce that thou'lt be held for a blasphemous liar if thou tell it. What say you to that?

A. I have thought the same, sir. I won't deny it. Yet humbly begging your worship's pardon, would believe her still till I know better. Set a thief to catch a thief, as the saying goes. For my part I know your liars, sir, being one myself, God forgive me. I smelt none there, as to repentance for her past.

Q. That might be. And what she told of the cavern, as false as it sounds. I shall have her yet, I shall know. Now I would have the subsequent course of events. You rode straight to Bideford?

A. No, sir, for at the first village we came upon, tho' all seemed asleep, there was a great barking of dogs, and a fellow cried after us, and we were sore afraid the constables or tithingmen might be upon us, and feared the watchmen of Bideford worse, should we come straight there in the night. So thought best to lie by our road till it was dawn, and enter the town more safe by day.

Q. You lay in the fields?

A. Yes, sir. On a bank we found.

Q. Did you speak of going to his Grace again?

A. I did, sir, for when all was told, she said I must see now we could not. I said I did not, I was certain we should be well rewarded. At which she said something strange, sir. To wit, that she knew my heart and that it spoke a different tongue; that if gold was all I believed in, though she knew I did not, then she had no less than twenty guineas sewn among her petticoats, and I had best murder her there and then, and take them. Well, sir, I said she mistook me, I thought most of my duty to his Lordship's father. No, she said, 'tis the gold. Now thou'dst call me liar to my face, I said, and that is poor reward for my help to thee. Farthing, she says, I doubt not thou art poor, and weak when such temptation shows; yet thou know'st it wrong. Thou mayst deny it, but the light falls on thee as well, she said, and would save thee. First save yourself, says I, 'tis the way of the world. And now she says, I have lived that way, and I tell thee it is damned. And we came to a stop there, sir, for I was taken aback she was so sure of me, and something of how she spake, which was not of accusing or reproach, see you, sir, 'twas more as my own conscience might have said. Then as I thought on this, she went on, Well, wilt murder me for my gold? 'Tis easy enough, and to hide my body, in this wild place. For this was spoken where we lay on the bank, sir, and no house within a mile. I said, Rebecca, thou know'st well I will not, but what of our Christian duty to tell the father what has become of the son? What is more Christian, she says, to tell him he is gone certain to Hell, or not? And I tell thee thou must tell him, for I will not; and I counsel thee not, for thou'lt get far more trouble by it than reward, and all to no purpose. It is done, his Lordship is damned and they'll be persuaded thou hast some part in it. And then she said, If it was money alone I needed, I was welcome to the half of what she had on her person. Well, sir, we argued thus for some time more, and I said I would think on it; that how whatsoever was done, if I was to be one day taken up and questioned, I should be in great trouble if I told truth and had no other word to prove it save my own; in which only she could help me. To which she said, she had given me her father's name and his place of abode, which she spake again, sir; and now gave me her word she would stand by what I said, if asked. And at that we were silent, sir, and slept as well we could. I know you will say I should have been more firm, but I was tired, why, all of that day seemed like a dream to me also, so far was it from what I had expected.

Q.   The next morning?

A.   We came to Bideford without trouble, and found us an inn behind the quay, which we chose for seeming less busy than the others, and so put up there, and brake our fast upon a star-gazy pie, that was stale, yet in truth I have not eaten better, so empty of belly I was. And there at the inn they said a ship sailed on the tide that very next morning for Bristol, which we went to ask when we had ate, and found it true. And I would take passage for us both, but she would not have it, and once more we fell to a skirmish or what you may call it, I saying I would not part from her, she saying I must. Well, sir, there were other matters I will not tire you with, but it came to my agreeing. I should for Swansea, she for Bristol, and neither of us to speak of what we knew, but should be ready to speak for each other, were either accused. I enquired and found I could be suited for Swansea two days thence, as I have told, with Master Parry. So we made for our passages with our two masters, then went back to the inn.

Q. Did they not ask you your business there?

A. Yes, sir. And we said we were fellow-servants, come from Plymouth, having lost our places by reason of our widow mistress's death, and so regaining our homes. And must leave the horse, and would pay a month's keep for it, until it was fetched; for we would not seem to steal it, sir. And I did not forget to send a message to Barnstaple at the Crown, as I had writ Mr Lacy, for where it now was; which your worship will find I did, and sent by a boy and gave him twopence for his pains.

Q. The name of this inn?

A. The Barbadoes, sir.

Q. This money she promised thee?

A. She was good to it, sir. She took me to a little room apart after our dinner and counted me ten of her guineas, tho' she said it was whoring money and would bring me no good; but my need was great, so I took it.

Q. And spent it so fast you had none a month later?

A. I spent some, sir. I gave most to my brother, for I found him in great need. You may ask.

Q. You saw her take ship?

A. Yes, sir, that next morning, and warped away, and sail.

Q. The name of this ship?

A. The *Elizabeth Ann*, sir. She was brig, the master Mr. Templeman or Templeton, I mind not which now.

Q. You are positive the wench did not leave it before sailing?

A. Yes, sir. I waited upon the quay, and she stood at the rail as they went out and raised her hand to me where I stood.

Q. Said she nothing particular on your parting?

A. That I must trust her, sir. And try to lead a better life, if we should not meet again.

Q. You saw no sign at Bideford of his Lordship?

A. Not one, sir. You may believe I watched well for him, and Dick beside.

Q. You sailed yourself for Swansea the day after?

A. Yes, sir. At full flood, then down on the ebb.

Q. Despite thy fear of the sea and of privateers.

A. Well, sir, there is truth in that. Salt water I never abode. But I had small choice, found where I was. I had liefer be in Little-Ease.

Q. Where I wish I might lodge thee. I tell thee thy first plan was a far better, that you should go to tell his Lordship's family, for all thy seeking thy own profit in it. I desire to know more of how this whore persuaded thee from it.

A. You may think I was cozened by her, sir, and it may yet prove I was. But your worship's respect, I must tell you again she I spake with that day was another woman from she I had spake to before. There was some great change upon her. Why, she was more friendly to me in a minute than in a day of her previous ways.

Q. In what manner friendly?

A. We talked much on our journey to Bideford, sir. And not only of our present.

Q. Of what else?

A. Why, of her past wickednesses, and how she had seen the light and would never return to her whoring. Of how Jesus Christ came into this world for such as she and I, to show us a path through its night. She asked me as well much of myself, sir, like we were met for the first time and she would know who I was and of my past life. Which I told her somewhat of.

Q. You told her your true name?

A. Yes, sir. And of my mother and family, that in despite of all, I had not forgot. And for the visiting of which she did strengthen my conscience.

Q. And also to be rid of you, is it not so?

A. I did believe her no liar in that, sir.

Q. You said earlier, she spake against her betters.

A.   Yes, your worship. Of the injustices of this world and what she had seen of them at Mother Claiborne's.

Q.   To wit?

A.   Sir, begging your mercy, I had spoken of some past faults of my own, and she said that the gentlemen who went to her bagnio were not better than us, but worse, for they did choose to live evilly when they might live well, while it was forced upon us, only to get our daily bread. That wealth was a great corruption in men's minds, a blindfold upon their true conscience, and the world a most damned place until such day as they see it.

Q.   She spake seditiously, in short?

A.   Your worship, she said there was no hope for the world while sin governs our betters, and they not punished for it. That we in humbler stations must look to our own souls, and not serve their wickedness.

Q.   Did you not laugh to hear such words in such a mouth?

A.   No, sir. For they seemed sincere, and she did not prate, and when I said, so I did, that it was not for us to judge our betters, she would persuade me gently, by putting me questions. Saying I'd not thought on it enough and that there was a world to come, which must be earned equally by all in this present one. For there was no rank in Heaven, she said, save in saintliness. She flattered my better side, sir. I know you deem those of my nation have none such, and are all wicked. Your worship's respect, sir, we Welsh are most desperate poor people, with so little natural advantage that our faults come most from our need. We are not wicked at heart, more we'd be friendly and religious, if truth be spoke.

Q.   I know thy friendship and thy religion, Jones. The first is all treason, the second all dissent. You are a plague among the decency of nations. A nauseous boil upon this kingdom's posterior, may God forgive you.

A.   At times, sir. When we know no better.

Q.   Which is all times. Spake she more of his Lordship?

A.   That she forgave him, sir, tho' God would not.

Q.   What right has a brazen strumpet to forgive her masters and to know God's will?

A.   None, sir. I walked almost sleeping, I was so tired and footsore. And what with all that had passed that day, I was much confused. It seemed somewhat of truth, as I led her.

Q.   She led thee, thou wretch. She rode the horse?

A.   Yes, sir. And here and there walked a little, to give me rest.

Q.   Were you so fatigued you no longer played the gallant? Why answer you not?

A.   Well, your worship, I see I must tell all, tho' 'tis nothing to your purpose. When we rested before Bideford, she was cold and lay beside me on the bank, with her back turned, 'twas but for the warmth, and saying she trusted me to take no advantage. Which I did not, yet told her as we lay, which is truth, I had married once, albeit it turned out ill for my own fault in drinking and my poor wife that died of the flux. And that I was no better than I should be and doubtless a poor figure of a man beside many she had known. Yet if she would take me, I would take her, and marry again, and we might live honestly and as she said she now wished.

Q.   What, she lies with Satan in the morning and thou'dst lie with her in the evening?

A.   Sir, she had lain with Christ since then, or so she said.

Q.   Thou gav'st lease to such blasphemy!

A.   No, sir. I believed her truly repentant.

Q.   And ripe for the practice of thy lust.

A.   Well, sir, I won't deny I envied Dick his use of her before. I have my natural vigours. I liked her much for her new candour, sir, as well as her flesh. And thought she might bring me to better ways, if I married her.

Q.   But this new-found saint would have none of thee?

A.   That she'd have none of being wedded to any man, sir. For she said I was kind to think of taking to wife one as defiled and sinful as she, for which she was grateful, tho' she could not; seeing she had promised at the worst of her trial inside the cavern, that she should never again have knowledge of any man of her own willing.

Q. That sufficed thee, for an answer?

A. Sir, I tried again on her going the next day — later that same, rather. And she said, I was a good man, she would entertain well of my offer if she changed her mind. Yet had no present desire that she should, indeed earnestly the contrary. And in all case first she must see her parents.

Q. Thou shouldst have unfrocked her piety whilst thou hadst the chance.

A. That tide is lost, sir.

Q. But I shall catch it. She'll not candour me with her soft looks and ranting fits. Quakery, quackery, by Heaven she won't.

A. No, sir. And I wish you well in it.

Q. I need no wishes from such as thee.

A. My pardon, sir.

Q. Jones, if thou'st lied in any particular of this. I'll have thee at a rope's end yet, I warrant thee that.

A. Yes, sir. I know it well. I wish I had told you all in the first place.

Q. Thou art too much a dolt and braggart to be a thorough rogue. That is all the good in thee, which is none, but by degree of wrong-doing. Now be off, until my further disposition. I have not released thee yet. Thy lodging is paid, and to it I sentence thee until all is done. It is clear?

A. Yes, sir. I thank your worship humbly. God bless your worship.

Your Grace,

My most humble concern for Yr Grace would, were I not also his servant, with duty above all else to bow to his gracious commands, beseech me to forbear the dispatch of this that is inclosed. Would that I might find some allay to it, yet cannot beyond that ancient saw of my calling, *Testis unus, testis nullus.* The more might it be applied to this present, that the one witness is known liar and transparent rogue, and here does inform of another we may fear to be a greater liar still. Yet must I in truth to Yr Grace state that though in all Jones doth most plainly merit the rope, I believe him no liar in the substance of our matter. Our hope and prayer must lie therefore in that the wench did cunningly deceive him.

All is on foot to discover her, and God willing we shall. Then shall she have such a riding as Yr Grace may guess. The rogue Jones describes himself in all he says, Yr Grace may picture his kind, that matches all that is worst, which is much, in his wretched nation. He is man of clouts, I will venture one hundred pound to a peppercorn he hath been no nearer Mars or my lady Bellona than

John o' Groats is to Rome, nay, further still. He is far more a frighted eel, that would slip from any pot, once caught.

This also I beg to submit to Yr Grace that knows his Lordship and that all in which he standeth blamable. There is no doubt, alas, that he is guilty of the most heinous of familial sins, in his conduct towards Yr Grace's wishes; yet always with this in his favour, as Yr Grace himself once in happier days remarked, that he hath seemed unsullied by those nowaday too frequent vices of his age and station; that is, by none so foul and dark as is now proposed. Yr Grace, I may believe gentlemen exist that would sink to such depravity; but not a one bearing the honour to be Yr Grace's son. Nor will my reason believe, as I doubt not Yr Grace's likewise, that such witches as these have been, these last hundred years. In short, I must exhort Yr Grace to patience. I pray he will not credit that such alleged infamy as here I send report of to him is yet determined truth.

Yr Grace's most saddened and ever his most obedient

Henry Ayscough

Bristol, by Froomgate, Wednesday the 15th of September, 1736

Sir,

I have received the honour of your letter and return your kind compliments an hundredfold, to which I trust I may add that your most noble client may be assured that I am ever his to command in anything that concerns him. I count myself no less fortunate to have been able to assist a gentleman of your eminence in our profession in the business of last year; as to which I may mention that I have just recently been at Assize (in another happily concluded suit) before Mr Justice G——— and that he did me the honour of asking me in private to convey his respects to our client and assurance of his most favourable interest in any further cause Sir Charles may choose to pursue before him; the which compliment, my dear sir, I felt gratefully obliged to transmit to you before I come to your directions in this present most sad and delicate matter.

Sir, you may furthermore assure his Grace that nothing is more precious to me than the good name of our nobility, that pre-eminent and divinely chosen bulwark upon which, conjoined to the King's majesty, the safety and welfare of our nation must always most depend; and that all shall be conducted with the utmost secrecy, as you request.

The particular you seek I have had most closely inquired after, and find she appeared in this city — and in that place she stated — about the time conjectured in your letter, though none my searcher spoke to could put more precise date upon it than the first or second week of May last. She was told what is truth, *viz.*, that her parents are gone this three years since to another meeting of their sect, it is believed in Manchester, and reside here no more. It doth appear that in Manchester a brother to her father dwells, who had persuaded them of better living (and a more pernicious enthusiasm besides, I doubt not) to be found there, and so they did take their three other children with them, thus leaving her no relations in this city. These three are all daughters, there is no brother.

The father's name is Amos Hocknell, his wife's is Martha, who was Bradling or Bradlynch before marriage, and is originary of Corsham, Co. Wilts. Hocknell was accounted here a good carpenter and joiner, though adamant in his heresy. He was most lately employed by Mr Alderman Diffrey, an excellent and Christian merchant and master ship-builder of this city, for the cabin furnishings of his vessels. I am acquainted with Mr Diffrey, and he tells me he had no complaints of Hocknell for his work; but found he could not leave his preaching and prophesying at home and was ever trying to subvert those around him from established religion, to which my worthy friend Mr D. is to his honour most securely attached; and that on finding one day Hocknell had secretly won two of Mr D.'s apprentices to his own false faith, he dismissed him; at which Hocknell cried injustice and persecution, tho' Mr D. had warned him many times he would not stand for what Hocknell had persisted in doing, as was now well proven. The man is as turbulent and rabid in his politics as his religion, Mr D.'s very words are these: *as steeped in false liberty as a cod-barrel in salt,* from which you may judge his kind; and by this that Mr D. also told me, of how when he dismissed Hocknell, he had the impertinence to exclaim, that *any man might hire his hands, but no man, not even the King, nor Parliament, should ever hire his soul.* It seems the fellow muttered for a time of taking himself and his family to the American colonies (where I heartily wish all such seditious fanatickals might be condemned), yet thought the better of it. The conclusion is, he may be found certainly by inquiry at the Manchester meeting-house; for 'tis, as you must know better than I, sir, an inconsiderable town to this great city that I write from.

The person stated she was come from London, and had there been maid by her work, tho' said no name nor place that is now remembered. To my best ascertaining she stayed no more than an hour in a neighbour's house, who informed her of the above, and then departed away saying she must journey on without delay to Manchester, as she wished with all her heart to rejoin her parents. Sir, I must explain that by a most malign mischance for our purpose, the neighbour in question, an elderly Quakeress, is dead of a dropsy three weeks before my receipt of your letter, and all is founded upon her tattle to her gossips. 'Tis accordingly tongue-worn testimony, yet I believe may be credited.

Of the person's past, my man could discover little more, owing to the closeness of her obstinate co-religionaries in this town, who deem all inquiry, however lawful, a threatened tyranny upon them. Howsoever he found one to tell him the maid was commonly considered slid from Quakerism, and lost to their faith and world, after being discovered in sin, some five or six years past, with one Henry Harvey, son of the house where first she had work here; was cast out by her mistress, then by her parents, who considered her insufficient in repentance; since it was she that led the young man to their sin. And was long disappeared, none knew where till this coming-back (of which none but the aforesaid neighbour knew nor spoke to her before she was gone off again).

Lastly I must inform you we are not the first to inquire after the person, for the prattler above told my searcher another came asking this past June after her, saying he was from London and had a message from her mistress; but neither his appearance nor his manner recommended him to these jealous and suspicious people, and he was told little beyond that she was believed gone to Manchester; at which the fellow went off and has troubled them no more. I trust you will know better what to make of this than I, sir.

I write in some haste before I leave on the other matter, which shall be done as prompt as circumstance allows. Pray rest assured I will write to you thereon as soon as it shall be possible. I am, sir, in all things your noble and gracious client's and your esteemed own most humble, most faithful and most obedient servant,

Rich'd Pygge, attorney at law

Bideford, the 20th of September.

Sir,

I have spent these two previous days at the very place of your most concern, and write while all is fresh in mind. This place is to my best computation two and a half miles above the ford upon the Bideford road and the valley thereto is known as the Cleeve, after its cleft and woody sides, that make it more ravine than vale, like many in this country. The cavern lies with a sward and drinking-pool for beasts before, in the upper part of a side-valley to the aforesaid, the branch path to which is reached in one and three quarter miles from the ford upon the high road. All is desart in these parts, and the valley most seldom used unless by shepherds to gain the moor above. One such, named James Lock, and his boy, of the parish of Daccombe, was at the cavern when we came; as he told us was his summer wont, for he has passed many such there.

This Mopsus appeared a plain fellow, no more lettered than his sheep, but honest in his manner.

The place has a mischievous history, being known to him and his like as Dolling's or Dollin's Cave, after one of that name in his great-grandfather's time who led a notorious gang of rogues that boldly resided here and lived a merry life in the manner of Robin Hood (or so said this Lock), with long impunity, by reason of the remoteness of the place and their cunning in thieving more abroad than in the neighbourhood itself; were never brought to justice that he knows, and in the end removed away. And in proof thereof he showed me inside the entrance to his grotto and rude-carved upon the native rock the initials I.D.H.H., that is, John Dolling His House. The rogue would have been a free-holder, it seems.

Sir, I run ahead, for he told me also of a superstition much older concerning the great stone that stands upright beside the aforesaid drinking-pool, which is that the Devil came once to a shepherd there to buy a lamb of him, or so he said, yet when a price was made and the shepherd said he might choose which he please, Satan pointed to this shepherd's young son (as Lock in telling me to his own boy), who stood nearby. Whereat the shepherd guessed with whom he truly dealt and being much afraid, lost his tongue. Why say you nothing, says Sir Beelzebub, did Abraham make such a to-do about a mere boy? Upon which our shepherd, seeing (as my rude fellow put it) he did speak with one who should best him in a barter over souls, bravely struck with his crook; which fell not on a human (or most diabolick) pate, but upon this stone, and was broke in half. For which loss the shepherd soon consoled himself, since his son's soul was saved from perdition, and moreover the Devil (not taking to this Arcadian hospitality) dared not to show his impudent face in the place again; thus ever since the stone has been called the Devil Stone. And perhaps for that reason the place is deemed accursed by many and some in the parish will not set foot in it. Not so this fellow Lock, nor his father (as well a shepherd) before him; on the contrary, good fattening ground and without mads or murrain, and the cavern apt for his summer living and the ripening of his cheeses. I trust, sir, you may not find me trivial in reciting this, since you especially desired me to omit no particular, however fanciful.

The antrum is fifteen paces broad in its mouth and rises to some twice the height of a man at the tallest of its exterior arch; and thence runs back some forty paces, there to make a most singular bend indeed (running upon a blank wall in first appearance) through a rough-hewn arch, which Lock believes formerly enlarged from nature, perhaps by the rascal Dolling and his band, unto an inner and more spacious chamber. This I paced and found it somewhat the shape of an egg, thus, some fifty paces at the longest and a pace or two over thirty at the broadest or beam, though not regular. The roof is tall and breached at one end to the air, for one may see a faint light at the place, though not sky, as in a crooked chimney; and the ground is damp thereunder, but not greatly so, Lock says in some manner it drains away. He uses not this retiring-room (if I may call it so), for the inconvenience of its darkness, except for his cheeses.

Now, sir, I proceed to your more particular enquiry. Advised by you I brought a lantern with me, and came by its aid upon ashes near the centre of this inner chamber, as of a great fire, or many such. Which Lock told me, before I had even asked, was made by what is called in the Devonshire vulgar didickies (that is, Egyptians), who come here with some regularity in their winter wanderings; for it seems some of their bands tend westward to Cornwall at that season and return thence eastward in the spring. Upon my further questioning Lock said that on his own returnings here, which passes most years about the beginning of June (and to which this present year is no exception), he has seldom not found such traces of their sojourn; and that it was so also in his father's time. Yet he has never encountered them (in this place) for they are secret people, with their own heathen tongue and customs; and never having done him harm nor disputed his summer possession of the cavern, they trouble him not; that he has even found store of burning and hurdle wood seemingly left dry and good for his use, for which he is grateful.

I must here remark that something in these ashes did stink

strangely of other than wood being burnt, I fancy somewhat of sulphur or vitriol, I can put no better name to it. It may be conceived the answer lies in the constitution of the bare rock on which these ashes reposed and that the heat of a strong fire draws forth some tarry emanation, whose effluvia linger on, though I am not competent to determine such matters. I asked Lock of this stink, but he seemed not to have remarked it and declared he could smell nothing uncustomary. Yet methought his nostrils were beclogged with the worse stink of his sheep and his cheeses, and that I was not mistaken. My own man, who was with us, was of my opinion; and we had further proof I was not wrong, as I shall come to, tho' with no better explanation. We disturbed the ashes somewhat to see if aught else but charred wood lay there, and found nothing. In one low corner or recess Lock showed us many bones lying as in a charnel-house, for the most part small, of rabbits and fowls and I know not what else, no doubt thrown aside by the uncleanly Egyptians in their regales and feastings. Lock says they use this inner room more than he in their winter stays, it may be with good reason, for the better protection from the winds and colds of that season.

I must add, sir, before I forget and in answer to another of your queries, that I searched all well by the lantern and found no other way from this cavern save that by which we had entered; and Lock likewise was positive there was none, other than the aforementioned chimney. To my best observation it is little more than a chink, for I later mounted above upon the slope where it issues, where it might pass a child, but not a grown man. Nor is it to be reached at the foot without a ladder. I saw naught else there, nor in the vestibule of the antrum, that spake of what concerns us.

Now I come, sir, to one last matter and that is the fire outside the cave. It lies some twenty paces off, a little to one side upon the sward. I had marked it on arrival, for Lock has encompassed the place with hurdles to keep his flock away. The ashes are washed out by rains, yet the soil remains dark and barren in this place, and nothing has grown upon it since it was burnt. Lock says in former years the Egyptians have not lit their fires so, outside the cave, and knows not why they are so departed from their usual custom this last winter. His sheep, when first he came, seemed driven to lick the superficies where this fire had been, as if something there tickled their animal appetites; and though none seemed to sicken for it, he had feared this sudden maggot in them and so barred them from it; yet said they would still on occasion try to thrust through, for all the abundance of sweet grass lying about them.

This ustulated patch is some nine paces across. I entered upon it and when I stooped was able to discern a similar sulphurous property to that I had smelled inside. I told my man kneel and scratch a little of the earth, whereupon he declared the smell was as strong as before, and the same; which I confirmed with a morsel (that I inclose) he handed me, and marked it seemed baked hard as a potsherd; *id est,* it had withstood the mollient effect of this season's great rains. I had Lock fetch a hurdle stake, with which my man digged down, and found all the soil in this bare place roasted curious hard for four or five inches' depth, and difficult of penetration without repeated thrust; which we could not put a cause to except by many and repeated great fires (for which there is provision enough of wood nearby, yet which I find not accountable to ordinary purposes of cooking and making warmth).

I asked Lock whether this absence of grass was not a strange thing, to which he said yes, and he deemed the Egyptians had poisoned it in making of their salves and potions. Now, sir, they are considered in this part of the Kingdom praeternatural wise in the preparation of simples and 'tis true get some living by sale of their pseudo-apothecarickal concoctions to the ignorant; but neither I nor my man will believe this, that so great a fire was needful if such alone were their business. My man truly observed it was more like earth at the bottom of a smelting-pit, though we saw no trace of metal or else besides. Nor, I think, is there utile ore known in this immediate vicinity. *Nota,* 'tis found in abundance upon the Mendip Hill, towards Bristol.

I fear I must leave you thus with a great enigma, sir, I assure you it is not for fault of my keenest perseverance at your command, nor for want of thinking upon it. Yet I can come to no sure conclusion. Not to be too long I will now answer your remaining matters.

1. There is no known previous visiting to this place by any curious gentleman or virtuoso. Its waters have no reputation whatso-

ever, and knowledge of it reaches not beyond the parish. Mr Beckford (who presents his most flattering compliments) had not known of its existence, before my asking him, e'en though it neighbours upon his own parish.

2. I questioned Lock close upon the hanged man and all that has ensued; which he lays upon thieves, and would not be shaken. For lack of a better 'tis the general but unreasoning opinion hereabouts. When asked what further evidence may be that such desperate thieves are about in this district, they have none; and fall back upon a silly tale that is now afoot of a landing of French privateers; notwithstanding there is no further evidence of it and that they should come this far inland is without precedent these past eighty years, without common sense besides. 'Tis their practice to land and seize what lies close to hand, then be swift away, as is too well known by our navy and water-guards.

3. Lock swore upon oath he had not seen nor remarked aught else unaccustomed in his summer sojourn; nor had more visitors, beyond his family, than I and my man. I have, alas, got no material new informations (beside speculations as the above of privateers) from the aforesaid Mr Beckford, or Puddicombe, or of any others of those you named to me.

4. I saw no fresh-dug ground about the place, such as might hide a person murdered; and neither Lock nor his boy knew of any in their far greater familiarity with it and its vicinity.

5. Such an overlooking vantage as your deponent describes may be seen. All else conforms well enough to his chorography. You may credit him in this at least.

6. Of what was left below, and the two horses, I found no *vestigia*, though this country is such rough wilderness in its bottom or lower parts I cannot be sure we searched where was meant; yet searched all that seemed most apt, beside the stream; and came away with empty hands. At the most neighbouring places naught seems known of the two horses unaccounted for, or what else was left. 'Tis thought most likely that the Egyptians might have come upon these horses; which did it so fall, they might well, if not most certain, steal them; and likewise what was left of baggage. Of your deponent's horse, I will anon.

7. As to witches, Lock declared to know of one in his village, but that she was of the kind they here call white, or benign, more given to the curing of warts and rots than of any evil conversation, aged and crippled besides. He knew of no covens, and was firm none came here in winter save the aforesaid Egyptians; that he had never seen female flesh about the place, in all his many visitings, apart that of his ewes and his wife and a daughter, who would now and then trudge up with provision for him and to pick whortles (which grow abundant there in August). Yet it may be he is here (as to witchcraft) less natural than most of his kind, for Mr B. tells me 'tis still most generally credited, and such noise as has reached their ears of the new repealing of the Act counted great folly. He has had one accusation, no more, concerning it since his coming here, and that proved baseless, caused by one crone's malice to another in some dispute between them. Yet still will most believe, as their grandsires.

8. One may proceed from the head of this valley across the Exmoor in seven miles to the road that goes from Barnstaple to Minehead. The path is obscure and unknown to strangers; those resolute enough might however pass it provided *qualibet* they bear north, when they must in one place or another come upon the high road, which here lies east and west. 'Tis most easy in summer, when dry. Minehead and Watchet, the only considerable places before Bridgewater and Taunton, may be avoided by one travelling in secrecy. I will return this way and inquire, with the discretion you enjoin, as also here; and write immediately if new evidence of moment is found; otherwise, upon my return to Bristol.

I am truly sorry, sir, that I cannot at present determine more to your advantage, and to that of your noble client. I have the honour to be your most humble, faithful and obedient quester and servant.

Rich'd Pygge

Bristol, the 23rd of September

Sir,

I fear I have had a barren return to Bristol, and have found no trace at the towns mentioned in my last, nor at many smaller on my road, of the noble person's having passed that way. I cannot alas positively say he may not have done so, for in truth the scent is grown too cold. Even were it the case of one who travelled openly (and were I able to conduct my questionings in the same fashion), I must respectfully advise that there would at this lapse of time be great improbability of a better result. Had his mute man been still with his Lordship, better hopes of publick memory might be entertained; but we lack that advantage. Barnstaple and Bideford are busy towns and much frequented in the more clement season for the trade in Irish wool, likewise Welsh coals, and no less the roads to them from Taunton, Tiverton, Exeter and even Bristol.

At Bideford the Collector, Mr Leverstock, was able to confirm me from his register that on the 2nd of May last the vessel *Elizabeth Ann,* master Thomas Templeford, sailed for Bristol and on the next day the coal-ship *Henrietta,* master James Parry, bound for Swansea, as your deponent told.

Likewise the same told truth as to the Barbadoes Inn, where I inquired, and found he and his companion was recollected, tho' little noticed, for their story was credited. He boasted to one after she was left that she was gone to ask leave of her parents in Bristol to marry him; naught else of import.

Now, sir, I must inform you also that the horse that was left there is sold, and the landlord would claim it within his right, for he kept it the month paid and a month besides, or so he says, and could keep it no more; nor would part with what he sold it for, tho' I threatened it should come to law and he be hanged for a horse-stealer; as I wish he were, he is an impudent, arrogant fellow, and

Mr Leverstock tells me, a great friend to the smugglers. You may wish not, for so small a sum, and so 'tis left in abeyance.

Sir, I await your further instructions *in re* and meanwhile respectfully attach an accompt of my fees and disbursements to date, in the trust that you will ever count me your most devoted and obedient servant,

Richard Pygge, attorney at law

London, the 1st October

Your Grace,

I write in great haste. She we seek is found, though she knows it not yet. My man is sure; for he took Jones to view her secretly, which he hath done, and now affirms most positively, it is she. She is late married to one John Lee, blacksmith, of Toad Lane in the town of Manchester; and is several months gone with child, it cannot be by him. Lee is said Quaker, like her. They live in poverty, in little better than a cellar, my man avers; for Lee has no regular work, but is called preacher by his neighbours. She now plays the housewife and very soul of piety. Her parents and sisters are likewise in the town, as Mr Pygge wrote. I trust I need not assure Yr Grace that I proceed there at once — and humbly pray he will pardon this present brevity, in the knowledge of its cause, and that I am ever the most forward in his service,

H.A.

I inclose with this copy of a letter received this day from Dr Hales, that is best known (these few years past) for his worthy anathemata upon the evils of spirituous liquors; yet I am told also of excellent report as a natural philosopher, though more such as botanist than chymist. He is friend to Mr Pope, that is one of his parishioners.

❧

The First of October, Corpus Christi College.

Sir,

I am pleased to assist any friend of the learned Mr Saunderson. I have examined the piece of baked earth, upon which you request an opinion, and regret I may come to no certain conclusion as to its nature. 'Tis clear that it hath been subject to great heat, and I doubt not great alteration of the original composition, that alas doth make the chymical analysis thereof (in even the best-furnished elaboratory) most difficult; for we may say in such matters that fire is as an anacoluthia in grammar. All natural logick of expression in the elements is made thereby interrupted and most obscure, howe'er so skilled and moliminous the adeptist. I may believe that before the incalesence the earth was admixed or drenched with some element of character bituminous, yet none has outlived the fire in sufficient size (upon colation) to allow of a closer determination. The Royal Society (of which I have the honour to be *socius*) doth hold in the collection of minerals and stones bequeathed it by the great chymist and philosopher the Hon. Robert Boyle some fragments from the banks of the Asphaltick Lake of the Holy Land (that is, the Dead Sea) that do bear some resemblance, if memory serves; and likewise have I seen pieces not dissimilar brought from the Asphaltum, or Lake of Pitch, that is found upon the Spanish isle of Trinidadoe in the Indies; indeed somewhat the same have I remarked where pitch is boiled and some portion has spilled upon the ground beneath the vats or coppers. But yet unless I mistake I detect a smell in these baked ashes that is neither of pitch mineral (as these examples that I have cited) nor of pitch of pine, or vegetable. Sir, if you can provide me of this soil a fresh portion that is not burnt (that may doubtless be found adjoining), I should be exceeding grateful, and may thereby the better enlighten you. Such soil is not hitherto reported to be found in these isles, and may be most apt to commerce, and of great enhancement to your client's (whose name Mr Saunderson did not vouchsafe) estates.

I am, sir, your most obedient servant,

Stephen Hales D.D.   R.S.S.

I am in Cambridge briefly, and may be the better addressed at my living, that is at Teddington in Middlesex.

THE TALL, GAUNT MAN SITS with an empty pottage bowl, wiped by bread as clean as if it had been well washed, on the scrubbed wooden table before him, and stares at the woman opposite. She is a less hungry, or more fastidious, eater, and does it with cast-down eyes; so, it seems, to declare the very act of eating vaguely immodest. The table stands before a huge grate and large chimney, but no fire is lit and the pottage the woman still eats is evidently cold. The fingers that hold the wooden spoon she eats with look cold; and are cold. The fingers of her other hand lie against the broken morning loaf, to gain some last warmth from its baking. That, the two bowls, two battered pewter mugs and an earthenware pitcher of water — only one thing else lies on the table, a little to one side: a large octavo book. Its brown leather binding is dog-eared, and it has lost its spine; and been repaired by a glued patch of old canvas, so that one may only guess at its contents.

The room is a half-cellar, paved with flags, many of which are cracked, with steps up to the street outside. The upper shutter of the door there is thrown open and lets in a weak and new-risen October sun; as do the two small windows beside it. The sun is needed, for the scene is one of great penury. The cellar-room has no carpet, not even a rush mat. The recently whitewashed walls are similarly without adornment, except that of patches discoloured by damp. There is no other furniture, besides the table and two chairs, bar a wooden chest against the inner wall, that rests at either end on rough-sawn baulks of timber, to keep its bottom off the flagstones. Two iron pans and an ancient chafing-dish hang on nails inside the chimney. There are the remains of a fire there, but it is very small, confined by old bricks, a paltry thing beside the large logs the seven-foot hearth must have been built to burn in its beginnings.

Through an inner and doorless doorway beside the chest can just be made out another and smaller room, and the end of a bed. That room has no light at all from outside. A shelf fixed to the beam above the hearth has one or two other necessities; an iron candlestick and two or three candle-ends, a square of mirror-glass without a frame, a tinder-box and salt-box. And that is all. A monastic cell could not have been more sparse.

Yet there are two strange things in this austere scene. One is physical, for the floor above the room, though not ceiled, is supported on two fine oak beams, almost black with age, and each delicately fluted and chamfered downwards to a narrow hanging edge; as if a century or more before, in James I's or Elizabeth's reign, the house had been a finer place, where even those who lived or worked in the half-cellar were counted deserving of such elaborate joinery. In truth it had served as shop to the merchant clothier who then lived above. It was his customers who were granted such noble beams.

The other strange thing is a virtue. Poverty is associated today with loss of morale; and that with dirt and disorder, both personal and domestic. This humble room is as clean as a modern operating theatre: no dust, no dirt, not a single cobweb, not a blemish on its strict tidiness. All is swept, washed, scrubbed, more thoroughly shipshape than the most demanding bosun's mate could want, as if its denizens have said to themselves: We have nothing, and so may be godly. There was an equivalent saying of the time: cruel to the flesh, kind to the soul. The virtue was not mere cleanliness in adversity, but a kind of wakeful resilience, a latent energy, a waiting will to change; a being set like a spring. We accept this now, we will not accept this for ever. The cleanliness was no more than a convenient and easily demonstrable symbol; a physical emblem of a psychological cleanliness, spare and hard, a dormant readiness for both martyrdom and militancy. That was why comfortable established Christianity so mistrusted the outward signs of a strict practical Christianity in Dissent.

The man, although only in his mid-thirties, is already going grey. He wears breeches and a loose white blouse, and an armless jerkin, scarred, like his forearms and hands, by countless smithy sparks. For this is John Lee, the blacksmith of Toad Lane; though he has no forge, and is far more given now to hammering something harder and more obdurate than iron — the souls of other men and women. A tall, gaunt man, with an abstracted face and seemingly far-seeing eyes. Something in them suggests he thinks too slowly ever to smile; must endlessly digest before he might laugh, or offer an opinion. He certainly does not look as if he has yet digested this other being and wife, Rebecca opposite, in her coarse grey dress and pure white cap; this latter an object as sober and sparse as the room itself, without lace or frill, close over her ears. Only her hair and her face have not changed; the grey dress and white cap cannot quite hide why she was what she was. Those gentle brown eyes, that opaque innocence in spite of all, that patience . . . yet she has changed elsewhere. There is now something also steadfast, almost learnt, in her meekness; perhaps learnt from the man opposite; a new self, defiant, determined by new circumstance and new conviction.

She pushes her bowl across the table to the man.

"Eat, thee. I have no stomach for it. And must to the neasery."

"It ails thee?"

"All shall be well, praise Jesus."

"Thy father and I shall stand witness outside, and pray for thee. If they'd stone thee for thy bygone sins, thee must bear it, and remember thee art the Lord's new-born."

"Yea, husband."

"They too shall be judged when He comes."

"Yea, yea. I know it."

He looks at the offered bowl, but clearly has more on his mind.

"There is a thing I would tell. I was given in the night, but feared to wake thee while thee rested."

" 'Twas well?"

"One came all in white upon a road, as I walked. And he held a staff in the one hand, the Book in the other, and greeted me. He said naught, beyond these words: Be patient, thee, for thy time is nigh. Yea, thus he stood and spake, most clear, as clear as I see thee now."

"And who should he be?"

"Why, John the Prophet, praise the Lord. And more, he smiled upon me, as his friend and good servant."

She stares gravely at him a moment. "The time is nigh?"

" 'Tis as Brother Wardley says. Be resolute in faith, and thee shalt be given signs."

She looks down, towards where her stomach swells a little, then up, and smiles faintly. Then she stands and goes to the inner room, to re-appear with an iron bucket, which she bears across the room and up the steps; unlatches the half-door, and disappears. Only then does he draw her half-finished bowl closer, and begins to eat what she has left. He tastes nothing, still thinking of his dream. It is thin gruel, watery oatmeal mixed with one or two specks of salt bacon and a few dark green leaves of fat-hen; the left-over of the previous evening.

As soon as it is finished, he pulls the book close and opens it; and it opens, as if by nature, at an inner title page, that of the New Testament. It is an old Bible, of 1619, and turned, by its most frequent usage, into a Tetrevangelium. The content words of the page are in a heart-shaped frame, heavily underlined in red ink for lack of proper rubrication. They are surrounded by tiny woodcuts of sacred emblems like the Paschal Lamb, the tented arms of the Prophets, portraits of the Apostles, and most closely by those of the four Witnesses. The man stares for a moment or two at the cut of St John, a distinctly Jacobean and moustached gentleman who sits writing at a table with a tame dodo — no, an eagle — sitting beside him. But John Lee does not smile. He turns on to the saint's gospel, and finds its fifteenth chapter: "I am the true Vine, and my Father is the husbandman."

He stoops a little to read. It is clear, without any ease, for his finger slowly traces what he reads, and his lips can be seen silently moving, as if these words cannot be understood unless they are also spoken in mind, not merely absorbed by it.

"Abide in mee, and I in you: As the branch cannot beare fruit of it selfe, except it abide in the Vine: no more can yee, except ye abide in me. I am the Vine, yee are the branches: Hee that abideth in mee, and I in him, the same bringeth forth much fruit: for without mee ye can doe nothing. If a man abide not in mee, hee is cast foorth as a branch, and is withered, and men gather them, and cast them into the fire, and they are burned."

The man raises his eyes there for a moment and stares across the room at the light in the doorway; then down at the ashes in the hearth beside him. He goes back to his reading.

Meanwhile Rebecca walks to the necessary, bucket in hand. There is a quickness and lightness in her walk that belie her condition; and are quite certainly not justified by Toad Lane. Though the Industrial Revolution has hardly yet begun, Toad Lane is an early forerunner of a familiar sight in many modern cities; a once fair street become a miserable slum of dilapidated houses, both they and their courts behind become warrens of one-room tenements, warrens of disease also. Its practical effects can be seen everywhere in the human denizens, in pocked faces, rickety legs, malnutrition, the neck ulcers of scrofula, scurvy . . . or would be so seen by a modern eye. Fortunately the victims were not then aware how much they were to be pitied. Such was life, and change not imaginable; and a more fundamental principle of resilience applied. One survived as one could, or must. This day the majority of those in the street and its doorways are women and very young children, for their men and children (though not more than five or six years old) with work have gone to their places. Some eye Rebecca a little askance, but it is for her sect-betraying dress; not her in herself, nor her errand.

The closets stand near the end of the street, on a common space:

a ramshackle row with their backs turned to the street, five noisome boxes, in turn containing even more noisome holes in the ground. Between them and a ditch below stands a heap of human dung, to which Rebecca adds, with something of an expert toss, the contents of her bucket. Nearby grows fat-hen, as always; another name for it is dung-weed. Then she goes to wait patiently by the necessaries, since all are occupied. They serve a population of nearly five hundred; as does the one water-pump, close by in the street.

Now an older woman, yet dressed rather as Rebecca, and with a similar very plain, close-fitting white cap, joins her in her wait. Rebecca smiles primly in recognition and then utters what must seem, in the circumstances, either a profound sociological need or something too obvious to require saying at all.

"More love, sister."

All that is spoken in reply are the same three words. It is clear they are not sisters, for the two women say no more, and stand still, rather apart. It seems this is no more than a stock greeting between fellow-believing neighbours, as banal as a good-morning. Yet it is not a Quaker formula; and exceptionally Mr Henry Ayscough's man (who at this very moment stands, as it happens, waiting near the half-cellar, with Jones at his side) has misinformed him on one matter.

When some fifteen minutes later John, who has put on a plain-brimmed hat and a threadbare black coat, and Rebecca Lee emerge from their cellar and walk towards the two men, the latter make no pretence of turning their backs and being in conversation, but stand and watch them approach. The tall clerk wears a small and sardonic smile, as one accustomed to his present role; Jones seems ill at ease. When they are only a few feet apart, Rebecca stops, though her husband walks on. She has no eyes except for Jones, who awkwardly takes off his hat, and looks sheepishly down at the gutter between them.

"I must. 'Twas as we agreed."

Still she stares at him, as at a total stranger; yet without anger, merely as one who sees him whole. Then she looks down and speaks that same phrase she had spoken at the necessary.

"More love to thee, brother."

She quickens her step to rejoin John Lee, who has stopped and now stares at these two strange men as if the last thing he feels for them is love. But Rebecca touches his arm, and they go on. The other two wait a moment, then turn and follow, like a pair of foxes who have marked their weak lamb.

The Examination and Deposition of
REBECCA LEE
the which doth attest upon her sworn
oath, this fourth day of October
in the tenth year of the reign of
our sovereign Lord George the second,
by the grace of God King of Great
Britain and of England, &c.

My name is REBECCA LEE, *I was born Hocknell, eldest daughter of Amos and Martha Hocknell, in the city of Bristol, on the fifth day of January in the year 1712. I am married to John Lee, blacksmith, of Toad Lane, Manchester. I was common prostitute in London until May of this year, and went by the name of Fanny. I am six months gone with child.*

◈

Q. You know why you come before me?
A. I do.
Q. That I enquire upon the disappearance of a noble gentleman in May last?
A. Yes.
Q. Then first this. Have you since the first day of May last seen, had news of, or held any communication whatsoever with his Lordship?
A. I have not.
Q. Do you have knowledge that he is or is most probably dead, in whatsoever manner?
A. None.
Q. And is what I have asked of his Lordship true also of his man Dick? You have no greater knowledge of his fate?

A.   None.

Q.   You are upon oath.

A.   I know it.

Q.   Now, my new-virtuous Mistress Lee, I will find out what you are before we come to what you were. And you will speak as plain as your dress. Your swelling belly shall not save you, if you rant religion. Is that plain enough?

A.   Christ shall be my witness.

Q.   Very well. And I counsel you, keep it well in mind that I have Jones' testimony concerning you before me. And your former mistress's, and much else besides. Now, when arrived you here from Bristol last May?

A.   On the twelfth day.

Q.   And found your parents?

A.   Yes.

Q.   Who forgave you your sins?

A.   I thank the Lord.

Q.   You told them of what you had been since they saw you last?

A.   Yes.

Q.   Did they not abominate you?

A.   No.

Q.   How no — are they not strict in their religion?

A.   Very strict, and so forgave me.

Q.   I take you not, woman.

A.   They do not abominate those who truly repent.

Q.   Did they not abominate you before and cast you out?

A.   Because I was wicked and did not truly repent. And I know now they were right, from what I became.

Q.   You say you have told them all. Do you mean by that, what happened in Devonshire immediately before you came hither?

A.   No, I have not told that.

Q.   Why not?

A.   Because I sinned not in that, nor would trouble them with it.

Q.   You are principal witness and accessary to foul and irreligious crimes, and are not to be troubled with them? Why answer you not?

A.   They were not crimes, I say.

Q.   But I say they were, and that you aided and abetted in their commission.

A.   I deny it.

Q.   You shall not deny me, woman.

A.   I shall, if I be falsely accused. There is a great lawgiver than thee. Is Jesus so poor a meter He cannot weigh true repentance in a soul? He is not so small, and soon the world shall know it.

Q.   Enough. Watch your tongue. None of your thouing and theeing. .

A.   It is our manner. I must.

Q.   A fig for your musts.

A.   We mean no disrespect. All are brothers and sisters in Christ.

Q.   Enough!

A.   It is truth. We are equal in this, if not in the world. Blame me not for defending my right, and God's word.

Q.   Your right and God's word! Shall I fetch you to a pulpit?

A.   I say they are one. Who takes my right steals from Christ.

Q.   You have no right to be stolen, you are a most notorious whore. I am not your new modesty's fool, I see whorish insolence still proud in your eyes.

A.   I'm no harlot now. And thee knows it, thee hast enquired of me. Christ is my master and mistress now. My pride is to be His servant, naught else.

Q.   You can buy remission of your sins so easy? Why, you should be at Rome.

A.   Thee dost not know my religion. I am repentance with each breath I breathe, until my last, or still I sin.

Q.   I know I'll have you whipped, if you throw more piety at me.

A.   I came not here to offend.

Q.   Then cease your impudence.

A.   When I was harlot I learnt those who would serve us worse than their horses or their dogs served themselves likewise; and those that were more kind left happier.

Q.   I should bow and scrape to you, is it so? I should call you madam and hand you to your coach?

A.   Thee may thunder and frown as thee will, but I think 'tis
more in thy manner than in thy heart.

Q.   Dost thou indeed!

A.   Yes. I pray thee, be not angry. I have met lawyers beyond
thee, and judges besides; and know their hearts are not all
flint. Nor would they rail me so for giving up my wickedness,
as if 'twere better I was their harlot again.

Q.   I wonder they ever came again to your bed, if you preached
so at them.

A.   Then more's the pity I did not.

Q.   Well, well, I see you have imbibed your father's poison.

A.   And my mother's. Who also lives in Christ.

Q.   And contempt of all secular rank and natural respect, is it
not so?

A.   No. Unless where rank and respect would forbid our liberty
of conscience.

Q.   That gives you no liberty to be pert in your answers.

A.   Then harry me not for my beliefs.

Q.   We waste time. I would know of your marriage. When was it?

A.   On the second day of August.

Q.   The man is one of your congregation?

A.   We are Quakers no more. He is Prophet.

Q.   What manner of prophet?

A.   French Prophet, descended of they who came from France
this fifty years past, called Whiteshirts by some.

Q.   The Camisards? Are they not lapsed?

A.   We are forty or more here who believe that Christ soon
comes, by prophecy, as they did.

Q.   You mean, your man is of French blood?

A.   No, he's English.

Q.   Your parents are grown such prophets also?

A.   Yes, and my uncle John Hocknell, who is friend to Brother
James Wardley, our elder and teacher.

Q.   Was Quakerism not extravagant enough for you?

A.   Not since I know Christ comes. But I will not speak ill of the
Friends. They are good people.

Q.   Your husband knew of your past infamy?

A. He did.

Q. That he wore horns to the altar, in the state of your belly?

A. He wore Christian kindness there, no horns.

Q. A prophetick saint indeed. He took you from pity, in short?

A. And holy love. For our Lord Jesus said, Neither do I condemn thee.

Q. Did you not tell Jones that you would hear of marriage from no man?

A. I did not know then I was by child.

Q. Then you are wed for your bastard's sake?

A. For his soul's sake or if it be she, for hers. And my own.

Q. And is it this, a marriage in form, without true conjugality?

A. I know not what that would mean.

Q. Whether your man has his fleshly rights?

A. He is content with what he has.

Q. That is no answer. I require yes or no. Why say you nothing?

A. My conscience will not allow.

Q. I must know.

A. Thee'll not know from me. Nor my husband, who waits in the street below, and thee may call him up.

Q. This is more defiance. You are to answer.

A. Of his Lordship thee may ask all, and I will answer. But of this, not.

Q. Then the imputation is this: the poor clown protects you, yet is denied your bed?

A. Believe what thee must. Where lies more shame? In my silence, or this prying where thee has no business? Of what I was thee may enquire, 'tis as whipping to that abomination I was, that she deserves. What I am since is no business of thine, nor any other man.

Q. Who sired this bastard?

A. His Lordship's servant.

Q. You are certain?

A. I was used by no other but Dick in that month.

Q. What, you are prostitute, and slept with no other man?

A. I had my courses, my flowers, then left the bagnio before I was used again, unless by him.

Q. Did not his Lordship have his pleasure of you?

A. No.

Q. No, what no is this? Did he not hire you?

A. Not for such a use.

Q. Did not the Devil himself have advantage of you in that Devonshire cavern? Why answer you not? Jones says he did, and that you told him so.

A. I told him what he might believe.

Q. And not what truly passed there?

A. No.

Q. You lied to him?

A. Yes. In that.

Q. Why?

A. Because I wished to lead him from meddling further. Because I would be what I am now become, an obedient daughter and a true Christian. And most, the last.

Q. Had you no thought of his Lordship's family, who are in despair of ever seeing him again?

A. I pity their pain, and their unknowing.

Q. Are you not its cause?

A. God is the cause.

Q. And doth He pardon those who most shamefully neglect their Christian duty? Answer.

A. I answer, He pardons those who do not speak a truth that none will believe.

Q. What none-will-believe is this?

A. What I am here to tell thee. It shall be seen, whether thee theeself will believe.

Q. That it shall, mistress, that it shall, and Heaven help thee if I do not. Which I will not, if you give me no better than these artful-devious answers. Now, it is true you know nothing of what is become of the begetter of that lump in thy womb — the man Dick?

A. It is true.

Q. I have your word upon oath?

A. Yes.

Q. Then I'll tell you. He is dead.

A.   Dead?

Q.   Found hanged of his own hand, and not three miles from that place where you last saw him.

A.   I knew not.

Q.   And have no more to say?

A.   I pray our Lord Jesus forgive him his sins.

Q.   Spare me thy prayers. You say, you did not know?

A.   When I saw him last, he lived.

Q.   Jones has writ you no letter since you parted at Bideford? Nor come hither?

A.   No.

Q.   Nor any other of your past world?

A.   None but Claiborne.

Q.   How is this, Claiborne? She swore upon oath she knew not where you were.

A.   Then she lied. She sent one Arkles Skinner, who is called her lackey, but is her bully-man.

Q.   Write Hercules. When came he here?

A.   Toward the end of June.

Q.   And lived to his name? He would use force to have you back?

A.   Yes, but I cried out and my husband John came running and struck him to the ground. And I had Brother Wardley, that knows letters, to write Skinner's mistress how I had told others all I knew, and if harm came to me, then worse harm to her.

Q.   And she has held her peace since?

A.   Yes.

Q.   Well, I may approve your husband's fist, if not his choice of wife. Where works he now?

A.   When he can with my uncle, like my father. They make grates and backs, and set them in, and the mantels, which is my father's part, who is joiner. They will do good work for any. But few will hire them, for their religion.

Q.   You are poor, then?

A.   We have enough. Those among us who have give to those who have not. The world's goods are to be shared by all who believe, so say we; and do.

Q.   Now, Mistress Lee, I'll have the part you played last April,
     and not a scene omitted. When came his Lordship first to you
     at Claiborne's?

A.   Near the beginning of that month, I cannot say the day.

Q.   And you had seen him never before — no matter where?

A.   I had not. He was introduced by Lord B———.

Q.   Knew you who he was?

A.   Not then. But soon after.

Q.   How?

A.   Claiborne asked me of him. And when I had spoken, she told
     me who he truly was.

Q.   And what else?

A.   That he was worth the plucking, and I must keep him close.

Q.   And how fared his Lordship? Liked he not his sport in your
     bed?

A.   There was none.

Q.   How none?

A.   No sooner went we apart to my chamber and I would put my
     arm around him, he took it away; and said it was in vain.
     That he had entered upon it only so as not to lose face before
     Lord B———. Then that he would pay me well for my si-
     lence.

Q.   What, would he not assay those arts and wiles you were once
     so remarked for?

A.   No.

Q.   Were you not surprised?

A.   The case is not so uncommon.

Q.   Is it not?

A.   No. Though few admit it so soon, and without trial. And
     most as well would buy our silence if they could, as they'd
     buy our boastings for them.

Q.   Of their gallantry?

A.   It was the custom, when they came down from us. Which we
     fostered, for our purses. Tho' among ourselves the saying was,
     Brag most, do least. And I think not only in that place.

Q.   We need not thy bagnio wit.

A.   More truth than wit.

Q. Enough. So, he would not, or could not. What passed then?

A. His Lordship was civil, and spoke with me, saying Lord
B——— had said well of me. And asked of my wicked life of
sin, and how I liked what I must do.

Q. Seemed he at ease, or embarrassed in his manner?

A. Unused. I would have him lie beside me; he would not, nor
even sit. But then at last, he sat at the end of my bed and told
me something of himself. That he had never lain with a
woman, that he suffered greatly for the knowledge of it and
the having to hide it from his family and his friends, that he
was much blamed for refusing advantageous offers of marriage, for he was a younger son and had no great expectations. I thought him more distressed than he showed. He
spake all with his face turned, as if in shame that he had no
more than one like me to confess it to.

Q. What said you to this?

A. I tried my best to comfort him, and said he was young, I had
known others in the same condition, who now had their normal powers. And that we should try. But I could not move
him to 't. And then of a sudden he stood away from the bed,
and when I went to draw him back, he said, Leave me, no
more, as he were angry and I was grown importunate; as
sudden again made his excuses, saying I was not to blame, I
did my best, that he was worse than marble not to melt at my
kisses, and suchlike. That if I would have patience with him,
he would like to make one more trial on another occasion, in
two days' time, for he believed himself on this first one too
wrought by his anticipations, not knowing what I should be
like, nor the place; but was reassured now, and conscious of
my charms, so be it he could not yet prove it. That is all.

Q. Another assignation was made?

A. Yes.

Q. And he gave you money?

A. He threw some guineas on my bed, as he left.

Q. Now, I desire to know this: in asking you of yourself, and
paying you compliments, was he out of the normal custom of
such libidinous encounters?

A. No.

Q. Was it not more usual for a gentleman to come, to take his pleasure of you, then away?

A. There were some such; yet more for pleasure of our company. I heard many say, Claiborne's had the best conversation in London, of the both kinds. She would take none of us who could not speak as well for ourselves out of bed as in it.

Q. You have known others speak and confide in you in this manner?

A. In their different fashions. They might say to us what they durst not say to their wives, God forgive them.

Q. Very well. He came again?

A. He came.

Q. And what passed?

A. The same as before, he would have none of me. But now declared he would watch his servant do with me what he could not. The which he spake of as one ashamed, yet forced to it, and feared I might refuse such an unnatural request; and knew it difficult to encompass, even should I agree. But so be it I should, he would pay me well, and gladly.

Q. Did he not propose this at that first meeting?

A. No. I am sure. For that second time he made me go to my window, that looked down upon the street, to see Dick that stood there opposite, and waited.

Q. What said you?

A. At first that I would not, he might buy me for himself, not for his man; that Mistress Claiborne was strict to our uses, she would never allow such a thing. At which he appeared much set down, and disappointed of his hopes. On which we fell to talking, and he told me he was advised to it by a learned doctor, and other things, which I did believe to be only excuses for what he wanted. Yet I doubted not he was in some distress, and had pity for him, and would have him lie beside me; tho' he would not, and fell to pressing me again, and told me of Dick, how they were like to twins, even born upon the same day, whatever so different in their station and outward.

Q. Was this not strange?

A.   Yea, yet I believed him more there than in this talk of doctors. And I will tell thee now, not half so strange as what I later learnt of them. Which was that they were two men as far apart in most matters as any in this world, yet of one soul. What one lacked, the other had, as it is with man and woman, tho' both were men. As twin brothers, tho' they were none.

Q.   On that I shall ask more, in good time. In short, he won you to his wish?

A.   Not then, another time, he came yet again. I will tell thee now what I said not to Jones. Whether thee believe me or not, I do not care, 'tis truth. Thee may take me for a notorious harlot, I will not deny it. So I was, may the Lord Jesus forgive me, and a great sinner, my soul harder than flint. Yet it was not dead, not quite dead, for my conscience told me I sinned and should not be forgiven. Most of my sisters in that house were blind, they knew not what they did; yet I was not in their case, I knew I was on the path to Hell and with no excuse save my own obstinacy in sin, that is none. There is a badder case than they who sin for their own selfish pleasure: it is we who sin in hatred of the sin itself. Not because we would, but somehow must, as a slave must do his master's will, though he hates both it and him. I tell thee this because I was in that snare when first his Lordship came. I sinned the more brazenly because at heart I would sin no more. The more modest I would be, the more impudently I did. And I pray thee remember we women are brought up to do men's will in this world. I know men will say 'tis Eve who tempts them into the stews. But 'tis Adam who keeps them there.

Q.   And Adam also who keeps most of 'em pure. Be done with this prating.

A.   I take heart thee won't look me in my eyes, 'tis sign thee knows I speak truth. It had become strong upon me that I must change my life, now saw I his Lordship was my prison's key. For when he came out with his scheme to take me away to the West, where I was born, I felt a great flutter in my heart, a new light and hope, and I knew my chance was come to flee where I was.

Q. You say, whatever might befall, you meant not to return to Mistress Claiborne's?

A. I do.

Q. And would mend your ways?

A. I will tell thee what I fain would not. To my everlasting shame I had use, to please the more wicked, to play the virtuous maid, that they might take the more pleasure in their conquests. And for that I was given a Holy Bible, that I might pretend the better; and that these men I served might show they believed not in God, and did mock His Word. For at the end I would hold it as if to forbid them; which they must tear aside to gain their will. What little conscience that still sprang in me knew I did do in that a most wicked abomination, tho' I could not stand against Claiborne, her willing that I acted thus. Yet I began then, when I was alone, to learn the letter of the Book I so misused.

Q. What mean you by that?

A. Its letter, that I might read it; which did come the more easy, that of some parts I had memory, that once I had heard read or spoken. God pardon me, for years 'twas not so. And Jesus' mercy was even then kind, for the more I read, the more the light came upon me: that what I did was great sin, and I crucified Him again in what I did. Still could I not bring myself to do what in my growing harlotry I came the more to see I must. I stayed too fond of worldly things; and would ever put away until the morrow. And thee must know that this pressed ever more upon me, like a great boil or sore place within my conscience, that must be lanced, or I should die of it.

Q. Did you tell his Lordship of this great boil upon thy everopen thighs?

A. No.

Q. Very well. Enough of thy tender soul. What pretexts advanced he for this journey?

A. First, that which he had already proposed, concerning Dick, and the greater commodity to it if we were removed from the bagnio. Then that he wished to take new waters supposed good for his condition, and so try two remedies for it at the same time.

Q. Did he name these waters?

A. No. Then told that his family and father thought the worst of him for having so far refused to marry, and spied upon him, and he greatly feared we should be followed if we did not hit upon some disguise for the journey. Which he said he had thought upon and found an answer to.

Q. To wit?

A. A scheme of a false elopement, where I should play lady's maid brought to serve his false intended.

Q. This was not told Claiborne?

A. No, for her 'twas said that his Lordship was upon a folly in Oxfordshire, to which he should bring me. All who attended were to bring one such as I.

Q. For which he fee'd her handsomely, did he not? And to thee did he promise more?

A. He did promise I should not regret the deceiving, that I took to mean I should not be the poorer for it. Heaven knows I was not, albeit I mistook then the fee he intended.

Q. You thought he spake of money?

A. Yes.

Q. Of what did he speak in truth?

A. What I now am.

Q. Am I to understand this — that you are now what you are because of his Lordship?

A. I will tell.

Q. Very well. First let us be clear — he made no promise of a fixed reward for your pains?

A. No.

Q. Did you not press for such?

A. No, for by him I hoped to escape, that was more than reward enough, and I did not care for the wages of sin.

Q. Were you not suspicious of so much deception?

A. I might have been, had I thought hard upon it. All I did see then was my own advantage. And e'en the same later, despite

I must do as I was bid, and was mistreated, as I thought: that it was the price I must pay, to change my condition and purge my fouled soul.

Q. Had you any suspicion, before you came to Amesbury, that his Lordship deceived you also as to the real purpose of this journey?

A. No, not none.

Q. Was he pressing that you should resolve yourself to this western journey? In all this did he rather solicit, or did he dragoon?

A. He pressed, but did not force. I told him the time of my courses was near. He accepted it must pass first, as happened.

Q. You say, the time of your going depended no more than upon the season of your menison?

A. Yes.

Q. It was not so appointed, that you should be in Devon on the first of May?

A. Not that I know.

Q. Now this, mistress. Is it not most often the case with such as you, that tops the licentious town in her trade, that her hope lies in leaving the stews and becoming kept woman of some nobleman, who may establish her for his use alone?

A. It was proposed me. I would have none of it.

Q. Why?

A. Such we called the militia, not trained soldiers like us. We might never desert, Claiborne would never allow.

Q. Were none that proposed this to you great enough to protect?

A. Thee were never in that world of Antichrist. She said she should find us in Hell, should we run off; and so she would, the devil.

Q. But she let you go with his Lordship?

A. Gold will melt iron.

Q. He offered more than she might refuse?

A. I doubt not more than she told me.

Q. What was that?

A. Two hundred guineas.

Q.   Had you in your house, to Claiborne or some fellow-whore, made mention whatsoever of his Lordship's fault?

A.   No, not a word.

Q.   And where were you taken, when first you left the stews?

A.   To St Giles i' the Fields, to Monmouth Street, that I might buy clothes at the second-hand, suited to a country maid. Which I did.

Q.   His Lordship fetched you to this?

A.   No, Dick his servant, with a closed carriage, as was arranged. It bore no arms, 'twas hired. Then out of the town to Chiswick, where his Lordship waited, within a cottage.

Q.   At what time of day was this?

A.   'Twas all after dinner. Past six of the clock, when we came.

Q.   What made you of Dick, now you had met?

A.   Nothing. He did not ride with me, but with the coachman.

Q.   How were you welcomed at Chiswick?

A.   His Lordship seemed pleased I was come. A supper was prepared.

Q.   Was any other person there?

A.   An old woman, who served us. She spake not, I think left when we were served. I did not see her again, in the morning when we set forth.

Q.   And what else passed, that evening?

A.   What was agreed, with Dick.

Q.   His Lordship was present?

A.   Yes.

Q.   Throughout all?

A.   Yes.

Q.   Where was this?

A.   In a chamber above.

Q.   Did it have the hoped-for effect upon him?

A.   I know not.

Q.   Did he not speak?

A.   Not a word. And left us so soon it was done.

Q.   He was not aroused by it?

A.   I have told thee. I do not know.

Q. Saw you no sign?

A. No.

Q. Had you done such an act before spectators before?

A. On occasion, may I be forgiven.

Q. What then?

A. 'Tis not thy business.

Q. I insist. Was there no lechery in his Lordship's conduct on this occasion?

A. No.

Q. Very well. And Dick?

A. What of Dick?

Q. Come, Mistress Lee. You are no innocent in this. Did he play his part sufficient well? Why answer you not?

A. He played his part.

Q. Sufficient well?

A. I doubt he had lain with woman before.

Q. Did not his Lordship complain on a later occasion — that you had failed to rein him back?

A. Yes.

Q. What answered you?

A. That he was green as a radish. No sooner in than out, if thee'd hear more bagnio wit.

Q. Yet later you chose to lie with him for pleasure, was it not so?

A. I felt pity of him.

Q. Those who were with you say more.

A. They may say what they list. It shames me not that I was kind to him, who suffered so by lack of natural parts. Given for my sins I was harlot still.

Q. He knew what you were?

A. He did not treat me so.

Q. Then how?

A. Why, not as a body bought for his lust, as I was used to feel, far more as one he loved, his sweetheart.

Q. How knew you this, since he could neither speak not hear?

A. There are more ways of speaking than with words. He would not brook me speaking with Jones, he would watch me with that in his eyes no woman mistakes, he would do all in his power to serve me.

Q.   And served you also in his Lordship's presence, is it not so? Saw you no resentment there? Do not true sweethearts abhor such a base value put upon the act of love?

A.   I say he was not as other men, more one that knew so little of this world he might have lived in the moon, and must take his Lordship as his guide in all here below. If his Lordship bade him, he must follow. I told thee, there was such closeness between them they needed no words, they were as one person, tho' two in body. I might almost believe his Lordship did enjoy me, despite he would not bear my touch, yet through Dick's enjoying.

Q.   Now, had you warning that morning you set forth from Chiswick that you had other companions on your journey?

A.   His Lordship told me that evening previous we should meet them, and they would come with us, Mr Brown and his man. And told me who he should pretend to be, a City merchant, tho' in truth he was the doctor he had spoke of; yet I must pretend I did not know such a thing, and take him for what he seemed. Which I did, yet so it happened I had seen him before, two months before in a playhouse where I was, tho' I could not mind me his name, notwithstanding his person and voice well enough. And that day as we rode Jones came up, and I knew by some gross hints he made that he likewise suspected I was not what I seemed, and I was much afraid. And when next I had opportunity, I told his Lordship I feared I was recognised.

Q.   What answered he?

A.   That I was to keep mum, and brave it out.

Q.   Seemed he set back, alarmed, I know not?

A.   No, not one whit. And he said that none of us were what we seemed. That I was to tell him if Jones was importunate again.

Q.   Did you not likewise tell him you knew Mr Brown for what he really was?

A.   No, for I must tell thee every step we took from London still lightened my heart. 'Twas to me as if I left the City of the Plains and Bristol was my Sion. And I thought, If his Lordship deceives me, I may the easier deceive him, when my time comes, and so it is better now to keep my counsel.

Q.   Very well. Now let us come to Basingstoke. His Lordship demanded what you had done before?

A.   Yes.

Q.   And where was it done?

A.   Within his chamber.

Q.   He watched?

A.   He found it too quick done, and he blamed me, after.

Q.   Was Dick present, when this was spoken?

A.   No, he was sent away.

Q.   His Lordship was angry?

A.   More as one who thought himself cheated.

Q.   He was disdainful of your supposed skills?

A.   Like one who was a practised rake, for all he could not be.

Q.   Did you remonstrate?

A.   No, beyond what I said. That Dick was too green to be managed.

Q.   What said his Lordship to that?

A.   That I was his now, and I should find he was worse than Claiborne if he did not get his money's worth.

Q.   You are certain — he spake thus?

A.   Certain.

Q.   What answered you?

A.   Why, nothing, I looked meek. Yet did not feel it, and counted him much changed, and not just, for he had seen how Dick came to it, like a poor beast with only one thought, and I could not stop him. I tell thee as I then believed. I know now he would be my good friend, but I saw it not.

Q.   How your good friend?

A.   I will tell in its place.

Q.   I will know now.

A.   Not by my mouth. 'Tis like the Book. We say, One threshing

will not yield its grain. Thee must wait till thee's heard all,
and as it was set down.

Q.   Came Dick to you privily in the night there?

A.   Yes.

Q.   And you allowed it?

A.   Yes.

Q.   Although he was no better than a poor beast?

A.   Because he was. And had enough wit to know he had no right
to ask. Shall I tell thee how many lords and dukes I have
served, master Ayscough? Why, even a royal prince besides.
I'll tell thee not one of them who came to my bed, yet knelt
there as he did, like a child with his head pressed down on the
coverlet, and waited to know my will, not force his own upon
me. Thee'll say for the first I was bought, I had no will, no
liberty, no harlot has.

Q.   I'll say thou art a most damned doctoress.

A.   No, I am not. Thee has thy alphabet, and I mine, that is all.
And I must speak mine. I tell thee why I took pity for Dick.
'Twas neither love nor lechery.

Q.   You lay together all that night?

A.   Till we slept. And when I woke, he was gone.

Q.   And every night the same?

A.   Not the next. After, yes.

Q.   I would hear of that next night, at Amesbury. Had you
warning of what would take place there?

A.   Not until we were arrived, no, more late still, we had supped,
it was eight or more of the clock, and I waited in my chamber, when Dick came to fetch me to this Lordship's, and I
must bring my riding cloak. Which did alarm me, I could not
think why that should be. And there his Lordship said we
must ride out later, in great secret, which alarmed me the
more, for when I asked why, he would not say and told me
sharp I was hired to do as he commanded, as the night before.

Q.   He had not spoken to you during that day?

A.   No, not one word, tho' before then all was under the guise of

my doing him a favour. He was courteous enough, and grateful I assisted in his designs. Now he spake so a master might
to a slattern servant, as in my sins I truly was. Then said I
might lie upon his bed, and sleep till he woke me. Which I
did, save I slept little at first, I was too frightened; yet slept in
the end till I was woken.

Q. What did his Lordship the while?
A. He had his box of papers beside him, and read before the fire.
Q. And Dick?
A. He went away, I know not where; and was returned, 'twas he
who woke me.
Q. When was that?
A. In the midst of the night. The inn was silent, all slept.
Q. Next?

꧁꧂

Rebecca Lee is silent, and does something she has not hitherto
done, looks down. The lawyer repeats his question.

"Next, mistress?"

"I would prithee drink a little water. My voice fails."

Ayscough watches her a long moment, then without looking
away speaks to the clerk at the end of the table. "Fetch water."

The clerk puts down his pencil — for unusually he writes with
that, and not a quill — and silently goes, leaving the diminutive
lawyer still staring in his speculative, robin-like way at Rebecca.
He sits with his back to the room's imposing battery of Jacobean
windows; and she faces their light. She looks up at him, into his
eyes.

"I thank thee."

Ayscough says nothing, he does not even nod. All of him seems
concentrated in his stare; clearly he would embarrass her, express
his doubt of this suspiciously untimely request. He surveys her with
all his education and knowledge, his judgement of human affairs,
his position in the world. It is true he does it partly from policy, as
one of his tricks or practices before difficult witnesses, and long acquired, like his bursts of bullying contempt, to compensate for his
puny stature; yet strangely she holds his look, as she has since the

interrogatory started. In all else of her appearance she seems modesty itself: her primly sober dress, her cap, her hands folded on her lap. But not once as she answers has she bowed her head or looked aside from his eyes. A modern lawyer might have found a sneaking admiration for such directness; Ayscough does not. She merely strengthens a long-held opinion in him: that the world grows worse, and especially in the insolence of its lower orders. Again we meet that unspoken *idée reçue* of his age. Change means not progress, but (as a child born the following year was one day to put it) decline and fall.

Without warning he stands and walks to the inn window. There he looks out. Rebecca gazes at that small back, but then drops her eyes to her lap again, and waits for the water. At last the clerk brings it and sets it before her. Ayscough does not turn to watch her sip it, and indeed now seems lost in what he watches outside: a square with many shops and central stalls, and busy with people, whose noise and cries have been constant background to what has gone on inside the room. Already he has noted a group of three men, who stand at the corner of a street entering the square, directly below where he stands, and stare up towards him, oblivious to the jostlings of the throng that passes by. He knows what they are by their plain clothes and their hats, and ignores them, once seen.

What he watches are a lady and her daughter. They are evidently of some rank and distinction, for they are fashionably dressed in town clothes, and preceded by a tall liveried footman, who carries a basket with their purchases and officiously gestures with his free hand at any who are slow to get out of the way of the ladies behind him; most, as if by instinct, stand aside. Some even touch their hats or bow their heads, though the ladies do not acknowledge them. Yet Ayscough, despite his watching, thinks less of them than of a recent literary memory they evoke, and especially the affected and self-assured younger of the two ladies. It had appeared in the *Gentleman's Magazine* for August, under the initials R.N., a satirist and evidently a misogynist, a seeming *abbé mondain* of the English church. Here it is, set in exactly the same form that Rebecca has just broken; it may serve also to remind of the reality of her world for the more fortunate of her sex; and how different from them she has chosen, or has been chosen, to be. The piece might have been entitled *Eternal Women of a Certain Kind,* but Mr R.N. was not so prescient.

PRETTY MISS'S CATECHISM

Q. WHO are you?

A. A lady fair of nineteen.

Q. 'Tis pretty difficult to understand what that is; therefore explain yourself a little.

A. No very keeping Ware, I promise you; *Stale Maids and stinking Fish* is, you know, a Saying never a whit the less true, because of its Antiquity.

Q. Is this the View you proceed upon?

A. Yes, truly; at 16 we commence thinking, at 17 love, at 18 whine, and at 19, if we can get the Man in the Mood (which, by the by, is a difficult Task) we e'en cry, Adieu, *Daddy,* and go off with our Spark. For, were we once to pass our Prime, we should run a very great Risque of taking up with some paltry, antique, undeserving Wretch of a most forbidding Physiognomy.

Q. Let me hear the Articles of thy Creed.

A. First then, I do believe, I came into the World by Mamma's Means, but not that I am one Jot obliged to her for that. In the next Place, I do hereby acknowledge myself bound (not in Duty, tho') to mind whatsoever she bids me, as also to obey that old Hunks, *Jack-pay-for-all,* my suppos'd Father; but for this very Reason only, that should I say nay, they'd force me to wear these scurvey Two-months - out - of - fashion Silks for half a Year longer, to my very great Mortification. And lastly, as for my Husband, that I shall hereafter condescend to bubble, I do verily believe he ought not to have the least Superiority over me; therefore am determined, that tho' Quadrille be my Religion, and Cuckoldom ev'ry Sabbath's Meditation; tho' I ruin him in Plays, Masquerades, Fashions, Housekeeping, &c, tho' I should even accept of my very Butler as a Coadjutor to him, he shall be mum. These are the chief Articles of my Creed, which I love, and will adhere to, to my dying Day.

Q. Have you any other Principles to steer by?

A. I act just as I've a Fancy, right or wrong, upon the Strength of my Beauty; follow all the new Fashions, be they never so ridiculous; devote myself entirely to Pride, Pleasure, and Extravagance; pray as often as a Lord pays his Debts; frequent the Theatre, &c. more than the Church; and laugh at every Body that go thither for their Devotions, believing it to be all Hypocrisy. 'Tis as natural for me to do all this, as for a Peacock to spread its Tail.

Q. Very right, but however, you know there is a World to come, should you not often consider of it?

A. No, not at all; because such Reflections are apt to give the Vapours; and Ladies ought never to molest themselves with any Thing serious, but only build their Faith on what an humourous Fancy suggests.

Q. But are Ladies then of no particular Religion?

A. No, indeed; for, at that Rate, we should be the most unfashionable Creatures breathing. Variety makes every Thing agreeable; and so for one half Hour, it may be, we assume the Christian, at other times are *Pagans, Jews, Mahometans,* or whatever best suits with our Conveniency.

Q. But what are those Principles, which, if adher'd to, will make a Lady's Life agreeable?

A. To pamper herself, her Monkey, or Lap-dog; to rail at and ridicule her Neighbours; to regard no Body; but to cozen and defraud the Poor, and to quit Scores with the Rich at the Expence of a neglected Husband's Reputation. To lie in Bed till Noon, and to chase away the Night at dear Quadrille.

Q. Hold, Hold — if you read the Form of Matrimony you'll see 'tis the Duty of Ladies to *Honour* and *Obey,* at least to respect and oblige their Husbands.

A. Marriage Form and Duty! A pretty Story! That Form's all of the Parson's contriving, and therefore not minded. Ladies regard only the Articles drawn up by the Lawyers, Covenants for Pin Money, or Allowance for separate Maintenance, and how to get an Addition to them with a good Grace. 'Tis quite out of Fashion to stand obliging an easy Fool of an Husband; but perfectly right and according to the Mode, instead of mending on their Kindness, to insult them the more.

Q. But is there any Reason for this Mode?

A. Yes sure, and a very good One. We claim our Wills while we live, because we make none when we die.

This piece had shocked Mr Ayscough when he read it. He knew it fairly described a spirit alive in many women of titled family and from the richer gentry, indeed was becoming only too prevalent lower down the social scale, in his own class. What had shocked him was not this; but that it should be said nakedly in public. His initial disgust for Lacy's calling sprang from precisely the same cause (although there, had he known, relief was at hand — in the form, only a few months ahead, of that abominable censor the Lord Chamberlain, about to begin his 230-year tyranny over the theatre). Both religion and matrimony were revealed in the Catechism as mocked, as was respect for man's superior status vis-à-vis womankind. What he saw in Rebecca's eyes, as indeed in some of her answers, was a reflection of this; that is, the effect of published laxity on high among the lower orders. It could lead one day only to the most abhorrent of human governments: democracy, that is synonymous with anarchy. The lawyer was possessed of one of the most unwelcome human sentiments: he was old, and glad he was old.

He glanced round and saw the tall clerk was back at his seat; that Rebecca had drunk, and now waited. She seemed a monument to patience, and humble submission. Yet he did not return to his chair. He continued the interrogatory from where he stood. It was only after he had asked several questions that he returned to his chair opposite her, and once more had to bear that undeviating directness of look; so direct indeed he knew he could not, and would never, believe it.

Q. Very well, mistress. Next?
A. We crept down and Dick led out the two horses, and we mounted outside, and were away. We rode a mile or more at a trot, and not a word was said, until we came to the standing pillars, or to a post some hundred paces short of them, where they tied the horses. 'Twas overcast, no stars nor moon, yet I saw them there in the darkness, like great gravestones; and I was near out of my wits with fear, not knowing why we should be in such a place at such a time. I knew hardly how to walk, yet must, for they made me. I saw some way off a light, a fire, as of shepherds, and thought to cry out, yet doubted they would hear, it was too far distant. Then, so, we came to the stones and entered within their circle, to the middle part.
Q. You would say, all three of you?
A. Yes.
Q. You told Jones, not Dick.
A. I tell now what truly passed. There his Lordship stopped, where there was a stone flat upon the ground, and he said, Fanny, kneel now upon that stone. And then I could no more, for I believed they must mean some great evil, sorcery, calling upon dark powers, I knew not what, and felt far more than natural cold, like to I was bound in ice, and about to meet my

death. So I did not kneel, nor could I speak, I was so chill and afeared. And his Lordship said again, Kneel, Fanny. And then I found my tongue, and said, We do evil, my lord, I was not hired for this. And he said, Kneel, it is not for thee to speak of doing evil. And still I would not, so they took me each an arm, and forced me to my knees upon the stone, that was hard, and most hurtful to kneel upon.

Q. You told Jones they made you lie upon it.

A. No, to kneel. And next they also knelt, beside me upon the sward on each side.

Q. How is this?

A. 'Twas so.

Q. With their hands set, as in prayer?

A. Their hands not so, but with their heads bowed.

Q. Wore they their hats still?

A. His Lordship wore his. Dick wore none.

Q. What direction did you face?

A. North, I must believe. For we rode the way west, and entered upon our right hand.

Q. Proceed.

A. For myself I prayed, and swore I should never more whore, should God forgive me and let me come safe away. I thought I was fallen into the Devil's hands, a far worse than the worst I had met at Claiborne's, and one who would not scruple to abuse my soul as much as my body and —

Q. Yes, yes, I'll imagine thee that. Now, how long knelt you all so?

A. Five, it may be more minutes, I do not know. But then there came a great rush in the sky above, as of wings, or a great roaring wind, and I looked up in terror, but saw nothing, no, nor was there wind that night, it was still.

Q. His Lordship and Dick — looked they up as well?

A. I was not fit to notice.

Q. How long did this rush, this roaring wind, sound?

A. A few moments. Not more than it takes to count ten.

Q. Did it grow louder in that time?

A. As it fell from the heavens straight upon us.

Q.   Not then as a flock of passing birds would, from one side to the other?

A.   No, from above.

Q.   You are most certain of this?

A.   Certain as Christ.

Q.   What next?

A.   Of a sudden it stopped, and there was silence, and in this pause there crept upon the air such a smell I cannot say, as of new-mown meadows and summer flowers, that was most sweet, most strange that it came not in their season, yet should spring from this cold and barren place. Then again of a great sudden there was a light upon us from above, a light more large than any human making, as of a sun, I know not, so bright I no sooner looked to it than I must look down bedazzled, why, near blind of it; and there I saw, who stood not fifteen paces from where we knelt, among the stones, a younger man and an old, that gazed upon us.

Q.   I will not believe this. I warn thee, I am not to be imposed upon.

A.   I speak truth.

Q.   No. Thou hast cunningly prepared this, to confound me. Thou and thy prophesying man, I'll warrant he put thee to this tale.

A.   No, he did not. I have never yet told him.

Q.   Yea or nay to that, still thou liest.

A.   No. I tell thee I saw them, they stood little further than this room is long. Tho' I saw them not well, for my eyes were made blind by the light, as I say.

Q.   In what posture where they?

A.   They stood, and looked on us. The younger man a little nearer, the older behind. And the younger stood with his finger pointed up, as if towards the light, yet methought his eyes did rest upon me.

Q.   With what expression?

A.   I could not truly tell, for the light went out before I recovered my eyes.

Q.   And the older?

A. I saw not, save that he had a white beard.

Q. What clothes wore they?

A. The older I saw not. The younger an apron, as masons and carpenters.

Q. You would say, he was ghost of the heathens who built the temple?

A. He was dressed as a working-man today; as might my own husband and father.

Q. Were they not painted figures?

A. No. They lived. They were no dream nor vision.

Q. Were they not most broad and tall?

A. No. Of ordinary figure.

Q. How long did this light last?

A. Very little. 'Twas nearer a lightning's flash than light proper. Enough to glimpse, no more.

Q. To glimpse, when you are already blinded, yet you may be so certain?

A. Yes.

Q. Were they not two of the standing stones?

A. No.

Q. Was there no thunder, no voice of Beelzebub?

A. No, not none. But as a gust of warmth, that was sweet-scented, as of summer fields, as I say, and more than sweet to the nose, sweet to the spirit. When all else was vanished, it remained. And I no more had fear, I knew this came not evilly, nay, the rather to comfort and solace me. Yea, it came like another light upon me, that what I feared, I feared no more. I felt more a sadness it had come yet gone so fast that I could not embrace it, nor look longer, with all my eyes. Yet must I cling to it in hope. For I tell thee it meant no evil, nor those I was with, evil. Thee must understand that.

Q. I understand one thing alone: I still cannot believe thee.

A. Thee shalt, when I have done. Thee shalt, I promise thee.

Q. When I shall call spent mutton fresh lamb, mistress, not before. Now I'll put thee closer to thy stinking meat. Whence came this light thou hadst this vision by?

A.　The sky above.

Q.　Did it light all about? Turn night into day, as the true sun does?

A.　No, the night stayed dark beyond.

Q.　Saw you candles and tapers in this great floating lantern?

A.　No, 'twas white as the summer sun, shaped as a rose, a circle.

Q.　And hung in the sky above the temple?

A.　Yes.

Q.　And moved not?

A.　No.

Q.　How high above?

A.　I cannot tell.

Q.　As high as the sun and moon?

A.　No, less. Not so high as those clouds above. As upon St Paul's round roof.

Q.　A hundred paces?

A.　I tell thee I cannot tell.

Q.　And how was this light so hung above, do you suppose?

A.　I know not, unless borne by some great bird.

Q.　Or some great liar. This sound you speak of before it shone out, you say first a rush of wings, next a roaring wind. They are not the same.

A.　I do not know to say it. Most of a passing wing that soughed.

Q.　Or a whip on thy back? Thou shalt hear that too, if I catch thee out. This pointing workman and his grandsire, carried they aught?

A.　No.

Q.　His Lordship addressed them?

A.　No, but did remove his hat.

Q.　What is this? Removed his hat to a carpenter and an old dotard?

A.　'Twas as I say.

Q.　Made they no sign back? Showed they no mark of respect to this courtesy he offered?

A.　Not that I saw.

Q.　And heard you, when the light went out, no movement?

A. No.

Q. Nor could see them still standing there?

A. No, for I was still dazzled blind.

Q. Was there no sound above?

A. All was silent.

Q. And what made you of all this?

A. That his Lordship was other than I had come to believe, as I say. For very soon after that he stood and helped me to my feet; and took my hands and pressed them, as one who is grateful, and looked me in the eyes, tho' 'twas darkness, and said, You are she I have sought. On which he turned to Dick, who was stood also, and they embraced, not as master and man, but as brothers might upon some happy outcome to their affairs.

Q. They exchanged no signs?

A. Nothing but a clasping to each other's breast.

Q. And next?

A. His Lordship led us from the stones. There he stopped and spake to me again, that I must not speak of what I had seen this night. It neither brought nor should bring harm to me; I was not to fear what must seem so strange. Then he took and pressed my hands again, most earnestly, it seemed to give proof this more gentle manner he showed me was more his true self than that I had known.

Q. What said you to this?

A. That I would not speak. To which he answered, Very well, now go with Dick. And thus I went with him, while his Lordship stayed. But before we were rid back to the inn, he came behind us. He stayed not long.

Q. Did you not ask him of what had happened?

A. He still rode some paces behind us for what short distance we had yet to make. And there in the yard bade me goodnight, and went to his room, leaving Dick his horse to unsaddle and stall. And I went likewise to my room.

Q. Dick did not join you there, when he was done?

A. I saw him not again that night.

Q. Very well. Now what of this — first that you told Jones his

Lordship did inform you of why you went to the temple, to wit, that he would use you carnally there, in pursuance of a superstition he would prove; and further you told Jones of a blackamoor perched upon a stone as if flown there like a great buzzard, ready to spring upon thy carcass, of a stench of carrion, I know not what else, a most satanick vision?

A. I lied.

Q. I lied, says she. I'll tell thee a truth of lying, mistress. Who lies once will ever lie twice.

A. I lie not now. I am upon oath.

Q. Why didst lie so greatly to Jones?

A. Because I must, to blind him, that he should think the worse of what was done, and dare not to speak, for fear he should be thought part of it. I will tell in good place, and why I lied to him.

Q. That you shall, I promise you. Now, that next day, did his Lordship's manner to you seem changed?

A. Save that once as he rode, he turned and waited until we came abreast of him, and then gave me a close look, and asked me, All is well? And I replied yes, and would have spoke more, but he turned and rode on, as it were to say, he would converse no further.

Q. What thought you to what you maintain to have seen among the stones?

A. That there lay some spell upon it, some great mystery. That it was a sign, and yet meant no evil. I have told thee, I knew no evil in it, nor fear.

Q. And what put you upon what you say his Lordship said afterward: that you were she he had sought?

A. There was that in me matched what he willed.

Q. To wit?

A. That I had sinned, and should sin no more.

Q. How is that — did he not keep you in sin and lechery?

A. That I should see it the better.

Q. Then what he willed was not what we suppose: a cure to his impotency?

A. What he sought was what came to pass.

Q. That a common whore shall provoke what passes belief? Is not that your sense? This visitation is made upon you, not him? Did he not kneel beside and below you?

A. Such was seeming. I was there of his will, not mine. I but served him.

Q. And who think you these two men to have been?

A. I shall not tell thee now.

Q. Enough of these shufflings. You are before the law, not at one of your prophetick meetings. I will be put off no more.

A. Yes thee will, Master Ayscough. For if I told thee now, and of his Lordship's will, thee would mock me, and not believe.

Q. Thy present obstinacy is worse than thy ancient whoring. Why smil'st thou?

A. Not at thee, I beg thee to believe.

Q. You shall not escape me, mistress.

A. Nor thee twist what God has given.

Q. Now what of Dick — seemed he changed upon that next day?

A. Not in his lickerousness.

Q. In what manner?

A. As we rode.

Q. What as you rode?

A. His Lordship was rid ahead, and Mr Brown and Jones lay behind.

Q. What passed?

A. I will not say. But that he was in a state of lust, as an animal.

Q. And you relieved him of it?

A. I will not say more.

Q. You mean by the roadside, among bushes?

A. I will not say more.

Q. What happened that night at Wincanton?

A. His Lordship called me not, except soon after we arrived, and then but to take a message to Jones, that his Lordship must speak with him at once.

Q. Do you know why?

A. No. I gave the message, and went to my room after.

Q. Jones did not speak to you concerning it?

A. No.

Q. And his Lordship did not ask further for you that night?

A. No.

Q. Did Dick come privily to you?

A. Yes.

Q. And you lay with him?

A. Yes.

Q. Were you not tired by then of his attentions?

A. I accepted them as before, tho' not as harlot.

Q. Out of pity, you would say?

A. Yes.

Q. Did he not arouse thy womanly lust? He did, is it not so? [*Non respondet.*] Stayed he long in your chamber?

A. As before. He was gone when I awoke.

Q. The next day you passed to Taunton. Spake his Lordship more with you on that day?

A. 'Cept once, when he rode a little beside and apart with us, and asked how I did, whether I was not sore from the riding. And when I said yes, for I had not the use of it, he said, Our journey is near done, you may rest soon.

Q. His manner was polite?

A. More as at the beginning.

Q. Did you not ask him then of what had passed at the heathen temple?

A. No.

Q. Was the moment not opportune?

A. I knew he would speak of it when he wished. And when he did not, would not. And I believed now I was under his protection, and more precious to him than he showed by his cruelty earlier, or seeming indifference. Tho' still I knew not why.

Q. And that day, did you satisfy Dick's state of lust again, as you rode?

A. No.

Q. Did he not attempt it?

A.   I would not have it.

Q.   Was he not angry? Did he not force you to it?

A.   No.

Q.   And bade his time until that night?

A.   Nor then neither. For we found no inn at Taunton that could
lodge us as we wanted, and must put up at a poor place, out
of the town's centre. There I must sleep with other maids,
and his Lordship and Mr Brown in one small chamber, and
Jones and Dick upon hay in the loft. I could not be apart
with either his Lordship nor Dick, even had they wished it.
Nothing passed. Unless the lice and fleas.

Q.   So be it. The next day?

A.   We rode all day, I think more distance than before. And
when we had passed Bampton, we went not by the high road.
By green paths and lanes, where we met few or none.

Q.   Did you not say you purposed not to return to Claiborne's,
and to find your parents and sisters again in Bristol?

A.   Yes.

Q.   Then why chose you to come this far? Is it not far west of
where you might most conveniently have escaped for Bristol?

A.   Yes, it is so. But I had not courage for it, nor saw means. At
heart I was whore still, may the Lord Jesus Christ forgive me.
A bagnio life makes hard in sin, soft in much else. We have
our servants and our needs looked to, as much as any lady.
And besides grow creatures of our humours, we think only of
today. We have no feet upon the rock, no faith to help us
provide against our future. I minded still to go to Bristol, as I
told thee, and to change my life; yet cared not at the time
that I went as I did, since it was ever more away from London, so be it at his Lordship's whim. Thee may scorn, I will
not deny it. When we rode from Taunton 'twas to be the last
day so. From that tomorrow I will not let thee scorn; or if thee
do, thee'll scorn theeself.

Q.   Enough. No more of this.

A.   Yea, I must. For else thee can't understand my soul's road,
nor his Lordship's neither. Thee must forgive, I tell thee not

the truth entire in one matter. 'Tis true I began out of force,
then out of pity for Dick. I came now to know he pleased me
more than that, yea, more than any man else I had known
since the first, when I was mere girl and in folly against all
my parents had taught me. He knew not the sinful art of love,
no not one whit; yet knew to please me more than those who
did. For he loved me the more, with all his strange heart, and
despite he could not say it in any words. And I have thought
since, in his no-words lay more speaking than in any spoken.
Which came not of what passed in the flesh, that is of our
fornicating and beastly selves, but of other times. When I did
sleep against his breast upon the road, of looks we passed, I
know not, when I heard what he would say better than if he
had spoke it out loud. He came to my bed on that last night,
and had his will of me; then lay a-weeping in my arms, and I
wept also, for I knew why he wept. As if we lived in two
prison cells, able to see the one the other and touch our
hands, yet no more. And thee may call it what thee will, I tell
thee this weeping was most strange and most sweet to me. For
I saw it freed me from my harlotry, my sin, my hardness of
heart, all I had become since first I lost my innocence. 'Twas
as if for those years I had lived in darkness, and made of
stone; and now was flesh again, if not yet Christian, and fully
saved. Believe me or not. Every word I say is truth.

Q. You loved the man?

A. I might have loved him, could he have shed his Adam.

Q. And what heard you in this speaking without words?

A. That he was a desperate unhappy man, as I was myself, tho'
for a different cause; and that he knew me so, and loved me
also that I did not mock and spurn him.

Q. Very well. Now did you not both upon this last day's journey
ride aside with his Lordship?

A. To the summit of a mountain, that lay beside the road, and
showed many miles to the land ahead.

Q. Did Dick not point in a certain direction? To a particular
place?

A.   I took it to be in show, to seem as he knew the country.

Q.   Did his Lordship ask Dick to point? Did they exchange some sign first?

A.   No.

Q.   Was not where Dick pointed, to that cavern where you were on the morrow?

A.   I could not say.

Q.   It was in that same direction, was it not?

A.   It was westward. More I cannot tell. It may be so.

Q.   This place was how far from where you rested that night?

A.   Two hours' ride or more.

Q.   And nothing else passed as you rode?

A.   His Lordship took offence that I wore violets beneath my nose. I put them in a band there for their sweet scent. He took it as an impertinence, I know not why. Tho' he said nothing till later.

Q.   It was not reasonable? You gave him no other cause than this, that you had picked a nosegay?

A.   I am sure not.

Q.   Now what said he later?

A.   He called me to him when we had supped, by Dick, and I thought for his old purpose. However, Dick was dismissed as soon as I was brought, when his Lordship would have me make myself naked before him; which I was obliged to do, expecting he would at last try his prowess upon me. But he would not, he made me sit on a bench before him, as I were a penitent, and called me impertinent, as I say, for the violets; then a whore, I know not what else, more cruel than ever before, like he was half mad, for he forced me to kneel, and make an oath that all he said was true. Then all of a great sudden he changed, and maintained his cruelty was no more than a test, that on the contrary he was well pleased with me. And spake of those he called the keepers of the waters, that we should meet tomorrow; and now said that I was brought by him to please them and must do so, he should reward me for it. I must put off my London airs, so he said, and appear as simple as I could, and feign I came not from the bagnio.

Q. By these waters you supposed those he had spoken of in London?

A. Yes.

Q. Said he no more of these keepers?

A. That they were foreign, and spake no English, nor other tongue of Europe; nor knew nothing of women of vice.

Q. He was not more particular — did he not name some particular place or country from which these persons came?

A. No.

Q. Did he never intimate where he had heard of them?

A. Only that he much wished to meet them.

Q. He had not met them before, was that to be understood?

A. Yes, when he spake of them. Tho' 'twas not said plain, he had not.

Q. Does this signify, it was to turn out upon the morrow that he had?

A. Thee shall hear.

Q. Did you not think this strange, that his Lordship now talked of giving you to others, as a pandar might?

A. Yes, in part.

Q. Why only in part?

A. I knew by then he dealt most in riddles.

Q. I would know this, before we proceed. Were you so given, on the morrow? Say yes or no.

A. I was given.

Q. Were you not on this evening made fearful again, even tho' you had believed what passed at the Wiltshire temple not evil in its purpose?

A. Still I saw behind his Lordship's dark humours no evil. I did not understand what he did, and most feared my own ignorance.

Q. I would know something more in general. Think you his Lordship knew of your amour with his servant? Was it done within his knowledge or behind his back?

A. He knew, for he accused me of it, that I had too great a fondness for Dick's embraces; as a master might say, You are bought for my pleasure, yet do find it in another's arms; and that I would have told him as much by the wearing of the violets.

Q. He knew you lay with Dick in secret, outside of those occasions he commanded?

A. What I had been hired for was done but twice, and then no more, so to say his Lordship gave up hope of it, and I was abandoned to his man; yet still was he angered that I took pleasure in it.

Q. You would say, that he saw your coupling answered not to his declared purpose, and so he cared no more?

A. His Lordship had more than one purpose, and one a far greater.

Q. What was this greater purpose?

A. I will not speak thereto yet.

Q. It shall be explained.

A. In good time.

Q. To the nonce: was it not singular that he should put upon you that you must serve to these important strangers, yet not say you must now put Dick by?

A. So it was, even so.

Q. That was his wish, as you conceived — that you should be these persons' whore if they so desired, and despite your appearance of innocence? Not less?

A. So I understood it.

Q. All this was said by way of command: that you must do it? Not that the choice lay with you?

A. As his wish, that I must obey.

Q. Nothing else was said to you by his Lordship?

A. No.

Q. You hesitate.

A. I sought my memory.

Q. And you say no?

A. I say no.

Q. Mistress, there is that in your answering I like not. 'Tis as if you would tease, and riddle me. This is no riddling matter, I warn thee.

A.   If I speak riddles, I was set them. If I confuse thee, so was I confused.

Q.   His Lordship dismissed you?

A.   Yes.

Q.   You saw him no more until the morning?

A.   No.

Q.   You went to your room, and then Dick came?

A.   I was asleep when he came.

Q.   And did you not think, I must lie in another man's arms to-morrow?

A.   I did not know the morrow then, Jesus be praised.

Q.   The morrow is close. Thou shalt put off no more.

A.   I know it.

Q.   Had you no warning that Jones would run away that night?

A.   No, none.

Q.   He spoke not of it to you?

A.   We spake little. I misliked him.

Q.   Why?

A.   Because he would pry when we started out; and would seem always to know more of me than he did; that I owed him a favour for his silence.

Q.   He did not lie in that?

A.   Notwithstanding. He would ever mock Dick for his dumbness and deafness. I liked not that, neither. He never said plain, till the end.

Q.   Knew you that Mr Brown should part also, so soon upon your setting out?

A.   No.

Q.   Were you not surprised?

A.   It seemed not strange. Their task was done.

Q.   Very well. Mr Brown rode away, and you set off upon the Bideford road. What next?

A.   We rode, and entered soon upon woods, a most wild place; and went there till we came upon a stream that fell across the road, and we must cross. Where his Lordship stopped and looked back upon Dick, for he rode ahead, and we behind;

and raised a hand with the forefinger stretched out so, the other forefinger so, as a cross. To which Dick replied by pointing ahead as we stood, which was not to the road we trod, that crooks back at where the stream crosses, but up the hill, or mountain, on the course the water fell by.

Q. What put you upon this?

A. That Dick must know this place, and his Lordship not; or was not so certain of it.

Q. Were other signs made?

A. His Lordship set his hands apart, as if to measure. And Dick raised two fingers. Which I understood not then, but I think now to have meant, It is two miles away. There came no more sign. Yet they moved not from where we stood, but stared still together, like two people tranced by each other's eyes. Till of a sudden his Lordship turned his horse, and rode away through the trees, up the hill where Dick had pointed.

Q. Said he nothing to you?

A. No, not one word, nor looked at me. 'Twas as I was not there.

Q. Had you seen them before stare in this manner?

A. Yes, once or twice, not so long.

Q. It was not as master and man?

A. More as two children will stare each other out.

Q. Then with a seeming hostility?

A. Not that, neither, not as an ordinary look. As if they spake, tho' their mouths moved not.

Q. Very well. You entered upon the valley above. Jones has told me of it, how it lies. Come to where first you stopped.

A. We must soon dismount, or our horses fall. And there it was Dick who led our pillion and the packhorse, and I walked after, and his Lordship led his own horse behind. The all in silence, save for the beasts' feet upon the stones, and we went beside the stream. And so for a mile or more, I know not. Where Dick of a sudden stopped and tied the two horses to a thorn branch, and took his Lordship's when it came, and tied it to another. And there began to unrope his Lordship's great box, from the seam the packhorse bore.

Q. Dick did not stop or do this last of his Lordship's command?

A. No, of his own will. Like as if he knew best where we went.

Q. Continue.

A. His Lordship came beside me, and said that my dress was not sufficient for who we met. That he had brought an other more suitable and now I must wear it, for we were close. And I asked, was there no better road? And he answered, no, there was only this. And then, that I should not fear, no harm would come if I did as I was told. The while, the box was upon the ground and opened, and his Lordship himself gave me the clothes from it, that lay upon the top.

Q. What were these clothes?

A. Why, a smicket and petticoat, then a fine white holland gown, ruffled with cambric upon its sleeves, where it bore pink ribbands also, in two knots. Fine clocked Nottingham stockings also, and white likewise. And shoes of the same. 'Twas all white and new, or fresh laundered.

Q. You would say, as a May dress?

A. As a country maid might wear, of dimity. Tho' finer made, and of finer cloth, as for a lady.

Q. And stitched also to your figure?

A. Well enough.

Q. You had no knowledge of these, before?

A. No, none.

Q. And next?

A. His Lordship said I must bathe, before I donned my new clothes.

Q. You must bathe?

A. That I must be pure of my body, with no taint of my former world upon me. And he did point a little back, to where the stream did deepen a piece, as a pond, albeit not so deep, and small; for most it ran shallow, upon stones.

Q. What thought you to this?

A. That it was too cold. To which he said I must, this stream should be my Jordan.

Q. He said these words: this stream shall be thy Jordan?

A. Yes.

Q. Spake he as in jest?

A. Thee shalt hear in what jest he spake. It seemed jest then, though no jest to me.

Q. You did bathe?

A. As best I could. For the water came only to my knees, and I must crouch in it, ice-cold as 'twas.

Q. You were naked?

A. I was naked.

Q. Did his Lordship watch you?

A. His back was turned, that I saw. And after, my back upon him.

Q. And then?

A. I dried myself upon the bank, and did put on the new clothes, and warmed myself in the sun. When his Lordship came to me again where I sat and gave to me a knife that Dick had used to carry, and said, It is May Day, and here is may enough. Thou shalt be queen, Fanny, but thou must crown thyself.

Q. He spoke again in good humour?

A. Passing good, so be it his mind was elsewhere. For he turned away some paces, and watched where Dick had gone.

Q. When was he gone? Was it before you had bathed?

A. As soon as the box was opened, and the horses better tied. Across the stream and up the steep side, where we could see him no more.

Q. The horses were not left tied as when you came?

A. No. For as I did go a little apart to bathe, I saw Dick a-tying of them to long tethers, which he put to the thorn-tree stems that were there; and that he had took off their saddles and harness and set them so that they might drink from the stream and take what grass there was.

Q. As to say, their stay would be long?

A. Yes.

Q. And you saw not Jones, when he was caught up and did watch you?

A. I had no thought of him, nor anyone, only of myself. I made my crown, as I could; then Dick was returned, and signed to his Lordship, who waited.

Q. A sign like this, was it not so?

A. No, not so.

Q. Jones says it was so.

A. No, it was not, and I doubt he could see so well, where he was hid.

Q. Then how?

A. With his hands clasped thus, before his breast. Which I had seen before, and knew it meant much like to saying, It is done; or, I have done what is commanded. So here it might mean, Who we meet awaits us above. For his Lordship came at once where I sat, and said we must go. As we did, tho' first I must be carried. The ground was most rough and steep, and Dick took me in his arms.

Q. Seemed he not excited, or in good spirit, when he returned from above?

A. No.

Q. Very well, enough for this present. We shall not yet mount with thee to the cavern, mistress. My man shall take thee to a room apart to dine. Thou'rt not to speak with thy husband, or none else, is it clear?

A. I shall with my soul's husband, that is Christ.

THE TALL, SLIGHTLY BENT-SHOULDERED clerk opened the door, and followed his prisoner out. But then she had to follow him, as he led the way down a short passage to another door. Only when she was inside the room, and turned back to look at him, did he speak.

"Ale or more water, mistress?"

"Water."

"You will not leave this room."

She shook her head, agreeing. He gave her a long stare, as if he doubted her word, then left, closing the door behind him. The room was evidently a small bedchamber, with only one window, before which stood a table and two chairs. She did not move to it, but beside the bed, and stooped, lifting the side of the coverlet and looking on the floor below it; pulled out what she was looking for and, quickly raising her skirts, sat upon it.

She did not have to remove any other garment for the very simple reason that no Englishwoman, of any class, had ever worn anything beneath her petticoats up to this date, nor was to do so for at least another sixty years. One might write an essay on this incomprehensible and little-known fact about their under-clothing, or lack in it. French and Italian women had long remedied the deficiency, and English men also; but not English women. All those

graciously elegant and imposing upper-class ladies in their fashionable or court dresses, whose image has been so variously left us by
the eighteenth-century painters, are — to put it brutally — knick-
erless. And what is more, when the breach was finally made — or
rather, covered — and the first female drawers, and soon after
pantalettes, appeared at the beginning of the nineteenth century,
they were considered grossly immodest, an unwarranted provoca-
tion upon man; which is no doubt why they so swiftly became *de
rigueur*.

Rebecca stood relieved, and pushed the earthenware jordan
back beneath the bed, and straightened the coverlet. Next she
walked slowly to the window and looked out, down upon the large
back courtyard of the inn.

A private coach was drawn up, its four horses still harnessed, as if
it had just arrived, on the far side. Its nearer door bore a painted
coat of arms, supported by a wyvern and a leopard; its motto and
closer detail, beyond two quarters of red diamonds, impossible to
read. There was no sign of its passengers or coachmen; only an
ostler's boy, seemingly left to watch the horses. Here and there
some hens and a gamecock scratched among the cobbles, and spar-
rows, and a pair of white doves, that the boy fed from a palmful of
grains, idly, as he leant against the coach. Every so often he would
put a fatter grain in his own mouth and chew it. Suddenly Rebecca's head bowed and she closed her eyes, as if she could not bear
to watch this innocent scene. Her mouth began to move, though no
sound came from it, and it became plain she was speaking to that
husband she had just given herself licence to address.

The movements of her lips stopped. There were footsteps on the
wooden floor of the passage outside. Her eyes opened again, and
she sat quickly, in one of the chairs, her back to the door. It opened,
the clerk stood there, staring a moment at her back. She did not
turn; some moments later, as if belatedly realising that no one had
come in, no normal sound followed that of the opening door, she
glanced back over her shoulder. It was no longer the sardonic clerk
she had expected: another man, elderly, of medium height yet
rather stout, a gentleman in grey. He stood neither in nor out of the
room, doom in the doorway, and watched her. She rose, but made

no other obeisance. He wore a plain black hat, and his right hand gripped a strange thing, a shepherd's crook, its foot on the ground. However, this was no shepherd; where the top of a working crook is of wood or horn, here it was of polished silver, like some staff of office; closer to a bishop's crosier than anything else.

Nor was his stare at her that of a normal man; much more that of a person sizing an animal, a mare or cow, as if he might at any moment curtly state a price that he considered her worth. There was something both imperious and imperial in that look, indifferent to ordinary humanity, oblivious of it, above all law; and something also that was unaccustomed, almost at a loss to be seen there. Without warning he spoke, yet not to Rebecca, though his eyes did not leave her face.

"Make her step forward. She stands in the light."

The clerk appeared outside, and beckoned urgently to her behind the man in the doorway; two swift movements of a bent finger. She came forward. The foot of the silver-ended crook was quickly raised, to keep her at a distance. So she stood, some six feet away. His face was heavy, deprived of any signs of humour, good or bad, and without generosity; or even, much more oddly, of any normal curiosity. One detected beneath it a hint of morose doubt that was also a melancholy. Even that was very largely obscured by the aura of absolute right, in both the ordinary and the ancient monarchical sense; an impassivity both habitual and imprisoning. He did not, now she was close, even look at her as a beast; but uniquely into her eyes, as if trying to read some almost metaphysical meaning through them. Rebecca faced him and gazed back, one hand upon the other in front of her belly; neither respectfully nor insolently; openly, yet neutrally, waiting.

Slowly the man's hand slipped down his crook and he held it out, without threat, almost tentatively, until the curved silver end lay against the close sidepiece of her white cap. Twisting the crook a little, he pulled to draw her towards him. This was done so cautiously, in other circumstances one might have said timidly, that she did not flinch when the silver end of the crook touched her, nor when it began to coax her forwards. She obeyed, until the pressure at her neck ceased, and their faces were barely eighteen inches apart. Yet they seemed no closer; not just divided by age and gender, but by belonging to two eternally alien species.

And now, as abruptly as he appeared, the man ends this wordless interview. The crook is jerked impatiently clear, and set firmly to ground again as he turns away, as if disappointed. Rebecca has time to see that he walks with a heavy limp — the crook-staff is no mere eccentric adornment, it is a necessity — and she has just time also to see the clerk step back with a deep bow, and Mr Ayscough also, with a lesser one, then turn to follow his master. The clerk comes and stands in the doorway, with a faintly quizzical look at her. Most unexpectedly his right eye flickers, in the ghost of a wink. He disappears for a moment or two, then returns bearing a wooden tray, on which is a cold chicken; a rummer and a small jug of water; a leather tankard, black with age; a bowl of green pickles, eldershoot and gherkins; a salt-pot, two apples, and a loaf of bread. These he sets upon the table, and produces from his pocket a knife and two two-pronged forks. Now he takes off his coat and throws it on the bed. Rebecca has not moved, and stares at the ground. The clerk sits in his shirtsleeves, and briskly seizes the chicken, knife in hand.

"You must eat, woman."

Rebecca moves and sits opposite him, at the window; when he would pass her the breast he has detached, she shakes her head.

"I would send it outside, to my husband and father."

"No. Feed your bastard. If not yourself. Come." Now he cuts a slice of the loaf, and puts the breast upon it, and places it before her. "Come. You are safe from the gallows till then." And again his right eye flickers, almost as if it is a tic, outside his control. "Your man and your father dine not so well. Yet they may dine if they would. I have had bread and cheese sent. What do they say? They say they will not eat the Devil's food. There it lies, on the street before them. Charity made sin."

"No, 'tis not. I thank thee."

"As I thee, mistress. For the absolution."

She bows her head a few seconds, as she had when she prayed alone; and grace said, begins to eat, and so does he, a leg, and a great slice of bread, folded round a forkful of the pickles; alternate bite by bite. It is a kind of wolfing, without delicacy. An acknowledgement of reality: that life is always near starvation, and plenty such as this not to be trifled with. She pours water into the rummer; and later, spears a gherkin from the pickle, and another; and finally a third. The second breast she refuses when it is silently offered; but takes her apple. She watches him opposite, and when he seems finally done, the chicken in ruins, the ale supped, speaks.

"What is thy name?"

"Royal, mistress. John Tudor."

"And where did thee learn to write so swift?"

"The short hand? By practice. 'Tis child's play, once learnt. And where I cannot read when I copy in the long hand, why, I make it up. So I may hang a man, or pardon him, and none the wiser." And once again she sees that tic in his right eye.

"I may read. I cannot write, save my name."

"Then you are saved writing."

"I would learn, e'en so."

He does not answer, but the ice thus broken, she continues.

"Are thee married?"

"Aye. And rid."

"How rid?"

"I married one worse than you, for her mouth. Who never spoke save she disputed or denied. She matched Joe Miller's jest. Should I forbid her another crooked word, why, she'd cry ram's horn to my face. Until one day I beat her as she had well deserved, and she would not brook it, and ran off. And did me a great mercy."

"Where went she?"

"I know not nor care not, mistress. Where women always go — to Hell or another man. She was not so fair as you. I was well rid." Again his eye flickers. "Thee, I might have asked after."

"She never came back?"

"No." He shrugged, as if he regretted having spoken. " 'Tis old water, well past the mill-wheel. Sixteen years gone."

"And have thee always worked for the one master?"

"Near enough."

"Thee knew Dick, then?"

"Nobody knew him, mistress. He was not to be known. Though he knew thee, it seems. More's the wonder."

She looks down. "He was man enough."

"Was he so?" She looks hesitantly up at him, aware that his question is sarcastic, yet plainly not understanding why. He stares away out of the window for a moment, then back at her. "Didst never hear of such, when thou wert what thou wast?"

"Of such?"

"Come now, mistress. You were not always saint. You have said as much today, and most credible, that you know your men. Did you not take one whiff?"

"I grasp thee not."

"What is most unnatural, and a great crime. Where servant may become master, and master, servant."

She stares at the clerk a long moment; he gives a small nod, to kill her doubt, and then again there comes that minute spasm of his eyelid.

"No."

"Saw you no sign of it?"

"No."

"Nor mayhap thought it might be so?"

"Nor that, even."

"Very well, God save your innocence. And do not you speak of it, unless you be asked. And never outside these walls, mistress, if you value your life." There comes from down below the sound of hooves on the cobbles, the heavy grating of iron-shod wheels, a coachman's cry. The clerk stands and looks down to watch. Only when the vehicle has drawn out, and without turning to where she still sits, does he speak again; almost as if to himself. "He'll hear aught but that."

Then he goes and picks his coat from the bed where it lies and puts it back on.

"I leave you now, mistress. Do your necessities, I fetch you again to Mr Ayscough shortly." She bows her head in a little sign of acquiescence. "Speak truth. Fear not. 'Tis but his manner."

"I have spoken truth, and shall. Nothing else."

"There are two truths, mistress. One that a person believes is truth; and one that is truth incontestible. We will credit you the first, but the second is what we seek."

"I must tell what I believe."

He walks to the door, yet there he stops and looks back at her.

"Thee, I should have asked after."

She receives one last tic of his right eyelid; and then he is gone.

Rebecca Lee further deposeth,
die et anno praedicto

Q.   Mistress, let us recommence. You rest upon oath, do not forget it. First I would ask you this. Know you what the vice of Sodom betokens?

A.   Yes.

Q.   Saw you ever, at any time since first you met his Lordship, any sign that he and his man were its victims? That they were guilty of practising it?

A.   No. I am most certain, no.

Q.   Was there no hint, when his Lordship first spoke of his failing to you, that such was the true cause of his insufficiency?

A.   No.

Q.   Nor later?

A.   No.

Q.   Did you never think, he may say what he likes, or not say, this must be the true cause?

A.   Those I have known said to be such have a different manner. 'Tis well known, where I was sinner. There are names for them, petty-masters or pretty-boys. They are more beauish than proper men should be. More foppish, and coxcombs, most often, more full of malice and scandal than aught else. 'Tis said, by resentment of what they are, and so must they damn all else, being damned themselves.

Q.   His Lordship seemed not like this?

A.   No, not one piece.

Q.   When Dick did use you before his eyes, he did not command it be enacted in manner unnatural?

A.   He was silent as stone.

Q.   Now, Mistress Lee, I respect your judgement here. You are certain?

A.   Certain he bore no common sign of it, nor report of it neither. Nothing was said of him to this wise at Mistress Claiborne's, though we had use to discuss all who came there, and most wicked freely; what their faults were, and every scandal we had heard of them. Lord B———— himself did question me, who has the most evil tongue in London, the most happy to hear ill of a friend. Even he made no hint of such vice. Only of his Lordship's coldness, his liking his books and studies more than flesh like mine; and whether I has surmounted this taste in him.

Q.   What answered you?

A.   What was false itself: that reputation was false.

Q.   Very well. Now come to the cavern.

A.   Still shall I tell truth.

Q.   As I shall doubt where I please.

A.   Doubted truth is no less truth.

Q.   Then no less truth for being doubted. Speak on.

A.   First as we mounted to where the cavern lay, tho' 'twas yet hidden from our eyes behind a fold of land, there stood sudden in our path, a lady in silver.

Q.   How, in silver?

A.   She was clothed, tho' most strange, in plain silver, that had no pattern to it, nor flowering. And more strange still, wore narrow trowse, as seamen wear, or northmen over their breeches, such that I saw once a-riding into London, yet more narrow, that fitted almost close as hose. And above a close-fit smock, cut of the same cloth, that shone like silver. And on her feet she wore as a man's riding-boots, yet shorter; as of black leather, without their tops. And thus she stood there, gazing upon us, as she had waited our coming.

Q.   Mean you to maintain she sprang from nothing, from thin air?

A.   So she had lain in hiding till then.

Q.   Why say you she was lady?

A.   She was no common person.

Q.   Was she attended? Was there no groom or servant?

A.   She was alone.

Q.   Young or old?

A.   Young and fair to see, with full dark hair, that was not bound, as black as a raven's wing; yet cut strange in a line above her brows, nor a curl to be seen.

Q.   Wore she no cap or hat?

A.   No. And I must tell thee her manner was strange as her appearance, for she moved and stood not as a lady might, more as a young gentleman, I mean of most simple and easy sort, that cares not for pomp and formal appearance; and did salute us in strange fashion also, so, with her hands held in front of her, so, as 'twere in prayer. Yet held thus for a moment only, as another might raise a hand to a friend, in light greeting.

Q.   She showed no surprise at your coming?

A.   No, not none.

Q.   What response made his Lordship?

A.   He fell at the once upon his knee, and did take off his hat, it seemed in respect. And Dick besides, and I must follow, tho' I knew not why, nor who she might be. Whereat the young lady did smile, as one who had not expected such courtesy; yet, being done, did welcome it.

Q.   She did not speak?

A.   No, not one word.

Q.   His Lordship addressed her?

A.   He knelt with head bowed, so to say he dared not look her in her face.

Q.   Thought you they had met before?

A.   He did seem to know who she was.

Q.   Made she no especial sign of greeting or respect to his Lordship?

A. No.

Q. Of what stuff were these her singular clothes?

A. Of none I have seen. They shone like best silk, yet fell more stiff, when she moved.

Q. You say she was young?

A. Of my own age, or less.

Q. How far from you stood she in this manner?

A. It may be fifty paces, not more.

Q. Seemed she of English blood, or foreign?

A. Not English.

Q. Then of what nation?

A. In looks she was most like unto one showed these two summers past in a tent beside the Mall, that they called the Corsair Woman. Who was taken from a ship captured in the West, and said as cruel a sailor as any man, tho' mistress unto the corsair's captain. He was renegade, and hanged at Deptford docks, she spared. And would stare at us who paid to view her so she would kill us were she not chained, yet was exceeding handsome and fine-figured. Claiborne thought to have her to the bagnio, and the taming of her fierceness as a whet to the boldest rakes; but those who kept her would not agree a price. And said besides, she would not bear such a thing, should kill herself rather than suffer it. This lady upon the path was not she, I pray thee do not mistake. This upon the path was gentle of face, not cruel.

Q. This woman you speak of in the tent, she was Moorish? A Turkess?

A. I know not, save she had dark eyes and hair, and a skin of olive. She wore no red nor ceruse, and had somewhat of the Jewesses I have seen in London; yet her manner not modest, nor seeming fearful as is their wont. Of she in the tent I heard some declare she was false, no true Corsair woman, but a common Egyptian paid so to pretend. I tell thee, I speak only of how it did come to my mind when first she stood there.

Q. Why say you she seemed more a young gentleman in her behaving?

A. That she made no affectation of elegant manner, as a London lady might; as she had no need of fashion nor airs to prove her state. She did seem at a loss at our kneeling, like she found it not necessary. For soon after, she placed her hands upon her hips, as a man might, like to say we puzzled her.

Q. She was angered?

A. No, for she smiled still, it seemed more we did amuse her. And then again of a sudden she did show with her arm behind her, in such a manner might one invite a stranger to a house or chamber, that he should enter at his will. 'Twas as the daughter of a house, before her parents' coming.

Q. Saw you no malice nor evil in this person?

A. I told ill of her to Jones, may God forgive me. I did see, as I say, strange dress and manner; in truth in all else innocence and beauty, that knew not England nor its ways, yet had a freedom and an ease no Englishwoman knows of.

Q. What followed?

A. She did make that same gesture with her hands, so; then did turn and walk away, simple and idle as within her private garden; for she did stoop and pluck a flower and raised it to her nose to smell. Thus might she had we never been there. Then his Lordship arose and we mounted where she had first stood, and we could see all before us, the cavern's mouth withal. Where she now did stand, and seeing us, did point towards the pool, so to say we should wait there; and turned and entered in its darkness and was gone.

Q. This path by which you had mounted — seemed it well trod, had others passed that way often?

A. 'Twas faint, or not at all.

Q. Did you not ask his Lordship who this person was?

A. Aye, and he answered, I pray she shall be thy friend. No more.

Q. Proceed.

A. We came to where a pool and stone did stand, before the cavern. There his Lordship a little apart, while I knelt by the pool, and bathed my face, and drank of it, for the sun beated down, and I was hot.

Q. Now I ask you, mistress, you were hot, were you not out of

your wits with the sun and your walking? I do not say you lie,
yet that there was some disorder in your spirits, and you saw
what was never in front of you, but had pushed forth from
your heated mind in the semblance of reality?

A.   No, I am sure not.

Q.   It is not heard of, that any woman whatsoever, far less a lady,
and one of foreign birth, should be alone in such a place.

A.   Much is not heard of, that is. Thee must judge when all is
said.

Q.   Then say it.

A.   His Lordship came to where I sat beside the pool and said,
The time is come, Fanny. The keepers await. Now I must tell
thee, as I sate there, my heart had of a sudden sore misgiven
me of what we did. I liked not that black cavern's mouth
across the grass, that seemed more fit for a gateway to Hell
than to curing waters. And when his Lordship spake, I answered that I began to fear. To which he replied, It is too late
now to fear. I would have him to assure me I should come to
no harm in what we did. To which he said, I should come to
more harm now if I disobeyed. I would know more of the
keepers, but he grew impatient, and said, No more of this,
and took my arm, so I must go with him to where Dick stood,
by the stone; and must as well put on my crown of may.
When Dick seized my hand, and I was straightway made to
walk by him toward the cavern, while his Lordship came a
two paces behind, like as it were to attend us, in my fears I
thought the better to prevent me, should I try to escape. And
now did I sink under great alarm that God forgive me I was
fallen into the hands of two devils, who wore the mask of ordinary men; and these waters they that are said to boil eternal for sinners in the deeps of Hell, and their keeper must be
the Devil, who I was now to meet. And all this swept upon
me with such force, I fell on my knees as we walked and
begged his Lordship to tell me the truth. I knew I had sinned,
but no more than many others, and begged to be spared, I
know not what. To which he told me quick I was a fool and
said, did I not suppose if they took me to Hell, the last thing I

should meet was punishment, on the contrary I should be welcomed with open arms, I had done their service so well. He said, had I not been the Devil's good servant? Should I not fear Heaven's anger far more? And then was I pulled to my feet again, and must move on.

Q. Did not his Lordship threaten you with his sword?

A. No, tho' he was drawn, and held it in his hand. He spake not in a rage, more as one impatient I should mistake their purpose so.

Q. I return a moment. Saw you, before his Lordship fetched you to this, a sign from the cavern that the time was come? The woman in silver beckoned not, nor servant?

A. I cannot tell. I looked not towards the cavern, I was too lost in my fears and thoughts.

Q. Did you not mark a burnt place beside the cavern's mouth?

A. Yes. I had forgot to tell.

Q. What did you observe of it?

A. It seemed new-burnt, yet was there no pile of ashes. It lay in a circle, as of a great fire.

Q. Very well. On.

A. First my eyes were weak after the brightness of the sun, and I saw only shadows, and knew not where I went save by Dick's guidance. Until of a sudden he made me turn upon my left hand.

Q. Why stop you?

A. The maggot.

Q. What maggot?

A. That floated in the inner cavern, like a great swollen maggot, white as snow upon the air.

Q. What is this?

A. Yea, like a maggot, tho' not. Its great eye shone down upon us, my blood did curdle in my veins; and I must perforce call out in my fear, ignorant that I was. Now his Lordship came beside me and took my other arm, and forward towards it, and then to kneel.

Q. You alone, or all?

A. All, as at the temple, and upon the path.

Q. I'll know more of this maggot. What appearance had it?

A. Of white, yet not of flesh, as it were wood japanned, or fresh-tinned metal, large as three coaches end to end, or more, its head with the eye larger still; and I did see other eyes along its sides that shone also, tho' less, through a greenish glass. And at its end there was four great funnels black as pitch, so it might vent its belly forth there.

Q. Had it jaws and teeth?

A. No, none, nor legs neither at that first, but six black holes or mouths beneath.

Q. It lay not on the ground? It was suspended — there were ropes, timber, could you not see?

A. No, none.

Q. How high in the air?

A. At twice a man's height, it may be more. I thought not then of measure.

Q. Why say you maggot?

A. So I first believed it to be. For it had a seeming head, and a tail, and was fat, and like in colour.

Q. Did it move?

A. Not when first we stood before it; then it hung in the air like to a kite, yet no string. Or a windhover, yet beat no wings, as they do.

Q. Of what girth or circumference?

A. More than a man in height. Two men.

Q. Ten to twelve feet?

A. Yes.

Q. And you say, as three coaches long or more? Why, this is entire fantastickal. Thou mak'st it up, 'tis not to be believed. How came this thing within a cavern whose mouth would not admit it, nor the passage to its inner chamber neither?

A. I know not, save that it was there. And if thee won't have it there, then I say no more. I will not lie. I am dammed as a stream is dammed, and must spill to waste.

Q. I may sooner believe thy three witches that was told to Jones, and the Devil at thy tail, than this.

A. That is, thee art man. Thee'd make me mirror of thy sex.

Dost know what a harlot is, master Ayscough? What all men
would have all women be, that they may the easier think the
worst of them. I would I had a guinea for every man that
hath told me he wished I were his wife, or his wife like me.

Q. Enough of thy licentious tongue. I'll not yet dam thy tale,
mistress, but I'll see thee damned for a liar yet. This most pre-
posterous maggot — bore it no marks other?

A. Upon its side was a wheel with figures thereafter, in a line;
and yet another, upon its belly, the same.

Q. How a wheel?

A. As 'twas painted upon its white skin, in a blue as of summer
sea, or sky; and that bore many spokes about its hub.

Q. And the figures?

A. I knew them not. They were in a line, as letters or numbers,
that might be read by those who knew. One was in the likeness of a bird, it might be a swallow flying; and another, of a
flower, as daubed upon a piece of china pot, not strict to the
life, though all of equal size. And yet another was as a circle,
divided in two halves by crescent line; its one half black, the
other left white, so the moon in middle wane.

Q. There were no alphabet letters, nor numbers?

A. No.

Q. You marked no emblem of Christianity?

A. No.

Q. Made it no sound?

A. There was as a humming, tho' low, such as a closed furnace
that flames, or oven before baking. Like also a hive of bees, or
a cat that purrs. And soon did I smell of that sweet smell I
knew at the temple, and guessed it to be the same light that
had floated above us there; and my heart had relief, for I
knew this must bring no evil, for all its seeming.

Q. How, you see a vile prodigy that denies all Nature's laws, and
deem it not evil?

A. No, I knew it not evil, by this smell; that it was the lion's carcase, and held honey within. And as I shall tell.

Q. What, you may tell good and evil by smell?

A. By this smell, yes. For it was of innocence and blessedness.

357

Q. Very fine. Now tell how innocent blessedness doth smell.

A. I could not say in words; tho' I smell it yet.

Q. As I thy self-weening piety, which stinketh over this thy manner of answering. I command you to describe this smell, as it might come to nostrils less blest.

A. All that was good in what does smell.

Q. But sweet, or more harsh? Of musk, bergamot, attar, myrrh? Of flowers or fruit, or made waters, such as they of Hungary or Cologne? Of what must be burnt or of what smells of its natural essence? Why answer you not?

A. Of life eternal.

Q. Mistress, had I asked another question of you, such as in what your belief or hope may lie, you may answer so. But not in this. You say that still you smell this smell. Very well. I'll not be foisted by this havering.

A. Then most of the white canker that grows in June in the hedge, which we did call the virgin rose when I was small, and a bride must carry in her posy, if she is wed within its season; that lasts but one day or two, and smells most pure when first it opens and is golden of its heart.

Q. The white briar, you would say?

A. She the rose that is weak, and falls if she is not supported, and less sweet of her perfume than they that grow in gardens. Yea, like to her, but yet stronger, as she were 'stilled. And yet this is no more than to say a man's soul by his outward face.

Q. Did there not burn upon the cavern's floor a great fire, as you told Jones?

A. No, yet a place as one had been, like that outside; but old, of darkened ashes only, long burnt away.

Q. It burnt not still?

A. No spark nor smoulder.

Q. You are certain? Was there no smell of burning also?

A. I am certain. There was no smell.

Q. Saw you not, now you were close, by what powers this great light shone?

A. No, for it was covered as by milk-glass, or thick muslin, that showed nothing behind. Yet more bright than any lamp or sconce I've seen in this world.

Q. How large was its expanse?

A. A foot.

Q. No more?

A. 'Twas so. But brighter than the sun. 'Twas not to be beheld direct.

Q. How close kneeled you while it hovered above?

A. Passing close. As to that far wall here.

Q. Do you maintain that this was some engine come from the temple to this place; that might mount into the heavens, as a bird?

A. Yes, and far besides.

Q. Though it had no wheels, nor wings, nor horses?

A. Thee must hear more, master Ayscough. Thee would have me out of my wits, and the fool of apparitions. Thee would have me put wheel and wing to God's breath. Thee can see I am a poor woman, and not well lettered; and a plain one besides, in my natural. I tell thee this came not in a dream, by sign obscure, but more like to those prodigies I have seen on show in London. Thee may say they are false, done by deceit and trickery; but not that they were not there to be seen.

Q. In all this, marked you his Lordship's behaviour? Seemed he alarmed, in fear of this monstrous prodigy?

A. The rather, in expectation. He had removed his hat once more, and carried it by his side.

Q. As one who knew he entered the presence of a greater?

A. Yes.

Q. And Dick the same? He appeared not frightened?

A. Terrified, his eyes cast down.

Q. On.

A. We were knelt, as I say, his Lordship with his sword before him, point to the ground, and his hands upon its hilt, so a gentleman of old before his king. Then came there a sigh from the floating maggot, and it did begin to fall, most slowly, like a feather; and came so until its belly rested nigh

upon the ground; and from that belly now there stuck forth
thin legs that had great dark paws, on the which it rested. No
sooner that than of a sudden there appeared upon its side towards us an open door.

Q. How, a door?

A. I saw none, while it floated; yet as it came to ground, such a
door was opened unto us, in its central part; and tho' I saw
not how, nor any person, there fell upon a cunning hinge a
set of stairs like for a coach that led to the ground from this
door. Of three steps or four, and all of silver latticed.

Q. What saw you inside?

A. Why, not of heart or bowels, but so it seemed a wall of precious stones, whose colours shone, of topaz and emerald, ruby
and sapphyr, coral and peridot, I know not what, yet more
clouded in their water than clear, it seemed lit with candles
behind, tho' I could see none. As of a coloured window in a
steeple-house, yet the pieces smaller.

Q. I would be clear. I repeat, this was no true maggot nor living
creature, but something of artifice, a machine or engine?

A. Yes. And this sweet balm stronger upon us, also, it issued
from therein. Now his Lordship bowed his head, so to say, he
that he called the keepers of the waters must now appear.

Q. These legs — whence came they?

A. From out its body, from those black mouths I spoke of; and
seemed too thin to bear such weight, yet did.

Q. What thickness had they? Had they thighs, calves?

A. No, all of one thickness, a flail or such, a constable's staff; that
looked as a spinner's legs, with such bulk above.

Q. On.

A. Now one appeared in the door, she in silver we had seen before. And in her hand she carried a posy of flowers, white as
snow. Smiled she and came brisk down the steps that led
from the maggot and stood before us, but there she did turn
her face, for of a sudden above her did appear another lady,
dressed as her, but more old, her hair grey, though she still
bore herself straight and upright; and did also smile upon us,
yet more gravely, as might a queen.

Q. How old was she?

A. Forty years, not more; still in her flower.

Q. Proceed, why stop you?

A. I have more to tell, that thee will doubt, but 'tis true, I give thee Heaven's word.

Q. Heaven sits not before me, mistress.

A. Then thee must believe its poor servant. For this second lady did the like come down the silver steps, and no sooner was she upon the cavern's floor, than yet another lady appeared in the doorway, as 'twere in her train, that was old; her hair white, her body more frail. Stood she and looked upon us the same as the two first, then came more slowly to the ground beside them. All three there gazed upon us, with that same kindly look. Then further marvel, 'twas plain they was mother and daughter, and daughter's daughter again. Thus it seemed the one woman in her three ages, so like were their features despite their different years.

Q. In what manner were these two other dressed?

A. Most strange, as the first, in silver trowse and smock. Thee'll think it immodest in she who was aged dame; yet it seemed not so, for all wore their garments as ones accustomed, not from mere foolery or the like, but as clothes it pleased them to wear for their plainness and their ease.

Q. Wore they no jewelry or ornaments?

A. Not one. Unless that the oldest bore a posy of flowers of darkest purple, near to black; and the youngest, as I say, of purest white; and her mother flowers of red, like blood. Else were all three as peas in a pod, spite of their ages.

Q. Saw you not toads nor hares, nor black cats about them? Did not ravens croak outside?

A. No and no. Nor broom sticks and cauldrons neither. Be warned, thee know'st not who thee mocks.

Q. I wonder, 'tis all thy picture lacks, with thy flying mawk and its attercop legs, thy scarecrow women.

A. I must yet tell thee worse for thy disbelief, master. Both young and old that stood beside she in the centre, they did turn towards her and made as a step to be the closer. And by some strange feat, I know not how again, were joined as one with her, or seemed to melt thus inside of her; disappeared, like to ghosts that pass a wall, and the one woman, she of the grey hair, the mother, left to stand where there were three, as plain as I see thee now. And did show her posy, for us to see it no more held her red and none other flowers, but now the three hues together; as if by this we must believe what our eyes must doubt.

Q. Mistress, this would tax the most credulous fool in Christendom.

A. Then thee must play that part. For I'll not tell thee any other tale, that is not true, howsoever a better friend to thy suspicions. Look not angry, I beg thee. Thee art a man of law, thee must play the hammer and the saw upon my word. I warn thee my word is of the spirit. Thee may turn its good plank to dust and chips, and then will be no wiser, in this world.

Q. That we'll see, mistress. On with thy farrago.

A. This lady, the mother I will say, did come to where we knelt, first to his Lordship, and reached her hands to make him stand; that he did, and she placed her arms about him, they did embrace, as mother might son that has been on long travel and she has not seen nor held this many a year. Then did she speak to him, in no tongue that I knew, her voice low and most sweet; to which his Lordship replied, in that same strange tongue.

Q. Not so fast. What tongue was this?

A. Not one I had ever heard before.

Q. What tongues hast heard in thy life?

A. Of Dutch and German, and French besides. A little also of the Spanish and Italian.

Q. This was none of these?

A. No.

Q. When his Lordship did answer in it, seemed it well, as one familiar?

A. As most familiar, and not in his previous self.

Q. In what manner not?

A. Why, more of respect and simple gratitude. As I say, so a son brought to his mother's presence after long absence. And I forget also what had been little foretold in him at the beginning, when first she came to him, that he had cast his sword aside, as 'twere something he needed to carry no more, its sash and sheath likewise; so might a man that had been abroad in dangerous places and comes now at last beneath his own roof, where he may be at his ease.

Q. You say he cast it aside, mistress — mean you rather he laid it carefully aside, or tossed it away, as if he cared not?

A. So he cared never to wear it again, for it fell ten feet away, behind, and the sheath and belt the same; like to they had all been disguise or mask till then, their purpose at an end.

Q. Now this — did they greet and speak as persons that had met before?

A. He showed too little wonder, had they not. Next he turned to present us, the first Dick, who remained upon his knees, but the lady reached her hand to him, that he did seize most fervently and press to his mouth. Then she did make him stand also, and now 'twas my turn. First I must tell thee his Lordship spoke to her in their tongue, and though I know not what was said, I heard my name most clear, and that one I was baptized, not Fanny, but Rebecca; which he had never used before, and I know not how he knew it.

Q. You had never told him of it, nor Dick, nor any other?

A. Nor none in the bagnio, unless it be Claiborne.

Q. Then he did learn it of her. On.

A. This lady was before me, where I knelt; and smiled down upon me, as we had been old friends long apart, but new met. And of a sudden stooped and reached out her hands to take mine and raised me to my feet; and so we stood close, for she would not loose my hands when I was risen, and still she smiled and searched my eyes, as an old friend might, to learn how much I had changed; and then passed me her posy of the three hues of flower, like it was her private favour she gave. And as 'twere in return, she lifted my crown of may from off my head, and held it to look at, yet put it not on, for she set it back upon me, with a smile, and kissed me gentle upon the mouth, in the old fashion, so to say I was welcome. In all of this I knew not what to do, yet must curtsey for her flowers and smiled her a little back, tho' not as she, who did so she knew me well, yea, as a mother or loving aunt might.

Q. Nothing was spoke?

A. Not one word.

Q. Moved she with ease and grace, as a lady?

A. With great simplicity, like her daughter, as one who did not care for the airs of this world, nor knew of them.

Q. Yet came of high estate?

A. Most high.

Q. What of these flowers she gave?

A. They were of the three colours, of the same kind, somewhat in look as they that grows upon the Cheddar rocks, that they bring to Bristol at midsummer, and call them June pinks. Yet not so, these were more large, and far richer scent; too soon in season, besides.

Q. You had seen none like before?

A. No, never. Tho' hope to see and smell again.

Q. How, see again?

A. Thee shalt hear. Next did the lady take my hand anew and would lead me to the maggot. I feared not her, yet I feared to enter, and looked to his Lordship that stood behind, over my shoulder, to ask what I must do. At which he raised a finger to his lips, to say I must not speak, and nodded also to she the mother who had greeted us, that I must give her my attention. And when I looked to her, she seemed to understand what I would ask, and did raise her hands before her breast, as her daughter had done, and did smile also, plain as plain to still my fear. So I passed on with her as she wished and mounted the silver steps and was conducted inside her coach, her parlour, I know not how to say, 'twas none such, but a place of great wonders, a chamber walled all of those gleaming stones I had seen through the doorway.

Q. His Lordship and Dick came also?

A. They did.

Q. The lady gave thee the precedence?

A.   Yes.

Q.   Didst not stand at a wonder to be treated so — thou, a whore?

A.   What should I be else? I was as one struck dumb.

Q.   Tell more of this chamber. How were these precious stones?

A.   Some shone more bright than others, and of many colours, cut both square and round, and all the walls and even a part of the roof or ceiling above was of them. And upon many were signs or marks, so to say each had some magic or secret purpose, tho' not that I could read. And many also had small clocks or pocket-watches beside them, yet the hands moved not, they were not wound.

Q.   Were not the hours marked?

A.   There were marks, but not as those of our world.

Q.   How large was this chamber?

A.   Not broad more than ten or twelve feet; more long, it may be twenty foot; and tall as broad.

Q.   How was it lit?

A.   By two panels upon the ceiling that gave a hidden light, tho' less strong than from that light outside, the maggot's eye.

Q.   How, panels?

A.   They seemed of clouded glass, milk-glass as I say; yet hid all behind, and whence came this light.

Q.   Were there no hangings, no furniture?

A.   None when we came. Yet when we were entered the lady touched her finger upon a precious stone beside her, and that door through which we had come closed of itself, as it had opened, upon some secret design; and the silver steps likewise folded back of their own will. And then she touched another stone, or the same; and there fell from both walls as 'twere a bench or sitting-places. I know not how, unless also by some spring, upon a hinge, like secret drawers in a chest. And there she invited us to sit, his Lordship and Dick on one side, I on the other. And mine I sat upon seemed covered with a white skin, finest shagreen, yet was soft as a down bed to my nether parts. Then went she to the far end of the chamber and touched another stone, which bared a cupboard, in which

stood many flasks and bottles in a cloudy glass, like unto a
'pothecary's shop, and some it seemed held powders, others of
liquid, I know not. One of these flasks she took, it seemed to
hold such as Canary wine, for it was golden, and poured of it
into three small crystal glasses, not cut, tho' marvellous light
to hold, they were so thin; and to each of us brought one, so a
serving-maid might. First I would not drink, fearing some
potion, for all I saw his Lordship did not fear to swallow, nor
Dick neither. Until she came back to where I sat and smiled
again down at me, where by taking my glass and drinking a
little of it, she made proof again I need fear for nothing; and
gave me the glass back, and so I drank. 'Twas not as it
seemed, of wine, but more of some fruit, it had of the taste of
fresh apricocks, or jargonelles, yet more sweet and subtle, and
soothed my throat, that was dry.

Q.   It tasted not of spiritous liquor? Of brandy or gin?

A.   Of juice from pressed fruit.

Q.   Next.

A.   Next came she and sat beside me close; and reached above
my head and touched a blue stone upon the wall. Of a sudden all was dark, there was no light inside the chamber, yet
some outside that passed through those small windows I
spake of at the first, that were as eyes — and I have forgot,
from this inside seemed not as from out, not of green glass,
no, clear as any, not flaw nor bubble. And I should have been
mortal afraid again, had not her arm fallen about my shoulder to comfort, and her other hand found mine in the darkness and pressed it, to comfort also. 'Twas plain she would
assure she neither meant nor would bring harm, but held me
as she might her child, to calm all these my alarms at what
did pass my understanding.

Q.   She held you close?

A.   In friendship or sisterhood. So we might sometimes at the bagnio, when we had leisure, or waited.

Q.   And next?

A.   There came a greater prodigy than all, for where was the
chamber's end, that stood before the maggot's head, was of a

sudden a window upon a great city we glid above, as a bird.

Q. What is this?

A. It was so, I tell thee.

Q. And I tell thee not, 'tis too much.

A. I swear by Jesus, it happened so, or so seemed.

Q. This fine chamber of precious stones flew out of the cavern in an instant and above a great city? I am not your green gosling, Mistress Lee, by the heavens am I not.

A. 'Tis in my telling I deceive thee. In naught else. I tell thee what I saw, tho' how I saw it I know not.

Q. This is more fit for chapbook than any ear of reason. I believe thee a cunning whore still, with all thy talk of hammers and saws, dust and chips.

A. I tell truth. I beg thee, thee must believe.

Q. Was there not that in the potion you were given which brought this fantastick vision?

A. I felt no drowsing nor sleep; and all most real, while we flew above this city, much else besides, as I shall tell. Notwithstanding it was done in part by some good magic, as in a dream, for I might see by those smaller windows we moved not from the cavern, its walls still stood outside.

Q. How great was this window by which you saw the city?

A. Three feet by four, more long than high.

Q. Yet you say you might see this machine you were entered in moved not from the cavern?

A. No.

Q. You were bewitched, or drugged, or both.

A. It may be, certain I was transported. Through this window we saw not as we might will, through glass ordinary. 'Twas as some other would have us see: here, from afar, here close; here to this side, then to another. I would fain turn my eyes to look aside, or back to see again; but could not. In vain my eyes would linger, I must see as it saw.

Q. A window cannot see, mistress. You were not in your proper senses. And what city was this you seemed to fly over?

A. Exceeding beautiful, like none upon this earth that I have seen or heard speak of. All built of white and gold, and everywhere was parks and plaisances, fair streets and malls, gardens and green orchards, streams and fish-ponds. 'Twas more rich-peopled countryside than city. And over all, there was peace.

Q. How know you they were orchards? Did you not fly far above?

A. Yet were they small trees set in rows, as orchards, and so I took them. And among them, that joined all, fair great highways that seemed paved of gold, where went people and shining carriages, tho' no horse pulled them. Yet they moved.

Q. How moved?

A. I know nōt. Nor walked they upon the golden streets, neither legs nor feet, and yet they moved, the very paving moved, and bore them along. Tho' they could move as we, for in a field we passed above were two rings of maidens dancing, and in another men also, albeit in lines; and others we saw that walked like us.

Q. How danced they?

A. It did seem they sang as they danced, and the maidens did show most graceful motions, so they did sweep a floor, then threw their faces to the sky in joy; and the men danced while they made to broadcast seed, then mowed it in pretence, the like, though with faster motion. This land did worship cleanliness of spirit, for many I saw swept in truth with broom and besom upon the paths and golden malls, so to show they could not abide uncleanliness. While others did launder by the streams. And the dancing men did rejoice in the bounty of the Lord. On all was a sweet order, in gardens and orchards, I doubt not in their houses also.

Q. Seemed they as us in their outward?

A. Of many nations. Some white, some olive or yellow, some brown, others black as night. I could not see all, they were too far below. 'Twas so we stood upon a great tower, and yet one that moved, it might have legs.

Q. And what clothes?

A. Why, all as the three ladies were dressed, in those same silver trowses and smocks, whether men or women. We passed above so swift I saw not all; for all was no sooner glimpsed than gone, and new appeared.

Q. Were not those that were black savages naked?

A. No.

Q. Saw you no churches?

A. No.

Q. No sign of God, nor His religion?

A. All sign, yet no wont sign. No church, no priest, nothing of such.

Q. Nor heathen temples, I know not?

A. No.

Q. No palaces or great buildings? No 'changes, hospitals, courts of justice?

A. None of those, save fine large buildings where it seemed all did live in common, without distinction nor difference. The most lay without fences or walls and scattered among the green, not crowded close nor smoking foul. All fair, each like to a great farmhouse in its field. All green, as high summer. And the sun shone on all, like to June eternal. So now do I call this happy land that we was shown.

Q. You call it how, mistress?

A. It is June Eternal.

Q. *Alias,* castles in Spain. In what manner were these their houses built — of stone or brick? Had they thatched roofs or tiled with slate?

A. Neither, for they were not of this world, such as I know. With walls of white, most smooth, so the inside of a sea shell, and roofed and doored in gold; and of all kinds, some of a figure of great tents, others with strange gardens upon their roofs, that were flat, yet others round, like great cheeses; and many fashioned else beside.

Q. How know you their doors and roofs and roads were gold?

A. I do not, 'tis what they seemed. And I saw also of these great common houses that each was for many to inhabit, and not the one family, as it is most often in this world; likewise some were for men to dwell in, and others for women alone, and this separation to be seen in all else beside. In one place there were many gathered, of both sexes, that did listen to one who spake, in the open air; yet did they sit most strict divided, the women upon the left, the men upon the right. So to say it was decreed they must be apart there, as they must live apart in their houses.

Q. Saw you no married couples, no lovers, whatever it may be?

A. No, none. It is not so, in June Eternal.

Q. What is not so? Do they live as Romish monks and closeted nuns? Did you see no children?

A. Not children of the flesh. The flesh, and all its sins, is not there. If it were, June Eternal could not be.

Q. Saw you none working?

A. No, unless within their gardens and their fields, for their pleasure.

Q. Were there no shops, no criers of goods, no markets?

A. No, none. Nor workshops nor mills, that I could see.

Q. Were there not soldiers, men who bore arms?

A. None bore arms.

Q. This is not to be believed, mistress.

A. Not to be believed in this world.

Q. And where was your lady, while this your aerial journey lasted?

A. Upon the bench beside me, and held me always, until I leant my head upon her shoulder as I watched.

Q. Was she warm of body?

A. Yes, as I.

Q. What made you of this phantasmatick city you was shown, albeit you dreamed?

A. That it was whence she came, and not of this world, but some finer one, that knows all where we know nothing. Its dwellers like us in some appearances; in others, unlike, and most unlike in their seeming peace and prosperity. For also saw I no poor, no beggars, no cripples, no sick, not one who starved. Nor saw I those who here parade more rich and magnificent, neither; 'twas plain all were content to be of a sameness in their circumstance, that none might be without; as they were chaste, that none might sin. Not as it is with us, each man and woman's heart cased in iron by their greed and their vanity, and forced thereby to act and live for themselves alone.

Q. I would have what you saw, mistress; not what your rebellious new-found democracy now puts upon it.

A. I know not democracy.

Q. Why, the rule of the mob. I smell it in thee.

A. No, it is Christian justice.

Q. Enough of it, call it how you will.

A. 'Tis true, I saw but passing outward of this world. Yet saw I nor soldiers nor guards, nor any sign else, such as gaols or those in chains, to show some did not agree with this, or did evil, and must be punished and prevented.

Q. I say enough.

A. Thee must doubt, I'll not blame thee. For then was I too in my this world's mind, and must doubt myself, and wonder men and women should live in such accord and harmony, when even they of one nation cannot do so here below, let alone they of many mixed. For there, was no sign of war, nor destruction, nor cruelty, nor envy neither; but life eternal. I tell thee, tho' I saw it not at the first, this was Heaven itself.

Q. Or what thou'dst have Heaven to be. That is not the same.

A. Thee must hear, master Ayscough. For now we flew lower and lower, more close to this blessed land of June Eternal, and came so to rest upon the ground, in a meadow of grass and flowers. Where stood about a tree three waiting, two men and a woman, to greet us. And behind them, at the meadow's end, I saw men and women mowing and cocking, and children, as upon a haymaking. Yet did I mark that all these were dressed unlike all others there, in robes and gowns of many hues; and the two men that waited beneath the tree were robed in white, and the woman beside in white.

Q. Did you not say, you saw none working? What is this else?

A. They worked not as we.

Q. How, not as we?

A. They worked because they would, not that they must.

Q. How knew you this?

A. That they sang and rejoiced; and some rested, or played with the children. Then did I see that those two men white-gowned beneath the tree were these same two, the young and the old, I had seen before, in that night at the temple. Now he the younger I called carpenter then, who had pointed above, he stood with a scythe upon his shoulder, he came fresh from the mowing; and the older man bore a white beard and stood with in his hand a staff of wood, in the shadow of this tree, yea, beneath its leaves and fruit, they were as oranges, bright among the green above his head. And he had the air of one both most gentle and most wise, who was lord of all he surveyed, yet now worked not; yet must all look to him as their father and their master.

Q. He seemed of what nation, this aged man?

A. Of all nation, neither blackamoor nor white, neither brown nor yellow.

Q. This is not answer enough.

A. 'Tis all I may give. There was a more wonder yet, for the woman that waited through the window was she I rested beside upon the bench within the maggot, whose hand yet lay in mine. Which did the so confuse me I must look back to her behind me as we sat, and lo, by some great miracle it was she I thought, that sat there still, tho' she appeared also outside the window, and different garbed, in her gown of white. And this beside me now smiled on me as a sister might; even as she might tease, upon some riddle placed, while she waits to hear its answer. Then of a sudden she leant forward and kissed me with her lips upon mine, in purest love, so to declare I should not fear what I saw in the window, that she both might hold me and stand where I saw her outside, beside the old man beneath the tree; who now did reach his hand to make her come closer. Which gesture did most plainly say, She is mine, of my flesh and blood.

Q. That she did appear in the two places at the once, doth it not make proof certain you dreamed?

A. Clear proof to thee; to me, no dream. And no dream that I too did seem to walk there, upon the meadow.

Q. In all this, what of his Lordship? Did you not observe how he watched this vision through thy window? Seemed he possessed by it, in belief of it; or disbelieving?

A. I thought not of him, nor of Dick, as it passed, and the least, at this moment that I say. Before, I did once look to where they sat across the chamber, and his Lordship looked then not through the window, but at me. 'Twas he would the rather watch how I was struck by all, as in a theatre, sat he near a lady, than watch the all himself.

Q. Doth this not suggest he had seen it before — that you were brought before what he knew already?

A. I know alone that he did smile, when he saw I looked to him, and showed with his hand toward the window, so to say, Behold this, not me.

Q. How did he smile?

A. As he had never smiled to me before; that is, as in friendship, as one might to a child, that she must watch to understand.

Q. And Dick, what of him?

A. He did watch as one 'mazed, like to myself.

Q. Very well. Return to this meadow.

A. As I say, it seemed I did walk upon it, for my nose smelt the flowers about us, and the sweet mown grass, and I heard the birds sing, throstles and larks their happy babble, and the haymakers likewise.

Q. How did they sing? Heard you words, had you heard the air before?

A. The air seemed such, one of olden times, that yet I had heard when I was small, though my parents brooked no music in their faith. Yes, it seemed to me my ears had heard it.

Q. Do you recall it still?

A. Alas, I do not.

Q. Speak on.

A. Then was it as I walked in Paradise, in life eternal and happiness everlasting, out of this cruel world and all its evil, out of my own most miserable sins and vanity, for which now I conceived I was about to be forgiven. I walked in a sea of light, all was light, I knew no shadow in my soul; and as I

went towards these three, it seemed no ordinary passing of
time; of one far more slow, like to the motions of a dream,
Then did I see the old man raise an arm and pluck a fruit
hung on a branch above his head, that he held out to she the
mother, and she took it from him, and held for me to take as I
came. Not as that great grace it was, more simple present,
that I might eat; which I did crave with all my soul. Yet tho' I
would hasten my step to take it, I could not; and it came to
me that he who stood with the scythe was son to the aged
man, and she also of a smiting likeness, they were of one family. Then it was when first some tongue, some utmost joyous
tongue, did stir in my mind, that I knew who these three
truly were. Master Ayscough, I speak of it to thee more plain
now than it was to me at this first, when it was but a trembling, a suspicion, a whisper, I know not, of what was to
come. Still I was as thee, I must doubt all the most strange
circumstance in which this had place. Thee must know I was
brought up Quaker, never to think so of divinity, as in bodies
or breathing persons, but of their spirit alone and their light
inside of me. For the Friends say, There is no true spirit in
image, and no image can be of the true spirit. Then too was I
not a great sinner, how should I expect myself worthy of this?
But now came the strangest, for he with the scythe pointed to
the uncut grass beside him, where I must look, and there hidden was laid his twin, it seemed asleep upon his back, with
his scythe beside him, tho' strewn with flowers as one dead.
Yet he smiled as he slept; and upon the face of he who
pointed was that selfsame smile. And yea, ten thousand times
yea, I will hide no more. These two men were one, the only
one, the man of men: our Lord Jesus Christ, who died for us,
yet was resurrected.

Q. What, you are in Heaven now? From whore you are grown
saint?

A. Thee may mock, thee may mock, I speak now what I did not
see till after. What others, the saints, might see in a trice, I
saw in confusion. 'Tis not as people say, truth may come in
one second; it may come more slow, and so 'twas for me. Yea,

374

I must mock myself, that I was so slow. I tell thee, undeserving sinner I may be, there was I brought certain, most certain, within the presence of the Father and the Son. Yea, though they stood simple as two labourers in the field, 'twas they; but there was I their simplicity's fool. And this beside, that still I did not know she against whose shoulder I lay. Yea, there was I fool most, alas, and blindest.

Q. No more of riddles. Speak now — who was this woman?

A. No woman, but queen of queens, greater than the greatest lady. She without whom God the Father could not have made His works, whom some would call the Holy Spirit. She is Holy Mother Wisdom.

Q. The Holy Mother, you would say? The Virgin Mary?

A. A greater even. Holy Mother Wisdom, 'tis she the bearing spirit of God's will, and one with Him from the beginning, that takes up all that Christ the Saviour promised. That is both His mother and His widow, and His daughter beside; wherein lies the truth of those three women grown one I saw first appear. She is that which liveth alway, and shall be my mistress alway.

Q. Woman, this is rank blasphemy. 'Tis writ clear in the Book of Genesis that Eve came of Adam's seventh rib.

A. Were thee not born also of a mother? Thee's nothing without her, thee are not born. Nor was Eden born, nor Adam nor Eve, were Holy Mother Wisdom not there at the first with God the Father.

Q. What, and this great mother, this *màgna creatrix,* doth hold thee in her arms, like to some fellow-trollop in thy bagnio? Didst thou not put it so?

A. 'Twas loving kindness, and her mercy. None so sinful they may not be saved. And thee forget, I knew her not in my blindness. Else should I have been on my knees before her.

Q. Enough of thy possibilities. What next?

A. Her kingdom shall come to be, and Christ's also, and far sooner than this wicked world allows. Amen. I am witness.

Q. Then witness, woman, an end to thy new-making sacred truth, thy preaching-prophesying. What next in the cavern?

A.   Most terrible, most bitter after sweet. I did run in the heav-
enly meadow, to take that fruit Holy Mother Wisdom did
there offer toward me, had believed it almost within my
hands. Of a sudden all was dark, yea darkest night. Then was
there light again, but on such a scene I pray I may never see
twice, for 'twas of most desperate battle, a field where men
fought like tigers, and the sound thereof about us, of clashing
iron, of oaths and cries, of pistol and musket and fearsome
cannon, and the groans of the dying intermingled, blood and
the cannons' smoke. I cannot tell thee all its gashly deeds and
cruelty, nor what terror I felt, for the battle did seem so close
its soldiers must break in upon the maggot's chamber where
we sat. Then would I turn my face to Holy Mother Wisdom,
in great horror at this change, to seek her solace; and found
greater horror still: lo, she was not there, nor his Lordship nor
Dick, no not nothing of what had been, all great darkness,
and I alone in it.

Q.   You were still in the maggot's chamber? This battle you were
shown was seen through the window, as before?

A.   Yes, tho' I had seen, nor heard nor felt, no other to leave. And
now was alone, nay, worse than alone, locked in most awful
prison with Antichrist for boon companion. I tell thee, there
was I forced to watch more evil and cruelty than I had known
possible, and each scene worse than the last.

Q.   It was more than this scene of battle?

A.   Of many, not all of battle, nay, of each foul crime and sin: of
torture, of murder and treachery, of the slaughter of innocents, never saw I Antichrist so clear, and the cruelty of man
more savage than the wildest beasts, a thousand times worse
upon his own than their worst upon him.

Q.   This is what you told Jones, tho' with different cause and circumstance to it?

A.   I told some, not all. 'Tis not to be told.

Q.   And you as one burnt in a sea of flames, it is not so?

A.   Yea, there was a girl-child of nine or ten years run from a
house put to fire by soldiers, most sorely burnt therein, her
clothes aflame, and it rent my heart not one there did take

notice of her agony, save to mock and laugh at it, I would I could have torn them limb from limb. I did spring from where I sat and ran to the window to succour, for she came toward me; but oh my soul in vain, I should have died a hundred times to reach her, for I saw myself in her, as I was before I sinned; yet stayed the glass stronger than a stone wall between us, dear God I could not break it, tho' the poor child was burning there not three feet from me and cried and wept most piteously. I see her still, I would e'en weep now for how she reached her hands for help, so she was blind, and I so close, tho' I had been ten thousand leagues apart for all I could avail.

Q. This and thy other cruel visions — were they in appearance of this world?

A. Too like this world, too like, there was no love; all cruelty, killing, pain. All meted upon innocents, upon women and children, and nothing to end it.

Q. I ask again. Recognised you face or place of this world among them?

A. I doubt it was this world; but not that such a world may be.

Q. They were not of this world?

A. Unless it were Cathay, for their faces were such they portray of Chinamen, upon pots and the like, more yellow skinned than we, the eyes narrow. Yet twice I saw beyond the window, what seemed three moons that shone upon a scene of carnage, and made all more dreadful by their light.

Q. You were not mistaken — three moons?

A. The one larger, the two other smaller. But stranger black marvels still: great carriages that bore cannon within, and went faster than the fastest horse; most swift and roaring winged lions, that flew as hornets in a rage, the which did drop great grenadoes upon their enemy and made untold destruction upon them — why, whole cities laid to ruin, like 'twas said London did look the morrow of the Great Fire. And else, great towers of smoke and flame that burnt all below, made hurricane and earthquake where they rose, visions so dire they make this world we live in seem kind by the comparison. Yet do I know all its seeds may be found in ours, all we lack are their devilish arts and ingenuity to be the same, as cruel also. Man is evil not by himself alone, nay, 'tis by will of Antichrist. The longer he rules, the more are we doomed, and all shall end in fire.

Q. Thou art like all thy kind, woman, ever thou'dst credit the worst most. Was there nothing but doom through thy window?

A. All cruel, all cruel.

Q. Therefore without God. How may such a world be truth? That some are cruel and unjust, it may be; that all are so, 'tis neither true nor seen.

A. 'Twas prophecy; so may this world become.

Q. A Christian God would not allow it to pass thus.

A. He destroyed the Cities of the Plain, for their sins and false idols.

Q. They were few among many. Those that worshipped truly, and believed His Word, He did not harm. But enough, return to thy well-called maggot.

A. I was before the window, the burning of that innocent girl, I must see her die before my eyes; whereon I sank in despair upon the chamber's floor, I would watch no more — nor could, for there came a great fog upon the window's glass, and silence, that in mercy hid all behind. Now of a sudden was there light within the chamber. At the far end I espied his Lordship, yet most strange, I first did not know him, for he wore as those from June Eternal wore, their silken smock and trowse, no wig beside. Yet he did look upon my face and sadness with kind pity, so to say he brought no more tidings of suffering, but relief of it; and came to where I lay, and lifted me to carry to the bench, where he did lie me gentle on my back, then stooped close above my face and stared into my eyes with a loving care and tenderness such I had never known in all my dealings with him. Forget me not, Rebecca, he said, forget me not; at that did kiss me soft upon the brow, as a brother might. Still did he stare into my eyes, 'twas as if his face was become one with He I had seen in the meadow in

June Eternal, that does forgive all sins, and to all despair bring peace.

Q.   I shall not forget thee either, mistress, I'll grant thee that. Is it this, thy crowning piece? His Lordship grows the Lord of All, the Redeemer?

A.   'Twill not fit thy alphabet, so be it. Yet so was it not to me. I knew such joy I must sleep on it; and did.

Q.   Must sleep? Who not doting idiot should sleep at such a juncture?

A.   I cannot tell, save I must close my eyes upon that tender face above, that our souls might join. 'Twas so a loving husband, that willed me with his love to rest.

Q.   Was it not more than your souls that joined?

A.   Shame on thee, to think it.

Q.   Did he not give thee some potion also?

A.   That of his eyes, no more.

Q.   Thy gossip Holy Mother Wisdom, did she not appear?

A.   No, nor Dick neither. 'Twas he alone.

Q.   And where didst wake, in Heaven again?

A.   No Heaven, but a sore bed to lie upon, the cavern's ground where first we came, tho' I knew it not at the once, and would believe myself still where I had slumbered, and most sweet rested. Too soon it came upon me I had suffered some great loss, was cold and stiff beside, for all my May-queen clothes was gone, every stitch. Next I did mind me of Holy Mother Wisdom, at first so she had come in a dream, as thee'd believe; then knew it no dream, she was departed and I most sore bereft, of worse than my clothes, my soul cast naked back in this present world. Then in a rush, so a tumble of autumn leaves, came further memory, of those three figures in the meadow, which only now I saw what they had been, our Father and His Son, both the living and the dead, and She beside, their haymakers saints and angels; nor did I forget he who had brought me to this holy knowledge. And misery, I smelled the sweet summer fragrance of June Eternal, that still lingered faint upon the damp cavern air, and knew certain I had not dreamed, but lived. My tears did flow, to think

such had come and gone from me before I knew them truly. I
tell thee I did feel it more cruel than all that other cruelty I
had seen. Yea, I was vain still, still the harlot, I thought only
of myself, one scorned and rejected, that had failed a great
test upon me. Poor fool, I knelt there on the stone and prayed
I might be taken back, where I had slept so sweet. No matter,
my soul is wiser now.

Q. Enough of thy soul — was there light to see within the cavern?

A. Small. I might see.

Q. The maggot was gone?

A. Gone.

Q. As I thought — thou wert practised upon. Such an engine
could never pass within, nor out. None of this had substance
outside thy woman's head; or what little it had thou hast
maliciously nursed and let grow inside thee like that worm in
thy womb.

A. Thee may say. Deny what I am become, do what thee will, to
me it matters not, nor to Christ's truth. 'Tis thy own soul
shall rue the day.

Q. Enough. Did you not search within the cavern? May his
Lordship not have been alseep in some corner, as yourself?
Was there no sign?

A. There was sign. When I made at last to leave, my foot did
stumble on his Lordship's sword, that lay still where he had
thrown it.

Q. Did you not pick it up?

A. No.

Q. And searched not to see if his Lordship might lie there?

A. He was gone.

Q. How gone?

A. Within where I last saw him.

Q. How know you this, were you not asleep?

A. I was, and I know not how, save that I am.

Q. Can you deny that he may have left some otherwise than in
your engine?

A. I cannot, in thy alphabet; in mine I can, and do.

Q. You say, he was brought to your June Eternal?

A. Not brought, he is returned.

Q. What that these your holy visions had stripped you of your clothes, like common thieves?

A. All Holy Mother Wisdom stole was my sinning past. That was no theft, she would send me back with new clothes for my soul, and did, for I wear them still, and ever shall, till I meet her again. I came out new-born from her spirit's womb.

Q. And most egregiously lied, did you not, so soon as Jones came up with you?

A. 'Twas not to spite him. Some are born broad and heavy, like ships, they may not be turned by their conscience alone, nor Christian light. He made it plain he would use me still, and I would not be used. I must make service of my wits, to escape his design.

Q. As thou dost now, to escape mine.

A. I tell thee truth, which thee will not have. In this thee's great proof theeself I must lie to be believed.

Q. Downright lies or unchaste parables, it is all one. Now, mistress, it is grown late, but I am not done with you, nor will I have you this night conspiring with your man to make more parables still. You shall sleep beneath this roof, in the chamber where you dined, it is clear? And shall speak to no man unless my clerk, who will watch you close as any turnkey.

A. Thee's no right, and least in God's eyes.

Q. I might have thee flung into the town gaol, mistress, where thou'dst sup on a crust and water, and sleep on lousy straw. Argue more, thou shalt see.

A. 'Tis to my father and my husband thee must tell that. I know they wait.

Q. Cease thy impudence. Be gone with thee, and thank Heaven for my mercy. Thou dost not merit it.

TEN MINUTES LATER THREE MEN STAND stiffly across the room
from Mr Ayscough, close by the door through which they have entered, as if to venture farther might risk infection of some kind. It is
clear they are a deputation of protest, and as clear that the lawyer
has changed his mind as to Rebecca's impudence. When she had
left with her turnkey, he had, as earlier that day, walked to the
window. The sun had only just set, and dusk had hardly begun,
but the square was far less busy than it had been that morning.
One thing in it had not diminished, however. Below the window,
on the facing streetcorner, still stood those same three male figures,
as sombre as the Erinnyes, and as implacable; but now behind and
beside them ten others, of whom six were women, three elderly,
three younger, and all dressed as Rebecca had been. One might
have assumed it a group chance-gathered, were it not for this
quasi-uniform, and even more in the way that all thirteen pairs of
eyes seemed fixed on one point only: the window where Ayscough
had appeared.

He was made out; and in a ragged but rapid sequence, thirteen
pairs of hands rose in prayer to their breasts. The prayer was not
offered. It was a statement, not a solicitation; an obscure challenge,
despite the lack of cries, of hostile or threatening gestures. The
group showed nothing but solemn, intent faces. Ayscough had

stared down at these pillars of righteousness for a few moments; then withdrawn in both senses of the word, to face his returned clerk, who silently showed a large key in his hand, that with which he had locked Rebecca in. He went to his desk and started to sort his sheets of scrawled, indecipherable paper together, preparatory to a start upon its laborious transcription. Suddenly Ayscough had spoken, it seemed crossly and curtly. The clerk had looked surprised at what was commanded, but said nothing; then bowed and left the room again.

The middle of the three men is the tailor James Wardley, who is the shortest, yet has visibly the most authority. His hair is grey, and as is his two companions', long and straight; his face worn and lined, that of a man older than his fifty years. He looks a humourless plain-dealer; or would have done so, did he not wear steel-framed spectacles. They bear peculiar pieces of dark glass on their stems, to shut out all side-light, and this apparatus gives an abiding impression of myopic but intent malevolence, for the eyes behind the very small lenses do not shift their gaze from the lawyer's. Neither he nor the other two have removed their Quaker hats, and unconsciously show that feature common to all members of extremist sects, whether political or religious, forced to consort with more normal human beings: an awareness, both defiant and embarrassed, of how locked away they are from conventional society.

Rebecca's husband stands gaunt as ever and visibly ill at ease. He seems, despite his prophetic enthusiasm, distinctly awed by this formal present — far less a potential rebel than a mournful outsider involved by chance. Unlike Wardley he stares at the floor between the little lawyer and himself. One might almost believe he had not wished to be present. But Rebecca's father is another matter. He wears a dark brown coat and breeches, and seems of Wardley's age: a strong, squareset man, who means not to give an inch, and is as determined in face as his son-in-law seems at a loss. If Wardley's stare is steady, his is bold, even aggressive; and his hands by his sides are clenched, as if for a fight.

Wardley is what he is by cantankerousness and love of argument; not that he lacks faith in his beliefs and visions, but above all he enjoys that part of their exposition and defence which allows him to mock his enemies' illogic (not least their smug contentment in a grossly unjust world) and also — how sweet is bile — then to dispatch them to future damnation. In him the spirit of Tom Paine — as of countless seventeenth-century quarrelers, in the past — is alive; he is not a true French Prophet only in as much as his eternal nature, nonconforming and uncomfortable, has found very different outlets in the course of history.

Rebecca's melancholy husband is in truth no more than an ignorant mystic, who has picked up the language of prophetic visions and yet is sure his utterances come by divine inspiration: that is, he is self-gulled, or innocently self-believing. To speak so is anachronistic. Like so many of his class at this time, he still lacks what even the least intelligent human today, far stupider even than he, would recognise — an unmistakable sense of personal identity set in a world to some degree, however small, manipulable or controllable by that identity. John Lee would not have understood *Cogito, ergo sum;* and far less its even terser modern equivalent, *I am.* The contemporary I does not need to think, to know it exists. To be sure, the intelligentsia of John Lee's time had a clear, almost but not quite modern, sense of self; but the retrospective habit we have of remembering and assessing a past age by its Popes, its Addisons and Steeles, its Johnsons, conveniently forgets how completely untypical artistic genius is of most human beings of any age, however much we force it to be the reverse.

John Lee *is,* of course; but as a tool or a beast is, in a world so entirely pre-ordained it might be written, like this book. He laboriously reads the Bible, and so does he hear of and comprehend the living outside world around him — not as something to be approved of or disapproved, to be acted for or against; but as it simply is, which is as it always would or must be, an inalienably fixed narrative. He has none of Wardley's comparatively emancipated, active and quasi-political mind, his belief that a man's actions may change the world. His prophecies may predict such a change, but even in this he is to himself but a tool, a ridden beast. Like all mystics (and many novelists, not least the present one) he is baffled, a child, before the real now; far happier out of it, in a narrative past or a prophetic future, locked inside that weird tense grammar does not allow, the imaginary present.

You would never have got the tailor to admit that the tenets of the French Prophets were simply convenient to his real nature and its enjoyment; and even less to consider whether, had some miracle brought him national power instead of the mere leadership of an obscure and provincial sect, he would not have been quite as grim a tyrant as the man his sinister spectacles vaguely foreshadowed, Robespierre. These various defects in his partners made Rebecca's father, the carpenter Amos Hocknell, the most straightforward and in many ways the most typical of the three.

Both his religion and his politics were ruled by one thing, the skill in his hands. He was a much more practical man than either Wardley or John Lee; a good carpenter. Of ideas in themselves he took little account, and regarded most as he regarded ornament in his sister trades of joinery and cabinet-making — superfluous, and transparently sinful in God's eyes. This marked tendency in Dissent towards severity of ornament, this stress on structural solidity, good workmanship, sobriety of taste (at the expense of fancy, elaboration, useless luxury and all the rest), came in the beginning, of course, from Puritan doctrine. The aesthetic of a society of God-fearing Sobersides had by the 1730s (or ever since 1660) largely been brought into contempt and discredit by the rich and educated; but not among those like Hocknell.

Plain carpentry had become a religious template with him; and so did he judge much else besides the working of wood. What mattered to him was that a thing, an opinion, an idea, a man's way of life, should be plain, exact to its purpose; well built, well pinned and morticed, well fitted to its function; and above all, not hidden by vain ornament from what it truly was. What did not fit these homely precepts taken from his trade was evil or ungodly. Aesthetic justness had become moral justice; simple was not only beautiful, it was virtuous; and the most satanically unvirtuous piece of work of all, grossly obvious beneath its unseemly and excessive ornament, was English society itself.

Hocknell was not such a bigot he refused to fit ornamental wall-cases, over-carved mantels, whatever it might be, on demand; but counted it all Devil's work. For fine houses, fine clothes, fine carriages and a thousand other things that hid or travestied or ignored the fundamental truths and elementary injustices of existence he had no time at all. His principal truth was the truth of Christ, which the carpenter saw rather as substantial and precious pieces of seasoned timber left abandoned in a yard than as a fixed structure or house. They were there to be properly used and built by such as him. The metaphors he used in his own prophecies tended very much to this kind of imagery; the present house was rotten and must fall, while far better materials lay to hand. His prophecies were plain beside those of his son-in-law, who seemingly had a close speaking and seeing acquaintance with the Apostles and various Old Testament figures. The carpenter hoped rather than firmly believed Christ's second coming was near; or believed, like so many Christians before and after him, that it must be true because it ought to be true.

It ought to be true, of course, because the Gospel may very easily be read as a political document; not for nothing did the medieval church fight so long to keep it out of the vulgar tongues of Europe. If all are equal in Christ's sight, and as regards entry qualifications for Heaven, why are they not in human sight? No degree of theological obfuscation or selective quotation justifying the Caesars of this world can answer that. Nor did the carpenter forget the trade Christ's worldly father followed; and indeed drew a fierce pride from the parallel, perilously close to the sin of vanity.

In ordinary terms he was a touchy, short-tempered man in many things, and adamant for his rights, or as he saw them. They had included the patriarchal right to command his daughters' lives and expel the one who had lapsed so flagrantly. Rebecca had feared his reaction most when she returned. She had had the sense to seek her mother's forgiveness first, and gained it — or rather, gained it if her father would allow. She was then brought straight into his presence by her mother's hand. He was at work in a new-built house, hanging a door; on his knees, about a hinge, and unaware of them, until

Rebecca spoke the one word, Father. He had turned, and given her the most terrible stare, if she were the Devil incarnate. She had fallen to her knees and bowed her head. Most strangely his face began to work beneath its terrible stare; he had lost control of it, and was in agony. The next moment she was snatched into his burly arms; and into a tide of mutual sobs stemming from a much older human tradition than that of Dissent.

Yet surrender to attacks of intense emotion was an essential part of both its being and its practice, perhaps not least because it stood so deeply against the aristocratic, then the aping middle class, and now the universal English tradition in such matters; which dreads natural feeling (what other language speaks of *attacks* of emotion?) and has made such an art of sangfroid, meiosis, cynicism and the stiff upper lip to keep it at bay. We may talk coolly now in psychiatric terms of the hysterical enthusiasm, the sobbing, the distorted speech in the gift of tongues, all the other wild phenomena found in so much early Dissenting worship. We should do better to imagine a world where, once again, a sense of self barely exists; or most often where it does, is repressed; where most are still like John Lee, more characters written by someone else than free individuals in our comprehension of the adjective and the noun.

Mr Ayscough walks from his table and sweeps past the three by the door — or more exactly, tries to sweep, since he is shorter even than Wardley, and can no more truly sweep than a bantam-cockerel could pretend to be the fierce old English gamecock of the inn backyard. At any rate he does not look at the three faces of Dissent, and manages to suggest by his expression that he is being very improperly put upon. The clerk gestures the trio to follow his master's back, and they do so, with the sardonic scribe behind them.

The five men file into the room over the inn yard, Mr Ayscough leading. He goes to the window, but does not turn. He joins his hands beneath his open coat at the back, and stares out at the now dusk-filled yard. Rebecca stands by the bed, as if hastily risen from it, and evidently surprised by this solemn delegation. She does not move to greet them, nor they she, and there is a moment or two of that awkward suspension characteristic of such meetings.

"Sister, this person would have thee rest here this night, against thy will."

"It is not against my will, Brother Wardley."

"He hath no right in law. Thee be not charged."

"I am obliged in conscience."

"Hast thee asked counsel of Jesus Christ?"

"He says, I am obliged."

"Hast thee not been ill treated in respect of thy state, both of soul and of body?"

"No. I have not."

"Hath this man not wickedly tried to break thee of thy faith?"

"No."

"Thee art sure?"

"Yes, I am sure."

"Hath he not told thee thee must say these things, or thee shall suffer after?"

"No."

"Be not afraid if he would taunt or corrupt or howsoever force thee from the light, sister. Speak truth entire, and nothing but Christ's truth."

"I have, and shall."

Wardley is clearly set back by this calmness. Mr Ayscough still stares down into the yard; one may suspect it is now partly to hide his face.

"Thee's sure that what thee dost is best in Christ?"

"Most sure, brother."

"We would pray with thee, sister."

But now Ayscough turns, and sharply. "You may pray for her, but not with her. You have her word, I do her no ill, are you not done?"

"We shall pray with her."

"No, you shall not, sir. You have the right to question her on what is pertinent. I gave no right to hold a praying meeting also."

"Friends, ye stand witnesses to this. Prayer is called impertinent."

The clerk, who stands behind the three men, steps forward and reaches for the arm nearest him, that of Rebecca's father, to encourage him to turn and go; but his touch is as if scalding, for Hocknell twists round and catches his wrist, clamping it as in a vise; then forces it down and stares fiercely at the clerk.

"Touch me not, thee . . . devil."

Wardley puts a hand on Hocknell's other arm.

"Still thy righteous anger, brother. They shall be judged hereafter."

Hocknell looks for a few moments little inclined to obey; at last throws down the clerk's wrist, and turns back to face the room.

" 'Tis tyranny. They have no right to forbid prayer."

"We are among infidels, brother."

Hocknell looks across at his daughter. "Daughter, kneel."

Rebecca does not move, in the silence that follows this abrupt paternal command; and nor now do the men, since they feel it below their dignity to kneel before she does. Her husband stares at the floor between them, more than ever as if he wished he were not there; while Wardley stares beyond her into a middle distance. Now she comes in front of her father, and smiles.

"I am thy daughter in all. Fear not, I shall not be bent again. I am Christ's daughter also, now." She pauses, then adds, "I pray thee, father, go in peace."

Still the three stand, plainly doubting whether a woman can, or should, decide such a matter. They regard the face before them with its innate meekness; and that has also something other, a kind of simplicity, a levelheadedness, almost a judging of them. A sceptic or an atheist might have suspected a contempt for them, for the way their faith had deformed them, and their sex also; in which he would have been wrong. She felt pity, not contempt, and in no way doubted the substance of the faith. Mr Ayscough has seemed largely indifferent until this point; now he may be seen watching Rebecca closely. It is Wardley who breaks the impasse.

"More love, sister. Christ's spirit be with thee."

Her eyes watch her father's still angry ones.

"More love, brother."

She picks up her father's hand and raises it to her lips; there seems some hidden allusion to a past event, some previous taming of his rancorous temper. He does not look appeased, and searches for something in her steady eyes, the faint smile, perhaps a simple answer to the question of why she knows him, but he does not know her. He is like a man shown, at this late stage of his life, a glimpse of something he has never recognised before: a lightness, affection, a last echo of her former life; a thousand miles from solid timber and moral judgements by setsquare, and so unplaceable by him. Yet there is no hint of this when it comes to her husband. She turns and takes both his hands, does not kiss them, or his face. Instead they exchange a look, that seems almost one between strangers, despite their joined hands.

"Speak truth."

"Yea, husband."

And that is all. They go, and the clerk follows. Mr Ayscough is left alone with Rebecca, and still watching her. She glances almost shyly back at him, then meekly down. For some moments he goes on watching her; suddenly, without a further word, he leaves. The door once closed, there is the sound of a key being turned in a lock. Rebecca listens as his footsteps die away, before turning to the bed and kneeling. Her eyes stay open, and her mouth does not move. She stands again, and lies on the bed. Her hands begin to feel her still only slightly swollen belly, and she cranes up for a moment to look down at it; lets her head sink back and smiles, much more fully than before, up at the ceiling.

It is a strange smile, strange in its innocence. It shows no vanity or pride, no sense that she has handled a situation well, no indication of a response to the awkward stiffness of her three brothers in Christ. It seems much more a reflection of some deep inner certainty; not of a kind she has actively earned, but of one she has been given, is simply now in, beyond her willing. Rebecca shares one thing with her husband besides a general faith: she too has a very indistinct sense of what defines and is common to every modern ego. She smiles in fact because Christ's grace has just granted her her first prophecy: the child inside her will be a girl. We should say today she has discovered she would like it so; and completely misunderstand what she feels. Her smile is not that of such a personal knowledge, and delight it in. It is the smile of one who has heard, is now written by, an annunciation.

The Examination and Deposition of
JAMES WARDLEY
the which doth witness but will not swear,
this fourth day of October
in the tenth year of the reign of our
sovereign Lord George the second, by
the grace of God King of Great Britain
and of England, &c.

My name is JAMES WARDLEY. *I am tailor by trade. I was born in the year of 1685, at Bolton on the Moor in this county. I am married.*

❧

Q.   Now, Wardley, the hour is late, my business with you is brief. I will not dispute with you over your beliefs, I wish to ascertain only some facts, that touch upon Rebecca Lee. She is one you count of your flock, your meeting, what you may call it?

A.   I am no bishop nor vicar, to count souls like a miser his guineas. We live in fellowship. She is sister, and believes what I believe.

Q.   You teach the doctrine of the French Prophets, is it not so?

A.   I teach truth, that this world is near its end by cause of its sin; and that Jesus Christ returns, once more to redeem it. That whosoever shall show faith in Him, and live by His light, shall be saved. And all else shall be eternally damned.

Q.   They to be damned are all those who do not follow you?

A.   All those that follow Antichrist, that has ruled since the first church of the Apostles ended; and hear not the Lord's word, revealed by grace of prophecy.

Q.   You say all religion since then is Antichrist?

A.   Until the Friends first came, this hundred years past. All else are possessed of the Devil's great I. Go off, great I, and come not nigh. So say we.

Q. Believe you not in predestination, as the Calvinists?

A. Nay, and nor doth God.

Q. What is false in it?

A. It saith man may not change in the living Christ, nor war the flesh and put a cross upon sin, if he so choose, as he should.

Q. Draw you this doctrine from the Bible?

A. Except a man be born again, he cannot see the kingdom of God. The Book is good witness, and much wisdom; yet is not all. So say we.

Q. How not all — is it not sacred truth, and infallible?

A. We say 'twas writ by good and holy men, they lied not by their lights. Such were of their understanding then; in some things, not certain truth. 'Tis but words, that are fallible in their season. The Lord was never beholden to letters, nor the Book His last testament; for that is to say, He now is dead; which is vile heresy put about by Antichrist, so the sinners may sin in the more peace. He is not dead, He lives, He sees all, and soon shall come among us.

Q. I am told, you have no belief in the Holy Trinity.

A. That it is all male, and woman no part of it, we will not credit.

Q. Christ may come again in the form of woman, is it not so you blasphemously proclaim?

A. What blasphemy lies in that? The first and greatest sin of all was the fornication of Adam and Eve, who were guilty both and equally. Man and woman that sprang from their loins, may be saved both; and may save both. Both may be in Jesus Christ's likeness; and shall.

Q. Believe you He may be seen now in this world, tho' it be in secret, brought from Heaven?

A. Christ is no secret. This world's present state doth answer thee. Had He been seen, it had not been as it is, all blindness and corruption.

Q. What of Holy Mother Wisdom?

A. Who is she?

Q. Do you not so call the Holy Spirit?

A. Nay.

Q. You have heard it so called?

A. I deny thee.

Q. Nor Heaven, the life everlasting, called June Eternal?

A. Thee's been sold more rotten eggs than good, master. Heaven hath no special season, 'tis no more June than any other month.

Q. You forswear all carnal pleasure?

A. The carnal nature is mansion of Antichrist, there will we not enter. What frees us of his chains is chastity, naught else. So say we, and do our best to live.

Q. This last I ask — doth by your faith the flesh of true believers survive death?

A. All flesh is corrupt, of those who have the light or not. The spirit alone is resurrected.

Q. This comes not of you alone, but of all who have declared themselves French Prophets?

A. Thee may judge. Thee may read of Misson and Elias Marion. Thomas Eames that be gone to the Lord nigh these thirty years past. Sir Richard Bulkeley likewise. Thee may solicit John Lacy, who liveth in this county till this day, that I know well, he is old now of seventy-two years; and hath witnessed to the truth far longer than I.

Q. Very well, to my present purpose. You are persuaded Rebecca Lee doth believe as you, and these you have named?

A. Yes.

Q. It is not by her husband's will, or her father's, to please both or either? As is common in all religion, not only yours?

A. She is of our faith of her own conscience, for I have questioned her thereon, and my wife also, who knows her better.

Q. Know you of her past — that she was whore in London?

A. She hath repented.

Q. I ask again — are you cognizant of her former life?

A. I have spoken to it with my brethren, and my wife with our sistren, and we hope she shall be saved.

Q. But hope?

A. Jesus alone shall save, when the doom is done.

Q. You believe her sincere in repentance for her past life?

A. Aye, most earnest for salvation.

Q. To wit, she fits your beliefs, and is fanatickal in them?

A. I will not answer thee that. I come in peace.

Q. Did you not quit the Quakers upon this matter of peace —
    were you not born one?

A. I was born a friend of truth, and shall die one, but with this
    difference, praise the Lord, for Christ's word I must fight. I
    treat not Christ's enemy as no business of mine, as they now
    have wont to do. If such a one deny me in matters of the
    spirit, I must deny him back.

Q. Did they not ban you from their meeting-house here?

A. I might still go if I was silent. Such is to say, a man may walk,
    if he will but wear chains. And I will not, for Jesus Christ my
    master's sake.

Q. Were you not ejected by force from their meeting, this two
    years past?

A. I would prophesy His coming, and they would not bear it nor
    hear it.

Q. Did you not say that civil authority was not be be borne by
    such as yourself, what you called true Christians? And that
    civil authority was most signal instance of the sins for which
    this world is doomed?

A. I said 'twas not to be borne when civil authority would make
    us do or swear against our conscience. I did not say it was not
    to be obeyed in all else. Should I be before thee if I believed
    other?

Q. I am told you would make all wealth and property to be
    shared commonly, and have likewise spoken so.

A. I have prophesied it shall be so, when God's vengeance is
    done, among those who are saved. I have not spoken it is to
    be done now.

Q. You maintain, it would be a better world, if it were done.

A. I maintain it shall be a better world, when it is done; as it
    shall be, by God's will.

Q. This world shall be a better place when it is overturned?

A. Christ overturned. We have good warrant.

Q. To bring riot and rebellion, is it not so?

A. Thee hast no proof for this, and there is none.

Q. You are how many here, of the French Prophets?

A. Some forty or fifty, and some where I was born, in Bolton. And in London some, also.

Q. Then you are not strong?

A. Many littles make a mickle. Christ had less, when He began.

Q. Is not the reason you are not in seditious rebellion this, you are too weak to bring it to success; but that you should, if you were stronger?

A. Thee shan't snare me in thy cunning supposings, master Ayscough. We obey the civil law in all matters civil, we hurt no man, unless it be in his conscience. We would make rebellion against sin, yea, we will go sword in hand against sin, which is the soul's saving. There is no law against that. And when we are strong, there shall be no civil rebellion; for all will see we live in Christ and shall join us. Then shall there be peace and true respect among men.

Q. The law demands obedience to the established church and its authority, does it not?

A. Aye. And Rome was once the established church.

Q. The Protestant and established church of this kingdom is as evil and corrupted as that of Rome, is it how you say?

A. I say all churches are made of men. Men are of flesh, which is born corrupt. I do not say all men of the established church are corrupt. Hast thee read *A Serious Call*? I will not judge he that wrote it, William Law, that is of thy church, an evil man. Nay, he puts most others in it to shame, that are blind as mouldwarps to Christ's light.

Q. Which is to say they are not fit for what they are. This is plain invitation to rebellion against them. Just so were our forefathers made to fall into their errors and intolerance this century past. You are damned of your own mouth, and of history beside.

A. And thee of thine own, if thee'd make an evil man, or a blind, fit to be what he is because he is what he is. Thee may call the

Devil good and fit, by such an argument. Thee'd not buy thy meat off a bad butcher, nay, nor go to one of my trade that sewed ill. But thee'll not qualm to hear the Word of Christ betrayed, coined false as by any forger. For lo, if he wear bands, and carry a dog's-tail of alphabet letters after his name, he may drink, he may whore, he may do what he will, for he is fit.

Q. Is this your peace and respect among men? Mr Fotheringay shall hear of it.

A. Is this thy no disputing upon my beliefs? And much good may it do him.

Q. Enough. I will know this. Hath the woman Lee prophesied at your meetings?

A. Nay.

Q. Hath she spoken in any way, publicly or privately, of what brought her to her new piety?

A. Save she had grievous sinned and stood sore shent by her past life.

Q. She hath not talked of any particular occasion to make her change her ways?

A. Nay.

Q. Nor place nor day?

A. Nay.

Q. Nor of other persons present, if there were such an occasion?

A. Nay.

Q. You are certain?

A. She is meek, as she should be; and lives now in Christ, or would live in Him.

Q. How, would live? Is she not persuaded yet?

A. She is not yet moved to prophesy. Which comes by Christ's grace, for which we pray.

Q. That she may rant with the best of you?

A. She may be given the glorious tongue of the light, and proclaim it, as my wife doth, and others.

Q. She is till now deficient in this?

A. She hath not prophesied.

Q. May it not be that she deceives you?

A.   Why should she deceive?

Q.   To pretend she is no longer what she was, though at heart she remain so.

A.   She lives for Christ, so she may one day live in Christ. She and her husband are poor, as bare stone are they poor, he earns not enough for them to live by. Why should she feign to live so, when she might live else, in luxuriousness and lechery, as she did in thy Babylon?

Q.   Do you not supply to their needs?

A.   When I may, and her brothers and sisters in Christ also.

Q.   Is this charity particular, or given to all in need?

A.   To all. For so said George Fox and the blessed first brothers, the soul's tabernacle must be decent fed and clothed before the light of truth may pierce to the soul itself. And I'll tell thee why they said, they saw about them the greatest most of mankind live in misery, worse than brutes; and saw also those who might and should relieve them, they that had more than sufficient to clothe and feed themselves and theirs, did not, from their selfish vanity and greed. And further, how this lack of charity did stink as a carrion in the Lord Jesus Christ's nostrils, and shall damn all who are so blind. Now call us rebels if thee will, for yea, we are rebels in this, and call our giving most good and fellowly, and best mirror of Jesus Christ's true commonwealth. Call us rebels, thee call Him rebel also.

Q.   Christ gave in compassion. This is not your case. You give to suborn they who know no better from their rightful station.

A.   Is rightful station to starve and go in rags? Why man, thee should walk in the street where the sister lives. Thee's eyes, hast thee not?

Q.   Eyes to see she is well hid behind your coat-skirts, and provided for, in this miserable town.

A.   So well hid, thee's found her.

Q.   She has been sought many months.

A.   Here, I have a guinea upon me I was paid but yesterday for two coats I have made. Lay one of thine to it, and I will give both in Toad Lane to those thee think in their rightful station, that yet starve and live worse than beggars. What, thee won't? Don't thee believe in charity, master?

Q. Not in such charity that goes to the nearest gin-shop.

A. Nor tomorrow, neither. I see thee's a careful man. Look thee, did Jesus Christ not give for thee, and far more than a guinea's worth? Think'st thee He was so careful as theeself and said, Mayhap I'd best not redeem this man, he is weak, my blood shall go to the gin-shop?

Q. You grow insolent, I will not have it.

A. Nor I thy guinea. We are well matched.

Q. I say, there is possibility she did great crime.

A. She has done no great crime, save she was born Eve. Thee knows it well as I.

Q. I know she is most suspicious close to a great liar.

A. Come, I know thee by thy repute. They say thee a fair man, though strict in thy master's service. Thee'd deny repute with me, so be it, I am well used to such. Thee'd break me and all who believe as I upon thy books of law, that are eleven inches in their foot no more than custom made iron to wall the rich against the poor. We shall not be broke, nay, try thy worst, it shall never be. All thy rods shall be but flails, to make us the better grains of wheat. I'll tell thee now a tale of my father's time, in the year of Monmouth, that was also of my birth, '85. For Jesus be praised, he was a Friend of Truth ever since he had met George Fox, who first saw the light, and his wife at Swarthmoor; and was brought to gaol upon a trumpery charge at Bolton. Where while he lay there came one Mr Crompton, who was magistrate and to judge him, and would exhort him to mend his ways and abjure the fellowship of the Friends. Whereat my father would not be swayed, and spake so well of his beliefs that in the end 'twas the magistrate was left the more shaken in his own. For in the end he spake to my father aside and said this: there are two justices in this world, and in one was my father innocent, which was the justice of God; and guilty only by the other, that was men's. And three years after was this magistrate cause of great scandal, for he threw off his chains and came to us, tho' it cost him

dear, great loss in many things of this world. Who did greet
my father thus when first they did encounter in fellowship,
saying, It is now for thee to judge me, friend, that I wove so
poor a piece before; yet now I know justice without light is
warp without weft, and will never make fair cloth.

Q.   The bench was well rid of him. A nation is lost which distin-
guisheth not law from sin. Crime is of fact, that may be
proven or not. Sin is for God alone to judge.

A.   Thee's blind to truth.

Q.   And thou art blind to what all men other have judged and
think. Once sin is made crime, gross tyranny doth ensue, such
as the Inquisition hath plainly shown among the Papists.

A.   Inquisition sits well in thy mouth, master lawyer. Men think,
men think — aye, most men think. And most to this life, and
what shall suit best their sinning lives in it. And little to that
court above, where all shall be charged. There shall thee find
whether sin is judged of a farthing's weight beside thy law,
that is given of Antichrist.

Q.   No more. Thou art a most obstinate fellow

A.   And ever shall be, so long as I am Christian, praise the Lord.

Q.   I will tomorrow have no unrest from thee or thy sectaries, is it
understood? No, nor standing there below. I warn thee, cool
thy mischievous temper. Else will I summon Mr Fotheringay
straight, who knows what I am about, and my enquiry just
and proper. Be off.

Historical Chronicle, 1736.

OCTOBER.

Friday 1.

ONE *James Todd* who represented the Miller's Man, in the Entertainment of Dr *Faustus*, this Night, at the Theatre in *Covent-Garden*, fell from the upper Stage, in a flying Machine, the Wires breaking, fractur'd his Scull, and dy'd miserably; 3 others were much hurt, but recover'd. Some of the Audience Swooned, and the whole were in great Confusion upon this sad Accident.

Lately, a large Grampus was drove a-shore at *Steaths* near *Whitby, Yorkshire*, the Lordship of *Francis Middleton*, Esq; the Head was 5 Yards long, the Finns 4 Yards each, the Tail 3, and the Body 17.

Thursday, 7.

A Man and his Wife, at *Rushal* in *Norfolk*, having some Words, he went out and hang'd himself. The Coroner's Inquest found it *Self-Murder*, and order'd him to be buried in the Cross-ways: But his Wife sent for a Surgeon, and sold the Body for half a Guinea; the Surgeon feeling about the Body, the Wife said, *He is fit for your Purpose, he is as fat as Butter;* and then he was put naked into a Sack, with his Legs hanging out, thrown upon a Cart, and convey'd to the Surgeon's.

Saturday, 9.

A great Storm did considerable Mischief to our Shipping, but was in *France* much more violent.

There had like to have been a Goal-Delivery at *Newgate, Bristol*, by the greatest Rogues, who propos'd to the rest, either to make their Escapes, or to have their Throats cut; but one *Smith* run up Stairs, gave the Alarm to the Keepers, and caused the Projectors to be secured, with their Chissels, Files, Iron Crows, &c. with which they were at work.

Monday, 11.

This Evening a Shoemaker in *Dublin* finding another Man in Bed with his Wife, desired him to take his Time, and not be in too much haste, and paid his Compliments with a brotherly Kiss, for the Labour he took off his Hands; but he was not so civil to his Lady, for he cut her Nose close off to her Face, desired her to follow her Gallant, and see whether he would like this Addition to her Beauty or no.

Thursday, 14.

The Parliament met at *Westminster*, and was further Prorogued to *Thursday*, Nov. 25.

Friday, 15.

At the Sessions, at the *Old Baily*, 3 Criminals received Sentence of Death (*viz.*) *Wm Rine* and *Samuel Morgan*, for the Highway, and *Mary Campton*, for stealing Goods; one was burnt in the Hand, 12 order'd for Transportation, and 12 acquitted. *Daniel Malden*, (See p. 550 E) received his former Sentence. The 5 *Spittlefields* Rioters were all found Guilty, order'd to be imprison'd for 2 Years and find Security for their good behaviour for 7 Years.

Saturday, 16.

Mrs *Mapp* the Bonesetter, with Dr *Taylor*, the Oculist, being at the Playhouse in *Lincoln's-Inn Fields*, to see a Comedy call'd the Husband's Relief, with the Female Bonesetter and Worm Doctor; it occasion'd a full House; and the following:

EPIGRAM.

While *Mapp* to th'actors shew'd a kind regard,
On one Side *Taylor* sat, on th' other *Ward*:
When their mock Persons of the Drama came,
Both *Ward* and *Taylor* thought it hurt their Fame;
Wonder'd how *Mapp* cou'd in good Humour be—
Zoons, crys the Manly Dame, it hurts not *me*;
Quacks without Art may either blind or kill;
But * *Demonstration* shews that mine is *Skill*.

---

* This alludes to some Surprizing Cures she perform'd before Sir *Hans Sloane* at the *Grecian* Coffee-house (where she comes once a Week from *Epsom* in her Chariot with four Horses) viz: a Man of *Wardour-street* whose Back had been broke 9 Years, and stuck out a Inches; a Niece of Sir *Hans Sloane* in the like Condition; and a Gentleman who went with one Shoe heel 6 Inches high, having been lame 20 Years, of his Hip and Knee; whom she set strait and brought his Leg down even with the other.

And

And the following was Sung upon ý Stage.

YOU Surgeons of *London*, who puzzle your
    Pate,
To ride in your Coaches, and purchase Estates,
Give over, for Shame, for your Pride has a Fall,
And ý Doctress of *Epsom* has out-done you all.
                Derry Down, &c.

What signifies Learning, or going to School,
When a Woman can do, 'bout Reason or Rule,
What puts you to Nonplus, & baffles your Art;
For Petticoat-Practice has now got the Start.

In Physick, as well as in Fashions, we find,
The newest has always its Run with Mankind:
Forgot is the Bustle 'bout *Taylor* and *Ward*;
Now *Mapp*'s all ý Cry, & her Fame's on Record.

Dame Nature has giv'n her a Doctor's Degree,
She gets all ý Patients, and pockets the Fee;
So if you don't instantly prove her a Cheat,
She'll loll in her Chariot whilst you walk ý street
                Derry down, &c.

Monday, 18.

The County Hospital at *Winchester* was opened; when Dr *Alured Clarke* preached before a numerous Congregation, many of them Gentlemen of Rank, who made an handsome Collection, besides their annual Subscription. It were to be wish'd such charitable Undertakings was encouraged all over *England*.

Tuesday, 19.

The common Crier made Proclamation at *Guildhall*, before the Lord Mayor, &c. for *Henry Fister*, Gent. to appear and answer to the Charge of Felony and the Murder of Mr *Darby*, or otherwise he would be Outlaw'd. — The said *Fisher* escaped out of *Newgate* some Years ago.

60 Horse Load of Tea amounting to 70 hundred Weight was seized in *Sussex*, by 3 Riding Officers, assisted by 3 Dragoons, and carry'd to *Eastbourn* Custom-house. The Smugglers were about 40, a good Part of whom after an Hours tipling, made an Attempt to regain the Goods, but were repulsed and several of them wounded.

Dublin. A Woman big with Child going into the Country to lie in, was taken with her Labour on the Road, no body being near but a blind Man and a Boy, she begg'd the latter to go for Help, he refus'd unless paid beforehand, she pull'd out her Purse, in which was some Silver and a small Piece of Gold, which the Boy seeing told the Blind Man of, he immediately knock'd out her Brains with a Staff, took the Purse and went off: A Gentleman coming by, and seeing the Woman murder'd, rode up to the Boy, and threatning to kill him, he confess'd the Fact, and both were sent to *Kilmanham* Goal.

Wednesday, 20.

At *Powderham*, *Devonshire*, a Toad-Fish was thrown ashore; it is 4 Foot long, has a Head like a Toad, 2 Feet like a Goose and the Mouth opens 12 Inches wide. One of this Kind was dissected at the College of Physicians in the presence of K. *Charles* II.

Thursday, 21.

A small Congregation of Protestant Dissenters met at *Brixworth*, *Northamptonshire*, for divine Worship, the Mob of the Town rose, dash'd the Windows to Pieces, threaten'd the Life of a young Gentleman of *Northampton*, who they supposed was to officiate there, seiz'd *William Beck* Master of the House, and threw him several Times into the Mud: It's hop'd that Persons of superior Character, to whom Application is made, will consider how much the Liberty of the Subject and the publick Safety are concerned in this Affair.

Friday, 22.

The Magistrates of *Edinburgh*, to make an exact Scrutiny into the late Riot and Murder of Capt. *Porteus* order'd all the Burgesses, Traders, &c. to appear before the Dean of *Guild*, and give in an exact List of their Servants and Apprentices. Five of the late Rioters have been committed to the Castle.

Came on before the Rt Hon. the Ld Chancellor the Hearing of a Petition of Mr *Allcock*, of *Waterford* in *Ireland*, Guardian to *Michael Aylmer*, an Infant about 6 Years old, Heir to a great Estate in that Kingdom, shewing, That the Mother, to bring up the said Child in the *Romish* Religion, did privately convey it away; and that the said Guardian coming to *London* after it, found the Mother, but not the Child: To which she answer'd, That she brought it over for Advice of Physicians, and that her Footman had, without her Privity, convey'd it away; but she was order'd to bring it into Court by the next Thursday, or she should be sent to the Fleet.

Monday, 25.

Mr *George Kelly*, formerly Secretary to the Bishop of *Rochester*, made his Escape from the *Tower*, where he had been confin'd 14 Years, but had lately the Liberty to take the Air with a Warden: He wrote a Letter next Morning to the D. of *Newcastle*, acknowledging his Majesty's Goodness towards him, and excusing the Attempt he had made to regain his Liberty, and another to a Gentleman in the *Tower* assigning over to him all his Books, &c. at his Lodgings. A Reward of 200l. is offer'd for apprehending him.

The industrious *Dutch* having this Year taken 589 Whales and 3 young Ones, the *French* and *Spaniards* 70; on this Occasion it was remarked, That if *England* has not had her Share in this profitable Fishery, she may boast of having out done all her Neighbours in *Horse-racing.*

Wednesday, 27.

At a Court of Common-council at *Guildhall*, it was Resolved that *Stocks market* was the fittest Place for building the Mansion-house for the Lord Mayor, and it was referr'd to the former Committee to prepare a Plan.

Several Persons have been apprehended on Suspicion of murdering Capt. *Innys* mention'd in our last.

EARLY THE NEXT MORNING Rebecca is ushered into Ayscough's presence, in the same room as the previous day. It is quite a large one, with a massive and bulbous-legged seventeenth-century table also. This is not a converted bedchamber, but used for an occasional dining-room, club-room, private meeting-place as the inn requires. Rebecca's place is six feet of polished black oak from that of her interlocutor. Most surprisingly he stands to greet her, almost as if she were a lady. He does not bow as he would have done to such a person, yet faces her and gives her a small nod of acknowledgement, and gestures her to her seat. Already a bone tumbler of water waits on the table before it; need there, it seems, is foreseen.

"You are well rested, mistress, you have broke your fast?"

"Yes."

"You have no complaint of your lodging?"

"No."

"You may sit."

She sits, but he remains standing. He turns to John Tudor, who has sat himself to one side at the end of the table, and makes a quick gesture of the hand: what first is to be said is not to be recorded.

"I must praise you for your conduct yesterday eve, that you gave no countenance to the troublous malice Wardley and your father showed. You gave good example there."

"They meant no ill."

"There we must disagree. No matter, Mistress Rebecca. An august parent may differ in all else from a humble one. But in this, the loss of a son, they are as one, and as deserving of our concern. Is it not so?"

"I have told all I know."

Ayscough looks down into those fixed and now obscurely puzzled eyes, lost by this change of attitude in him. After that last answer he tilts his head and wig slightly in his characteristic way, as if he expects her to say something more. But she does not, and he walks away to the window and looks out thoughtfully; then turns to face her again.

"Mistress Rebecca, we lawyers must be thrifty. We must glean our acres more than other men, we must hold the smallest grain of truth precious, the more so when there appears great dearth of it. I would ask more of what your present piety must find offensive to have made quick again."

"Ask. I would not forget I sinned."

Ayscough contemplates the waiting, unyielding face in the light of the windows he stands by.

"Mistress, I will not rehearse the tale you told me yesterday, it is fresh in your mind. I would say this first, before we begin. If, having had this last night to reflect, you should now wish to change your sworn evidence, you shall have no blame. If aught of consequence was left out, if you told not exact truth by reason of fear for your state or any other cause, you shall not suffer. On that I give you my word."

"I have told truth in all."

"To the best of your belief all passed as you say?"

"Yes."

"His Lordship was transported to Heaven?"

"Yes."

"Mistress Rebecca, I might wish it were so, nay, I wish it so. But I have an advantage of you. You knew his Lordship for scarce more than a month, when he did hide much from you, as you have admitted. I have known him these many years, mistress. Alas he I knew, and many others likewise knew, was not he you portray."

Rebecca makes no answer. It is as if he has not spoken. Ayscough waits, then continues.

"I will tell you a little of him, in great confidence, mistress. The attention he bestowed upon you would astound his own family or circle, who counted him the churlishest man alive towards your sex. Why, in that he was called Poor John, closer to dead fish than human flesh. Nor in his previous life, mistress, had he shown the least respect for established religion, despite his rank. He was no more seen happily on his knees in church than swallows out of their winter mud. I may believe you were eager to leave your former life, most inclinable to approve whatever should assist you in that, very well. It is his Lordship providing that assistance, and you but a common strumpet, mistress, which he had never set eyes on in his life till a month before. That, on my life, I cannot credit."

Again he waits for her to reply, again she does not. He walks back to his chair across the table, with her eyes still on his. He might perhaps have hoped for some weakening, some defensiveness in them, but they retain that same strange blend of meekness and fixity as before, almost as if she is deaf to all reason. He goes on.

"I speak not of much else, mistress, that I likewise cannot credit. Of your being brought to a chief place of pagan idolatry to meet Our Lord and His Most Sacred Father, in most impious circumstance, and scarcely the less at a Devonshire cavern, and there more improbable still in all else. Of poor husbands and carpenters being made divine, this female figure the Holy Spirit beside; why, that Wardley tells me is not even known among your own prophets, nor your June Eternal neither. Mistress Rebecca, you are no common fool; nor woman that has not seen the world. Would you not, if you heard such a tale as yours from another, doubt either the teller's reason, or your own? Would you not cry, I cannot and will not believe this absurd and blasphemous tale, it must be got up to bubble and deceive, to blind me from some much plainer truth?"

Still Rebecca will not answer beyond staring at him, though clearly she now must make some response. What happens is in fact what has happened a number of times in this interrogatory. She is extremely slow to answer. It is not the look, or seems not the look, of one searching for words, hesitant and embarrassed; but much more a strange pause, as if she must have Ayscough's words first translated from a foreign language before she can frame a reply. She lacks completely Wardley's aggressive promptness and sharpness of repartee; on occasion it is almost as if she answers not for herself, but waits until some mysterious adviser puts one in her mind.

"I answer that most doubted or disbelieved when Christ first came. I have told truth plain, I can no more."

"You are too modest, mistress. Why, Claiborne said you had as well been actress as what you were. Have you not admitted there was no truth in what you told Jones? You may say it was forced upon you to lie, but not that you did not lie."

"It was not falsehood upon great matters."

"To be brought to Paradise to meet God Almighty and His Son is no great matter?"

"So great it may hardly be said in words. I knew not then how to say it in words, I know it not still, to thee. Yet so did it come to pass, and I was given sight of Jesus Christ and His Father; which filled my soul with balm and greatest joy by Their presence, yea, a pleasure more than mortal."

"The Almighty a yeoman, the Redeemer a haymaking labourer, is that seemly?"

"Is God the Holy Father not so because He sits not in glory on a throne, is Jesus Christ not Jesus because He groans not on a cross? Angels not angels because I see them not with wings, because they bear sickles in their hands, not harps or trumpets? I told thee, I was brought up to count all image of godliness false, of Satan. What I did see was shadows of the light alone, seen of my body; of my soul I saw the light, and first-last object of my love."

"You may see with your eyes what you please, since all you see is counted false? Is it not so?"

"What I see with my eyes is of the body carnal, not certain truth, which is of light alone. I see no less true or false than thee in carnal seeing, or any other man and woman."

Ayscough is left, after this exchange, in a dilemma, though he conceals it. A modern person would not have had a shadow of doubt that Rebecca was lying, or at least inventing. Gods, except for an occasional Virgin Mary to illiterate Mediterranean peasants, no longer appear; even in Ayscough's time such visions were strongly associated with Catholic trickery, something good Protestants expected and despised. Yet his England, even his class of it, was still very far from modern certainties. Ayscough, for instance, believes in ghosts; he has never seen one himself, yet has heard and read too many accounts, and by no means all from old wives and dotards, not to credit some of them. Ghosts and spirits did not then come from an idle and fancy-nursing imagination, they came from the very real night, still largely unlit, of a lonely England, that still held fewer human beings altogether than a fraction of modern London.

Ayscough has certainly supported the repeal of the Witchcraft Act (though not for Scotland) in this very year. But this is largely because he now associates the witchcraft cases he has heard of, even attended as a younger man, like the occasional uses of the ducking-stool, with defective law and always disputable evidence. He does not say to himself there has never been witchcraft; rather that its worst aspects have lapsed. That some malign and wicked coven in a remote part of Devonshire still follows ancient practices remains very far from the bounds of possibility. He may feel, he does feel, Rebecca is nine parts hiding truth in her holier vision (against which he has his own knowledge of his master's son to argue, and an ancient dislike of him, muted behind respect for rank); but there remains an irreducible one part, of possible truth, he cannot quell. He will never reveal it; yet there it sticks, a nagging thorn in his side.

"You will not change your evidence? I repeat, you shall not suffer."

"Nor from truth shall I suffer. I will not change."

"Very well, mistress. I give you this great favour, that were we in a court of law, you should not have. Yet you will not have it. So be it, and upon your head if you prove false. Now we shall begin upon oath." He sits down and glances to John Tudor at the table-end. "Write all."

***

Q.   Let us keep to thy carnal seeing, for all its words may be false. Are you certain you had never, before his Lordship came to you at the bagnio, seen him?

A.   No, I had not.

Q.   Nor heard speak of him?

A.   No.

Q.   Your service was often taken in advance, was it not so?

A.   Yes.

Q.   Was it so with his Lordship?

A.   It was writ in Claiborne's book, friend of Lord B———, under my name.

Q.   How long in advance was it writ?

A.   She told me nothing of it till the morning of when he came.

Q.   This was her usual custom?

A.   Yes.

Q.   And you saw not what was entered, but was first informed by what she read out?

A.   I knew not who he was till after, as I said.

Q.   You went out sometimes upon the town? To routs, ridottos, the theatre, elsewhere?

A.   On occasion, but never alone.

Q.   Then how?

A.   In larking, when we must always be with Claiborne and her bully-boys about us.

Q.   What is larking?

A.   To snare sinners to the bagnio. Those who were lured and asked for assignations were told they might have them at the bagnio only.

Q.   You or your companions never made private assignations?

A.   We suffered if we were found to cheat her.

Q.   You were punished?

A.   We should dine with the bully-boys. 'Twas called so. And then were we treated worse than any punishment by law. She ruled us thus. Better die than dine, we were used to say among ourselves.

Q. You yourself were never so treated?

A. I have known who were.

Q. None the less, you were to be seen in publick places. Might not his Lordship have first seen you so?

A. If he did, I saw him not.

Q. Nor Dick?

A. No.

Q. After you had met, did his Lordship never say to suggest he had seen you before? That he had long sought to meet you, or words of that ilk?

A. No.

Q. He might have heard of you, notwithstanding? There was gossip of you about the town?

A. Alas.

Q. Now this — did you ever, to any whatsoever, confide you were not happy with your lot and would be rid of it?

A. No.

Q. Not in the bosom of some fellow-whore?

A. I might trust none. Nor any else.

Q. Was not his Lordship's assiduity after you had met, when he could take no ordinary pleasure in you, most unaccustomed?

A. He had pleasure in hope, so it seemed.

Q. He gave you no sign you was chosen for a purpose other than the hope then alleged?

A. No. Not one.

Q. He asked you of your past, did he not?

A. Two or three questions, not more.

Q. Did he not ask you of your life in the bagnio? Whether you were not tired of it, perchance?

A. He asked of it, but not whether I was tired, tho' most men do. 'Tis nine parts fear of their own sin.

Q. How is that?

A. Is it better a man fears he sins, yet still will sin? Some did like to call whore and still worse at the height of their animal passion; others by the names of those they love, yea, even to those of their wives and, God forgive them, their mothers, sisters, daughters. And others be speechless animals like those they use. All that dwell in the flesh are damned, but those last, not most.

Q. What doctrine is this? They that sin as coarsest brutes are less to be blamed than they who sin with conscience of their culpability?

A. God is now; or He is not.

Q. I follow you not, mistress.

A. He judges men by what they are, not what they would be; and most blames not those who know no better, but those who do.

Q. God has seen fit to open His mind to you concerning this, is it so?

A. What harm have we done thee, master Ayscough? We mean thee no harm, why should thee be so resolute to harm us, to scorn when we speak plain? Our beliefs come from God, yea; but we are humble in them, also. We do not say they are revealed to us alone; nay, to all else beside, so be it they worship not the Antichrist. I say this: they who dwell in the flesh are damned, more great or more small it matters little, they are damned.

Q. To my point. Believe you, before you had left London, his Lordship had made especial enquiry to find if you were apt to his purpose, to wit, you would quit the bagnio if you might?

A. I had no inkling before the temple.

Q. Must he none the less not have discovered such? Were you not chosen, mistress, take that how you will?

A. I was saved, not chosen.

Q. That is one. You must be chosen to be saved.

A. I knew not one nor t'other then.

Q. Very well, let this rest for now. I will follow where you'd lead me with your damning. May man and woman not dwell sometimes in the flesh, if they be lawfully wed? Why answer you not? Come, are they not enjoined to procreate?

A.   They shall not live in June Eternal.

Q.   Did you not say you saw children there?

A.   Of the spirit. They were not carnal flesh, as us. Thee'd scorn we do abhor all sin of the flesh, and would cross it. I tell thee all I saw there in June Eternal were spirits of they who did fight while they lived against this evil sin, and are now rewarded. In their reward lies holy proof of what we believe.

Q.   Is this the doctrine of the French Prophets?

A.   And of Christ beside, that married not.

Q.   All pleasure of the flesh is sinful?

A.   Most this one, it is the source of all sin else. Unless we cross it, we shall not be saved.

Q.   I ask again, mistress. Is your man one with you in this, or the rather, not one?

A.   I'll answer thee again. 'Tis between Christ and us, 'tis not thy business.

Q.   Why should you not answer, Yes, he agrees, we live in Christ? Is it this: you may not agree? [*Non respondet.*] Very well, let your silence speak for you. What make you now of his Lordship's part in your story? Why think you he should choose you? Why, of all others he might have saved, if it were his purpose, did he come to you, and none other?

A.   I was in need.

Q.   Are others not in as great a need, and far the less sinners?

A.   What I was is ashes, it is punishment for my long and wilful blindness.

Q.   That answers not my question.

A.   Christ's mercy comes oft where it seems least deserved.

Q.   There I'll not dispute, mistress.

A.   It cannot be for what I was, nor what I am, tho' that is better than what I was. It shall be for what I do.

Q.   What shall you do?

A.   What women are in this world to do, whether they will it or not.

Q.   All this has taken place that you may be with child?

A.   The child I bear is but the carnal sign.

Q.   Sign of what?

A. More light and more love.

Q. The child shall bring them, or you by giving it birth shall do so?

A. She shall bring the more.

Q. What, are you so certain she shall be of your sex? Answer.

A. I cannot, in thy alphabet.

Q. Mistress, there is one and one only alphabet, that is plain English. How are you certain of this?

A. I know not, save I am.

Q. And when she is grown, I doubt not she shall preach and prophesy?

A. She shall be handmaid to Holy Mother Wisdom.

Q. Is it not to a most wicked and blasphemous greater station still that you aspire for her? [*Non respondet.*] Have I not plumbed thy depths? Is it not so among thy prophets? Do they not most impiously assever that when Christ is come again, He shall be changed to woman? May God forgive me for uttering the very thought, dost thee not in secret believe there is now carried in thy womb such a woman-Christ?

A. No, no, I swear no, I am not so vain, I have never said this, even to my inmost heart.

Q. Said it, thou mayst not. I wager thou'st thought it.

A. No, I say no. How should such a one come from so great a sinner?

Q. How indeed, unless she believed herself grown saint — as well she might, having been vouchsafed to meet God and His Son, and the Holy Spirit beside. Do you deny that by your prophetick lights such a Christ in petticoats may come?

A. I deny with all my soul I have believed it she I carry.

Q. Be not so modest, mistress. You have been honoured by the most high. Why should you not believe a diviner seed than that of Dick at work inside you?

A. Thee would snare me. Thee knows not what it is to be woman.

Q. I have a wife, and two daughters both older than you, and granddaughters besides. What is woman? Mistress, I have heard that riddle, and had it answered.

A. No riddle. As I was used when whore, so I may be used still. And all women beside.

Q. How, all women are whores?

A. Whores in this. We may not say what we believe, nor say what we think, for fear we be mocked because we are woman. If men think a thing be so, so must it be, we must obey. I speak not of thee alone, it is so with all men, and everywhere. Holy Mother Wisdom is not heard nor seen, nor what she might bring if she were let.

Q. What she would bring, we'll pass. I'd know what you would bring in the womb, mistress.

A. She I carry, yea, she shall be more than I, I am but brought to bring her. That she shall be Jesus Christ who comes, I say I am not worthy, nor so vain. Whoever she shall be, I shall not weep, no, but shall thank the Lord with all my heart I was given her. And 'tis time I tell thee this more. His Lordship was not lord in this world alone, but in a far greater, that he must conceal. What I took as his cruelty was his kindness, tho' I saw it not at the first, and sign also he saw this world's people do live in the night of Antichrist. He spake most often in such manner he might not be obliged to say what he was, unless to those that grace awakened. Yea, he was as one that finds himself in a country at war with his own, where he must dissemble his true allegiance; yet would not hide all, to those he might trust or had hope in. Mistake not, I do not say he was He of the Book. I say he was of His spirit, and both spoke and did for Him, in His name. I spake this yesterday of his Lordship and his man, how in much they seemed as one. And now do I see they were as one in truth, Dick of the carnal and imperfect body, his Lordship of the spirit; such twin natures as we all must hold, in them made outward and a seeming two. And as Jesus Christ's body must die upon the Cross, so must this latter-day earthly self, poor unregenerate Dick, die so the other half be saved. I tell thee now again I believe that other self shall be seen no more upon this earth, no not ever as he has been; yet is he not dead, but lives in June Eternal, and is one with Jesus Christ, as I saw. There,

I have said it plain, too short and plain, and thee will not believe.

Q.   You say, his Lordship was carried away upon this maggot-machine, it was sent divinely to bear him from this world?

A.   Yes.

Q.   Despite he first hired you and set you to great lewdness?

A.   So I might see there lay the road to Hell. He took no part nor pleasure in it.

Q.   Despite his other self, this carnal self you speak of, this brute Dick, did take such pleasure?

A.   For which he must die. It became not, after that first, base or lewd pleasure; but as I said, pity and affection, which it surprised me I felt so strong, as I said; and could not understand it should be thus. Now I know he who wept in my arms was the fallen half, the flesh, the shadow beneath the light, and suffered in such knowledge; so Christ, when He cried He was forsaken.

Q.   Despite most of all, that none other has seen this in them? I gave you truth there, mistress. The master disdainful of all expected of his noble rank, disobedient of his gracious father, disrespectful of God, rebellious to family duty, the servant closer kin to a beast than to a human being — so might be said of them, so were they to all the world save you.

A.   I care not what other people believed. I know only what I believe myself; and shall do, till I die.

Q.   You say his Lordship must conceal, he must dissemble his true allegiance, to wit that he is, or was, of the spirit of the Redeemer. How is this, mistress? Is it so Our Lord conducted himself — did He not most eximiously hold truth above all else? Why, does the Evangel ever bear report of Him concealing and dissembling, like some two-faced spy in fear for his own skin? What say you to that? Is it not blasphemy even to think it?

A.   The Pharisees are grown strong.

Q.   What mean you by that?

A.   Christ cannot come as He would to this world, it is too dark with sin. He shall come when it is purged of Antichrist, in all

His glory. In these presents He should be crucified again, if He were known to be among us, and did teach as He taught before; and the more so, should He come as woman. All would be as thee, and put him to mock and scorn, crying that God cannot partake of the sex of Eve, it is blasphemy. He shall come when Christians are grown true Christians again, as they were at the first. Then shall He come as He is, or She as She is.

Q. Meanwhile there are ventured only surrogates and agents, is it so?

A. Thee'd see all by this world's lights. Hast thee not read the Apostles? Except a man be born again, he cannot see the kingdom of God. Things seen are temporal; unseen, is eternal. Faith is the substance of things hoped for, the evidence of things not seen. So did God frame this world. Thee'd keep me still cunning harlot, thee'd keep his Lordship still disobedient son, and Dick, mere beast. If so thee see, so it must be, thee cannot change. Once only born, thee must live by thy lights, willy-nilly.

Q. Mistress, this stinks of rank pride, for all your face of humility.

A. I am proud in Christ, but naught else. I will speak for His light, notwithstanding I speak it ill.

Q. And in defiance of all common and prescribed belief?

A. Christ's kingdom is not must. If a thing must be, it is not of Christ. A harlot must be always harlot, is not Christ. Man must rule always over woman, is not Christ. Children must starve, is not Christ. All must suffer for what they are born, is not Christ. No must by this world's lights is Christ. It is darkness, 'tis the sepulchre this world doth lie in for its sins.

Q. Now you would deny the very heart of Christianity. Doth the sacred Bible not prescribe our duty, what we must do?

A. It tells what it is best we do, not what we must; for many do not do it.

Q. Must we not obey Christ?

A. If first we are free not to obey Him; for He would have us choose Him freely, therefore we must be free also to choose evil and sin and darkness. There is no must in that. So have I heard Brother Wardley speak. Christ dwells always in tomorrow, in hope however much we sin and are blind today, tomorrow the scales shall drop and we be saved. And further, how all His divine power and His mystery must lie in this, that He tells us man may change of his own will; and by His grace, so be redeemed.

Q. This your belief you have taken of Wardley?

A. Also of my own mind, when I look upon my past life, and this present.

Q. Does not this belief, that man may change, the which any reasonable man may approve in matters of the soul and its redemption, not show itself a most opprobrious and dangerous principle when it is carried into matters of this world? Must it not lead to civil war and revolution, to the upsetting of all lawful order? Does it not become the most wicked notion that every man must change, and be brought to his change by bloody force and cruel tumult if he will not do so of his own free will?

A. Such change is not of Christ. Even tho' it be done in His name.

Q. Is not this why the Prophets have parted company with the Quakers — who will not take sword in hand for their beliefs?

A. 'Tis no more true than wheaten bread is brown. We would conquer by our faith and by persuasion alone; not by the sword. Such is not Christ's way.

Q. Then now you deny Wardley. For yesterday he did proclaim to me he would go sword in hand against those who did not believe as he did; and made other contumacious threats upon the present government of this nation.

A. He is man.

Q. And seditious.

A. I know him better than thee. Among his own, he is kind and compassionate. And of good sense, except where he is threatened by persecution.

Q. I tell thee, he has no good sense, and one day soon shall suffer for it. No matter, enough of thy sermoning. Let us come now to Dick. You would make more of him than any who knew him before. Do you say behind his outward there was hidden one less lacking?

A.   He did suffer for what he was, he was no beast in that.

Q.   Do you say as much, he understood far better than most supposed?

A.   He understood he was fallen.

Q.   And else beside? You have said most high things of his master. What make you of this: was it not Dick who did seem to lead on the last morning? He, not his Lordship, who seemed best to know when you should leave the highway, as when you should dismount and proceed afoot? He who did first mount above while his Lordship and you did wait below?

A.   Some knowledge in him there was that more complete men, even such as his Lordship, lack.

Q.   You saw nowhere evidence to conclude either had been in these parts on previous occasion?

A.   None.

Q.   It must seem that Dick had known the place, by what he did? You have no suspicion, by what means he knew?

A.   He knew not of God by rote; yet of his heart. As beasts may return home, though lost at great distance from it, and no man to guide them.

Q.   Do you maintain your June Eternal and your visions was as home to him?

A.   He did greet Holy Mother Wisdom when first she came to us so a faithful dog long kept from its mistress, who now must fawn upon her.

Q.   Jones said he did run from the cavern before you came out yourself as one in great fear and horror, that had but a single thought, to escape. What dog does so, having refound its mistress?

A.   One that cannot cross its sin, and is not fit.

Q.   Why doth your Holy Mother Wisdom, that shows such kindness and mercy to you, show none to this poor creature? Why is he let to run off and commit this great sin of *felo de se?*

A.   Thee'd have me answer what only God can answer.

Q. I'd have thee answer what I may believe.

A. I cannot.

Q. Then I'll put such an answer in thy mind. Might he not in his ignorance be moved by one likely cause alone, that he did see his Lordship killed before his eyes, or snatched away, in some manner henceforth lost to him as protector?

A. I know not what passed, I slept.

Q. Mistress, first, he leads you to this place, which doth further lead to the presumption he knew what should pass there; yet despite this, what doth pass doth bring him to end his days. Is this not most dark?

A. All is dark if God wills it.

Q. And dark also, woman, tho' falsely so, if you yourself will answer thus, and play the self-elected saint among the clouds, above such flim-flam things as common reason. I marked it when first I told you Dick was dead. What woman hears the father of the child she bears is dead, and makes so little cry and to-do as you? As if she but hears of a nobody's death? Yet who declares herself later more enamoured of him than of any other, she, why she of all women, who's known more lovers than stinking flesh has blow-flies? Who answers now she cannot tell, she cannot know, the matter is of no consequence? What of this?

A. This of it, I do bear his child, and yet my heart rejoices he is dead; and that for his sake, not mine. Now he shall rise again, without his sins.

Q. Is this your Christian fellowship?

A. I say again, thee'd have me mirror of my sex, that thine has made. I will not suit. I have told thee I was harlot still, I did sate his lust; for so was he, lust incarnate, as bull or stallion. Can thee not see I am changed, I am harlot no more, I am Christ's reborn, I have seen June Eternal? I will not suit. By faith the harlot Rahab perished not with them.

Q. Thou art worse than reformed harlot. Thou art bishopess, woman, why, thou'dst dare to make a theology of thy flibberty-gibberty fancyings, thy foolish dreamings, with thy

June Eternals here, thy Holy Mother Wisdoms there — what right hast thou to coin such names, when even thy fellow conventiclers know them not?

A.   I have told them to none save thee, nor shall not. Other names beside I have not told thee, nor shall not. All are no more than words in this world, tho' signs to greater than words hereafter. Are thy steeple-house hymns and anthems evil, that use words to rejoice in the Lord? Are they not to praise Him, 'less licensed by government?

Q.   Watch thy tongue.

A.   If thee'll watch thine.

Q.   This is brazen impudence.

A.   'Twas not I that provoked it.

Q.   Enough. It was this, to thy mind Dick died by guilt of his lust for thee?

A.   So he might cross and deny his fleshly self, that sinned.

Q.   Thou wert never by child before?

A.   No.

Q.   Though with more than ample chance. How many times wast thou ridden, of a busy night? [*Non respondet.*] A pox on thy piety, answer. [*Non respondet.*] No matter, I may guess. What of this bastard thou'dst palm off on thy man?

A.   My barrenness was Christ's will; and His will, that I am what I now am. My husband shall be her father in this world, she shall be no bastard.

Q.   What of its father not in this world?

A.   Truth may not be said of seen things.

Q.   I will have it said.

A.   Thy world is not my world, nor Jesus Christ's neither.

Q.   I will have it said what thou'dst hide from me, woman. Which is the most father in thy unruly mind — is it Dick or is it his Lordship?

A.   His Lordship is what he is, no less, no more; which is not father in this world.

Q.   But in another thou dost count him so?

A.   Of the spirit, not the seed.

Q. Is it not divinely appointed it is sin to rebel against the authority of man? Witnessed in the Almighty's first act, and ever after?

A. 'Tis reported so, by men.

Q. The Holy Bible is false witness?

A. Witness from one side alone. Which fault lies in man, not in God nor His son. Eve came of Adam's rib, so 'tis said in the second of Genesis. In the first 'tis said God created man and woman in His own image, male and female created He them. Which Our Lord Jesus Christ did further speak of in the Gospel of St Matthew, the nineteenth chapter; and there nothing of ribs, but of Moses, who did allow men to put away their wives. And Jesus Christ said, from the beginning it was not so. Equal were they made.

Q. I do not believe thee a new-born woman, no, not one tittle, beneath thy plain cap and petticoat. Thou hast found a new vice, that is all. Thy pleasure's now to fly in the face of all our forefathers have in their wisdom told us we must believe; there hast thou malignantly found shot to weight a base resentment. Thou wert drab to serve men for their pleasure, was it not so? And now thou'dst have them serve thine, and put off the old as a ribband, a last year's fashion, thou cunning jade. Religion is thy mask, no more. 'Tis all the better to have thy unwomanly revenge.

A. Thee'll not snare me so.

Q. Snare, snare, what snare?

A. Thee'd have me say I am lost in revenge, as termagant or virago; and cannot answer to the good reason for fear it be taken for the bad.

Q. I smoke thy evil purpose.

A. I'll tell thee my evil purpose. Most in this world is unjust by act of man, not of Our Lord Jesus Christ. Change that is my purpose.

Ayscough stares at her, this assertion once made. Now it is he who is slow to reply. She sits bolt upright in her armless wooden chair, hands as always on her lap, intent on his eyes, as if she faced the Antichrist in person. Her eyes may hold still some hint of meekness, but her face seems pinched, determined to be obdurate, to concede nothing. Ayscough speaks at last, it seems rather more of her, than to her.

"Thou art a liar, woman. Thou art a liar."

There is no reaction in her expression. John Tudor looks up at her from his shorthand, as he has often in the interrogatory, during such pauses. She stares. So it has gone, since the beginning; always the lawyer on the attack, always Rebecca staring, slow-answering in her manner. It has become obvious Ayscough's patience grows thin. He had opted to begin in a kinder, more polite way than on the previous day; yet as things wore on, he knew she did not give to such pretended respect. Neither soft nor hard words would break her, reveal the enigma she hid: what really happened. Once or twice his mind slipped back to the days of the real question; interrogation aided by rack and thumbscrew. By that method at least one had got to the bottom; but the Bill of Rights had ended such procedures in England. Except for high treason, they survived only in wicked and degenerate Catholic countries like France; and for all his faults Ayscough was English, not French. That did not prevent him feeling a growing ill-temper.

With Rebecca it was less, as it might be today, that she felt herself and her religion insulted and disbelieved; she would have been surprised had they not been, and acutely suspicious. Such scepticism and persecution were commonplace. It was far more that this interrogation did not let the religion be fully seen — its right, its reason, its crying need, its fierce being now. In truth these two were set apart from each other not only by countless barriers of age, sex, class, education, native province and the rest, but by something far deeper still: by belonging to two very different halves of the human spirit, perhaps at root those, left and right, of the two hemispheres of the brain. In themselves these are neither good nor evil. Those whom the left lobe (and the right hand) dominates are rational, mathematical, ordered, glib with words, usually careful and conventional; human society largely runs on an even keel, or at least runs, because of them. A sage and sober assessor of evolution must regard those dominated by the right lobe as far less desirable, except in one or two very peripheral things like art and religion, where mysticism and lack of logic are given value. Like Rebecca, they are poor at reason, often confused in thought and argument; their sense of time (and politic timing) is often defective. They tend to live and wander in a hugely extended now, treating both past and future as present, instead of keeping them in control and order, firmly separated, like honest, decent left-lobers. They blur, they upset, they disturb. So truly are these two human beings of 1736. They speak for opposite poles, though long before such physical explanations for their contrariness could be mooted. Rebecca is driven now to the very brink of her left-handed self, that is her kind. At last she speaks, it seems almost to herself.

"Thee play blind. Thee play blind."

"Address me not so. I will not have it."

She falls.

"Thee will not have it, thee will not have it. Thee's cloud, thee's night, thee's Lucifer with thy questions, thee'd blind me with thy lawyer's chains, that blind thee worst theeself. Can thee not see this world is lost? 'Tis not new sinning, 'tis oldly so, since time began. 'Tis cloth a thousand and a thousand times rent and soiled, 'tis sin every thread, I tell thee it shall never be washed clean nor newed again. No, never newed again by thee and thine, nor its evil ways thrown off, that corrupt the innocent from the day they are born. Can thee not see, thee and thine are blind?"

Ayscough rises abruptly from his chair.

"Silence, woman! I say silence."

But Rebecca now does the unheard-of. She stands also, and continues her denunciation; not slowly now, but rapidly, almost to the point of incoherence.

"How dost honour Heaven? By turning this present world to Hell. Can thee not see we who live by Christ are thy only hope? Flee thy ways, yea, live Jesus Christ's ways now forgotten. Thy sinning world doth mock and persecute, yea, it would bury them; thee and thine are certain damned, and each day more. Yea, it shall come to pass, yea, His way shall be resurrected, yea, so shall the sinners see, yea, we of faith shall be justified; and thee and thy legion of Antichrist accursed for thy blindness, thy wicked ways. By this we shall conquer, I tell thee Christ returns, it is prophesied, yea, His light shall shine through every deed and word, the world shall be all window, and shining light, all evil seen thereby, and punished in Hell, and none of the damned like thee withstand it."

"I'll have thee thrown in gaol and whipped!"

"No, no, thee evil dwarf, thee'd bind me in thy evil snares, thee shall not. I tell thee time past did never once return, thee cling to it in vain, 'tis now, 'tis now, I tell thee a new world comes, no sin shall be, no strife more between man and man, between man and woman, nor parent and child, nor master and servant. No, nor wicked will, nor washing of hands, nor shrugging of shoulders, nor blindness like thine to all that breaks thy comfort and thy selfish ways. No judge shall judge the poor, who would steal himself, were he them; no, nor greed shall rule, likewise not vanity, nor cruel sneers, nor feasting while others starve, nor happy shoes and shirts while any go naked. Dost thee not see, the lion shall lie with the lamb, all shall be light and justice, dear God dost thee not see, thee cannot be so blind to thy own eternity, thee cannot, thee cannot . . ."

Ayscough throws a look at John Tudor, who has remained head down, rapidly scribbling his shorthand.

"For God's sake, man. Stir thyself. Stop her tongue."

Tudor stands, hesitates a moment.

"I tell thee I see, I see, dost not see I see, it comes, it —"

Tudor moves to silence her; almost at once he stops. Something extraordinary has happened. At that last "I see," her eyes have suddenly shifted. From staring at Ayscough, they look away, to the corner of the room to her left, some fifteen feet from where she stands. A small side-door there apparently leads to the adjacent room. It is exactly as if someone has entered by it and now stands there, making further speech impossible. The impression of this is so vivid that both Ayscough and his clerk look swiftly to the side-door. It stands silently there, unopened. No one has entered. Of one accord they look back to Rebecca, to see her still staring as before, it seems rooted, struck dumb; yet not dumbfounded or amazed, on the contrary, tamed, like one grateful to be silenced. All that previous pinched and obstinate quality in her face has mysteriously passed away. Whatever she sees, her expression is more that of a dawning smile, curiously timid, childlike and expectant, brought unexpectedly face to face with someone she trusts and loves.

Ayscough looks quickly round to the door again, then to Tudor, who answers his unspoken question.

"Not a soul, sir."

The two men stare a moment at each other. Ayscough looks back to Rebecca.

"She is in a fit. See if she may be woken."

Tudor moves closer, then stopping a yard short of the tranced woman, gingerly reaches out a hand and shakes her arm, as if she were a snake or some dangerous animal. Still Rebecca stares towards the door.

"Harder, man, harder. She won't bite thee."

Tudor goes behind her, and moving her chair back, takes both her arms. At first she seems oblivious, but as he continues to shake there comes a small cry from her, as of pain. It is low, more of an unbearable loss, bizarrely like an intimate sigh at the end of love, than true pain. Slowly her eyes find Ayscough's, who still stands facing her across the table. They close immediately and her head sinks.

"Make her sit."

Tudor places the chair behind her.

"Sit, mistress. It is past."

She sits as if will-less, her head sunk deep; then raises her hands to her face, and begins to sob, it seems at first in shame, as if she would hide this collapse into emotion. Ayscough leans forward, hands on table.

"What is this, what saw you then?" Her only answer is a deeper sob. "Water, give her water."

"Let her be, master. 'Tis like the vapours. 'Twill pass."

Ayscough scrutinises the sobbing woman a little longer; then goes abruptly to the side-door to open it. But there he is defeated; though he tries twice, three times, with increasing irritation, it is locked. He walks more slowly back to the window, and stares out. He sees nothing outside; that irreducible one part of his mind stands crowing over all his reason and he is as shaken as Rebecca herself, though he does not admit it; nor looks back as her sobs rise, become unshameable, racking her body, rending in their intensity. Only when they become less frequent, does he turn again. He sees his clerk has managed to persuade her to drink, and stands with a hand on her shoulder, though she still sits with her head bowed. After a minute Ayscough goes back to his chair. He watches her bent head for a few moments, then gestures Tudor back to his seat.

"Are you returned within your senses, mistress?" She nods her bowed head. "We may proceed?" Again she nods her head. "What came upon you then?" She shakes her head. "Why stared you so, towards the door?"

At last she speaks, though without looking up. "At what I saw."

"There was none there. Why answer you not? I will forgive you your ranting and your insolence, your words most insulting of me. I would know what you saw, that is all." He folds his arms across his breast, and waits, but in vain. "Are you ashamed of what you saw?"

Then he has Rebecca's eyes, as she straightens up to face him, and once more puts her hands on her lap. Her face gives him a shock, for it holds a faint but perceptible smile. He will long remember it.

"I am not ashamed."

"Why smile you?"

She continues smiling, as if it is sufficient answer.

"It was a person?"

"Yes."

"A person of this world?"

"No."

"Did you believe it to be Our Lord, the Saviour?"

"No."

"She you call Holy Mother Wisdom?"

"No."

"Mistress, no more of this coyness. You did stare, it seemed at one who stood, that had entered, that you knew. Is it not so? Come, who was it?"

Her face has lost its mysterious smile; it is as if only now she remembers where she is, before an enemy. Yet in what follows of the interrogatory, Rebecca is not to seem the same. One knows she will not win, and cannot win; neither in this historical present, nor in the future. One knows, and she does not.

A. He you would find.

Q. His Lordship? You maintain you saw his Lordship stand here in this very room?

A. Thee will not believe.

Q. What expression bore he?

A. As my friend.

Q. What clothes wore he? As those he wore when you travelled into Devon? As those in your dream?

A. As those he wore of June Eternal.

Q. He came then as a ghost, an apparition, that takes no account of locks and wood, what is obstacle to ordinary flesh?

A. He came.

Q. Did he not speak?

A. He needs no words.

Q. You were not surprised to see him so? Answer me, mistress. Is it not this — you have seen him on other occasion since the first of May? Is it not so? Answer. It is so or it is not? Have you not told me false at the beginning, when I asked if you had had communication with him? What is this else?

A. Thee will not believe.

Q. Such is no answer. Have you or have you not seen him, it may be not as here today, none the less so you may say, I have seen him?

A. He is my friend.

Q. So you may say, you have seen him?

A. I have known him close.

Q. As a less fanciful might say, I have felt his spirit close?

A. Most close.

Q. Have you as here, seen him as it seemed in the flesh?

A. What is the flesh?

Q. I grow angry. This you must know.

A.   He was not in this world's flesh; yet as he is.

Q.   Has his Lordship never, on such occasion you felt his spirit close, addressed you?

A.   Not by word. In the spirit.

Q.   How in the spirit — has he ever said, Do this or that, believe this or that I tell you?

A.   In the soul.

Q.   Your soul is told what it must do and believe?

A.   That what it does and believes is right.

Q.   Has the spirit or what you will of his Lordship never spoken of himself, where his flesh might now be?

A.   No. It has no need.

Q.   You are certain it lies in your June Eternal?

A.   Yes.

Q.   Have you told any other, your man, your parents, your friends and gossips, whosoever it might be, of these conversations?

A.   No.

Q.   None can bear witness to this, that you have had such visions, spiritual conversation, what you may call it?

A.   None but he, and our master Jesus Christ.

Q.   How often has this been since the first of May? Shake not your head, mistress. You may say in the general. Is it often, or not? Many occasions, or few?

A.   When I have need.

Q.   Often, or less?

A.   Often at the first.

Q.   The more rarely the more latterly?

A.   Yes.

Q.   Is it not most usual among your co-religionaries that they make common their visions among you, thereby to prove the efficacy of their conviction? Why said you nothing of this to anyone, mistress?

A.   It is not of such presence they may believe.

Q.   Did you not say, his Lordship is of the spirit of Jesus Christ? Is that not presence enough?

A.   It is not time he was seen.

Q. Your fellows should not acknowledge him, if you were to tell of what passed this last April? They should not understand this great worth you put upon him? They see not so far as you?

A. I have seen him among us, where we meet; most plain, yet my brothers and sisters not. He would not yet be seen by all.

Q. Shall you tell them, in time to come?

A. They shall be told.

Q. By whom, if not you?

A. Truth will out, and all but the damned shall see.

Q. Why dost thou ever speak the word as a cat laps cream? Is this Christian, that you should so often rejoice in the damnation of others?

A. I rejoice not. 'Tis thee and thy kind most in this world that do rejoice; yea, that nothing may change, that thee and thine have brought about a hell worse than Hell itself for all below thee on this earth. I ask thee plain, is this Christian? Thee knows I am a simple woman, thee's a subtle man of law. Can thee and thy law answer the plain question? Thee knows 'tis so. Can thee tell why, can thee justify?

Q. To each his deserts. It is appointed so.

A. The most rich deserves the most. Yea, it is appointed; but not by will of God, by will of rich men alone.

Q. Were it not God's will, He would not allow it.

A. That He has not yet struck is no proof He shall not. Thee'd twist His patience into a justifying.

Q. And you, mistress, His anger to satisfaction of your own resentment.

A. Mercy is money loaned. One day it shall be paid back, or he who pays not shall suffer for it, and be made most terrible example of. All shall be dust and ashes, all shall be such fire I saw.

Q. Still you prophesy. Of what may come you speak as it were come already; which speaks far more to your present intemperate desire than to what time shall bring in truth. I ask again. How shall you change this present world?

A.   By living as we should and would, which is by Christ's light and word.

Q.   If you prove so contrary and obstinate in all, mistress, then I prophesy you shall be forbid, and with good cause. Answer not, I will be led no more into such idle disputation. I am almost done with you, for the now. First I admonish you, and most severely, of these following matters. You shall not speak of what has passed here, nor of what passed earlier this year. Neither to your man, nor your father, nor Wardley, nor any else beside. Nor shall you speak of those same things to prove your faith, to make of his Lordship in your meetings what he never was. In this you shall not now or ever more be prophetess. Is it understood?

A.   As Herod must be understood.

Q.   I will not have truth nor untruth from you. But silence, in the both cases. I demand your sworn oath thereon, and signed upon this paper before me. Have you letters to write your name?

A.   If thee and thine think they may prison God's truth, I'll be thy bar to prove thee wrong. I may write my flesh's name.

Q.   I warn thee. Think not you may speak despite this, I shall not know. I shall know, and shall make you curse the day you speak.

A.   So I, that I did break my given word.

Q.   This is not all. I require likewise your oath sworn and signed upon what you did swear at the beginning: which is, you have not in any common sense, that is, without your visions and spiritual conversations, seen or spoken with his Lordship since the first of May last, nor had communication with him, nor news by third party whatsoever of him. You may state no more than this: what is become of him, you know not.

A.   I will sign.

Q.   Do you smile, mistress?

A.   Thee'd pin me fast upon the least, and toss aside the most.

Q.   I'll have thee pinned in gaol, if thou dost make light of this.

A.   I would make light of all.

Q.   I warn you one last time. If you have lied and I shall at any future time discover such, it shall be with you as you said yourself of mercy not paid most duly back. All the just wrath of his Lordship's family, and my own, shall fall upon you. You shall be made most terrible example of.

A.   I shall deserve no less.
[*Here was the said solemn affidavit read to the deponent, that she did sign with her name, and it was witnessed duly.*]

Q.   Very well. You may go, I'll have no more of you at this present. Think not you are free. You shall attend, if called upon, to answer further.

❧❦❧

Rebecca stands. John Tudor looks slowly up from the end of the table at his master, as a man watches, even though it is his master; things are not as expected, in something they surprise. Ayscough stops Rebecca as she would move.

"There is another matter, that is done against my advice. I would the rather see thee flogged for thy insolence, had I my way." He pauses. "I am instructed to give thee this, against thy lying in."

Ayscough feels inside a waistcoat pocket, then pushes a small golden coin across the table, a guinea.

"I do not wish it."

"Take. It is commanded."

"No."

"Thy new pride wishes it not. Nothing else."

"No."

"Take. I shall not ask again." Rebecca looks down at the coin, then shakes her head. "Then I give thee what thou must take." They stare at each other. "A prophecy. Thou'lt be hanged yet."

Still Rebecca stares at him.

"Thee's need also, master Ayscough. I give thee more love."

She goes, and Ayscough begins to collect his papers. After a few moments he reaches for his rejected guinea and shoots a fierce glance towards John Tudor, as if he would vent an anger on him. But that worthy is no fool; his head is down.

Manchester, the 10th October, '36.

Your Grace,

Your Grace will here read much I doubt he will credit, yet I trust
he will give me leave to say that I think we deal not here with a tis-
sue of cunning-ordinary lies, or such a tale as a common female
rogue might invent to save her skin; for were she truly cunning of
the kind, she should surely have found better than such extravagance as this, nor thereby put her wretched skin at such risk. In
brief, in so much as the woman Lee is concerned, we may say as the
ancient father, *Credo quia absurdum,* it is most (if at all) to be believed
because it is impossible to be believed. For much it is plain she was
grossly practised upon by his Lordship and his man, and that their
practice did but swell and ripen those unseemly resentments she
had gained from her life in the bagnio. I am persuaded she lies little in any ordinary sense, that is, as to what she believes of these
events and their nature and meaning; as *non obstante* I am persuaded
that her evidence is false in the substantial truth of what passed.

Here I must first state to Your Grace what is not clear writ, of
her fit of seeing. This appeared to me neither malignantly re-
hearsed, nor else in its nature than is said common among her kind

435

of superstitious sectary. I did find more suspicious a manner upon her when she was recovered; as to which I may not easily explain, 'twas as if she now put on anew a part of her hid till then: a strumpet's insolence, such as I did meet with in her former mistress, Claiborne. It is recorded, she did smile: but not her ill-disguised scorn that I should ask her if she were not ashamed at what she saw. Yet even this impudent and forward contempt in her was neither politick nor cunning if she but purposed to deceive. I should rather believe this, her fit made her more determined in her wilful pride, or the more careless of what her manner might betray of disrespect for my enquiry.

Yr Grace will observe she shows little and often no reason nor logick in her beliefs, and he may censure me that I pressed not more hard to expose such patent muddled foolishness (well might I write maggotry). I pray Yr Grace will take my word, such as this may not be humbled so, nay, are driven by it farther into their apostacy, and finally grow bound irrevocable to it. I know her unlettered kind, they would rather first be burnt at the stake than hear reason or recant; they are obstinate to death, most blindly *opiniâtre*, as fixed and resolute in this, tho' it be in unreason and for all their womanishness in outward, as any man in a far better cause. They are like those put under a spell by some legendary romance, that once heard, they cannot shake off; but are its foolish slaves thenceforward. Nothing shall persuade them it be false. Lee is the more strong in this her perversity, Yr Grace will divine, for that the *rota fortunæ* did bring her greatly above her destined station, notwithstanding it were by vice and immodesty. She was never, as is the commonalty of her sex, brought to know God's wisdom in decreeing for them their natural place as help-meet to man, in house and home alone.

In short Your Grace may believe me this, she is not to be broken easily of her new ways. There was, apart from that instance I have cited, in her general manner of answering less pertness and contradiction than may appear in the written words, as almost to say on occasion she was sorry to answer thus boldly, yet must by her faith. I count this small pence in her favour, who loses far greater sums in all else. In most she is of an obstinacy of belief Yr Grace's servant hath seldom encountered; as is seen in what she declared of his Lordship's secret nature and character, which (Yr Grace must know but too well) most signally denies all credible knowledge; likewise in what she would hope of this bastard she carries.

'Tis plain this borders upon, nay is, the rankest blasphemy; yet to her it counts (tho' she did not, like a veritable madwoman, claim full certainty) as not without plausible expectation. Yr Grace may feel she is eminently prosecutable in this her claim, it is most easy proven vile insult upon all decent religion. Yet time, I doubt not, shall soon enough make sufficient example of her culpable foolishness therein, and punishment for it of a kind her arrogance may least bear; besides that I trust Yr Grace will upon reflection agree, such a plainly impious assertion is best not published. Such gross delusion of prophecy, 'tis well known, doth always attract its adherents among the idle mob. Dogs the like are best let sleep in silence; I need not to point out to Yr Grace what further consequence might ensue were this most infamous one awoken, and let run in the publick street. Such as she are far less dangerous when they are common miscreants, the base dross of this world, *puellæ cloacarum,* than when brought to a specious piety.

I judge all of her religion here in this town pernicious, and so also doth Mr Fotheringay, that hath had more dealings with them, for though they honour in outward the civil law they show no respect for it among themselves, nay speak of it as tyranny and say it shall be overthrown in time to come. To all argument of those that would remonstrate or dispute with them, they are deaf — Mr F. says, as if they speak not a common tongue, and are French exiles still among us. Wardley has been heard say so much: that it is futile and nugatory to dispute religious matters with ordinary Christians, for they are Turks in their ignorance and shall be damned for it.

Mr F. has a spy among them, they are close watched, and he tells me he shall act to prevent them so soon as good case be found; the which he doubts not long in coming. But they are close people, and bold in their own defence, Your Grace may deduce it from this present case. Yet to our purpose, I do believe Lee, howsoever misled, firm in this her quarrelling new faith. She refused Your Grace's charity not as one that was notwithstanding tempted to take it, but one who saw (may God forgive her) the Devil's money, and would not have it, though offered in pity. That she is of strong will, for all her sometimes guise of meekness, there is no doubt. When Your Grace did say, upon his view of her, this was no ordinary woman, he was as just as he is accustomed. I will add no more on her account.

Your Grace did me the honour to say, this one week past, that I should not hide my conclusions by reason of the natural reverence I must harbour for his most eminent rank. I shall now, tho' it be with the greatest disinclination, obey his wish; and tears also must I weep, that the most probable truth I have come to should be so bitter. Your Grace, I shall compendiate it thus: I may hope, yet may not in reason believe, his Lordship still lives. This I must ground not only upon that of which Yr Grace is already cognizant: his Lordship's having drawn upon no part of his allowance nor revenue since last he was seen in this world.

I take also into account the death of his man Thurlow. Your Grace knows what devotion the fellow showed to his master through all their lives together. I cannot credit he died of his own hand by any cause except this: like the dog in human form that he was, he knew his beloved master dead and wished to live no more. It is true he did not as in most cases, he did not die in melancholy at his master's side. Yet must I still assume that such a death was what drove him to the most desperate end he then gave himself. The place where his *felony de se* was done was well searched, and in my presence, as I said. But I fear now we were mistaken. I may conjecture it passed thus, in brutal simplicity; that Thurlow saw his Lordship die within the cavern; did then run from it in extremest horror, as Jones did report; but did later, after the wench and Jones was gone, and it may be not before the next morning, return there to see what in his simple wits he could not believe he had first seen; and finding there what he had most feared, his master's corse, did inter it in that place, or more likely carry it as he could to some place other we know not of; then only, that most direful task done, did he run off and hang himself in his despair. Upon this conjecture must I alas hazard further, which I shall come to, as to reason for his Lordship's death.

To this must be added what is proof only by negation, yet must grow in strength with passing time; to wit, no word is heard of his Lordship since the dark first of May, neither of his then taking ship nor of his being now settled in some foreign city. It may be said he was most able to embark in secret, perhaps from some port other than Bideford or Barnstaple, and where we have not enquired; and may now live in equal secret where he went. Why then should he not take his servant? In such matters, where we have no certainty, we must judge by probability. It may not, alas, be said that it is more probable he doth now live in retirement abroad. As Your Grace knows, not one of those our agents and ambassadors to whom I have written on this behalf hath made such answer as we hoped.

Yr Grace's command doth now oblige me, if he will thus far grant me my most melancholy supposition, to state how his Lordship may have come to his tristfully ill-starred end. Yr Grace, I would believe him foully murdered, if I might; by the hand of any of those we know to have been there, I cannot; by hand unknown, again I would believe, were there any evidence or probability to it. Yr Grace knows as well as I, there is not; nor that Thurlow should not defend him, were either such the case. *Horresco referens*, I am reduced to this: his Lordship's death was self-given. In this Thurlow did but do as in so much else, that is, did follow in his master's footsteps.

I will not repeat all in his Lordship's past Your Grace knows better than I, and that has so often excited Yr Grace's disapprobation and paternal distress; yet must I believe here we may best ground explanation of what occurred last April — I speak not only of those philosophick pursuits his Lordship has these last years followed in such headstrong disobedience to Your Grace's wishes; but more deep, in the most contrary spirit that allowed, nay drove, his Lordship to indulge them.

It is but too well known from history such pursuits may lead their follower out of the noble world of reason, of commendable and useful enquiry, into the black labyrinth of the Chimaera; into matters most plainly blasphemous, and as plainly forbidden to mortals. I must believe now, this is what passed with his Lordship.

He did seek wickedly to pierce some dark secret of existence, and moreover grew besotted by it, it may well be because he could not accomplish his grand design, as is most often the case. I do not say the account the woman Lee gave Jones is to be believed exact; yet may it be nearer truth than what I am myself here told by her. I do not say she lied knowingly in this; yet was led by means obscure to credit the opposite of what was truly intended. Your Grace will ask by what means, and there I cannot answer him, save I do not doubt there was a natural proclivity in Lee that his Lordship had observed, and did see also it might be made his tool, to further his own ends.

Nor do I doubt as to the general drift of the grand design. I will not weary Your Grace by adducing how much in his Lordship's past must suggest there was ever in him some perverse principle that drove him to deny what reason and filial respect might have most expected him to believe — nay, not only to believe, but in view of his most fortunate rank, to maintain and uphold. We have all on occasion heard words and opinions from his Lordship's mouth that offend both divine wisdom and its reflection in this world below — I would say, the wisdom by which this world doth best conduct and govern itself, its sagacity in matters civil and political. It may be his Lordship felt a respect for his noble father which did most often prevent him from speaking before him in his darker vein. Even when he did, in other circumstance I have been witness to, I have heard the ladies declare him a tease, no more; and discerning gentlemen not find in him beyond a fashionable cynick, who cares more for the mark he makes in polite society than for his immortal soul. Even with those juster in their censure, I have heard the blame for his views put upon his being a younger son, and his holding a (but too familiar) rancour thereat.

I may here repeat what Sir Rich'd Malton did remark recently to me in London, upon the abolition of the Act against Witchcraft, which was this: that tho' the old hags be counted gone, there were impudent libertine philosophers enough to take their place. There are many such in London, Your Grace, who make no bones in professing to believe in nothing beyond their own pleasures in debauch; that care outwardly not a farthing for Church and

Religion, nor King and Constitution neither; that would turn Musulman to gain a place or particular favour. Yet these are not what Sir Rich'd spoke of, they are no more than slaves of a pernicious fashion of the times. *Nos hæc novimus esse nihil,* for there are worse beside, far worse. These above do declare themselves openly what they are. These I speak of do most largely conceal behind a mask what they truly believe and would work upon in how this world is managed; or more subtly they but show enough to make themselves believed fashion's slaves, as is his Lordship's case above. They make their outward impudence their mask, as foxes, the better we may not see where they truly tend, nor their true black tergiversation beneath.

This twelve-month gone I did chance to ask his Lordship upon what he was engaged in his enquiries, and he did answer, I thought then in his manner half in sour jest, Why, how I may make a man of a toad, and a fool into a philosopher. Upon which I remarked it seemed he would usurp upon divine prerogative. To which he replied I was mistaken, since the world showed us it was easy enough to make men into toads, and philosophers into fools, and so must it be the Devil's prerogative he would usurp. I must now believe, Your Grace, that in that exchange lay some part of a confession he might have declared, had the occasion not been trivial and in passing. In truth he would doubt all: birth, society, government, justice, so to say in some more adept world their present provisions and dispositions should be found evil and corrupt. Yet he was ever not bold enough, or too cunning, to speak these things outright.

By such weakness or fear, Your Grace, must I believe he did come finally to what passed in April. He would persuade one who was in this comparatively innocent, nay, gullible besides, to prove the point he dared not make himself, in her guise of seditious religion. In plain words, this world that is must be upset. Now that this one was a she, and whore besides, may seem a madness in him, to launch such a venture on so small and miserable a bark; yet it may be she was freighted but for a first proof and essay, to see if a simple woman of pleasure might not be turned into the fanatick she is become, to serve his secret ends. Those are such no thinking man could countenance, for they place the judgement of a person's worth not upon his condition, but upon himself; not on birth, but upon the mere fact of being. This is clear behind the drift of our French Prophetess: all are to be counted equal. Such as she may place such dangerous belief upon religious grounds. It is plain their general spirit is rabid political, of the mob, to destroy the sacred laws of inheritance, among much else. They would break this nation to pieces. I doubt his Lordship cares one whit for their religion; these their other desires, they are his also.

Yr Grace, by such sad presage must I come to this: in that he would break the world which bore him, and to which he owed all, why, even unto those means that allowed him to pursue such ends, was his Lordship broken himself. *Fiat experimentum in corpore vili;* and in that doing he did become vile to himself, he was hoist on his own petard. In what is said of him and his behaviour upon his journey, we may see he was oft in secret doubt of it, his enterprise misgave him long before it was concluded. How can he not have perceived he forsook the pursuit of scholarship for common trickery, such as at Stonehenge? Whereby he raised the light into the sky and made appear those two figures blasphemously passed off as the Almighty and His Son, we know not. He stayed behind when all was done, I doubt not that those he had hired should be paid, and all evidence of trickery cleared away in the night; and likewise at the cavern, though there it is to be noted we know not what passed except by Lee's testimony, which is more of gross fantasy than credible fact; and I believe there put upon her not by any outward malfeasance and deceit, but far more likely by means of drug or potion, or by black art of some kind.

Here I must believe conscience did mercifully put a stop upon his Lordship's venture; that at the last he did acknowledge to himself he was upon madness, in unholy union with all decency abhors; and driven to it by a malevolent and unreasoning hatred and resentment not only of his noble father, but of the sacred principles of all respectable society and belief. His Lordship's youngest sister did once remark to me that her brother was as a pendulum, never to be still nor found in the same humour from one minute to the next. In that black Western cavern 'tis most probable he did find himself to swing away from all he had done, and to regret it with a violence unaccustomed even in him; and in such violence did end his wretched days. Your Grace, I cannot say it was so. Yet must I guess it most likely so, and with this only to commend it: that coming to recognise he had sinned most heinously, he must condemn himself to no less than he did, as only proper expiation of his awful crimes.

Your Grace will not, I trust, take offence I put my conclusion so baldly, since it is at his behest. He himself, as he will no doubt recall, did once vouchsafe to this his most humble servant that were it not all evidence denied, and not least the unimpeachable testimony of physiognomick likeness, he should believe his Lordship a changeling. I fear Your Grace was not mistaken: he may justly conclude that in all matters but of blood, his Lordship was indeed as a changeling, and not his true son.

Your Grace did also ask me in what manner he should best broach this matter to his most esteemed spouse; and here I shall respectfully propose to him there is one consolation to be drawn, *viz.*, in this our unknowing we are not obliged to declare the worst of his Lordship, as I have here with great reluctancy but upon best probability stated. We may not easily believe what the woman Lee declares him to have been and to have become, against all past belief and family knowledge; yet Yr Grace may judge it should be allowed some colour of extenuation, to allay maternal concern. And furthermore, that he is now disappeared, it may be said it is because he knows himself not worthy to be Yr Grace's son, and would but relieve Yr Grace of his presence. May it not be said that perchance he lives still in some foreign land, where none may break the secret of an incognito; where he may now acknowledge to himself that he has given Yr Grace great hurt, and would trouble you no more? And advanced in hope that he reflects upon the injustice he has done, and shall in due time return to ask Your Grace's forgiveness?

These lines are written in some haste, not to delay dispatch, as Yr Grace will understand; and will know in what sadness also and fear of having failed Your Grace, in not bringing matters (despite most diligent effort) to more happy conclusion. Man would of his nature know all; but it is God who decrees what shall or shall not be known; and here must we resign ourselves to accept His great wisdom and mercy in such matters, which is that He deems it often best and kindest to us mortals that we shall not know all. In the bosom of that great mystery, I most humbly suggest, should Your Grace seek comfort; as in the more earthly solace of his noble wife and noble son the Marquis (who doth, unlike his poor brother, so preeminently enshrine his father's virtues), of those most charming ladies his daughters likewise. Alas, the one flower may wilt and fade; the others still may console the more.

I shall be before Your Grace very soon upon his reading of this dispatch, and his to command. In closing now, I beg Yr Grace to accept my most respectful sympathy for this unhappy conclusion upon enquiry; and ever the most sincere assurance of untiring diligence in all his affairs, from his humble servant

FROM THE ROOM OUTSIDE there comes a murmur of voices, mostly female, a group waiting quietly for some event; though the event of this twenty-eighth of February, as it happens, has taken place, and the three men present, Wardley, Hocknell, John Lee, are but new admitted from where they were recently sent, which was to stand in Toad Lane outside. Rebecca lies alone on the rough bed in the inner cellar; on her back, her face spent, impassive, seemingly almost sullen now it is over. It is noon, a strange time to be abed, and already she would rise; yet knows she cannot and must not. Of a sudden the voices outside cease; they listen. Now there is a shadow in the door, and she cranes her head up. John Lee stands there, with the new-swaddled baby clasped tight in his right arm, posing for a picture of a man at a loss; a picture he does not lessen by removing his hat, slowly and as if by reluctant afterthought, before this echo of a far greater birth, though in similar humble circumstances. She looks only at what he holds cradled in his right arm. His grave and awkward-peering face would seem to be about to announce the end of the world; but then again, by afterthought, it shows the ghost of a wintry smile.

"All is well, thee?"

"Most well, husband."

"I prayed for thee, and her new soul."

"I thank thee."

And now he steps forward and taking the new-born infant, as absurdly tight-bound as a parcel, in both hands passes it down to the hands raised to take it. The appalling custom of swaddling was, among the more emancipated and thanks to the philosopher John Locke, already near its end; but not yet, alas, among the poor. The blacksmith-prophet watches while the parcel is set beside her, and as she stares at it with that strangely paradoxical intensity, half love, half doubt, both objective and subjective, both certain and wondering, of the young mother first faced with what has come from inside her . . . this long-drowned creature risen from the ocean depths, yet miraculously still alive. It is very plainly not divine; its face crinkled, obstinate, still more in the sea than the air. It opens its eyes for a long moment, it seems almost stunned by the revelation of this wretched and shadowy world it is born into; yet already there is a hint of azure, of vacant sky, in them. A time will come when people shall remember those eyes, their blue candour and their brisk truth, that was far from vacant.

John Lee replaces his broad-brimmed hat.

"I have bought thee both a handsel."

She takes her eyes up from the child, and smiles faintly, secretly incredulous at such secular grace.

"What is it, then?"

"But a bird. Would thee see?"

"I would see."

He turns and goes back into the other room; then returns at once holding a small square object, swaddled with cloth as the child, and which he holds by an osier handle. Now he holds it above the bed where she may see, and pulls the cloth away. It is a goldfinch, in a tiny wicker cage, barely seven inches square. The brilliantly coloured little bird takes alarm and flutters against the brown bars.

" 'Twill grow more tame, and sing."

She reaches up her free arm, timidly, to touch the minute cage.

"Thee must hang it by the door, in the light."

"Aye."

And he stares still for a time at the bird, which now cowers in a corner, as if it means more to him than the face beside Rebecca's on the bed. But then he swathes the cage in the cloth again and holds it down by his side.

"The Lord has given me this last night a name for her."

"How a name?"

"Mary."

"I promised the Lord she shall be Ann."

"Wife, thee must obey. We are not to deny the gift. It spake clear."

"I deny no gift."

"Yes, thee would. It is not fit, at such a time. What the Lord has given, we must receive."

"What else was given?"

"That she shall see the Lord Jesus come again."

"We may call her both."

"Two names is vanity. One sufficeth."

For a moment she says nothing, staring up at him. She looks down at the rough blanket that covers her. "I tell thee, John Lee, when the Lord Jesus come again, He shall be She, and the mother most shall know Her name."

He stares down at her without answering, uncertain whether such levity deserves reprimand or is so far-fetched it may in these circumstances be ignored. At last he stoops and lays a clumsy hand upon her shoulder, a quarter in blessing, a quarter in forgiveness; and a full half in sheer incomprehension. Like so many seers, he is blind to the present. He straightens.

"Sleep. And when thee wake, thee'll know to obey."

He leaves, carrying the cage; and for a moment or two more the young woman on the dark bed still stares down at the blanket. He speaks in a low voice outside, perhaps something about the goldfinch. There is a silence, then the voice of the bird, from by the cellar door: a silvery little tintinnabulation, its flight-call, piercing the sombre rooms like sunlight; and conscience-piercing also. But William Blake is yet to come.

Now Rebecca looks down at the tiny creature in her arms. There is something of a wonderment in her eyes, at this other, this intruder into her world; she bends and very gently kisses its pink and wrinkled forehead.

"More love, Ann. More love, my love."

Now the infant's features begin to contort, a preparatory paroxysm to crying. It begins to bawl. A few seconds later, its mouth brought for a first time to the mother's breast, the bawling has stopped. Outside, the low voices start again. Rebecca nurses, with her eyes closed, sunk within feeling, this affirmation of her selfness no words she knows can describe, or that she would have had describe even if she knew them. For a moment she opens those meek brown eyes and stares into a dark corner of the room, as if someone stood there watching; then closes them again. After a while she begins slightly to rock, and there comes the barely perceptible sound of a hum. She has begun a slow lullaby, the baby lies stilled. It is very simple, and seems to be of two repeated phrases only.

Vive vi, vive vum, vive vi, vive vum, vive vi, vive vum . . . it is clear they are not rational words, and can mean nothing.

EPILOGUE

READERS WHO KNOW SOMETHING of what that Manchester baby was to become in the real world will not need telling how little this is a historical novel. I believe her actual birth was two months before my story begins, on 29 February 1736. I know nothing in reality of her mother, and next to nothing of various other characters, such as Lacy and Wardley, who also come from real history. They are here almost all invention beyond their names. It may be that books and documents exist that might have told me more of them in historical terms than the little I know: I have consulted none, nor made any effort to find them. I repeat, this is a maggot, not an attempt, either in fact or in language, to reproduce known history.

I have the greatest respect for exact and scrupulously documented history, not least because part of my life is (in a very humble way) devoted to it; but this exacting discipline is essentially a science, and immensely different in its aims and methods from those of fiction. I have mentioned Daniel Defoe (who died in 1731) only once in these pages; which is poor recognition of the admiration and liking I have always felt for him. *A Maggot* is not at all meant to be in any direct imitation; he is, in any case, inimitable. To following some of what I take to be the underlying approach and purpose in his novels, I happily confess.

My text is maggot also in how it came to grow from that primitive image of travellers I mentioned at the beginning. One day one of the mysterious riders gained a face; that is, by chance I acquired a pencil and water-colour drawing of a young woman. There was no indication of artist, simply a little note in ink in one corner, which seemingly says, in Italian, *16 July 1683*. This precise dating pleased me at first as much as the drawing itself, which is not of any distinction; yet something in the long dead face, in the eyes, an inexplicable presentness, a refusal to die, came slowly to haunt me. Perhaps it was the refusal to die that, improbably in all other ways, linked this real and unknown woman with another and known one I had much longer respected; and whom you have just seen born.

Such gross inconsequence, jumping from a picture of a seventeenth-century Italian woman (and prostitute, I have a strong suspicion) to the memory, later in history, of a remarkable and saintly English one, must defy all normal notions of how one goes about making a novel. At the least I owe it to those readers whose ears have not pricked at the name Ann Lee, nor know what she became far outside these pages in the real world, to end with a word about her, my other presiding spirit.

A convinced atheist can hardly dedicate a novel to a form of Christianity. None the less, this one was partly written out of a very considerable affection and sympathy for the United Society of Believers in Christ's Second Appearing, better known as the Shakers, of which Ann Lee was the founder. To most people now, I imagine, Shaker means little more than a furniture style and an ultra-puritanism superficially akin to the asceticism of some monastic orders (such as the Cistercian) from the opposite religious extreme. Orthodox theologians have always despised the sect's doctrinal naïvety; orthodox priests, its fanaticism; orthodox capitalists, its communism; orthodox communists, its superstition; orthodox sensualists, its abhorrence of the carnal; and orthodox males, its striking feminism. I find it one of the most fascinating — and proleptic — episodes in the long history of Protestant Dissent.

This is not only for social and historical reasons. Something in

Shaker thought and theology (not least in its holding that a Holy Trinity that has no female component cannot be holy), in its strange rituals and marvellously inventive practical life, in its richly metaphorical language and imaginative use of dancing and music, has always seemed to me to adumbrate the relation of fiction to reality. We novelists also demand a far-fetched faith, quite often seemingly absurd in relation to normal reality; we too need a bewildering degree of metaphorical understanding from our readers before the truths behind our tropes can be conveyed.

England had already, of course, had an age of outspoken dissent (and self-discovery) in the 1640s and 1650s; Ann Lee's came late, historically. Only a very few years after she was born, in the April of 1739, a dissatisfied yet ordained priest in the Church of England stood on Kingsdown, a hill then outside the city of Bristol, and spoke, rather than formally preached, to a gathering of the Bristol poor, consisting mainly of miners and their families. Many of his listeners began to weep, others were so disturbed and moved they fell into a catatonic trance. To be sure they were very rough, illiterate, easy to work upon; such cathartic phenomena are now both anthropologically and psychologically well understood. But on Kingsdown something more than the speaker's charisma was involved. Quite simply his audience was being given light. It was as if they had all been blind or (as many of the miners truly had) living in darkness till then.

I suspect we owe quite as much to all those incoherent sobs and tears and ecstasies of the illiterate as to the philosophers of mind and the sensitive artists. Unorthodox religion was the only vehicle by which the vast majority, who were neither philosophers nor artists, could express this painful breaking of the seed of the self from the hard soil of an irrational and tradition-bound society — and a society not so irrational it did not very well know how much it depended on *not* seeing its traditions questioned, its foundations disturbed. Can we wonder the new-born ego (whose adolescence we call the Romantic Age) often chose means to survive and to express itself as irrational as those that restrained it?

Now, I hate modern evangelism, with its spurious Madison Avenue techniques and general loathsome conservatism in politics. It seems almost always unerringly based on the worst, most backward side of Christianity, an insidious supporter of whatever is retrograde in contemporary thought and politics; and thereby denies the very essence of Jesus himself. Nor do I think any better of this same trait in many other religions, such as Islam. But what happened with John Wesley (the man above) and Ann Lee and their like in the eighteenth century is quite different: an emotional enlightenment beside, almost in spite of, the intellectual (and middle-class) enlightenment the *siècle de lumières* is famous for. They had, Wesley by his energy and transparent strength of conviction, Ann Lee in her obstinate (and immensely brave) determination and her poetry — her genius for images — a practical vision of what was wrong with their world. Ann's vision was more thorough-going than Wesley's, a fact that we may attribute in part to her sex, but perhaps above all to the fact that she was uneducated; that is, unsullied by stock belief, learned tradition, and the influence of the other kind of enlightenment. At heart people like Ann were revolutionaries; one with the very first Christians of all, and their founder.

Their efforts (especially John Wesley's) were, as always, one day to breed a narrow-minded bigotry, an inward tyranny as life-stultifying as the tyrannies they first tried to end, or fled from. But I speak here of that first fuse, that spirit that was in them at the beginning, before the organised business of religious conversion and gaining adherents *en masse* came, and dimmed and adulterated their fundamental and highly personal example and force. One of the saddest ironies in all religious history is that we should now so admire and value Shaker architecture and furniture, fall on our knees like Mies van der Rohe before the Hancock Round Barn; yet totally reject the faith and way of life that made these things.

The Shakers had purely English roots, but were very soon persecuted out of England. In Manchester the real Ann Lee was first to be a mill-girl, then fur-cutter for a hatter, then a cook in an infirmary; she was to marry (Abraham Stanley, another blacksmith) and to bear four children by him, all of whom died young. She set out for America in 1774, accompanied by only a tiny handful of fellow-believers. Her husband deserted her almost at once there, and for several years her "family" was harried as much as in England. The growth, maturity and decline of the United Society all took place in America. Much of both the fixed dogma and the practices of the Society in its gathered communities was developed after Ann's death in 1784, by disciples like Joseph Meacham and Lucy Wright; but behind all (not least in the great revival of the 1840s) lie the seeds of Ann's very special personality.

It is easy enough now to dismiss much of the aftermath of her memory, the spirit drawings, the dictated songs and music, the trance states, as unrestrained religiosity, and at least partly a product of the sexual abstinence for which the Society was famous (and whose dangers it was well aware of, in terms of the conversation and other rituals it evolved to compensate for that deprivation). A similar wild and suspect religiosity may be found before Ann's time, in those early French Prophets whose names I have Wardley cite.

Yet something haunts the more serious side of the United Society's life that cannot be so easily dismissed. It is an aspiration, a determination to escape mere science, mere reason, convention, established belief and religion, into the one thing that excuses an escape from such powerful social gods, the founding of a more humane society . . . all that is conveyed in "more love." It was almost as if Ann Lee and the early Shakers foresaw that, if not Antichrist, then certainly Mammon, the universal greed in each for more money, for more personal wealth and possession, would one day rule this world and threaten to destroy it. Our present world is as deaf as poor Dick to Ann's appeal for simplicity, sanity and self-control. Gathered or community Shakerism is now virtually extinct, its faith too plain, its rules too radical, for twentieth-century Adam and Eve. Yet for me something else in it does not die.

Dissent is a universal human phenomenon, yet that of Northern Europe and America is, I suspect, our most precious legacy to the world. We associate it especially with religion, since all new religion begins in dissent, that is, in a refusal to believe what those in power would have us believe — what they would command and oblige us, in all ways from totalitarian tyranny and brutal force to media manipulation and cultural hegemony, to believe. But in essence it is an eternal biological or evolutionary mechanism, not something that was needed once, merely to meet the chance of an earlier society, when religious belief was the great metaphor, and would-be conforming matrix, for many things beside religion. It is needed always, and in our own age more than ever before.

A historically evolved outward form, adapted as in a plant or animal to cope with one set of conditions, is doomed when a new set appears; as in my view not only the United, but Western society as a whole, only too plainly shows. What the Shakers "crossed," or condemned, in the society and world they had to inhabit may seem to us quaint and utopian, their remedies hopelessly unattainable today; but some at least of the questions they asked and the challenges they flung seem to me still unanswered.

In so much else we have developed immeasurably from the eighteenth century; with their central plain question — what morality justifies the flagrant injustice and inequality of human society? — we have not progressed one inch. One major reason is that we have committed the cardinal sin of losing the old sense of mediocrity: that of a wise and decent moderation. It is betrayed in the way we have twisted and debased the word (as our sense of individual self has grown) to its modern sense. This is the hidden price, as in the Greek gift at Troy, put by nature upon our twentieth-century consciousness of and obsession with self. A species cannot fill its living space to absurd excess in number; and still so exalt excess, the extreme, non-mediocrity, in the individual. When excess becomes synonymous with success, a society is doomed, and by far more than Christ.

I have long concluded that established religions of any kind are in general the supreme example of forms created to meet no longer existing conditions. If I were asked what the present and future world could best lose or jettison for its own good, I should have no hesitation: all established religion. But its past necessity I do not deny. Least of all do I deny (what novelist could?) that founding stage or moment in all religions, however blind, stale and hidebound they later become, which saw a superseded skeleton must be destroyed, or at least adapted to a new world. We grow too clever now to change; too selfish and too multiple, too dominated by the

Devil's great I, in Shaker terminology; too self-tyrannized, too pledged to our own convenience, too tired, too indifferent to others, too frightened.

I mourn not the outward form, but the lost spirit, courage and imagination of Mother Ann Lee's word, her Logos; its almost divine maggot.